A Fighter's Chance

No Frills
<<<>>>
Buffalo
Buffalo. NY

Printed in the United States of America

Gonzalez, Gabriel

A Fighter's Chance/Gonzalez- 1st Edition

ISBN: 978-0615810058

1. A Fighter's Chance – Fiction.   2. New Author – Boxing. 3. Sports.
1. Title
ISBN: 978-0615755427

1. Steep Drop – Fiction.   2. New Author – No Frills. 3. Social Fiction.
1. Title

Cover Image by Paul Clifton
Cover Model Mike Del Zappo

No Frills Buffalo Press
119 Dorchester Buffalo, New York 14213
For more information visit Nofrillsbuffalo.com

A Fighter's Chance

By Gabriel Gonzalez

Dedication

To my longtime trainer Ray Casal, for all the hard work and dedication that he has put into the sport of boxing. Ray has been an inspiration to a lot of young kids for the past thirty years. He has put his heart and soul into training professional and amateur fighters. I dedicate this book to him, and thank him for helping me become the man I am today, and for giving me the inspirations that it took to write this novel.

Chapter One

The sound of the bell jars my thoughts as I make my way to the corner of the ring. I place my arms on the ropes and wait as Trey positions the stool. The look in his brown eyes is confident as he slips his lithe body between the ropes without touching them.

My white gloves are pasted with spots of dried-up blood. Taking deep breaths hurts my lungs. It feels as though a 400-pound man is dancing on my chest. My body is covered in so much sweat it looks like I've just gotten out of a pool.

The last four rounds have been a war. Taking a seat on the hard stool, I realize how tired my legs are. It's been a long fight. I think it's round eleven but I'm not entirely sure. The pain in my head is like a nagging headache that never goes away. My right eye is swelled up, although my vision is clear. I can feel the electricity of the crowd and it makes me realize one thing: this has been one hell of a fight!

Trey covers my back with a bag of ice, making me jump, and the soothing cold spreading across my back helps me regain focus. Henry Brass joins Trey in aid. Mr. Brass' gray, healthy hair and clean-shaven face look rich. Not nearly as rich as his pockets though. Mr. Brass smiles at me. He was one of the reasons why I was here.

His daughter sits a few seats over in the front row. With bright green eyes so elegant that they can be noticed from where I sit I can't help but take a peek over. Her blonde hair looks amazing with her black dress. She's the most beautiful girl in this arena, at least in my eyes. She's not showing her usually stunning smile; instead, she looks worried.

Coach Kay is talking to me. I can hear what he is saying but somehow I ignore it. It is the eleventh round, which much is clear.

I can't help but look out into the vast crowd; it's the biggest I've ever seen. People are screaming, and many of them are looking at me. I can only hear them in between rounds, for when the fight in the ring starts, everything goes blank.

According to the promoters, every single seat has been paid for. I glance at promoter Grey Bones and distaste swells in my mouth. I wish it were him on the other side of that ring so I could pound his face in as soon as the round starts again. The hair on his head is mostly black, with streaks of grey that try to give way to his age. He's a tall man that perhaps kept in shape in his younger years. The man has more money than God, and more deceit in his eyes than Satan himself. Boxing is his gold mine. Everything he's done, everything he has tried to do, and everything he plans on doing in this sport bothers me. There is only one way to beat him, and that is to beat the man across from me right now. That victory would shatter Bones' world.

Juan Riviera is sitting a few seats away. Dressed in a dove-gray suit made precisely to his liking, the once boxing sensation is looking at me with worried eyes. Many compare me to him, saying that my good looks and boxing abilities are everything the sport needed after Riviera retired. Even though his black hair and dark brown eyes are the complete opposite of mine, I can't help but see the similarities between us.

Disputes often broke when speaking Juan Riviera's name. He used to be the face of boxing and the people loved him. However, a stunning knockout loss sent him to retirement so early in his career that many debated whether he was even worthy of entering the Hall of Fame. He hadn't let retirement ruin his good looks, and he seemed like he could still get in the ring and go a few rounds. Juan was looking for me to take his place as a superstar in the sport. But I still don't trust him fully. Perhaps I never will. Promoters are very hard to trust, and even harder to become friends with. Still, if Juan released me tomorrow, I would walk over and hug him, thanking him for everything he's done.

I'm not sure if I'm losing or winning the fight, it's been so close. Judging by Juan's eyes, though, I am losing. The fact that it's been this close has surprised everyone, I'm sure.

"Look at me, son!"

Coach Kay finally gets my attention. He has the most distinct, demanding tone I have ever heard. I look into his strong and determined eyes. His black skin shines in the lights that hover above the ring. His tall body always seems smaller when he is hunched over, cleaning me up. Taking the end-swell, he rubs my eyes as he grabs the towel and wipes the sweat from my face. I feel like smiling at the old man but I can't. If Mr. Brass saved my life, then Coach Kay changed it. The man has been everything I could ask for in a trainer, and perhaps even a father. We have been through it all, Coach and I. It hasn't been an easy road but is it ever? The hardest part is yet to come. We will tell our secret after this fight. The secret that I have fought so hard to keep buried inside of me, the secret that will change my life forever. I realize I have to quickly dismiss that thought, though. If I let it distract me, I will surely lose this fight.

"He's tired, you understand me?" Coach barks. "He's damn

tired! If you win these last two rounds, you will win this fight! Do you understand me? I need you to go after him now. These are the championship rounds, son. This is what we train for. Take the fight to him!"

The words ring through my head. I'm winning? Or am I losing and I need the last two rounds to win the fight? I would never ask. My face is all over the television and I wouldn't want their corner to see any doubt in my eyes. Each round has been close. I know that I won a few rounds, and I know of some rounds I lost, but they go by so fast I can't count how many. The close rounds are hard to judge because, as a fighter, I can never tell if I won or lost the round unless I completely dominate. Even then you never know what these judges are thinking especially if one of them is corrupt or just plain stupid.

Looking across the ring, I stare into the eyes of my opponent for a moment. His face is swollen and his right eye is cut. He's breathing heavy. I have watched hundreds of tapes of him and have never seen him breathing the way he is right now. He has never been cut. The most distinguishing thing, though, is the look in his eyes. He's usually confident, cocky, and poised, but he's none of those right now. For the first time ever, I see fear in his eyes. He's worried. He's tired. Coach Kay is right. I can win this fight! It was a fight very few people thought I could win.

He glances at me and I look away. I take a few deep breaths. My legs don't hurt now as much as before. I can't tell if my mind has tuned the pain out or if the one-minute break between the round has helped. It might be the fear in his eyes that has given me the energy to continue.

Standing up, I can hear the crowd going crazy. I've ignored all of the celebrities sitting ringside. It's my first fight they've attended, but I know they're not here to see me. They paid a ridiculous amount of money to come watch him as they usually do. Money was something that I once hated more than anything, something that nearly drove me to end my boxing career, and almost my life.

Tonight, I have to steal his spotlight. I have to take his crown. I have to show the world that the pain they have seen in my life the last couple weeks on television has made me stronger than I've ever been. My story has spread quickly; so tonight, despite being the underdog, I am the crowd favorite. I may never know if it's because they feel sorry for what I've been through or if they truly like me. Regardless, people who didn't even know my name weeks ago now want me to win.

I take one last look into the arena. A faded image of my father appears in the middle of the crowd. I can't deny that I look like him:

dirty blonde hair, light green eyes, and a smile that could steal any woman's heart. His tall, muscular figure towers over everyone around him. He is not cheering, just smiling at me like he used to. There is only one thing I once hated more than money, and it was him.

A second later, the image of my father is gone and I see my mother. I almost laugh. I must be delusional after one too many punches to the head. How could one image that I hated lead into another? They say you should always forgive but not forget, but what she did to me I can never forgive. Every single time I stare into that woman's eyes, the hatred in my soul burns.

Then I remember that I had invited her to come. And I suddenly realize that my mother is actually in the crowd, sitting timidly a few rows back from the ring. Her being here, I tell myself, is a small step toward making amends for the devastation she brought upon my family.

The bell rings. It's the eleventh round of the championship fight, a fight that the whole world is watching. I have come to love this sport more than anything, but it was the pain that started me on the journey to get here.

Chapter Two

I press my hands on the wood table to hear the creaking sound. Looking at my grandmother, she does not turn back towards me. Her attention is on the meal that she is cooking. Her grey hair is long and healthy yet her body seems to be getting smaller. Her strength has faded over the years as she struggles to walk back and forth to prepare.

The cupboards look to be as old as the table; the paint has faded so much that it's hard to tell what color it used to be. The sink is clean but nowhere near to being new. It probably should have been replaced years ago. The entire kitchen is about the size of a car. The fact that she was able to fit a table in it eludes me.

Putting my head underneath the table, I again press down as hard as I can. The creaking noise is louder now. I still have no idea where it is coming from. How would a 13-year-old boy know what to do, anyway? Even if I did find the reason it was creaking there would be no way I'd know how to fix it. My grandmother could barely afford to buy food so paying someone to come fix it wouldn't be an option.

I press one more time and the leg closest to me cracks, sending the table falling on me as I use my strength to hold it up. Now I've really done it! It's broken. My grandmother turns around at the sound of the crack and walks over slowly to see what I have done.

"Well, I'll be," she says gently, shaking her head. "Forty years and finally it gives way to the curiosity of a boy."

"I'm sorry, Grandma, I thought if I found out what it was I could fix it." My apology is sincere. She doesn't say anything as she walks into the living room. As quickly as her feet allow she comes back with a book and hands it to me.

"Place it underneath to prop it up. It should work." I grab the book and look at the table leg. The book is thick enough to make the table even. I snap off the rest of the broken leg so the book can fit underneath properly. Positioning the book under the leg, I look up.

"See?" she says, smiling, as she finally brings two plates over.

I look at the meal in front of me. She sits down across the table and I smile. I don't have to smell the food to know what it was. I don't even have to see it. Every meal, every day and every night, is always the same: rice, beans and, if I was lucky, some chicken added.

She couldn't afford much else. The best meal of the day is usually at school. I always looked at the school lunch menu to see what special things I would get to eat. Pizza, chicken fingers, pasta…they are all so good. Thinking of them now is making my meal look dull.

The kids at school usually make fun of me because I always take their leftovers. I love to eat, mainly because I never get the chance to. I try to ignore their jokes until they start adding ones about my cheap clothes, old sneakers, and the same pair of dirty jeans that I have worn for the last two years. Those jokes usually angered me, which always resulted in fights and school suspensions.

I never complain about the lack of food in the house. Each time she serves a meal I say the same exact thing, "Mmm, smells amazing, Grandma." It's not what I am thinking or what I want to say, but I understand that she tries her best to keep us sheltered and fed.

Just as I grab my spoon, she smacks my hand. "You know the rules," she scolds. I always forget. She closes her eyes and folds her hands and reluctantly I follow. "Lord, bless this food we are about to receive, bless the lives we have lived and the lives we are going to live, and pray that our lost loved ones watch over us, not just in our darkest hours, but in our greatest ones as well. Amen." It's the same prayer every night. I could recite it in my sleep. I probably do.

"Amen," I add a bit late, prompting a glare from her.

"I looked over your homework," she says as we start to eat. "There are a few things we should go over after dinner. Most of it looks right. You are doing better, from what your teachers say." She's been watching me the last couple of weeks. I can't help but be annoyed by it. "Of course, your math is perfect, as usual. I don't understand how you can do so well in math yet struggle with everything else."

"I like math. It's easy and fun to do. Just like gym."

"Well, gym and math aren't going to get you to be a college student. Or even out of high school. You need to find a way to interest yourself in your other subjects. Otherwise, we will never get you out of this area."

She always ends with that. There is one wish my grandma has for me, and that is to leave the city of Niagara Falls, New York. I know why she doesn't like it. Crime is high in Niagara Falls and trouble brews everywhere. We don't live in the best area of the city either. My frequent run-ins with the cops don't help my situation. It's never really my fault. My friends always want to do stupid things.

"Don't worry, Grandma," I say, taking a bite from my plate. The rice is very good, as usual, although I don't know if it's good because I am hungry or because I actually still like it after all these years. "I'll get out of here one day."

"Not without good grades you won't."

"I don't like some of my teachers," I complain. "They're assh…mean." Her snare makes me lower my eyes. I take a drink of the cold water sitting in front of me. Usually I drink milk but because the price has gotten so high we can't afford to get it like we used to. That made eating cereal in the morning a huge problem. Often I eat it with water.

"Well, you should stop goofing around with your friends." Her scolding look could have been seen a mile away. "Getting into all these fights at school, and having the cops bring you home outside of school. I didn't raise you to be like this."

"The cops brought me home two times. Neither time was my fault." I try to defend. "It's not my friends Grandma. I really don't like some of my teachers."

"It's never your fault Aiden. Then you learn to like them. There will be a lot of people that come through your life that you don't like. You need to learn to deal with them. I know you have a free soul and you like to do what you want with no regards to authority, but school is something that you need. I don't want you ending up like all the other boys around here, selling drugs and going to jail. Or worse, dead. You are better than them."

"But my friends are the only thing I have, other than you," I protest. She doesn't understand that. I can't live my entire life just with her and doing homework. I'll go bonkers!

"I know this area isn't the best but you should stay away from them boys you hang around with. They are trouble. Your father would never approve, you know." She shakes her spoon at me. My father. The mere thought of him destroys the appetite that I have worked up.

"Well, he's not here, so he doesn't have a say." My stern reply stops her from going any further.

After dinner, I help clean up and then I leave the house. It's a nice night out, after the cold, brisk winter during which I tried my best never to leave the house. This rare warm day at the beginning of spring isn't something that happens often so I have to make the most of it. As always, my grandmother advises me to be as careful as possible. There have been a lot of crimes lately and she doesn't want anything bad happening to me. I am one of the few white people in the area, which makes me a target to the African-Americans and Hispanics that don't like white people.

Walking down the street, I notice a few people here and there. Some are begging for money, some are just hanging out, and others are going about their business. Nothing seems to have changed. A few cars pass by and I try not to make eye contact with anyone around me. I look at the old warehouses that have been closed for years. There are abandoned cars in some of the lots that look as though someone has given up on fixing them. Many of the houses are boarded up, with homeless people sneaking in and out of the back. A lot of people wouldn't believe places like this exist in the country, yet some wouldn't think anything else is normal.

A city like Niagara Falls takes on a life of its own. It's a community that has learned to survive with close to nothing. There are nice areas in the city but none of them are anywhere close to where I live. The wealthiest person in the next twenty blocks is most likely a drug dealer. That's what my grandmother always tells me.

Oddly, I notice an old abandoned building has some activity brewing in it. I stop at the sight of lights in one of the rundown warehouses that used to be abandoned. There is a sign but it's too far away for me to make it out. A business? That would be strange. A few cars are parked outside. Running around to the back of the building, I try my best to find a window but can't.

In the front of the warehouse there is a window just a few paces away. I slowly approach, hoping I'm not seen. I don't know what's going on inside but there is a good chance it's not something I am supposed to see. It if's a drug-deal I am going to get into a lot of trouble if I'm caught. For a moment I think of turning back. As usual, my careless curiosity gets the better of me. I take one last look around to make sure no one is watching me and then finally peek through the window.

To my surprise, it's not what I expected. Long chain ropes are hanging from the high ceiling. At the end of the ropes are large boxing bags that a couple of men are punching. There is a boxing ring in the center of the warehouse. People are everywhere. Inside the ring I spot an older-looking black man that is holding some sort of pads and a younger man is hitting them with his boxing gloves.

I have never seen a boxing gym before. My emotions are tingling as I watch everyone work out. It's amazing. The people punching the bags seem so poised and full of energy. They look angry, yet controlled. Their focus is one hundred percent; their only intention is on hitting the bags. Some are doing other things, like jumping rope or sit-ups, but every single one is working hard. They almost look like an army being trained. I have never really paid attention to the sport of boxing, mostly because I never watch television because we don't have one. I immediately decide that I like this sport.

There isn't a single white person in the gym, which suddenly frightens me. I probably shouldn't be watching this. I could get into a lot of trouble. As I peer at the ring one last time, I see the trainer look right back at me. Shit! I've been spotted! I push away from the window, falling over an empty pail that I hadn't noticed was next to me. I get up and run as fast as I can down the street toward my house, all the while thinking how much I wish I didn't have to. But there's no way I can stay. I am white and I have no money. There is no way I can go back.

Chapter Three

There was no escaping my curiosity. My grandma always said I had a free soul destined to do whatever it desired at the moment. So for the next two weeks, I ditched my friends after school, decided not to take the bus home, and walked by the boxing gym every day. Each time I passed, I walked around to the back of the building where I had found a window, crept up to the window where I always stood, and watched as the fighters trained.

My grandmother thought I was staying after school to get help with my homework. I began to come home after dinnertime and she was a little upset with me. Time went by so fast when I was watching the guys box, I didn't even realize when an hour had passed. My initial amusement with the sport became an obsession. Every night before bed I would practice all of the punches I was watching them throw. I watched their foot movement, watched their hands and elbows, and watched as they glided from side to side. Their training became my training.

Only two weeks in and I could already see my body changing a little. I wasn't sure if it was just my mind playing tricks on me. At night I would spend at least two hours practicing what I had learned that day from watching them.

I leave the house early Saturday morning because my grandmother goes shopping with her friend every other Saturday. I usually have a few hours to spare before she gets home and I use that time to go to the gym. The sun is shining bright and the cloudless sky makes it hot. I run to the gym as fast as I can despite knowing that my shirt will be dripping with sweat by the time I get there. It doesn't matter to me though. The way I see it, the faster I get there the more time I have to watch and learn.

Once I get there I notice there aren't as many cars parked in front. Damn! I wonder if they are open. The hours on the door said they are open Saturday mornings. I remember because I snuck by the door quickly one time just to get a peek at it. Strolling around to the back I look through the window and notice there aren't as many people there as usual, but they are open. The coach isn't around. A few fighters hit bags; they seem to be taking it easier than usual laughing amongst each other.

One guy, however, is much different. I had been watching him since the first day I came to the gym. He is tall, with dark black skin and a mean-looking face. His build is huge, like a bear. When he punches the bags, they fly from side to side as if someone were pushing them. Each punch is thrown with anger and intensity. His speed is amazing and his determination is untested. He has been there every single day that I had come to watch. He never leaves before I leave, and is always there when I get there.

When he gets into the ring, people in the gym usually stop what they are doing to watch. From what I can tell, he usually wins each round that they fight. Most of the guys in the gym that step in the ring with him get knocked down when they are boxing. He always helps them up after though. The guy's boxing skills are amazing.

I continue to watch him hit the bags and I study his movement. His hands are always kept high and his feet separated. He moves from side to side, always keeping his eyes on the bag and looking to pinpoint each shot with force. Of everyone in the gym, I try to mimic him the most. Sometimes I catch myself in the window, throwing punches without even realizing it.

"You know, most people just come in." The words of a man make me stumble as I fall off the can but catch myself before I hit that ground. Fear crosses my face as I look around. His big brown eyes are gentle; his grey curly hair ages him. He's tall, but not too tall. I recognize him as the coach, the same man that caught me staring through the window the very first night. The only thing I can think of is that I am in so much trouble. "Very well." He takes a step forward as I take a step back. There's a chance I can make a run for it. There is no way he can catch me.

"My name is Joe Kay, but the guys call me Coach Kay. What's your name, son?" His words seem generous and his voice is distinct. I am scared and thinking of running.

"Aiden," I answer timidly. "Aiden Walker."

The man smiles. "Well, Aiden, do you like what you see in there?" His question makes me wonder what his intentions are. He seems genuine. I remain silent, still thinking about running. "I've seen you here every day for the last two weeks. Now I am not going to make you come in, son. But you are welcome to come give it a try."

This entire time I thought no one had seen me, yet he had been watching. Running isn't an option anymore. Not just because I know I will never be able to come back, but because I want to go in.

"It's ok, I don't bite, I swear." He leads the way. His mocking comment draws no comfort from me.

Slowly I follow him to the front of the building. Two glass

doors lead inside. On the glass doors are posters of upcoming fights. I see the big guy that I have been watching the last two weeks on one of the posters. Coach Kay turns towards me and opens the door, allowing me to walk in first.

"Welcome to the Star Boxing Gym," he says as I enter. The size of the warehouse is much bigger than it is from the window. The ceiling is as high as I can see, the bags circle around the ring, and weight machines are off to the side. There are pads on the ground where the guys do sit ups and pushups. My eyes are open so wide they hurt. The sounds of bags being hit echo through the entire room. A few people walk by me and nod their heads, while others don't even look my way. The ring is huge. I walk towards it slowly, staying far away from the people hitting the bags around it. They look very scary. I don't want to get in their way while they are training. No one seems to care that I'm white.

Towards the back of the place I notice a little office that Coach Kay usually stays in when he is not training. I had seen it the past two weeks while I watched. My focus turns on the ring. It feels amazing being close to it. My heart is racing. Circling around it, I can't help but smile.

"Never seen a ring before?" Coach Kay mocks. The only time I have is here. "You can go in if you like, the stairs are right there." He points a few paces ahead and I see a set of stairs leading up towards the giant ring. I look at him again. He smirks. "Go on, son," he repeats, waving his hands forward.

Taking a step onto the first stair I realize they are shaky. I try to ignore it as I walk up into the ring. Spreading the two middle ropes like I see the other boxers do, I enter the ring. I notice Coach Kay nod to someone. Ignoring it, I walk around the ring in amazement. So this is what it feels like to be in a boxing ring! My excitement is not hidden from my face, at least, I don't think it is. I bounce around a little like I see the fighters do and I hear a laugh.

"Been watching well, I see," Coach Kay says. He has a pair of red gloves in his hands that the guy he nodded to gave him. The older Spanish looking man with the dark mustache is the assistant trainer. That is what I think anyways. His height matches Coach Kay's but his build is a little less intimidating. So is his gentle face. "These should fit you ok. Put these on. Let's see what you got."

I hesitate. These are real gloves he is going to let me wear, not the ones I made from pillowcases in my room! I can't help but wonder if I'm dreaming. Is this really happening? Why is this man allowing me to do this? He walks over to me. I put my hands forward, allowing him to put the gloves on.

My right hand slides in first. It fits perfectly. I squeeze a fist. The feeling is awesome. My left hand slides into the other glove as I stare at them both on my hands. They are lighter than I thought they would feel. I feel like a real boxer. I can't help but smile and Coach Kay catches it. He ties up both gloves and walks away, leaving me in the center of the ring.

"Now, you don't have wraps on so I don't want to do this for too long. I'm just going to teach you a few punches, and you listen to everything I say. Do you understand?" I nod my head. "Well, you don't talk much. That is going to have to be remedied." His mocking words don't make me speak. He steps towards me and I immediately put my hands up like I have been watching his fighters do. My feet spread a bit and my knees bend. My left hand is forward and my right hand is behind it. Coach Kay's face is surprised and he looks to his friend watching outside of the ring. The Spanish man raises an eyebrow.

"Well, well. Someone has been watching us. Your power hand should be behind you. Right handed then?" I nod. He smiles. "Ok, ok." Getting closer, he straightens up my elbows. "Hands up, elbows in, body turned. I like it. Let's see how well you've been watching. When I say jab, I want you to throw that left fist into my hand. Align your shoulder with your chin. This helps you avoid a counter punch. Jab!" His quick order makes me throw the punch into his hand. His hand is so hard that it feels like I have hit a wall. My knuckle immediately hurts, but it feels good to punch. "That's some power you got, son." I can tell he is a bit shocked by it. "Straighten up your body. Step into the jab a little harder. Glide into it. Turn the fist over like you're cork screwing it in. Bring it right back to your chin and make sure your right hand stays up for protection, got it?"

I do exactly as he says. "Jab!" he barks. Again I throw the jab, this time just the way he asks. I can feel the difference in the punch.

"That is one hell of a jab you got," Coach Kay says. "Boxing is strategy as much as it is power and as much as it is speed. Your jab is the most significant punch you have. A good, strong jab puts fear into your opponent. It's the punch that sets up your power hand, which is your right. However, if you can get a man to fear your jab, then he will fear your power hand more, even if he has not felt it. Jabs win fights, and separate the good from the great. Do you understand?"

"Yes, Coach." The word slips out. He looks at me awkwardly. I don't know why I said it. It just came out so naturally.

"Next is your cross, your power hand. This is the punch that knocks people out. It's your power hand, the hand that you do everything with – write, swing, throw a football. After you throw your jab, I want you to throw your cross. Extend the punch as much as you can; turn your hip and your body into it to maximize your power. However, do not overthrow it. Jab. Cross!" I glide into the jab, slamming his hand, and immediately follow with the cross down the middle into his other hand. I feel his hand fly back at my cross. His friend outside the ring raises an eyebrow again.

"It's a little off, but something we can work on. You've got some hard punches for a kid. How old are you, son?" Coach Kay asks.

"Thirteen," I answer. I'm not supposed to give my age or name to people I don't know. I love this sport, though, and Coach Kay seems like a man I can trust.

"Do you like this place?" Coach asks, looking around.

"Yes."

"Good, because I want you to come here every day you can. I'm going to teach you how to fight, how to box. Is that something that you want to do?"

Really? He wanted to train me? I try and hide my excitement, except for a smile. I feel like jumping up and down. "Yes, yes it is," I answer. Then suddenly I realize something that stops my excitement. "But, I can't pay you."

My sad tone makes him exchange looks with his friend and his face turns grim. Walking over to me, he bends over looking into my eyes and grins.

"Let's make a deal. I will train you for an hour every day and then when we are done, for one hour you can help me around the gym with whatever I need. That will more than pay for your gym fees. Deal?" He sticks out his hand.

I don't know how I am going to do it, but as long as my grandma thinks I am getting tutored after school I think I can swing it. I want to do this sport. I want to be a boxer. With my gloves still on, I grin and shake his hand. He chuckles.

Chapter Four

I kept to my word, and so did Coach Kay. Every single day after school I ran to the gym as fast as my feet would allow me. Coach always said that a good run was a perfect way to build up endurance for a fight. All of his fighters had to run. Some days he wouldn't even allow them to hit the bags until they ran a few miles down the road and back. I listened to everything he told me. I learned how to throw a good jab and cross. He wouldn't teach me any other punch. For weeks I had to throw jabs and crosses on the bags.

Once a day for twenty minutes, he would take me into the ring and teach me as he held the punching mitts. He only allowed me to throw the jab and cross. There was no other punch, and if he saw me trying to mimic one of the other fighters that were throwing different punches, I would get in trouble.

After five weeks of throwing the same punches, I had become annoyed. There was frustration with each and every punch I threw. At home before bed, I would sit in my room and shadowbox. Even in my room, away from Coach Kay, I only threw the jab and cross. For some reason I felt as though he could see me from wherever he was, and that if I tried to throw an uppercut or a hook, I would get in trouble. It was a strange thought that haunted me. Listening to someone that wasn't even watching me was a discipline I could not explain. In school I wouldn't write down something that I didn't want to even if the teacher was watching me. Now I was listening to a man that couldn't even see me.

Shadowboxing was something I loved to do. I took everything I learned in the ring and applied it to thin air. I moved around my room, throwing punches, bobbing and weaving like he taught me. Moving the head from side to side was an art. It looked easy watching other fighters do it but when I tried it for the first time I couldn't do it as well or as fast. I had to learn how to move my head away from the punch, and at the same time position myself for the counterattack. Coach Kay had taught me that every single second of the round, and every single movement my opponent made, was an opportunity. My job was to create those opportunities, and hit as hard as I could when I got them. The problem was that he was only allowing me to throw jabs and crosses, which I knew was limiting my ability to counter.

If I dipped my head to the right, then I had to line up my cross to be thrown straight down the center. Sometimes I could loop the cross if there was an opening, but very rarely did he let me do it against him. Dipping to the left was hard. My body felt weird doing it. I couldn't do it very fast and sometimes he would hit me in the head because I would drop my right hand, another thing I seemed to have a problem doing was keeping my hands up. I learned that boxing wasn't as easy as getting into the ring and throwing punches. It was a craft that one had to learn to perfect. Every movement, every punch, was part of a strategy to help land the best possible punch against your opponent. It was like a chess match.

I hadn't even been in the ring to fight anyone and I seemed to be years away from getting a chance to fight.

As usual, I run to the gym after school. I am more tired than usual due to the humid, hot weather that covers the day like a blanket. By the time I get there I am sweating. The doors are open and a few people stand outside chatting.

"Aiden, what's up, white boy?" Hector says. White boy. It is the name all of the fighters and people in the gym call me. I was the only white boy there. Hector is a good fighter with a load of talent. He is much bigger than me but his weight isn't high. He isn't as intimidating to look at on the street as he is in the ring. Even though he thinks he is the greatest thing to happen to boxing, he will never make it. Coach Kay likes him a lot but Hector is not dedicated the way he is supposed to be. I hear it is because of drugs.

As arrogant as Hector is, he was one of the few people in the gym that was always nice to me. I smile and give him a handshake, which is a slap that turns into a fist. "Not much," I reply, shaking my head. "It's so hot today I can barely breathe." Most of the people in the gym have adapted to me being there. Most of the other kids my age ignore me. The older ones make fun of me a lot. I wear the same clothes every day which doesn't make me very popular. I can't afford anything else though. I am ok with it. It only fuels my anger to punch things.

"Shit, wait until you get in there," he responds. "It's like a sauna up in that bitch." I didn't like the sound of that.

Walking into the gym I try my best to ignore everyone. The sound of bags being hit isn't as intimidating as it used to be. No one is paying any attention to me anyhow. I walk up to the ring and watch the heavyweight hit Coach Kay's mitts. His power is amazing, his footwork is perfect, and his punches seem flawless. He moves side to side quicker than the eye can catch sometimes, his hands are always to his chin, and his execution of combinations is dangerously fast.

His name is Tracey Jury. I found out my first week here that he is the best prospect Coach Kay has at winning a world title as a professional boxer. His record is 6-0 as a pro. All six victories have come from knockouts before the sound of the third round ever came to be. He's got the best promoters in the world looking to sign him.

Despite dark brown eyes and eyebrows that work together to give a look that can kill, he is, surprisingly, very respectful to everyone in the gym. His genuinely polite attitude reflects the emotion of the entire gym. There are a few cocky, arrogant fighters here and there. Tracey usually puts those guys in their place when he enters the room.

Coach Kay stops and looks over at me. "Get your gloves on," he says. "I'll be done by the time you're geared up."

Quickly, I run into the locker room to get ready. I take off my school clothes and put on the only pair of shorts I have. The guys in the gym always make fun of me for wearing the same shorts. I can't afford to buy new ones. My grandmother doesn't realize that I wake up in the middle of the night to wash them every night. My shirts rotate between three different choices. I don't have boxing shoes like the rest of the guys so I wear broken-down sneakers with holes in them that draw more than a few laughs from the guys. One day I hope to get real boxing shoes.

After getting my gloves on I enter the ring. Coach Kay is sweating a ton. Holding mitts for Tracey must be hard. I assume my stance. Left foot forward, right foot back. Hands up.

"Cross, hook." His words stun me for a second and I hesitate and drop my hands. Immediately, a mitt strikes the side of my face. "Don't drop your hands," he demands as I put my hands up to block his next strike. "I said, cross, hook!" he barks. I throw the right hand down the middle as hard as I can, then turn my hip and my body, rotating my arm into the hook.

"Good!" he says. "You're dropping the right just a tad when you throw the hook. Other than that, you are throwing it perfectly. Twist the body into it, just enough so that you're not overthrowing it, and so that you can come back with a cross or another hook. The hook is a very dangerous punch because a strong, fast one surprises opponents. World champions often have amazing hooks that can knock people out. We need to work on perfecting your hook."

I am glad to hear him say that. I've been watching these guys throw hooks for the last two months. My punches seem stronger as well.

"Jab, cross, uppercut." Again his words surprise me, but I

keep my hands up. I throw the combination he asks for, finishing with the uppercut coming from underneath my stomach and drilling it up into the mitt. "Dip the head when you throw the uppercut. Just a little bit. Then strive it up the middle like a missile. The shoulder dips, too, like a quick dance move. Let's do it again."

I throw it exactly as he says. He smiles. "It feels good to finally throw other punches," I admit.

"It should. Your shoulders have been built up well since you started. Your footwork is good. Hooks and uppercuts are easier to throw when your form is right. That is why I made you wait. Focus on form first, and punches after. Your left hook is a very dangerous punch because it is powerful, as well as your jab. Now I usually don't say this about people that have been here only five weeks, but I might have you sparring soon. I have some people your age and weight that you could give it a try with."

Sparring?! I am so excited I can barely say anything. My smile says it all. Coach Kay's grin returns my look. "C'mon now," he says. "Let's keep going."

After six rounds of hitting mitts I am exhausted. The humidity alone can be credited for the loss of about nine pounds from my body, I'm guessing. I clean up the best I can and begin to do chores around the gym. Coach Kay has me do a lot of little things. I clean the floors, the bathrooms, and sweep his office. I put away the gloves and things that people leave out. Some of the guys crack jokes and make fun of me. I ignore them as best I can, never letting their jokes get the best of me. I don't allow myself to lose my temper with them, no matter how much they make fun of me. Mainly because they could all kick my ass. I never clean the bathrooms unless Tracey is there, though. He usually keeps the guys from doing things to mess with me.

At the end of the night most of the people are gone, except for one man, who usually stays until 8:00. He is the only man that stays later than Tracey, because he arrives late every night. He is bigger than Tracey and taller, too. In fact, he is one of the biggest men I have ever seen. He hits the bags with anger, and I have never seen anyone talk to him.

"His name is Kenyon Martin," Coach Kay says, sneaking up on me as I watch from a distance.

"What's his deal?" I ask bravely. "I never see him talking to anyone, even you."

"I don't know," he admits. "One day I'm sitting in my office and this man walks into the gym. The biggest man I have yet to train. Of course, the first thing I think when I see him is that I have the next heavyweight champ of the world. He's about six-foot-eight, 290

pounds of pure muscle. I have never seen a man like him before."
Coach Kay begins to walk around the gym and I follow him. "So he
comes into my office, asks me how much a month he needs to pay to
come work out. I ask him about fighting, and he immediately cuts me
off and says no, he just wants to work out. He says that he will not
talk to anyone, and he don't want anyone talking to him."

I scratch my head and look at the mysterious man. "So you
know nothing about him?" I ask.

"I know as much about him as I do about you, Aiden," Coach
Kay replies, peering at me with a raised eyebrow.

"You never asked," I respond quickly.

"Most people walk into this gym and within five days are
telling me things about them that I do not wish to know. Things that
no person should know about people." Coach walks into his office
and I follow. He takes a brown paper bag and pulls out a sandwich.

"There's nothing really to know about me."

"Aiden Walker," Coach Kay says. "A white boy living in the
ghetto, coming to a boxing gym all on his own. Wearing the same
clothes every day. I honestly thought you were homeless at first. But
you're smart, and you hit like an eighteen year old." He pauses,
taking a bite of a dry-looking sandwich. "There's not too many white
people that live in this area. So I ask myself, 'Now how does this
young boy end up in this situation, and where is his family'?" He
pauses and his next words I know are going to bother me. "The only
Walker family in this area is Barry Walker's family. Which makes
you Barry Walker's son." My heart skips a beat and I look down to
the ground.

"What your father did," he continues, hesitating as he looks
around, "well, not too many people would have done the same thing
in his shoes."

"I don't have a father," I respond angrily. "He abandoned us."

"Abandoned?" Coach Kay asks, shaking his head. "Is that
what you call it?"

"Yes," I answer hastily. "I don't want to talk about it."

My anger seems to have gotten Coach Kay's attention. He
looks oddly at me, then just nods with his chin up.

"Very well, son," he says. "Very well."

Chapter Five

After dinner, I decide to go out. My grandmother would never let me leave so late at night. So, as usual, I sneak out. I run a few blocks to meet my friends at the grocery store parking lot. Summer is starting to kick in and the temperatures are becoming unbearable. At the gym, sweat usually begins to seep through my clothes as soon as I enter the building. It's going to be a long, hot summer at that place.

At the parking lot I see three of my most trusted friends: John, Rasim, and Big T.

John has been my friend since I've been able to walk. They say his father and mine were like brothers. My grandmother is wary of him. According to her, he is a bad influence on me and always seems to get me in trouble. It's not like she's wrong. I've met the cops a few times hanging out with him. John was my boy though. I could never turn my back on him or stop hanging out with him. He has the look of a fighter even though he has never boxed before. He doesn't wish to, either. He'd preferred to brawl in the streets.

Rasim, an Indian guy, started coming around a few years ago. He is nice with very thick, dark eyebrows and eyes to match. We often make fun of his family claiming that they own every corner store from here to New York City. They actually might. We spend some afternoons hanging outside his uncle's store. Sometimes we are there for hours as we watch people go in and out of the store. We sit around making fun of each other, laughing, and getting ourselves into trouble. Rasim is so skinny you would think he came from a family that couldn't afford food instead of me.

Big T is taller than I am and about three times my size. His big belly never stops wanting food. That's where the name Big T came from. His dark face is fat but his features are gentle.

This is my main crew. My boys. Trouble doesn't follow us, we go create it and not on purpose. We are poor. In order to get nice things we have to steal them. In order to eat nice meals we have to take them. There is nothing complicated about it. This is life. A life, that because of Coach, I was being forced to leave. His number one rule to stay in the gym was not to get into mischief. Staying away from my crew was a must if I wanted to stay out of trouble. So why was I here right now? I had no idea.

"What's up, boxer boy?" John says, giving me the traditional handshake. "You haven't been around lately. Still going up to that gym, trying to be a fighter?"

John is sixteen. He has been in jail over a dozen times already. If anyone needs to get into the ring and let off some anger, it's him. Him mocking me for fighting is something I have gotten used to over the past few months.

"Always," I answer. "I love it there."

"I should go be a boxer," Big T jokes, dancing around a bit. "I could tear some people up."

"The only thing you're tearing up is a hamburger, son," Rasim says, laughing and smacking hands with John. I chuckle, too, patting Big T on the back. He frowns and looks down at the ground.

"It's all good, man," I say.

"That boxing shit ain't gonna get you nowhere, man," John says. "You may as well just give it up, fool. The real money is to be made out here." He pulls a few hundred-dollar bills from his pocket.

"Damn! Where you get that from?" Big T yells.

"Back off, fat boy," John answers, pushing him away. "This is my money, fool. I might be able to let you get in on some of it, though. All of you. That is, if you can handle it." He looks over at me with grim eyes and a smirk.

"Not interested," I reply immediately.

"I am," Rasim says. "I'm trying to get paiiiiiid!" I shake my head.

"What about you, Big T?" John asks. "Don't tell me you're gonna be punk-made like Aiden."

"Yo, man, I'm trying to get in on that, too," Big T says without hesitation.

"Looks like you lose, Aiden," John mocks, putting the money back in his pocket.

"I don't need to be getting in trouble with all that. I'm trying to do good in school, boxing, and get up outta this place," I admit. The boys don't like those aspirations, especially John.

"Say what you want, but you're gonna need this money right here one day," he says, smirking again. "I'll be waiting for you when you do."

"Enough of this crap," Rakim interrupts. "C'mon, let's go."

John leads the way to the back of the grocery store. I don't know where we are going but it doesn't seem like a good idea to keep following them. For some reason I can sense there is some trouble looming, but I haven't seen my friends in a long time and I can't back out on them now. If I stop hanging out with them then I will be alone with no one to protect me if I get into trouble.

We run around to the back of the building. There is a dumpster up against the store. I don't have to ask to see where this was going.

"No, no way," I say.

"C'mon, man, don't be a chicken," John says. "There's an opening at the top. We did this a few days ago. The store's closed so we can break in and steal whatever we want." His determination is absolute. And mine is broken.

"No, man, I'm not stealing anything."

"You better come, Aiden, I'm not letting you sit behind," John says, jumping onto the dumpster.

"Listen, dude," Big T says to me, shaking his head, "this ain't money we're stealing…it's food. I know you can use it, too, man. We don't got money to be eating what we want; my family sure as hell don't. I know your grandmother doesn't. Let's just grab some good stuff to eat and bounce. It's simple. We'll be eating steaks and chocolate later." He licks his lips with a smile.

I know that I am going to do this no matter how much I don't want to. Big T is right. We are poor. This opportunity didn't come a lot. My stomach is turning, telling me to turn around. But part of my stomach is excited as I can taste a juicy steak. Chocolate. I love chocolate. The boys jump onto the dumpster and climb up the ladder, disappearing onto the rooftop one after another.

"Let's go." Big T waves me to come. I slowly climb my way up the dirty dumpster. The smell is horrific. I try to cover my nose. Big T helps me grab the small ladder that leads the way to the rooftop. I reach the top and watch John and Rasim run to the door at the top of the building, which is pried open. John must be doing this a lot.

I run across the top of the roof, get to the door, and enter. A set of stairs leads down into the back of the store. We get down the stairs and look around. It's like heaven for a poor, thirteen-year-old boy.

Pallets of food lay everywhere – every brand of every type of food and drink. Cereal, canned goods, chocolate, everything. It's all ours for the taking. I still feel sick about this but if we aren't going to get caught, then why not? I think of the beans and rice I have been eating every day, my entire life. My poor grandmother can't afford to buy stuff like this for me. She will be thrilled to see this food in her refrigerator and cupboards. Of course, she won't be happy if she finds out how I got it. I will have to lie to her.

The boys begin to stack up. John has wool bags that he passes to everyone and I grab mine without hesitation. The first thing I go for is pop. No drinking just water for the next couple weeks! I stock up on Pepsi and Coke. It makes the bag a little heavy, so I put some back and follow John down the back hall. He stops where the candy is. I start to fill up as well, taking as much as I can. The canned goods are right behind me along with cereal. I grab as much as I can of that as well, filling up my bag.

"The steaks and stuff are this way," Big T says. I follow him through the back of the store into the cooler area. As we enter, I stare in amazement. Steaks, turkeys, lobster – all kinds of meat are sitting there, ours for the taking. I can't believe how easy this is. We grab as much as our bags can hold.

"Sweet, all done, let's roll," John says as we make our way back to where we came from. I am a little excited to have all this to eat when I get home. I realize this probably isn't the last time I am going to do this with them. My grandmother tries so hard to provide for us. This is a good way to pay her back.

I see that Big T is struggling and breathing heavy as he goes up the stairs. I run back down and grab his bag from him.

"Just a little bit more," I say. Nodding his head, he follows as fast as he can.

We run across the top of the roof and start to climb down the ladder. Suddenly, I see lights shining as two cop cars pull into the parking lot. I'm still on the ladder. John and Rakim are on the ground.

"C'mon!" John yells.

"But Big T is still up there!" I shout back.

"Forget him!" They say. I can still jump down and make a run for it; I might get away. My heart is racing and my hands begin to shake. "Man, forget ya'll, I'm out of here," John says, looking toward the cop cars that are close at hand. A few seconds later, John and Rakim are running down the lot.

As I make my way back up the ladder one car pulls up to the building, pointing a huge light up at me. I know he has seen me. The other car chases after Rasim and John. I get to the top of the roof. I'm trapped. Big T is lying down with his bag next to him.

"We're dead, we're dead," he groans. "We're going to jail. Oh, no, no." His wailing stops as I put my finger to my mouth to quiet him.

"Listen, he didn't see you. Just me. You stay here until we're gone, ok?"

He looks awkwardly at me. "What you mean until we are gone?" he asks.

I grin at him, stand up, and run back towards the ladder.

"Put your hands up!" the officer on the ground shouts up at me. He's standing next to the car, his hand on the pistol at his side. I put my hands up and slowly come down the ladder to the ground. "Looks like your two buddies got away. Anyone else up there?" he asks.

"No sir, just me," I say, dropping the bag right in front of him. He turns me around and snaps handcuffs on my wrists. They are too big for my small hands but manage to stay on. "Ok, let's go." He puts me in the car and reads me my rights as we head to the police station.

I'm nervous but I'm glad at least Big T got away. I know they can't arrest me. This is not my first run-in with the police and I've paid attention enough in school to know that I'm a minor and unless I kill someone there is no way I can be arrested. Plus, John has been arrested a dozen times and they always just bring him home after. I'm more nervous about what my grandmother is going to say. Again.

The last time I got caught with John stealing bikes down the street, she was so upset she didn't talk to me for an entire week. She made me feel bad about betraying her trust. She's going to kill me.

The police station is quiet as I wait for my grandmother to pick me up. The wait isn't as long as I expected; my heart drops to the floor and I lose my breath as I see Coach Kay open the door and walk in with a police officer. It's not the one who arrested me. I know this man. His name is Mike Harver. He comes to the gym. He's short, plump and clean-shaven, with a bald head.

"I noticed he was one of yours when I saw him come in," he states.

"Ah, yes. He is definitely one of mine. Thank you, Mike." The look on Coach Kay's face scares me. My hands are shaking.

"No problem, Coach," Mike says, shaking his hand. "Just keep him out of trouble."

"Oh, you bet I will."

Coach's words frighten me. I face the ground, unable to look him in the eye. He sits down next to me.

"Mike says this isn't the first time you've been here," he says. I stay quiet, still looking down. "I know how important friends can be to you young folks. But bad friends, friends that let you get in trouble, and that bring trouble your way, are not friends at all."

I look up and nod my head. Suddenly, my grandmother storms into the station like a mad woman. She rushes into the room and looks angrily at me. Her frail body moves faster than it ever has before.

"This is the second time in four months!" she exclaims, shaking her head. "I can't believe you make me come down here in the middle of the night. Was it John? Is that who you were with? I swear, if I get my hands on that boy…" Her words fade as she notices Coach Kay. "Who's this?"

"Forgive me, ma'am," he says politely, "my name is Coach Kay. I am Aiden's boxing coach."

I shake my head for him to stop but it's too late. Now I'm really in for it.

"Boxing? When did you start boxing?" she asks me, her words drawing an odd look from Coach. I'm too ashamed to look at either of them. "I thought you were staying after school every day to get help."

I shake my head, trembling. "No, Grandma, I've been going to the boxing gym every day after school and training."

"He's a very talented fighter, Ms. Walker," Coach says. "And he is dedicated and works at the gym as well. We love having him there. He works hard. Had I known he had friends that were getting him into trouble, I would have walked him home to you myself every night."

Coach Kay's words shock me. It's the first time he has ever said anything like that about me.

"I didn't tell you because I knew you wouldn't let me do it," I tell my grandmother, defending myself before she has a chance to argue.

She glances at Coach Kay, then at me. She suddenly seems more relaxed.

"Coach Kay, can you excuse us for a minute?" she asks.

"Of course, ma'am," he responds, walking toward the door. "And just so you know, ma'am, he's a good kid. You've done a fine job raising him."

Once he's gone, she sits down across from me. "Those boys are trouble," she begins.

"I know," I say. "I haven't been hanging out with them, I swear. I've been at the gym every day." My pleading will probably get me nowhere, but I still try.

"Boxing, huh," she says. "It's a dangerous sport. You can get brain damage or beat up. In my old days, I would never allow it."

I don't know how to take her response. I just sit there. She shakes her head and grins.

"Oh, your grandfather is probably looking down at me right now with a big smile on his face," she continues. "He loved boxing. He would sit in front of that television every weekend watching the fights. Drove me crazy." She chuckled a bit.

"He did?" I had no idea.

"Oh yea, God knows he loved his boxing. Your father did too.

33

They used to watch it together." Her words surprise me. I didn't care that my father did, but I always heard great stories about my grandfather.

"So does that mean you don't care?" I ask cautiously.

She sighs. "I would never tell you that you can't do something in life. I tried that with your father. Tried to get him to…see the world the way I did. Told him that he had to do certain things in life, growing up, things that would make him money and get him out of this God-forsaken town. In a way, he listened to me. And I can't help but think that maybe if he hadn't…Oh, I don't know. Maybe if he hadn't listened to me he would still be alive today."

"It's not your fault he died, Grandma. It's his own fault. I blame him for abandoning me."

"Partly it is," she continues. "I pushed him to do something he wasn't sure about doing. And he listened. People push people – parents, friends, coworkers, bosses – to make decisions that can affect the rest of their lives, for better or for worse. If a father pushes his son to go to a family party that he don't want to go to, and the son does it just to please his father but dies in an accident on the way there, is it the father's fault for pushing him? No. At least, that's what most people would say. But deep down inside, the father will always blame himself." She looks into my eyes. "My point is, I don't want to push you into any direction, Aiden. I want you to make your own decisions in life. That is the way to live, which is the only way to live. If boxing is what you want to do, then that is fine. As long as you keep up with your school work!" Her words are gentle and rest in my heart – I will never forget them.

"Yes ma'am," I slyly respond.

Just then, Coach Kay walks back into the room.

"I don't mean to interrupt, ma'am, but the officers need this room."

"That's ok, we are finished," she responds. "Don't let him get into any more trouble, you hear me, Coach Kay? There are a few boxing moves this old lady has picked up over the years."

Coach Kay laughs. "I wouldn't dare test my skills against yours, ma'am. I'll watch him as if he was my own son."

I look at Coach Kay. He's got that look in his eyes. That look that I know I'm forgiven but I will pay for this when I get to the gym. I'm not sure what his punishment will be for me getting arrested, but I'll bet it will involve a lot of running.

Chapter Six

Standing in front of the mirror, practicing my uppercuts and hooks, I can't help but think how good they feel and look. If a movement feels wrong, I try to perfect it. I'm dipping into my uppercuts, then rolling my upper body out and coming back with a hook. My body flows so well that it almost feels like one movement. When I finish the combination with a cross down the middle it looks perfect.

When I am boxing, nothing else exists. The resentment I have towards the life I have lived fuels my energy to keep pushing, even when I am exhausted. *I can do this*, I always say to myself when the mirror reflects my image. Boxing has consumed my life.

It reminds me of the first day that I came to the gym window. When I looked in, no one saw me. They were focused, determined. I can finally see why. Boxing has a way of taking over the mind. The amount of dedication it takes to be a fighter is more than I had originally thought, and harder than I could have ever dreamed. Without having one fight, and not even a sparring session, I can see how this sport is so brutal. The obsession that it takes on the mind is beyond comprehension.

When I eat at the dinner table at night I am thinking about bobbing and weaving my head. When I dream, I dream of fighting. When I walk to school, I feel as though I should be running to gain more endurance. Sometimes I do run. In class, I look up the history of fighting in the library and search the top fighters as soon as I get to a computer. I watch old videos of great fighters studying every move they make, wondering if I should mimic some of them. Everything in my life has become boxing. I can think of nothing else. I am only thirteen years old, but it has hold of me.

My fighting in school has stopped. The kids have stopped making fun of me. I'm not sure if it's because they know I can fight now or if it's because when I first started boxing I knocked out bully Bob Donne the last time he tried to fight me. Coach ripped me a new one when he found out about that.

It didn't matter. Not one bit. My feelings towards things have changed. If the kids at school are making fun of me now, I ignore them. Boxing has taught me self-discipline. I know I can beat up the kids that tease me and because of that I find myself more inclined not to do it.

"Gear up!" Coach Kay yells towards me. I look at myself one last time in the mirror. My body is beginning to tone into a fighter's. Realizing what he just said, I turn with a confused look. My gloves are already on. I am already geared up. I glance around to see if he was talking to someone else. "I said gear up!" he shouts again. This time he goes to the edge of the ring and tosses a headgear towards me. I'm going to spar!

My heart begins to beat faster; I can feel it coming out from my chest like in the cartoons I used to watch when I was younger. I am going to spar! This is it – the moment I have been waiting weeks for, when I get to go in the ring and fight someone for the first time! I can't hold back my excitement as I run over to the ring, nearly tripping on my way there.

I run up the stairs and jump into the ring with the headgear in my gloves. Coach Kay walks over.

"Excited?" He smirks.

"Yes, very," I answer. "I've been waiting forever for you to say that." For weeks I've been asking Coach to let me spar. He just kept saying not yet. When the other guys would, I couldn't even focus on the bags because I just watched them. Sparring was the first step to getting my first fight. Suddenly, my stomach started to turn a little. I could feel my hands begin to shake. Great, I'm nervous.

"Good. Now, listen up." He grabs my full attention. "He's a little older than you, and a little more experienced. He's also a little heavier. I want you to listen to me as I tell you what to do. Start out sticking that jab in his face. Don't just throw it to throw it. Make it swift, strong. Make him feel the power behind that jab just like I told you when you first started throwing it. Don't get nervous. Don't get anxiety. If you are wild with your punches in there you will get hurt. Keep your composure. Pretend you're hitting pads but defend yourself. This is your first time so I don't expect much."

"Yes, sir," I reply as Coach puts in my mouthpiece.

He straps on the headgear. It's so tight I can feel it pressing against my skull. It's also cut off my vision. I try to adjust it but it doesn't move. The feeling is off. It's the first time I've ever worn it. There is not one thing I like about wearing it. Coach always expresses safety first but I'd rather not be wearing it.

Across from me is a young black kid whose name is Trey. I've seen him around. He's fifteen years old and he's had a couple fights. Trey's comical personality always draws laughs in the gym. Humorous tactics don't define his boxing skills though. Trey is good. I'm nervous. My hands are starting to sweat and shake.

"Go!" Coach Kay yells. It's the start of the round. Trey and I walk to the center of the ring and tap gloves. I can feel my heart racing even faster than it was before. For some reason I can't shake these jitters. My hands are up, guarding, the way Coach Kay taught me. Trey throws two jabs at me. Both of them land through my gloves into my face. The second one stings a bit, but neither of them hurt. Getting hit actually doesn't feel as bad as I thought. Everything is moving so much faster. My anxiety is starting to get the better of me as I move around not throwing any punches. Trey throws a few more jabs that land on my gloves.

I throw my jab back at him, and he backs up so I miss. He's a lot quicker than me on his feet. As he steps to the side, he throws a cross down the middle, hitting me in the gloves. I am able to block it. Again he comes at me, and I throw a cross straight down the middle, which lands on his nose. I can tell by the look in his eyes that he isn't happy. He comes forward this time, bad intentions behind his punches. He throws a jab, cross, and hook, very fast at my head. All of them land against my face, but none of them hurt me. Before I can gather myself, he comes forward again, throwing and landing the same combination.

"Keep your hands up!" I hear Coach Kay yell. My hands are down for some reason. I didn't even notice I had dropped them. "Move your head. He's going to land those damn combinations all day if you don't."

"Yes, sir," I say, glancing at him. My mouthpiece distorts my words.

"Don't talk to me while you're in there! Don't look at me, either! Listen to my words and focus."

Again, Trey throws a combination of four punches. I am able to block the first two, but the second two hit their mark landing against my nose and skull. I am sick of getting my head hit. Breathing is starting to get difficult. I'm used to wearing a mouthpiece but now I feel like I can't breath at all. All of my training doesn't seem to mean anything. The first round isn't even over and I'm exhausted.

I hop around to get my legs under me. It's time to focus. Looking at Trey coming for me again, I move my head to the right; his jab misses. I throw a hook to his body and back to his head. The body shot lands but he blocks the headshot. He comes at me again. I back up, making him stretch out his jab. I step to the left and throw a cross down the middle, landing it again, and immediately follow with an uppercut to the body and hook to the head. He blocks the head shot again, but the body punch lands. He is getting frustrated. I'm exhausted! The only thing keeping me going is my desire to fight.

"Very good, son!" Coach Kay yells without realizing that I feel like I'm going to throw up. "Come back with the cross after that, it was open. Trey, he's figuring you out. You need to do something different. It may be his first time sparring but he damn sure ain't acting like it."

Trey nods his head. This time, he doesn't come forward with the jab. He leads with a cross straight down the middle, landing it on my chin. It's the first punch he has thrown that actually hurts me. He does the same thing again, except follows with a hook to the head and another cross. Each one of them lands. I can feel my head starting to hurt, and it's ringing.

"Move your head, son, I don't know how many times you want me to say it! Watch for those punches."

Trey comes at me again, landing three more punches. He's slow to get his hands back to his chin for protection after the uppercut lands. Instinctively, I throw my right as hard as I can to his chin. It lands cleanly. Trey's eyes roll and his legs buckle, sending him to the canvas. Oh my God! I knocked him down! Looking over to Coach, his face is stunned. Suddenly, I look over to Trey who isn't moving.

Spitting out my mouthpiece I rush over to him and kneel down.

"I'm so sorry!" I plead loudly. "Are you ok? Are you ok?"

"Relax, Aiden," Coach Kay says as he enters the ring and goes over to Trey. His eyes are open and he's staring at the ceiling. "You ok?" Coach Kay asks, rubbing Trey's head as he takes the headgear off. Trey lifts his head up and stares at me.

"Yeah," he says, brushing his glove against his bleeding lip. "That was one hell of a punch."

I stare at him, thanking God he's all right. I'm not sure what got into me or how I was able to land a punch so cleanly after getting hit so many times. His skills were far more advanced than mine. All I could think of was how much harder I needed to train. I had to be faster, stronger, more focused.

Coach Kay gave me a look I would never forget.

Chapter Seven

As fast as I can, I throw a right hand over the top of Jordan Graves' cross. My punch lands again. His nose is bleeding and his eyes are bloodshot. I struggle to take a deep breath. Graves has all but given up. Stepping forward, I lean my shoulder into his, pushing him against the ropes. I unleash a five-punch combination starting with lead cross that lands flush on his chin again, and ending with hook that lands on his forehead. My speed, and power, have developed well over the years. All five punches land and I can see the Referee looking at Graves. The final bell rings. I take a deep breath and run over to my corner. Coach Kay smiles as he takes off my headgear and rips out my mouthpiece. I find it hard to catch my breath and my arms feel like rubber. That fight was intense.

"Good job, son. You won that fight easily," he assures as he begins to take off my headgear and gloves.

"I'm tired." My heavy breathing distorts my words. I should have trained harder. Despite what Coach believes, that fight was not easy.

"You'll always be tired after a fight no matter how hard you train. You didn't get tired in there nor did you look it so don't worry about it."

"No, I need to train harder," I say, taking off my gloves.

"You train harder than anyone in that gym. Relax. What you need to learn is to move that damn head of yours. I don't know how many times I have to tell you. You're exciting to watch but you take too much unnecessary damage."

"It's easier just to keep my hands up and block the punches." I argue rolling my eyes.

"I don't care, it's not healthy. Moving your head creates openings for counter punching. You need to understand that." Coach's words go ignored as I look over to the center of the ring.

The Referee calls me over as the announcer grabs the microphone. "And the winner is, out of the blue corner, Aiden Walker!"

The announcement makes me smile and the crowd begins to cheer. This win makes me 48-5. Not bad for a twenty year-old. Most amateur boxers that start at an early age can get to as many as 200 fights before they go pro. Unfortunately for me, the area I live in doesn't have many opportunities for a boxer. We have to travel far for our fights and over the years Coach Kay hasn't been able to move as much as he used to. So we take what we can get until I am able to afford to go to a national tournament.

"That a boy," Coach Kay says as I walk over to him. "Keep winning these and we will be on our way to a national tournament in no time!"

The card was a small show. I was the main event; Jordan Graves was from Flushing, where we had had to travel to fight him. I didn't understand why the crowd had cheered for me when I won. Coach always said that an exciting fight will draw cheers from the winner whether they like him or not. There was no argument that I was the most exciting fighter in our gym mainly because of my knack for brawling.

"There you go, white boy!" Trey yells. I can hear the other guys from the gym who had made the trip chanting "white boy." I was the first white boxer to fight out of Star Boxing Gym; the name had stuck with me since I was thirteen. I knew I'd never get rid of it.

I step out of the ring and sit down to catch my breath.

"Get up and put your arms up," Coach Kay demands. "You're still getting hit too much. It may make fights exciting but if you run into someone that packs a heavy punch you're gonna get your head clocked."

"He didn't hit hard," I reply, taking a sip of water and then pouring it down my shirt. "I had to get inside on him and take some shots. He was fast at first."

"That's why you need to listen to me. Back him up with the damn jab. Jab, jab, jab. I don't know how many damn times I need to say it, son. You walk in there trying to put him on the ropes without throwing the jab and you are going to get hit. Unnecessary hits. You've got the best jab I've seen in years and you can move your head so fast. I don't understand why you don't do either of them!"

"I feel like I'm slower than everyone in there when it comes to dancing around the ring." I fire back. "Walking them down and banging with them makes me more comfortable than trying to jab and move my head."

"That's 'cause he's white, coach," Trey jokes cutting in, rubbing my head. "He don't got those quick, black people feet."

"Whatever, I don't need them when I spar you," I say, smiling as I push him away. The group around us laughs and mocks Trey.

"If you continue to not use your jab when you turn pro it's going to get you into a lot of trouble. Great fighters have great jabs.

Remember that." He's done with the conversation as he grabs my things and walks away.

Coach and I have been arguing a lot lately about what I've been doing in the ring. He always tells me I did a good job but then comes back with a million things I did wrong. He can make me feel like I lost a fight even when I won. It's starting to bother me. I let him vent, trying to ignore what he's saying. I am winning fights. That's all that matters to me.

The three-hour ride home is quiet. I'm so amped up from the fight that I offered to drive. The only thing I can think of is getting back into the gym so that I can train for my next fight. It's a far drive back home but necessary. We can't afford to stay overnight in the hotel. Coach borrowed the car from a buddy of his just so we could get down here to begin with. The older vehicle feels like it's going to break down with every mile that passes.

Everyone in the car is sleeping. Trey is passed out and snoring like an old man. He has become my best friend over the years. He is funny and a pretty good boxer when he isn't joking around or trying to sing his way to a record deal. Most of our training is done together. Trey spent a lot of time at my house over the years. His parents aren't around so he sleeps on my couch a few nights a week. He sometimes disappears for days at a time, which worries me a bit. But he always comes back and is always at the gym. He loved my grandmother too, and took a mutually feeling from her as the years passed.

Next to him is Sergio who was another decent boxer, though undedicated. He's a Puerto Rican kid with a knack for trouble. His dark brown eyes and smooth skin gave away his nationality with just a glance. Rumor's had it he was hanging with my old friend John, selling drugs. Judging by his nice watch and diamond earring I'd say that was true. The first time we sparred he was so nervous he threw up in the middle of the ring. To this day we make fun of him for it. He fought a few fights before me and won, but his record isn't as good and he doesn't fight as much as I do. His dedication to the gym is back and forth. Sergio's private life is secure. There are months at a time that he takes time off from the gym. No one ever knows where he goes or what he's up too.

"Tired?" I ask Coach Kay looking over to him as he looks lost in the outside.

"No, this coffee will keep me up all damn night."

"That's why I don't drink that stuff. The first time I took a sip

I spit it out all over the table. My grandma was so mad." I chuckle as I think about it.

"It's an acquired taste," he admits. "My mother started letting me drink it when I was three years old."

"Three years old!" I bellow.

"Oh, yeah. She said I was so addicted to it that when she took it out of the cupboard I would bang on my chair until she gave me some." He chuckles a bit as he loses himself to the memory for a second. "What she say again?" He reminisces. "That's right. 'I felt like I had committed my three year old child to a drug problem.'" He laughs at the thought. "Yes, it's one of my few addictions."

"That's crazy. I'm too broke to be addicted to anything."

"Broke people are often broke because of their addictions. Drugs, gambling, alcohol – those are the things that usually make people broke."

"Well, not me, Coach. I have the pleasure of being broke because I was born into it. Although, it was my mother's addiction that made us broke, so I do see your point." He responds with an awkward look. "Sergio had a good fight," I say, quickly changing the subject. He had fought on the card a few fights before me.

"Yes, he did," Coach Kay agrees, turning his attention out the window.

"He'd be good if he stuck around more. These guys come in and out of the gym so much. I just don't understand. You've had so many good fighters over the years." I shake my head.

"I'd have a lot of good fighters if they stuck around more," Coach says, continuing to stare out the window.

"Why don't they?"

He looks over at me and grins. I didn't think it was a comical question.

"Pull over for a second, son. Right up there." He points as we pull up to a bridge.

"Another bathroom break? Coach, I know you're getting old but I don't need to get you to a nursing home already, do I?" My joke draws a smile followed by a mocking remark.

"Boy, if you don't pull this car over…" I immediately pull over to the side of the bridge. He gets out of the car.

"C'mon," he orders. "Turn off the lights."

"Where are we going?" My curiosity sparks as I look around. The night is quiet. Finally I get out of the car. "Coach I know I didn't do things right in that ring but you don't need to kill me. I'll listen to you more from now on I swear."

"Just c'mon." He orders as I follow him to the railing of the

42

bridge. There are no lights around and the sky is clear, with brilliant stars and a bright half-moon shining through the silent night.

"Beautiful, isn't it?" he asks.

"Yeah, but we could look at the stars almost any night, Coach. Why'd you make me stop?"

He doesn't react to my sarcasm. Instead, he looks up at the night sky. It's a little cold even though it's the middle of summer. I don't have a jacket on so I fold my arms to keep warm.

"You know, when Tracey Jury died, a part of me died, too," he says. "A part of the gym died." With the mention of Tracey, my thoughts become more serious.

"Big heavyweight prospect," he continues. "Had Grey Bones and Juan Riviera looking to sign him. He had everything it took to be the champ. Worked harder than an ox and trained every day. I always thought to myself, 'Man, this kid is going to be it. He's not going to be like the rest of them.' The rest of them, like Trey and Sergio, that come and go whenever they want."

"No. Not Tracey Jury – 16-0 and an unstoppable wrecking force that even the heavyweight champ all the way from Spain had heard about. He was going to be the champ, he was going to put the heavyweight division back on track in the United States." Coach's sad tone was untested. Everyone knew that Tracey was going to be a star.

"I remember the day he died," I reply. "It was the saddest day at the gym I had ever seen. He was my idol. I tried to mimic his style in everything. I miss him, too, Coach."

I did. Tracey had always had my back when the other kids gave me a hard time. They were scared to make fun of me when he was around. Once I started to get good at boxing, I didn't need him anymore. I had earned respect. By training hard like him, and dedicating myself to the sport like he did, I had become good. He had been my inspiration to train that hard.

"He got caught up in a life that I had no idea about," Coach continues. "Drugs and the streets, a boxer's biggest Kryptonite. This is a poor man's sport right now. Mostly blacks and Hispanics that grow up in ghettoes, broke and angry. Fighting is their way to suppress that anger. To rise above it. There is hatred and anger towards something in their life. So they fight to forget it. But, eventually, they all fall back into those lives. Very few learn to put their dark pasts behind them so they can achieve greatness." He pauses. "That is the answer to your question. That is why fighters don't stick around. Fighters like Sergio will never make it because of that. Because boxing is a sport that demands your full attention. It must be your life. You must live it, you must sleep it, you must breathe it. There very thought of existing outside of the ring cannot exist. And while these boys that come into the gym with all this talent may seem like they are ready to be pros and win titles, once they fall back into the streets they are consumed by them." He looks up at the stars. "They are stars because at times they shine brighter than anything in the world. But there are other times…times that they are covered by clouds and darkness, some never to be seen again, and others that on a very clear night will come back to shine again, brighter than even before."

Suddenly it hits me. "Star Boxing Gym," I say, shaking my head with a smirk. He puts his hand on my shoulder and smiles. That's where the name of the gym had come from.

"That's right, Star Boxing Gym."

"Well, Coach, you don't have to worry about that with me. I'm never going to leave you. You're stuck with me till the day I become champ!" I pat him on the back grinning. Boxing is my life, I think to myself. I am consumed by it and I won't allow anything to get in my way.

"Are you guys going to jump?" We suddenly hear Trey say, sticking his head out the window. "'Cause that wouldn't be a good idea, and I don't have a license to get us back." We both laugh. Coach and I head to the car and prepare for the drive home.

Chapter Eight

When I get back to town, I drop everyone off and, as usual, drive to the cemetery. The car itself seems intimidated by the dark night; it shakes as I drive slowly through the graveyard. I have music playing in the car, soft rock. Usually I'm consumed by rap music. Rap music pumps me up to fight. It gets me amped in the ring. Soft rock has the total opposite effect. It soothes me, which I need very much at times. Especially right now.

I park the car, get out, and slowly walk towards the grave. I pass a few huge gravestones that look very pricey. I can't help but think that, even in death, people need to spend money to make their gravestones better than the person's next to them. I try to ignore my anger. Money. My whole life I have had none, and because of that I hate it more than anything.

I reach the stone I am looking for. Helen Walker (1923-2004). She lived a long life. Next to her is my grandfather, Gary Walker. He died long before I came around but the way she had talked about him made me feel I knew everything about him. My grandmother hadn't died sad. She had been in good spirits during her last days in the hospital. She said she was happy to finally be going to see her husband, and her only regret was leaving me alone.

I had assured her that I wasn't alone. The people at the gym had become my family. I didn't need to share their blood – they supported me just as much as she did. She knew that. She and Coach Kay had talked a lot in her final days. She had probably told him everything about me, including things that I didn't want him to know…how I hated my father, and my mother even more so. She probably told him that if I ever saw my mother again, I would turn the other way, or perhaps even call the cops on her and get her put in jail.

"I won again, Grandma." I whisper as if she didn't already know. She would be upset that I wasn't going to church every weekend like I had told her I would. That would have to wait. God was not there for me; there was no reason for me to pray to Him. He had taken everything from me. I resented Him to the point where I didn't want to believe in Him. I put him in the same category as my mother and father. I detested all of them. Perhaps God is an illusion. If he wasn't then he surely didn't care about me. "I hope God's watching you better than he is watching me."

I remember the flowers I have in my hand, and place them on the grave. I miss her. There isn't a day that goes by that I don't think of her.

When she had been alive, I hadn't known that the reason we were always broke was because she had been saving money. When she died, she left enough so I could live in the house for at least a few years. But the money was running out. If it wasn't the furnace that needed to be replaced, it was the roof or bad plumbing. Every single time I felt like I was getting ahead, something happened to set me back. Boxing wasn't giving me any money even though I was training every day for hours. I picked up a part-time job at a local delivery warehouse to keep the bills afloat. It helped but I would have to leave there soon if something didn't change. The fact that I owned a house so young was a step up from everyone else in the neighborhood, who were living on welfare and in government housing. Even so, I didn't feel like I was in a better position than any of them. Pretty soon the bank would be after me for the mortgage, and the government for back taxes. I was all but broke.

I go home. My house is clean; I always keep it that way. My grandmother was a clean freak and it rubbed off on me to the point where I am worse than she was. My friends and Coach Kay make fun of me for it. My crazy habits have invaded the gym as well. I spend most of my time training, and the rest cleaning the place. I don't know what it is. Coach Kay told me years ago that I didn't need to clean anymore to pay my gym fees, but I can't stop. I lay down on the couch, not even making it to my bed before dazing off.

The following night I go out with my boys to a local nightclub called Rave. Over the years Star Boxing has brought in all sorts of people. I'm not the only white boy anymore, although the name still sticks. Coach Kay isn't just training poor, local fighters, he is training people from the city as well – white, middle class men with connections and money. A good amount of guys my age come to the gym to work out, too. They like to party and they invite us out a lot with them. Tonight's one of those nights I actually decide to go.

"It's a nice night," Wes says as we all walk down the street toward the club. The warm air felt good to the skin. It was dark out but the lights and music from the street ahead could be heard.

"A perfect night to party!" Tom agrees slapping Wes on the back.

Tom Frone and Wes Grayson have picked up me, Sergio, and Trey. Tom is 6-foot-2 with bright blue eyes and blonde hair. He's 220 pounds of pure muscle. I can understand why most women find him attractive. Wes is a little smaller than Tom but bigger than me. He has light brown hair with eyes to match. He is also a catch with the ladies.

Tom's dad is wealthy, from what I have heard. The fact that Tom picked us up in a brand new Lexus makes me believe the rumors are true. He is 22 and Wes is his best friend. They are two of the most popular people in the city's party scene. They know all the girls and the bar owners. Everyone likes to be around them.

They both started boxing a few years ago. Their first day in the gym was not very pleasant. They came in with cocky attitudes, thinking boxing was a sport they could pick up easily. They asked to step into the ring the first day and spar without learning a single thing from Coach. He let them, and allowed me the honor of fighting them. Needless to say, Tom couldn't finish the first round because of his lack of endurance. I was able to hit him with a punch whenever I felt like it and he hit air with just a fraction of a movement. It had been like fighting a punching bag.

Wes came in right afterwards and I did the same to him. They were both off balance and even though they were big, they had no power in their punches. I easily beat both of them; I could have knocked them out but I chose not to. Although Coach Kay wanted to teach them a lesson, he didn't want them to leave the gym and never come back. So making them look stupid in the ring was the next best thing to teach them, but not hurt them bad.

It worked and eventually both of them became my friends. They have been at the gym for years, coming a few days a week to work out. Despite their economic status, which everyone at the gym knew about, they were accepted. The Star Boxing Gym had become a much friendly place than when I had started.

I am no longer the kid that everyone picks on. In fact, I've become one of the top fighters in the gym. Coach's theory about young boxers from the ghetto has proved to be right. Most of the fighters over the years have disappeared from the gym. Some of them have been murdered, others just disappeared, and others are spending their lives behind bars.

Turning my attention back to the party scene we finally walk up to Prary Street. I admit, the party scene is out of my comfort zone, as is hanging out with Tom and Wes. I have to dress nice, which means buying clothes I'm not used to wearing – a collared shirt and a nice pair of jeans, which cost what I would spend on food for a week. I hate the fact that I spent $60 just to fit in with the local, popular white people. Trey and Sergio, both also dressed properly, follow cautiously behind me, Tom, and Wes. I'm almost positive Trey stole his clothes. Sergio probably used the money he was making from selling drugs with my old friend John to buy his. He might have even paid for Trey's.

The club is on one of the city's main streets. The streets are lively. It's like a huge party in the middle of downtown Buffalo. People from the local Catholic college, along with the city kids that like to go out and have fun, make Rave one of the best nightclubs in the city. Within a two-block radius are many other nightclubs. Most of them have fenced-in patios packed with smokers. Pizza places and sub shops stay open most of the night to accommodate the drunken people that get hungry after a night of partying.

I'm bewildered by the amount of people that are out. There are many beautiful women; my eyes can't focus on just one. Some of them are wearing barely any clothing.

"Welcome to the party, boys." Tom's confident voice rings out as he smacks me on my back. I look over at Trey and Sergio. Their eyes are wide and they look around like they've just landed in paradise. Girls bump into them, so drunk they don't even realize, and laugh with their friends as they stare at me.

"I knew bringing you was a good idea," Wes says, looking at the girls who just passed.

"What do you mean?"

"Girls love you, Aiden. Every time I show them a picture of us on my phone they ask 'Who's that guy? He's hot.'"

"Uh oh, my boy Aiden is about to get some girls tonight," Trey adds. "I don't know about you guys but this is like all them spring break shows I been watching on MTV. It's time to introduce the ladies to their savior! Let's go!"

I don't know what to think. Girls were attracted to me in high school but I'd never really had a girlfriend. I dropped out at 16 when I lost my grandma. Coach became my legal guardian, even though I hadn't lived with him for any of those years. After that I had dedicated myself to the gym, with no time for girls.

We enter Rave through the VIP line. The music is blaring and the club is packed with people dancing and lining up at the bar like starving people waiting for food. Two more floors above us are swarming with people, too. I follow Tom and Wes closely, making sure my two friends are still behind me. We come to an area blocked off with rope. The bouncers gaze at us oddly but let us pass. Ahead of us, there are bottles of liquor, ice, and cups all over the table. A few people are sitting on couches, looking like they're ready to start drinking.

"Let the party begin!" Tom announces.

A few hours pass. After walking around for a bit, I take a seat on a couch by myself. I've managed to sneak a few bottles of water in between the drinks Tom is mixing me in the VIP area in an attempt to keep myself sober. It's working but not as well as I'd hoped. I can see Trey and Sergio dancing with some girls, and they are not sober at all.

"So, this dude right here is going to be the next world champ." Tom's slurred words make me grin as he walks over and sinks onto the couch next to me. "Aiden Walker, Super Middleweight Champion of the world!"

"I wouldn't say all that yet," I mumble. The well-dressed guys Tom walked up with stare down at me. I stand up and extend my hand. They politely do the same, introducing themselves as Matt Soyer, Anthony Shiner, and Rick Corple.

"Listen, bro', you are the shi…man, just listen," Tom announces drunkenly. "One day you'll…"

All of a sudden, I am caught off guard by the sight of a girl walking over to our group. Her green eyes are bright even in the darkness of the club and her smile is absolutely stunning. As she comes to stand before us, I can see that her hair is blonde. Her two friends are also pretty, but I can't keep my eyes off of her.

"Hello, Tom," she says softly. "I see it's the usual Saturday night for you."

"This…is Vanes…Vaness…Vanessa Brass," he says to me, ignoring her mocking words. He looks like he's ready to pass out.

"Hi, I'm Aiden," I say, standing up and shaking her hand. She seems stunned by my introduction.

"Aiden Walker. The boxer, right?" Her friends smile as she asks.

"Um…yes."

"Yep, that's right!" Tom stands up, nearly falling backward onto the couch. I grab onto him. "Aiden Walker. Big, bad boxer." He sinks back onto the couch and his eyes shut.

"I'm really sorry about him," I apologize. "He's been drinking a lot."

"He's always like that," Vanessa answers. "You don't have to apologize for him." I realize there is something about her that I like, her tone, her attitude, everything.

"I, um, how did you know who I was?"

"I've seen you in the papers a few times. My dad is a huge boxing fan. He actually follows you. I swear, every time he sees your name or picture somewhere he says, 'That boy right there is a great fighter, he's going to be an exciting pro if he keeps his head on straight.'" Her tone makes me grin. "I'm sorry. I sound like a creep, don't I? Here I am, this stranger that knows things about you and you have no idea who I am."

"No, no, that's ok. I didn't realize I have a fan club. It's cool in a way."

It was odd that someone followed my career, someone I had no idea even existed. I knew I was in the papers a lot. When I entered the Golden Gloves tournament the local news did a story on me. I lost the New York state finals, although I believed I had won. Coach Kay had, too. He had complained for hours about the stupid judges after that fight.

"So, Aiden, what brings you to Rave?" Vanessa asks.

"Him," I say, pointing at Tom, who is almost asleep on the couch. "This is my first time here, actually. It's not really my thing. To be honest, I'm kind of bored." It was the truth, although I hoped that telling her didn't make me seem like an uninteresting person.

"Really? Well, that's good. At least I think so. Someone like you can have a good career in boxing. I would think drinking and partying wouldn't help that."

"No, it definitely doesn't mix." Shaking my head I smirk. "Are you a fan of boxing?" I ask.

"Actually, no. I don't watch it at all." Her friends start to drag her away. "But maybe now I'll have a newfound interest in it." Her smile makes it seem like she's flirting. "I have to go now, Aiden Walker. I hope I'll be seeing more of you."

"Me, too," I say as she walks away. I can't take my eyes off her until she disappears into the crowd. I have to see her again. Tom knows her, so he should be able to help me out. I sit back down on the couch and look at Tom as his eyes open.

"You like her, huh?" he mumbles.

"She's pretty," I casually reply.

"Yes, and rich, too. Her father has more money than God. Huge boxing fan, too. You should get close to her. She might be able to help you guys out with the problems at the gym."

I look over at Tom in surprise. My mood immediately changes. "What are you talking about?"

"C'mon," he says, sitting up to grab his drink. "The gym's broke. Don't tell me you didn't know. My mother works for the city. She says he only has a few months left and they are going to have to shut him down. I tried to get my dad to help him but Coach Kay refused. Stubborn old man. Said he will take care of it and not to worry."

Could this be true? I knew Tom wouldn't lie, especially when he was wasted. I thought Coach Kay was doing well now that he had opened up the gym to people like Tom so he could get more money. That was the whole point of allowing people to come just for the workout. I allow myself to sink into the couch, lost in my thoughts trying to ignore the rest of what Tom says.

"Once the state cut all the grant money 'cause of the economy' he started refinancing things to pay for the fees," Tom continues. "Turns out he can't pay any of it back. He's broke."

I had known something was up with Coach as of late. I thought it was doctor visits, but now I knew it wasn't a health issue. He was in financial trouble. I thought of Vanessa, not just because I wanted to see her again, or because her father was rich, but because of what she had said. Her father thought I would be a great pro. I believed I was ready. That would be the quickest way to get money. I had to do it. The time had come to take my career to the next level.

Chapter Nine

"No," Coach Kay says adamantly, searching his desk. As usual, his office is a mess. His desk, which looks like it could break apart at any moment, is covered with papers in no particular order. The office walls are plastered with boxing posters, just like the rest of the gym. The one I notice most is Mike Tyson. His fierce look could never be tested. So much anger, so much hatred, yet after every knockout he showed so much compassion. Hanging next to the poster is a pair of vintage gloves signed by the great Sugar Ray Leonard.

"What do you mean 'no'?" I argue. "Why not?"

"Because you're not ready," he insists. Still rummaging through the papers, he looks at me. "I mean, you're ready, but you're not ready."

"How does that make any sense?"

"Professional boxing is different. It's more political. Way more political. It's like the government except more corrupt and more like a dictatorship. They try to control who makes it to the top and who doesn't. And if they don't know who you are, then your chances of making it to the top are not good."

I've always known that but it wasn't going to stop me. "I know you're in financial trouble, Coach."

My words make him stop what he's doing. He looks at me strangely.

"Who told you that?"

"It doesn't matter who told me. It's true."

"I'm always in financial trouble. Have been since I was 10 years old, son. Nothing will ever change that. I'll get out of it like I always do. There is no need to worry. This gym isn't going anywhere."

His determination is admirable. The strength in his voice makes it easy to believe he will find a way. But I've done some research since I talked to Tom. There is no way out of this one. He's behind a lot of money, with no way of getting it.

"Coach, let me be your way out. I can do this."

He finally gives all of his attention to me.

"Sit down, son," he sighs as I take a seat opposite his desk. "We haven't won a national title. We haven't even won the first round of a national tournament. Do you know why? Two fights, both of which we know you won but they say you lost. Do you know why you lost? Not because you got beat, but because they don't know who you are. The judges favor who they know. We need national recognition before you go pro so we can get a promoter to help you grow. Then we will start off with the easy fights, and work our way up. That's how professional boxing goes."

"I don't need to be babied from the start like the other guys," I say angrily. "That's what you did to Travis. Gave him all these easy fights to build him up. I don't need that. I can beat the best guys right from the start."

"It's not that easy, Aiden. Your first fight can be against someone from the Olympic team or trials. They will try to use you as an opponent because they do not know who you are. And it's not that I don't believe you can beat anyone in this country. It's that the judges won't favor you in close rounds because they do not know you. They won't even favor you in a round that you win. You'll get ripped off early in your career. And after that it'll keep happening."

He sighs again. "Listen to me carefully. This is not like any other sport in the world. It is only you in that ring. Your fate in every fight rests on three judges' impression of you. You need to make them believe you were better that round. You need to show them that you are in control. You need them to like you. Those judges control your career. Unfortunately, a lot of them are corrupt as well. Not only do you have to deal with that, you need to deal with the fact that you cannot lose. In any other sport, you can learn from your losses, and come back and be stronger. In boxing, one loss, one bad game, and it can be all over. The chances of coming back are slim, especially with no promoter to back you up."

The room is silent. My mind is made up, and there is nothing he can say to change it.

"I guess I'll just have to knock everyone out then," I smirk. He is staring at me. My determination must be gleaming in my eyes. "I'm not taking no for an answer."

He sighs, leans back in his chair, and glances around the room before looking at me. Suddenly the entire atmosphere in the room changes, and Coach seems more serious now.

"You really want to do this?" he asks. His eyes are staring so deeply into mine that I think he can see my heart.

"It's the only thing I ever wanted to do."

"We won't make any money to start. I'll be lucky to get you eight-hundred dollars your first fight. Your amateur record might work in my favor at first, but trust me, after a few fights, they are going to put you up against the best there is."

I can tell he's still trying to talk me out of it. I stand up and head towards the door. Just before I get there I turn to look at him.

"I'll give you all the money for the gym. And if that's all you're going to get per fight then you better line up two fights a month."

I walk out of the office and shut the door behind me. I can see him leaning back in his chair with his hands folded. I don't know what he's thinking but he'd better be ready. I know I am.

A couple weeks pass with no word of a fight. I manage to get my professional license. After completing a few tests, the doctor clears me. I never knew getting a license would be so much hassle. I took more tests at the doctor's than I had in high school.

I'm still training every day. I have picked up my work ethic. I run eight miles every morning. I spend one hour working on the heavy bags, eight rounds hitting pads with Coach, and another two hours doing sit-ups, push-ups, medicine ball drills, chin-ups, running cones, hitting the tire, and every other drill I can think of. My body hurts every second of every night yet I cannot stop training. Coach could tell me tomorrow that he got me a fight for the weekend and I would have to fight.

In the meantime, Tom manages to help me with Vanessa. He's told her that I'm interested in meeting up with her one night so we can hang out. Surprisingly, she has accepted. Unfortunately for me, there is no way for her to contact me. I can't afford a cell phone. I can't afford to take her out to dinner, either. These things remind me how much I hate money.

So instead, Tom told her to meet me by the falls at 7 o'clock. Niagara Falls, one of the biggest wonders in the world, very romantic to walk through, and luckily it's not far from my house so I can walk there. Tom told me to wait at the entrance of a bridge that crosses onto an island that is known as Goat Island. I tried to dress as nicely as possible in a pair of shorts and a shirt. The night is peaceful. I could sit by myself and watch the water all night long. I have before during runs.

"Hey." Vanessa's voice startles me. She smiles as she approaches where I'm sitting.

She gives me an awkward hug and I shyly hug her back. She looks beautiful, just like the first time I saw her, in a pair of jeans and a pink shirt. Her green eyes are as bright as I remember.

"You snuck up on me," I tease.

"Sorry, I saw you from my car and figured that beeping the horn would probably be a little much."

She puts her keys in her purse. I'm no shopping expert, but I would bet her purse is equal to a month's rent at the gym and her Mercedes is worth more than the entire building. Tom had said her parents are rich.

"Niagara Falls," She smiles taking in a breath of air and looking around oddly. "God, it's been so long. I forgot how beautiful it was here. I have to admit, this is the first time a boy has ever asked me to come here to hang out. I don't think I've been here since I was a kid."

"Really?" That's odd to me. I've heard a lot of people say that even though they live in the city, they rarely go to see the grand Falls. "I come here a lot. Actually, I work out here a lot. This is where I do my running. It settles me in a way." We begin to walk over the metal bridge. It's not a normal bridge that most people would see. The odd structure is built with metal flooring and tall fences to prevent people from jumping, not that there isn't a million other places to jump into the falls if someone really wanted too. There were many different paths that someone could take to get to the water. Trails lead all over the place, through the trees, and down to areas that would allow someone to literally put their hand in the water that fall over the falls only hundreds of feet away. In recent years there have been restrictions put down by the State Police, but that didn't stop people from doing it. It could be very dangerous if not watched carefully. History has proven that people have accidently fell in and went over the falls. Some people have actually survived the plunge over.

"I remember when I was a little girl my parents would take me down there by the water and let me play. It's so surprising to me now that they allowed that. I feel like every time I turn on the news someone is jumping or falling in." She shakes her head.

"I'm sure your parents were very careful though. My mother used to walk me across this path every day when I was little, and she held my hand so tight that I felt like she was cutting off the circulation. Even when we weren't anywhere close to the water." My words trail a bit at the end. I didn't know why it came out. Talking about my mother. I hate my mother and talking about her only makes me angry.

"So, enough about that," I say. "What about you?"

"What about me?" She oddly laughs giving me an awkward eye.

"I don't know, tell me something about you. Something interesting." I wasn't about to get caught talking about my horrible life that I was embarrassed of.

She looks up at the sky, suppressing a smile as we exit the

bridge and begin our walk around the quiet island. There's tons of people around but it still seems quiet. Right now the only thing that exists to me is her. "Well, let's see. I'm 21 years old. I'm going into my fourth year of college at the University of Buffalo. I am studying to be a marine biologist. I graduated high school with a 4.0 and captain of the cheerleading team. My favorite color is pink, my favorite food is pizza, and I love movies and reading books. Oh, and I dropped out of Harvard after finishing two years there with a 4.0 as well. That's something my father will never let me forget."

I'm shocked that she gave away so much about herself in one paragraph.

"You're studying to be a marine biologist?"

She doesn't seem like the type of girl who would be interested in that type of field. What intrigues me most, though, is that it was a subject I was always interested in. There was something about the ocean that I found fascinating.

"I...uh...yeah," she stutters.

"Something wrong?"

"No," she giggles. "No, not at all. It's just that usually when I tell someone I dropped out of Harvard after two years, their eyes blow up and their mouth drops to the floor."

"Well, that was going to be my next question," I admit with a smirk.

"Oh, so you were just pretending to be interested in my career choice," she teases, playfully nudging me.

"No, I really am interested in it. I've always loved the study of the ocean and the animals in it. I love animals."

"Well, I guess I forgot to mention that I love animals, too. Maybe we should have gone to the zoo on our first date."

Her words make me stop. I wasn't sure if this was a date. A girl like her was probably used to getting fancy dinners on a first date.

"I've never been to the zoo," I admit.

"Really?" she cries.

"Nope."

"That is crazy. I thought everyone has been to the zoo. Your parents never took you when you were younger?"

"No. Not once."

She seems to notice the change in my voice. I have to change the subject.

"So, Harvard, 4.0, and dropped out?"

"Yeah," she sighs, looking at the ground. "I was going for business so I could take over my father's company. It just wasn't something I wanted to do. I also missed my family, my friends, and living in this stupid place."

"I would love the opportunity to leave," I say, thinking how much I hate the ghetto. There's so much violence, unending problems, and never knowing which friends I could trust. Even though it was home, I wouldn't mind leaving it all behind. It had to be different for her though. She probably lived in some fancy house in a peaceful neighborhood.

"Oh, I did. There was no one that wanted to leave more than me, trust me. But when I did, it was totally not what I expected. Nothing will ever be home. You don't realize how much you miss the little things until they are not there anymore. Mostly family and friends." She stops for a second. "So now that I've told you a lot about me, tell me some more about you."

There is a bench a few feet ahead and she sits down.

"I, um, well…" I pause for a moment. "I guess there's not much to say. I started boxing when I was 13 years old. Dropped out of school at 16. My life is at the gym. I don't do anything else, really." It was sad, and I could tell by looking into her eyes that she felt it was, too. For the first time in a long time, I felt stupid.

"No, that is so unfair," she protests. "I basically gave you my life story in ten seconds. There has to be more than that. C'mon, tell me something else. What's your favorite television show?"

"I don't have a television."

Her odd look makes me feel worse. What must she think of someone who couldn't even afford a television? I would be lucky to make it to a second date after this.

"Why did you drop out of school so early? You don't have a high school diploma?"

"Nope. My grandmother was taking care of me and when she died I didn't feel the need to continue. Coach became my guardian. I knew what I wanted to be when I grew up and that was that. Coach didn't agree with it but he couldn't contest it. It probably makes me look stupid, huh?"

"No, not at all! If my memory is correct, some of the wealthiest, most successful people in the world didn't finish high school or college. What about your parents?"

"My father died when I was eight years old, and I haven't seen my mother since I was nine. My grandmother took me in after my mother left."

"I am so sorry."

"It's ok. You didn't know." I don't get upset when people ask about my parents. I've learned to bury that hatred outside of the ring. I just didn't like talking about it for more than a few seconds.

"It's so amazing." Her words catch me off guard as I finally look over to see the sight of the Falls. We had made our way around the island and now we were staring at hundreds of thousands of gallons of water pouring over the falls, maybe even millions. I had no idea how much water was actually going over but she was right, it was an amazing sight to see.

The falls was lit up with lights that changed colors every couple seconds. The mist that came back from the water reaching the bottom of the falls stretched to the top of the hill where we were, getting us a little wet. It felt so comforting to be standing there watching it. Like nothing else in the world mattered. Every problem, every struggle, nothing bothered me in this moment. Life ceased to exist as I stood here watching the water crash down into river. Even the miraculous sight of the Canadian side of the falls with all their lights and buildings doesn't take away from the beauty of the water.

"So what did you do after you grandmother passed? I mean, how did you live? Where did you live?"

Her questions weren't what I wanted to hear, but she was interested. I had never talked about it before. Maybe it would be good to get some of it out for once.

"My grandmother saved money so I could survive. She left enough for me to cover the bills, mortgage, and things like that for years. Coach Kay helped me with everything. We did some illegal things to make the state believe I wasn't living alone. I wasn't going to let them send me to a foster home or some orphanage or anything. I told Coach that I wasn't leaving the gym no matter what."

"You're close with him, aren't you?" she asks.

"Yes, he's like a father to me." My words catch in my throat for a second. I look towards the water. "After my grandmother died, I was broken. I think that finally, for the first time in my life, everything had caught up to me. I had this build-up of anger that I couldn't control. That's why Coach said I was such a good boxer. I couldn't even stay at the house. Every night I went to the gym, grabbed a pillow and blanket, went into the ring, and fell asleep. I don't know why. It was the only place that I could fall asleep." I had never told anyone that before – Coach was the only one who knew. "Finally, after an entire year, I was able to go back home."

Her eyes didn't leave mine. I couldn't tell if she was scared or sad.

"I'm sorry. This is probably the worst first date you have ever had, having to hear these ridiculous stories."

"No, no," she says, walking over to me. "That's nonsense."

"Yeah, right. You're probably used to all these guys with

money and security taking you out on fancy dates and promising you the world. And here I am. I can't promise you anything. I can't even take you out on a nice date. This was a mistake."

I begin to walk away but she grabs my arm.

"Hey," she says, "you're right. Most guys will take me to a fancy dinner and promise me the world, and then they will do that to the next girl, and the next. They all tell the same stories in different ways and the entire time I'm there I can't help but wish I were doing something else. Today isn't like that. You're different. I am more interested now than I have ever been before."

I want to smile but I can't, because telling her my story has made me realize how sad my life has been. Hopefully, turning pro will change all that.

"So that's a good thing then, huh?" I ask.

"Maybe." She grabs my hand as we resume our walk. "Let's see how the rest of the night goes. If you're lucky, you might get a second date."

Her wink makes me smile.

"Yes, ma'am."

Chapter Ten

    I sit in the chair facing Coach Kay as he wraps my hands. He carefully weaves the light white wrap in and out of my fingers, around my wrist, and around my knuckles. The nerves in my body are playing tricks on me. For a couple of minutes, I feel nervous, almost as if I have never been in the ring before. The fight plays over and over in my mind. I have to think about how I am going to react in every situation that is thrown at me. What happens if his jab is very good, what if his punches hurt me, am I in good enough shape? All of these questions circle around my head like a tornado. I'm told that this is normal. Even though I have been in the ring plenty of times before, this is my first professional fight.

    The nerves subside and excitement kicks in. I'm ready for this. I want this. I don't care what he is going to do because whatever it is I am going to do it better. He will not hurt me, he will not be faster, he does not have the resilience I do. In no way, shape, or form am I going to lose this fight. I am ready. I have trained for weeks for this. No one can beat me at this level right now. My heartbeat slows, making me more comfortable. Then, just when I feel like I have everything under control, my nerves kick in again, making me wonder about the very same things I was just so confident about.

    In the battle that is about to take place I have to be victorious. The training for this fight has turned my body into a machine that can resist pain. I have to be smart, quick, confident. Bad intentions must be put onto all of my punches. I have to strategize in the ring and be ready to adjust properly. I have to hurt this man, I have to knock him out, I have to kill him. Even though I have never met my opponent, my only thoughts are to inflict as much pain on him as possible until he is not standing anymore. I think of my mother and father. I brush my thoughts towards money. My hatred for them fuels me.

    After Coach Kay finishes wrapping, he puts on his final touches. The inspector working for the commission carefully watches to make sure there is no foul play with my wraps. The locker room is small. It feels smaller when I am shadowboxing to warm up. It feels like the walls are closing in on me.

    I am sharing the locker room with other fighters on the card that I am going to fight on. They separate the fighters into two separate locker rooms. One group of fighters shares one, while their opponents share the other. Whispers of the coaches around us find my ears as I listen to the advice given to the fighters. I size up every fighter I see, even if they are not in my division.

Even though they have other professional fights under their belts, they seem to be feeling the same way I am. It makes me wonder if being a professional boxer means that every fight feels like the first. Will these feelings ever go away? Or will they one day settle in my system so that I actually feel comfortable going into the ring?

"His 3-1 record is a little deceiving," Coach Kay whispers, talking about my opponent. His name is Justin Smith. Coach Kay doesn't know much about him. He claims it's hard to find out a lot about fighters in the early stages of a professional career. He tries to tell me that it's just like amateur boxing, where you don't know anything about your opponent most of the time, and that we just have to make the proper adjustments in the ring. My first fight is a four-round, three-minute battle. It's a little different than the three-round, two-minute fights in the amateurs.

The day before the fight I faced off with him at the weigh-ins. There is nothing overly concerning about his image. He weighs in at 168, the same as me. His build isn't much different than mine although my arms are bigger and more cut. I am taller than him, which gives me a slight advantage. My reach is longer, too. Trey made fun of me, saying that because Justin is black I am going to have to dance a little more than I am used to. I just laugh. Trey and Sergio always mess with me because of my white skin. Because of them, I have taken the professional name Aiden "White Boy" Walker. I'm not sure how long I will be able to keep that name. As I get a bigger name in the professional industry, I assume I will have to change it due to its racial overtones. For now, it is funny. It's a name I was given at the gym the very first time I went in there. I liked it now.

"It doesn't matter," I say to Coach. His record doesn't mean anything to me. Whether he is 3-1 or 10-0, I just have to be better than him tonight.

"I hear his right hand doesn't come in straight. He loops it. You should be able to step back and land a hook. We'll have to see how he throws it but keep your eyes open for that. His footwork also isn't that great. He won't dance. Just keep putting pressure on him, cut the ring off, son." Coach seems just as nervous as I am.

"I thought you said you didn't know anything about him." My comment makes him grin.

"I have a few connections here." Finally, he's finished wrapping my hands. "This promoter does a few shows a year. If we look good tonight, he'll keep on putting us on his shows."

"It's not that far from home, either."

"No, it's not. This is a very good contact to have. I think I have another fight for you in a few weeks but we have to see how this goes first. It's out of state, but the cost shouldn't be too much. They'll cover some of it."

"Good, the more fights the better."

He smacks the top of my hands as the commissioner looks at them. The commissioner takes a marker and nods. He looks like some normal guy you would see standing in line at a supermarket. He adjusts his glasses.

"All set," he says. "Good luck."

Coach Kay stands up. "Ok, let's get warmed up."

After twenty minutes of shadowboxing I've built up a good sweat. My body feels good and my hands are flowing nice. Coach finally puts the small gloves on my hands. Ten-ounce gloves are the rule for my weight class. They feel tight, light, like nothing is on my hands. The knuckles on the gloves make my fist seem harder than if I didn't have them on.

I am used to sparring with sixteen-ounce gloves. Already I can feel the difference in speed as I hit Coach Kay's pads. The red color of the Everlast gloves makes me think of blood. I realize I could end up bleeding in this fight, and so could my opponent.

In the amateurs, the headgear protects us from cuts. The professional game of boxing is a different story. There is no headgear to protect me from anything. Surprisingly, even though it is my first fight with no headgear on, I'm not nervous about it at all. I have sparred without it lately and everything feels better. My vision is better and my defense has improved because it is easier to move my head. I preferred not to wear it. That is one thing about the pro's that doesn't make me nervous.

"Let's go, you're up."

I didn't even see the commissioner walk back into the locker room. This is finally it. My heart begins to race again. Coach Kay walks over to me and puts his hand on my shoulder.

"Ok, this is it. Deep breath." I do as he commands. "This is just like amateur boxing, son. Stay focused. Listen to everything I say, even if you don't think it's right. I can see things that you can't. If I say it'll work then you better believe it will work. I know that you're the fighter in there but this is a team effort. You'll notice that more in the pros than in the amateurs. Understand?"

"Yes, sir." Even though I always listen to what Coach says, sometimes I let my hard head win out. He doesn't like it. Because it is my first fight, maybe I should listen to everything he says tonight. I don't want my nerves to get the better of me in the ring like they are right now.

Butterflies fill my stomach as I walk down the aisle. Shockingly, there are a lot of people at the show. The ballroom is small but it is filled to the max. An Eminem song blasts over the speakers; no one is really paying attention to me. I didn't even pick a song to come out to. Trey seems to have taken that responsibility. That was the last thing I was worried about.

My black and gold shorts sparkle a little. Coach Kay says I need a little bit of spunk to get the attention of the crowd. My shoes match my shorts and they both add to the black and gold coat that has the star of my boxing gym embroidered into it.

I don't pay attention to anything or anyone around me. My opponent is already in the ring. He moves side to side as he warms up. I run up the stairs and enter between the ropes into the ring. My concerns are fading. This is where I feel relaxed. My sanctuary. I remember sleeping in this square for over a year. This is my home. I move side to side, shadowbox, and stretch out my jaw. I give myself a few shots to the face to get the feeling going as I pace back and forth in my corner.

The announcer introduces my opponent and his record. Then he announces my professional debut. As he centers us in the ring, I glance down at the ground, not looking my opponent in the eye. It doesn't matter what he looks like. I don't care. I am here to fight and to win. By choosing to look down I show myself that it doesn't matter who he is, only who I am. After the Referee's instructions, we tap gloves and I go back into my corner.

"Calm and focus," Coach Kay says. I nod my head and the bell rings. Slowly I walk towards the center of the ring as the crowd cheers. Immediately, I throw two jabs – one to the head followed by one to the body. Both of them land, backing him up. All of my nerves have vanished. The crowd has ceased to exist. My heart rate is normal. Now I feel good. Now I feel comfortable. This is where I feel the most right in my life.

He throws a jab back that lands right on my gloves. His speed isn't faster than mine. I can feel a little power behind his jab but I don't think it's enough to hurt me. He comes forward after his jab. I step right into him and throw two shots to his body and come back with a hook to the head. He blocks the hook as he backs out. He dances around a little, tossing his jab as I walk him down. He throws the right hand and misses. Coach Kay was right. He is looping and overthrowing his right hand.

I toss my jab again to the body as it lands. Body shots are key to wearing the fighter down. Coach always teaches that and I listen. I throw a jab and cross, both to the body, and again they land. Already, I see him start dropping his hands from his head. He doesn't like the body shots. He throws a double jab, backing me up, and then surprises me by finishing with a cross that lands on my nose. It doesn't hurt but I need to be careful of it. Coming forward again behind the jab, I drill two more body shots and finish with a cross to the head. The crowd is cheering for this exciting first round.

He comes forward, throwing the right again, but he misses. I counter with my hook and land a good shot right on his chin. It's easy to land over his cross. If I load up that hook, I can really land a good shot. Backing up, I throw a light jab to keep him honest. He comes in again with a jab and then back with his looping right. This time I load up the hook and fire it over his cross. It almost seems unreal as I connect. His legs falter and his body falls onto the canvas! I can see his eyes roll back into his head as he goes down. The crowd goes nuts and the Referee counts only to 3 before realizing that he's not getting up. I WON!

Excitingly, I run to my corner. Coach Kay is already on the ropes, smiling.

"I did it!" I yell, giving him a hug. Sergio and Trey are jumping up and down as they rush up to the corner of the ring.

"You sure did, son, nice work," he casually states. It is a first-round knockout! Not even two minutes into the fight! The crowd is staring at me. I notice women smiling at me as well.

"Well, if they didn't know who you were before, they sure will next time you fight here." Coach Kay's words ring in my head.

"You said I had to make an impression," I grin back. I did just that. The crowd is excited. Because I am the first fight of the show, I have opened it up well. They love to see good knockouts. I look Coach in the eye as he takes off my gloves. He smiles. I can tell he's excited even though he will never show it. I run over to my opponent who is slowly getting up to make sure he is ok. My only hope is that this is the start to a road of victories that will fulfill my dream of becoming the champion of the world.

Chapter Eleven

Earning my first professional win was the best thing that had happened to me. For the first time in my life I felt like things were starting to turn in my favor. Things were going well with Vanessa too. We had hung out a bunch of times at the falls again, and a few more at my house. Everyone's spirits at the gym were high, but money still was not.

I fought five more times in the coming months, building a 6-0 record with 6 knockouts. None of the guys I fought could handle the power of my punches. Even though each fight had been scheduled for four rounds, none of them went past the second. I was all over the local newspapers and even in the local T.V. news a few times. The gym was getting more people coming to work out, and people were starting to take up the sport of boxing. My growing popularity was helping to bring the sport of boxing back to Niagara Falls, New York. Boxing had once been huge in the area and it was my hope to restore that passion!

Coach Kay had been right – despite my good record and the excitement I brought to every fight, I was only making $800 to 1000$ a fight. Some of that money was going to expenses just to get to the fight and pay for hotel rooms and such. Not every promoter would cover those costs when traveling very far or out of state. I was giving it all to Coach but he was so far in debt it was never enough. To make things worse, I had run out of the money my grandmother had left me for the house. I was behind on the taxes and barely keeping up with the mortgage. My part time job wasn't cutting it. I didn't know what else I could do.

I hear a car beeping in front of the house, which breaks into my thoughts. I run to the bathroom and look in the mirror. My button-up shirt is properly ironed and my face is clean-shaven, which makes me look even younger than I am. I grab my sneakers and head towards the door. A Mercedes is parked in my driveway. Vanessa smiles as I enter on the passenger side. Stepping outside I realize the warmth that has still trickled away from summer in this October month.

"Hi," she says, giving me a quick kiss before backing out. Her striking green eyes are hard to ignore. The beauty of the Mercedes interior is no match for hers.

"This is nice," I say. It's the first time I've been in her car.

"Yeah, my dad got it for me a few months ago," she responds casually, like it's no big deal. Money isn't a big deal to her family, unlike the struggles I have.

"So where are we going?"

"Well, that's the thing," she says, looking over at me with a grin. "Just don't be mad, or weird."

"What?" Her smile is always gorgeous, even with a hidden agenda behind it. "What?" I ask again in response to her silence.

"We are going to meet my family. Is that ok?"

My eyes widen and I'm instantly nervous. Had she told me before that this is what we are doing tonight, I would have made up a reason to get out of it. I couldn't meet her rich family! What would they say when they saw her with a poor ghetto boy from the streets?

"I didn't want to tell you because I didn't think you would come," she continues. She's starting to know me better than I thought she did. I can't say no now, even though I want to. Would I meet the standards of her family? Absolutely not.

"I...uh...no, I don't care. I'm just a little nervous, that's all."

"Nervous? You?" she snickers. "Aren't you a big, popular, professional boxer now?"

"Not even close."

"Well, still, you shouldn't let them scare you."

Music plays on the radio but I can't think of the name of the song, even though I hear it at the gym all the time. One thing I've noticed about her is that she's in tune with her music.

"They don't scare me," I say, realizing that the only person who does scare me is Coach Kay. Vanessa's father is a rich and powerful man; money is nothing to him. If he finds out I'm a poor kid who lives in the ghetto and that I barely have enough money to eat every day, he will surely steer Vanessa away from me. That is the reason I don't want to meet him. He probably already knows about me from reading the newspaper articles. The media wasn't shy about putting my problems out there for the world to see, that's for sure.

"Have you told your father about us?"

"Kinda," she admits. "I told him that we were hanging out a lot and that we were friends."

"But nothing else?" I pry.

"Well, I think he knows that we are sort of dating. He doesn't really ask a lot of questions so I try to avoid telling him things."

"Why?" I ask. "Is it me?" Maybe she is embarrassed because I don't come from money like her. Her four years of high school cost more than my house.

"No, of course not. I just don't really have a close relationship with him. Now my mother, I tell her everything. She knows everything about you."

"What does she know?"

"She only knows what I tell her," she smiles, grabbing my hand.

"And how does she feel about it?"

I feel like my questions are becoming annoying, but I'm so nervous I can't help but wonder what this experience with her family is going to be like.

"She's fine, stop worrying!"

The ride there is fun, as is every minute spent with Vanessa. She tells me things about her friends and college, things I know nothing about. I listen to every word, ask questions, and try to understand her life. I want to know everything about her. After we've been on the road for twenty minutes, we pull in to a parking lot that's obviously not her house.

"The zoo?" I ask, dumbfounded.

"Yes, my father is throwing a party here tonight, a benefit party for someone he works with. I figured if you are going to be my boyfriend then you might as well start being my date for these types of events. Besides, didn't you say you have never been here?"

Stepping out of the car, I can't help but think this isn't a good idea.

Music is playing, people are everywhere, and there are tons of food and drinking tents. She introduces me to various people as we walk around the vast place. Tents are set up everywhere selling and giving away things. I look into the eyes of every person she introduces me to in order to properly and politely greet them. The odd thing is that some people know who I am. A couple of them make remarks about getting my autograph before I leave.

"I can't believe how many people know who I am," I whisper to Vanessa in between introductions.

"These people watch the news and read the papers every day. They wouldn't miss one article. If you're in there, they will remember who you are."

"Yeah, but it's weird to me. These people don't know who I am yet they are treating me like I'm special."

"You are special."

I see a man look over at Vanessa and smile. He is wearing a black suit and talking to people that look important. He glances at me for a second but doesn't pay much attention. He has grey hair and green eyes that match his daughter's. The man is tall, and has a strong determined face on him sort of like Coach's. He ends his conversation and strolls over to us.

"Daddy," she smiles, kissing his cheek.

"Hello, daughter," he answers, hugging her.

"I want you to meet a friend of mine, Aiden Walker."

"Yes, Mr. Walker, I have heard a lot about you." He shakes my hand.

"It is an honor to meet you, sir. Vanessa talks so much about you."

"I hope it's all good," he jokes. "And please, call me Henry."

"Yes, sir," I say. I can't help but be proper. I have been around intimidating people my entire life, people much scarier than him, but there is something about her dad that sets me back. I am more intimidated by him than I ever was by the gangsters and thugs that came through the gym. I wonder if it's because of Vanessa.

"So, Aiden, I must admit I am a very big fan. I have followed boxing my entire life. It's very nice to see someone from the area become such a good pro. When's the next fight?"

I remember Vanessa telling me that her father was a huge boxing fan. He knew all of the top fighters and everything that was going on. I could only hope that would work in my favor.

"November 9th," I answer.

"Is it around here?"

"No, it's down in Rhode Island. It's hard to get fights around here."

Most of my fights had been hundreds of miles away.

"Yes, this town loves boxing but the market seems low. Who are you fighting?"

"His name is Victor Sanchez. He's 11-2 with five knockouts." Talking boxing made me calm. I didn't know much more about my opponent. Coach managed to borrow a computer so we could look up YouTube videos of him. We only found one fight and it wasn't enough to develop a game plan. The fight was three weeks away and I couldn't get my mind off of it.

"That's a pretty good test. Isn't Dominick Cayman in your weightclass?" Cayman was a name that was talked about a lot in the boxing world. He was in the class above mine. The face of boxing is what people referred to him as.

"He's close to mine." I respond.

"I'd love to see you get to him one day. Cayman is amazing but..."

"Daddy," Vanessa cuts in, hooking her arm in mine. "Do you think I can have my friend back?"

Her father laughs as he stops in his tracks. "Sorry, hun, you know how I get when I talk boxing. You two go have fun. There are tons of things to do. We can talk boxing later." He winks as he shakes my hand again.

"Pleasure to meet you, sir."

Within seconds someone else had grabbed his attention.

"See, that wasn't so bad," Vanessa joked.

"No, not at all. He loves boxing."

"There you are," a woman's voice cries. I turn around to see an older, pretty woman staring at us. She has blonde hair and blue eyes. There's no mistaking who she is, either. She looks like Vanessa, except twenty years older.

"Hi mom," Vanessa says. "This is Aiden."

"Hello, Aiden," she says, putting out her hand.

"Hello, ma'am." I bow my head. "Nice to finally meet you."

"Vanessa has talked so much about you, Aiden." Her voice is gentle, just like her daughter's, but there is something negative about her as she looks me up and down. She's dressed very nicely and her makeup is done well. Her jewelry shines everywhere as if she needs the world to notice it. She doesn't like that I'm poor; I can tell that just by looking at her.

"Mom, please," Vanessa pleads.

"Well, it's true. Anyways, Aiden, I hear things about you over the news. Boxing is such a brutal sport. Is it something you plan on doing your entire life?"

"Hopefully." I know she is going to hate my answer. "It's not as bad as it appears to be."

"Getting punched in the head for a living, I mean, how bad can it get?" she jokes, laughing with one of her friends.

"Well, when you grew up where I grew up, ma'am, it can get much worse than that." She raises an eyebrow at my sarcastic comment.

"Where do you live again?" she asks, not looking me in the eye.

"7th street."

"Well," she says, looking over at her daughter, "that's not a great neighborhood. Vanessa, have you been going over to his house? I don't really feel safe with you going down there. Maybe you two should start coming to our house."

"Mom, I'm fine, and we are leaving. Goodbye, have fun, we'll see you later!"

She grabs my arm and pulls me away. "Vanessa!" Her mom yells one last time before we are out of her sight.

"I think we lost them," I joke as she looks over her shoulder to see how far away we've gotten. "Your mom doesn't like me, does she?"

"That's nonsense."

"Really? As soon as I said where I live, her eyes lit up. Not to mention the fact that she hates my job."

"She's just not used to me dating, that's all. I mean, she's used to me dating a certain type of person." She grabs my hand. "She'll learn to love you. Trust me."

Rich people. I'm not going to say anything else about it. We walk slowly through the vast zoo, holding hands.

"Now that I have you all to myself. What should we go see first?" she flirts.

"I don't know. What's your favorite animal?" I like all animals but I've never been to the zoo so I don't know where to go or what to see first. After walking around and talking for a bit, visiting a lot of the animals I finally feel comfortable again.

"Come over here." She runs ahead and I slowly follow. I notice a bear's den to the right. A grizzly bear paces behind a large opening in the floor that separates it from the railing where I stand. It is restless. I know the feeling I think to myself.

I follow Vanessa to the lion's habitat.

"Hmm, she's not out." Her disappointed tone reflects her expression. "C'mon!"

We can't see where the lion is so we walk around to the back, and enter a building. After a few twists and turns we come up to a door that reads, "Personnel only."

"C'mon," she says, opening the door.

"I don't think we are supposed to…oh, ok." She is gone before I can finish. No one is around so I follow her. Just ahead is a cage where the lion is laying down, staring at us. Vanessa gets close. The lion doesn't move.

"You should be careful," I advise.

"Don't worry. She's harmless." Vanessa stares at the lion. "I've been coming here since I was a teenager, watching her grow as I grew with her. She was just a baby back then."

"You know her?"

"Yes, they call her Sapphire. She's the only lion within five hundred miles."

"I like that name."

"When she was born, she was sick, really sick. The vets in the area didn't know what was wrong with her, but they said she wasn't going to live much longer unless she got special doctors to come and take a look at her. And when I say special, I mean expensive. I took a school trip to the zoo and found out she was sick. I begged my father to come here and donate the money to help save her life. At first he refused. But after coming here and taking a good look at what she meant to the people that worked here, and the zoo, he gave in. He saved her life. The vet said if we had waited another couple days, she would have died."

"She got lucky, huh?"

"Yes." Vanessa puts her hand on the cage. "I was sick that day. I wasn't going to go to school. At the last minute I made myself go, only because I knew we were going to the zoo. If I hadn't made myself go, she would have died. That one decision changed the lives of the people in this zoo, and the lives of the community that loves to come see Sapphire."

"I suppose we all come across decisions like that in our lives." I say.

"Yes, but I wanted to show you to her because as I stand here, I can see you as this lion."

"What?"

"People around here love boxing, and they're looking to embrace someone like you. This is a sports area, you know that. Our football team is awful, the baseball team left, and our hockey team falls short every season. Think of what you could do if people started thinking you could become champion of the world! Think of the support the community would give you! They would come to see you for the same reason they come to see Sapphire, for support and hope. Young kids would look up to you. Aiden you have a generous nature regardless of the sport you partake in. People will fall in love with you."

Her point is foreign to me. I'm just a poor ghetto boy from the streets. I have been arrested six times for misdemeanors. No one will support me if they find out who I truly am.

"I don't know. I still have a long way to go. I don't think anyone can ever look up to me the way they do to the football team or the hockey team."

"I think they can," she says, peering at me. "If you don't mind me asking, what happened to your parents? You have never spoken about them and when you mention them the subject gets changed very quickly."

I had known it would only be a matter of time before she asked about my parents again. Even though she had gained my trust, I still wasn't ready to talk about it. I looked at the lion and got lost in its eyes. Perhaps she was right. I did feel a connection as I stood looking at this fierce animal bound by the walls of this cage, and this zoo.

"Do you know what I see when I look at her?" I say to Vanessa, pausing to make sure I have her attention as I continue to stare at the lion. "I see a lonely animal with no family and no one to properly raise her except a bunch of people that need to prop her up so she can bring them money. I know you saved her life, and maybe people love to come and see her, but when I look into her eyes I see a caged animal that should be allowed to live her life freely with the family that created her, where she belongs."

Vanessa grabs my hand and moves closer to me. I suddenly ask myself, do I box because I love it or because it is all I know? If I had been raised in a family of Vanessa's stature would I have taken up the sport? Am I the one caged in, by the gym and money, because I have nothing else in my life? If I had a chance to break free, and put boxing behind me forever, would I? I hesitate before looking into Vanessa's eyes.

"There is no heroism in what I do. Put another lion in that cage, bring people to the zoo to watch them fight each other until one is badly beaten…then you will have me."

Chapter Twelve

Sticking a stiff, hard jab into the bag, I follow up with a cross straight down the middle and a hook to the body of it. Then I side step to the side and throw another combination. Trey throws his fist from behind the bag, trying to hit me in the head. I block it, then drill two hard body shots into the bag. My shoulders are strong and my legs feel as though I can run a hundred miles without stopping. The punches are flowing naturally. The bell rings. I nod to him as I wipe the sweat off my face.

"Nice work," he says, following me towards the bench, where I take a seat. I pour water over my head and allow the soothing sensation to trickle down my body. Another day is over.

I notice a giant man making his way over. As Kenyon Martin walks by and out the door, he doesn't even glance at us.

"I think that's the closest he's ever got to us," Trey laughs. "Nine years he's been coming here and hasn't said a word to anyone."

"I don't even think he looks at us," I agree, grinning. "I could literally walk up to him in a store or something and he probably wouldn't even know who I was."

I remember the story Coach told me about Kenyon when I first laid eyes on him one of the first weeks I started boxing. At first I thought it was some sort of joke. A man who came here every single day and never spoke a word to anyone baffled me. When new people joined the gym they would try to talk with him, only to be met with silence or a menacing look that frightened them so much they wouldn't work out anywhere near him. Kenyon showed no remorse for the kids he scared, either.

"To each his own, I guess," Trey says, shaking his head.

"This is going to be a tough fight. This guy has never been knocked down."

"He's never faced someone who's 11-0 with 11 knockouts, either," Trey responds. His confidence in me is sound. Now that I'm 11-0, people in the community are really starting to talk. I'm still not to a level that will make me the money I need to keep this place open, though. Even my upcoming fight is only going to give me $2,500. It will buy another month for Coach Kay, but it's not going to help me out in any way.

No matter how hard I try to sway my thoughts, money is all I ever think about. If I'm not boxing or hanging out with Vanessa, I am thinking about how to make more money. I'm sure she is getting sick of doing things that don't cost a lot. When we do something nice, she usually pays for it. It makes me feel weak. That anger comes with me every single time I step into that ring.

"I need to get bigger fights, Trey," I say, wiping my face with a towel.

"They will come, man. You just have to work harder than the rest of them, that's all."

His words do not reassure me. "I don't get it. I'm 11-0 with 11 knockouts and no manager or promoter has shown interest in me. I know there are a lot of undefeated fighters out there, but still, someone should be interested."

Getting a promoter meant more money. And that meant an answer to our problems.

"Coach Kay told you before you went pro how it was going to be. You haven't left any of those fights to the judge's decisions, thank God, but if you had you might not be undefeated. They've put undefeated fighters in front of you your last three fights and now they are putting a fourth one. They want you to lose. You have to rise above it."

Although Trey isn't very educated about boxing, he is right. The fighters are getting better. Coach Kay told me they had me losing on the scorecards my last fight, even though I had been clearly winning. That was because I had faced someone in his hometown, where one of the bigger promoters was looking to sign him. I knocked him out in the sixth round, and drew tons of cheers from the fans. They loved me.

"It's ridiculous." I shake my head. "So now I'm being used as a stepping stone for bigger guys." This industry was tough if you weren't well known. It wasn't easy to get noticed. Only a handful of promoters controlled ninety percent of the boxing world. If you weren't in with them, you were fighting against them. Right now that was exactly what I was doing.

"No, it's boxing. It's corrupt and political. Without national tournament experience or a few connections, you are going to keep on getting these undefeated fighters until someone realizes how talented you really are. That day will come."

"Yeah, but I've beaten them. And still no one is interested. I just don't understand. By now someone should have showed interest. What if I lose, Trey? Then it's all over. What if I can't knock someone out and I get ripped off? Then it's all over. Everything I have worked so hard for, gone in one fight."

"Then you don't lose. What's with all the pressure on yourself, Aiden? Take your time, bro. You haven't worried about all this stuff before."

"Yo, Trey," Sergio yells from near the doorway, "Let's go." I didn't realize everyone had left the gym. Trey runs over to pick up his bag before looking over at me one last time.

"Relax," he says, "you'll be the champ one day."

Sergio yells goodbye to me and I nod in return. The gym is quiet with no one around. This next fight is going to be big. I need to train harder.

I wake up in the middle of the night and can't get back to sleep, so I get dressed and run to the gym. It's three miles and I manage it in less than 15 minutes. I gear up and start hitting the bags. I envision the videos we watched of my opponent. My right hand is going to be the key to winning this fight because he's a southpaw, which means he fights backwards because he's left handed. It's my first professional fight against a left-hander and they make everything so much more complicated. My only advantage is my experience with them in the amateurs. I fought tons of southpaws there. He has a tendency to leave himself open down the middle. I need to step to my left and throw the cross straight down the middle to land cleanly on him. The main thing is to keep my lead foot outside of his. The uppercut will also work well on the inside. I heard he hates fighting on the inside, though, so he'll try to keep the fight to the outside.

My jab is better than his as well as my power. His speed is my only concern. He's the fastest fighter I have ever faced. A speed disadvantage is a huge concern in boxing. Faster fighters can often beat you to the punch, making it difficult to get punches off first. Speed is neutralized by two tactics: a good jab and timing. I was very good at both. He isn't taller than me so I don't have to worry about that. Body shots will be good, too, as long as I can cut the ring off on him and force him onto the ropes or into a corner. If I do, I plan on unleashing a barrage of punches to the body so I can slow him down.

"Can't sleep?"

Startled, I turn around to see Coach Kay standing behind me.

"Something like that." I continue to hit the bag.

"You know, there is such a thing as over-training," he tells me. I ignore him and resume my punches. "The body can become weak if you train too hard. Then, when the fight comes and you are going through those late rounds, it fails on you because you have spent so much time training."

"That won't happen to me."

"I'm not saying that it will. I'm just saying, don't push it. You are ready for this fight, Aiden. No more extra work is required." My combinations keep coming as anger fills me while I continue to hit the bag. "Aiden." He grabs the bag as I look up to him. Finally I get what he is saying so my punches stop. I need a shower. With the amount of training I've been doing, I shower about five times a day.

"What are you doing here, Coach?" I ask, surprised he's at the gym this time of the night.

"I come clean up once in a while. Good gym needs to be clean."

"The gym's spotless every night. I make sure of it." I assure looking around.

"It may seem that way but there is dust everywhere."

"You've taught me a lot of things, Coach, but lying isn't one of them. What's going on?"

"Don't you worry about me, son."

I look towards the upstairs part of the gym where nobody is allowed to go, even me. Finally, it clicks.

"No, don't tell me you are living here now, Coach." He begins to walk away and I follow him, taking off my gloves. "Coach, are you living here?" There's no reply as he walks towards his office. "Coach, answer me!"

He stops and slowly turns around, his confident expression never faltering.

"I might be staying here for the time being. It's good for me, you know. I can focus on this place more."

"C'mon, Coach, how come you didn't tell me it was this bad?"

"What would you have done?" he asks, shaking his head. "What more can you do? You already give me everything – you haven't kept one dollar of your checks from fighting. I got in over my head, son, way before you ever came into the picture. Now I have to face it. It is my battle, and no one else's. I can't bring you into it."

"I am into it, Coach. I'm giving you money to keep this place open and I'll keep doing it until it isn't a problem anymore."

"You are keeping the gym open, son. My personal problems, however, are my own. I don't need anyone else to worry about them."

"Why don't you charge more, Coach? You're letting half the people that come here not pay you a dime. We need money. You need money. Every little bit helps." Now that Coach was getting money from some of the city people he was starting to allow the younger kids with no money from the ghetto's to train for free. While the intentions were good, it wasn't paying the bills. His cliental with the city people wasn't big enough yet.

"They can't afford it."

"Then they can't join. It's simple. We need the money."

"What would you have done when you first came here if I'd told you you had to leave because you couldn't afford the gym fees?"

I have no reply. He's right, I couldn't afford it when I was younger. Hell, if I wasn't fighting I still wouldn't be able to afford it. I'd probably be selling drugs with John. Or dead or in jail. With the path that I was on those were the only options I had growing up until I found boxing.

"I hate money," I say under my breath.

"Money is money. Don't let it bother you. Most of this country lives day to day with no money. It's just the way it works. I'll find a way to make it, as I always do. This isn't the first time I've been homeless, you know."

"You don't deserve to be, Coach." I look at him. "You don't. You give people a gift that can't be learned anywhere else…confidence. You take kids away from the street, even just for a little while, and you help them. You show them there's a world besides drugs and gangs. And you ask for nothing in return. Hell if it weren't for this place God knows where I would be right now in my life."

"There are thousands of people in this world that have money but don't deserve it. You are not one of them. You shouldn't be living like this. We shouldn't be living like this."

"It's ok."

"No!" I yell, angrily. "It's not ok! We deserve better. You deserve better."

"Is something else wrong, son?"

Coach's cool stare calms my anger. I can't hide it anymore.

"I'm broke, Coach." My admittance brings a look of sadness to his usually stern face. "All my money is gone. They are going to take my house if I don't pay the taxes on it. I'm behind on the mortgage. I've got a job lined up, but it will cut into my training."

"Why didn't you tell me?" he asks angrily. "I wouldn't have taken any of that money from you had I known that!"

"I didn't have a choice! We didn't have a choice! I'll train at night and continue to fight. Just until we can catch up."

"No, you won't be able to do it. It'll be too much. I'll find a way."

"There is no other way, Coach. You have nothing else to give. For God's sake, you're living here now."

We both calm down a bit. His face is still sad but I can tell he's trying to be strong. I take a deep breath. "Please, I can do this," I say. There is no way I am going to give up. I can do both, I know I can.

Coach walks over to the ring and leans up against it. "Do you know what drives someone to fight, son? Do you know why someone like you decides that he wants to fight for a living? That he wants to risk his own health and body so he can hurt people?"

His questions baffle me.

"Anger," he continues. "Anger, hatred, pain. That's what draws people to this sport. Yeah, a lot of people want to learn. And they will try, spar a little, and have fun. But true fighters, the ones that want to get into the ring and hurt people, are different. They do it because of a burning anger inside of them that they can't seem to let go. Whether they are poor, orphans, gang members, whatever the case may be, they box to escape their lives. They channel their hate towards their opponents."

He sighs and stares ahead. "For you, it's your parents. It always has been. Your hatred for them drives you. You don't hate money, you hate your parents for leaving you the way they did. Because no matter what anyone says, money doesn't buy happiness. Sure, it makes paying the bills easier, but it doesn't fulfill that happiness within yourself. Your anger may pave the way to the championship, son. But to become champion, to become a good champion that people will embrace, you must overcome the demons that pave the way for you. You must rise above them. Only then will you ever become happy with yourself, and only then will you become the champion you have always wanted to be."

He pauses for a moment then looks over at me. "Do what you have to do. Just remember what I said."

I nod. Regardless of what Coach says or thinks, we need more money. Perhaps he is right, but I can't think of that right now. I can work and train, even if it's just for a few fights. I only pray that a promoter will see what I can bring to the table and will give us enough money to fight our way to the championship.

Chapter Thirteen

I took a job at a local factory. The money is decent. After a few months I am starting to live comfortably. I'm not rich but I am able to afford everything I need in life. I even managed to take Vanessa out on a few dates and pay for them myself. I have only fought twice and had won both easily. My knockout of the undefeated Jesse Nest – the fighter I'd been so worried about the night I talked to Coach – was the first. I also won my first decision, against Bernice Thompson. His record had been 12-4; he is the only fighter I haven't knocked out.

We have a new problem, though, one that I hadn't seen coming. Coach believes that since I have knocked out four undefeated fighters in a row, no one in the area wants to fight me, and no promoters want to put their undefeated fighters against someone as dangerous as me.

I am making a name for myself around New York State and in a few areas out of state as well. Coach predicts that my next couple of fights will be against guys like Bernice Thompson who have some losses on their records and want to fight just for the money. These are the ones I should be most careful about, he says, because they are fighting for their livelihood, as I am.

I don't tell Coach how tired I am. My 21st birthday came and went without any celebration. Me and Coach got a small cake at the gym for everyone to eat but my mind was barely there because I was so tired. Between trying to box and work, sleep has become a thing of the past. I'm lucky to snag five hours a night. I am training at least three to four hours a night after work, and my body is exhausted. I try to make it up on the weekends but it is catching up to me. The people at the gym are noticing and I think Coach is, too. My punches lack the power they usually have behind them. My training is subpar; I take a lot of breaks in between and don't push myself as much as I want to. Since I don't want to get too tired while training, I am slacking in areas I shouldn't be. The only thing that keeps me going is the idea that I can quit the job soon.

"I'm glad you're coming with me today," Coach Kay says. The drive has been quiet for the most part. I can't help but notice the abandoned buildings, ragged streets, and homeless people – things I wouldn't have noticed before I met Vanessa. Being a part of her

79

world makes me realize how sad it is living in mine. The homes in her neighborhood are stunning, with beautiful yards and swimming pools. There are no beggars asking for money or drugs. The streets are perfectly paved, without a pothole in sight. These are things I never saw growing up in the ghetto.

The other difference is the general atmosphere. People are nicer. The businesses there attract people with money who can shop and help the city prosper. I can't understand how people like Vanessa can live so close to people like me, and yet it seems like we come from totally different worlds. It was odd that I could actually run to Vanessa's house within an hour if I wanted too.

"Well, you asked," I say. "You know I never say no to you, Coach."

"Oh, you never say no to me? You sure as hell don't listen to me in that ring."

He is referring to my most recent fight. I had kept trying for the knockout even though Coach persistently told me to just get the rounds in and work. I had ended up tiring myself out in the last two rounds. I easily won the fight, but he had been mad at me at the end, although he always seemed that way after fights.

"I still don't say no."

"Just 'cause you don't say it don't mean that isn't the answer. When I tell you to do something and you do something else, that means you are saying no."

"I always listen to you, Coach, but sometimes I just have to go with my gut feeling."

"Well, you've been having a lot of 'gut feelings' lately. When I tell you to do something it's 'cause I know. I see something that you don't. There's a reason for it. You need to trust me when you are in that ring."

"I do trust you, but even if I did everything you told me, down to the damn period in your sentences, you would still have something negative to say after the fight! You always have something to say that I did wrong. Always!" I yell.

"That's because we need to improve every fight! Every single fight is different and I see something new that we need to work on. I'm trying to better you! You take it too personal, that's your problem. You should take criticism with an open ear."

We finally pull up to the church. I'm surprised to see a lot of white people. I hadn't realized we have traveled a little farther than my comfort zone. When I see the sign that says Mother Theresa's Roman Catholic Church, I nearly laugh out loud.

"You're joking, right?" I ask.

He puts the car in park. "What? I told you we were going to church."

I can't help but smile. "This is a Catholic church."

"Yeah, so what?" He gets out of the car and I follow.

"Don't you go to a black people church or something, where everyone sings and dances and stuff?" I am still smiling, and so is he. As usual, our argument has ended in laughter.

"All of a sudden you can afford a television and now you're stereotyping?"

"Ok, well, whatever," I laugh. "Let's just get this done. Oh, and I still can't afford a television."

I'm more intimidated by the massive building than I was the first time I looked at a boxing ring. The cross on top catches my eye, along with the huge windows featuring paintings of religious figures I don't recognize. If there is one thing about churches that I do like, it's their structure. They are amazing.

At the same time, churches scare me. My first step inside makes me remember when I was a child, when my father and mother used to take me. Oddly enough, I feel like I remember this place.

I try to pay attention to what is going on, I really do, but church isn't something I am too thrilled about. My father believed that God was the key to everything around us; He was the reason we became who we are and He directed us in the right direction when all seemed lost. I didn't believe any of it. My grandma had always gone, too. Every Sunday morning she would wake me up and ask if I wanted to go. I always said no. I thought she would eventually stop asking, but she never did. Even on her deathbed, she made me promise that I would start going. I'm sure she is staring down at me right now with a smile on her face.

I don't know why I said yes to Coach. I feel bad about everything that has happened. Coach is still living at the gym and there is no way I'm making enough to get him out of there. For now, I feel the best way to keep his mind off his problems is for me to hang out with him, even if it means going to church.

After a long hour of standing, sitting, and kneeling, the mass is over. At times I felt the priest glare over at me, like I was doing something wrong. I hadn't paid attention to anything. I couldn't remember one word that had come out of the priest's mouth. Coach had sung along with the choir and said all the prayers. I had just sat there, thinking I should have taken a Sunday morning shift at the factory to make a little extra cash.

People stick around afterwards and a lot of them talk to Coach. He introduces me to various people, most of whom know who

I am. I even sign some autographs and pose for a few pictures. It is an awkward feeling. I don't know how to smile in the photos, or even if I should. Do people want me to look serious, with a fist up 'cause I'm a boxer? I don't spend much time outside the ghetto or the gym. I didn't realize how many people actually follow boxing and know who I am.

"Coach Kay." The voice of the tall, older-looking man is crisp. His suit looks very expensive. "How are you feeling, Coach?"

"Better," Coach answers. "This is the boy I was telling you about, Aiden Walker. Aiden, this is Dr. Brad Brudge."

"Pleasure to meet you, Aiden."

"Nice to meet you, too, sir."

"Aiden, I need to talk to the doctor alone for a second," Coach says awkwardly. "Why don't you go to the car and I'll be there in a second."

I feel strange as they both look at me. So it is true – Coach is having problems. All of those visits to the doctor weren't just check-ups because of his age.

I doubt it is too serious, though. It has been going on for four to five years. Maybe he has diabetes or something and just isn't telling anyone. Coach isn't exactly the type to open up his problems to the world, or a single person for that matter. The visits have been fewer lately. I don't know if he is on any medication but I suppose I will have to pay attention and find out.

As I walk out, I gaze around at all the statues and paintings. For some reason, this feels so familiar. Suddenly, something to the left of the exit catches my eye. It is a small statue of Jesus sitting on a older looking table. His face is bleeding from the crown of thorns on his head. His eyes are sad and His frown could rip the soul right out of a man. I have seen sad statues of Jesus before, but this particular statue is very familiar.

"Your mother donated it after your father died," I hear someone say. I turn around to see an old woman walking toward me, leaning on her cane. "She said she wanted the church to have it."

I turn back to the statue and suddenly realize that it had been in my house for years, right in the middle of our dining room table. When I was younger, when I still had a family.

"You should watch it," I say. "If she knows it's still here, she will try to steal it back and sell it for money." I start to walk away.

"She was a good woman, you know," she replies. "She just got lost on a very dark path. Perhaps you should pray for her."

"She came here?"

"Yes, for an entire year after your father died. She sat in front and prayed every Sunday, mostly for you, she would say." The woman pauses, knowing she has my attention. It finally hits me! This was the church they used to take me too as a child. "Said that you were lost, that you were angry at your father and that she had no idea how to deal with it. That no matter what she tried to do to make you happy, it didn't work."

"That's no excuse to become who she is today."

"No, child, it's not. But God teaches forgiveness. You do not have to accept your mother for who she is today, but you can forgive her for it. And maybe one day, when you have found the compassion in your heart, you can try to help her."

"I'm sorry, ma'am, I appreciate your thoughts," I say, suddenly angry, "but my parents are dead to me, and so is God." I head towards the door, but stop to turn and look at her. "If God is this all-powerful being that wants to help her, then tell Him to do it Himself."

Chapter Fourteen

I grab a mitt from the counter and pull the chicken out of the oven. It's hot and smells like it does every night. I place it on the plate next to the spinach. It's not the best meal in the world but I need to lose a few more pounds before the fight. Cutting time in my training has made making weight an issue for me. I'm not used to having to lose weight before fights; I usually train so hard that it naturally comes off.

I grab the glass of water and walk over to the table. Finally, after a long day of work, I can relax and eat.

Fight night is one week away. I can't sleep, I can't focus, and my training is less than where it needs to be. Double shifts have opened up at work, allowing me to make double the money by putting in overtime. I thought I would be able to finally start saving money, but each time I tried something happened where it needed to be spent. I was just starting to catch up with the IRS when they managed to find out I actually owed more money than they originally thought. Both my washer and my dryer are broken and the porch is falling apart. I don't have the money to fix any of it. It's so frustrating.

Coach made it known he is not happy with the way I am training. Some days I only manage two hours of gym time. I wake up at 6 a.m. to get to work by 7. Then I work until 7 at night and shoot to the gym right after so my body is exhausted before I even begin to work out. I train from 8 to 10, but not hard. Then I go home but can't fall asleep until 1 or 2, especially when Vanessa is over. For three weeks I have been doing this and my body is no longer cooperating.

Sundays aren't days off anymore. I run, sometimes pick up a 4-hour shift at work, and then train at the gym. My friends are starting to notice the effects. I'm often short with them, not talking and joking like I usually do. Coach and I fight a lot. What bothers him more than anything is that I'm not in shape for this fight like I have been in the past.

The fight is against Pedro Garcia. His 28-5 record isn't bad. He's fought some of the top guys in my weight class but he got knocked out by boxing superstar Dominick Cayman. Beating Garcia in good fashion will definitely get me noticed by more than a few promoters. The fight is also on the undercard of boxing prospect Tony "The Terror" Rocks. He is in my weight class and is Bones

Promotions' next big star behind Dominick. ESPN is showing his fight as the main event; mine will be right before the air, meaning I won't make it on television. Even so, a lot of important people will notice me. I have to look good.

The doorbell rings. I wipe my face and walk over to the door and open it.

"What's up, bro?" Trey asks. "Can I come in?"

"Yeah, of course."

It's a little strange that he's here. I remember when he used to spend days on end here slouching his body on my couch for nights, when my grandmother was still alive. The smell of cooking food and him being here reminds me of how much I miss her. He walks in and looks around.

"Man, it's been a long time since I've been here."

"I know, that used to be your bed," I laugh, looking at the couch.

"That's right. I miss your grandma's breakfasts, man. She really knew how to hook a brother up." He sniffs the air as if he can smell her cooking.

"I mean, if you want to stay the night I can cook you breakfast," I offer. "Not sure what it'll taste like." I walk to the kitchen and he follows.

"Hell, naw, I'm good. You couldn't cook if Betty Crocker herself came here and showed you how to."

"That's true," I agree. I only know how to cook chicken, rice, and vegetables because that's what I grew up on. It wasn't really cooking either, more like warming it up. "What you doing here? I can't even remember the last time you came by. Looking for a place to crash for the night?"

Even though Vanessa is on her way over I would never tell Trey he couldn't stay. He is one of my best friends.

"Naw, just came to see what's up with you," he says, sitting down at the table. "Coach Kay is a little worried about your endurance for this fight. Plus, I noticed you're irritated lately."

"I'm good. Just working a lot. I feel good. I can go eight rounds easily." My friend raises his eyebrow; he doesn't buy my lie.

"You know, I worry about you, bro. Demarcus won his first fight tonight." Shit! I was supposed to go to the amateur card tonight downtown and sign autographs. I totally forgot!

"Oh, man, I forgot there was an amateur show tonight. Damn."

I had promised Coach I would go to the fight, but I'd gotten caught up late at work and then went for a run. The fight had totally slipped my mind.

"Yeah, it's all good. You're busy. He looked good, though. Said he wants to be just like you when he gets older."

The idea makes me laugh. "Broke and angry?" I joke. I don't know why anyone would want to be like me. Demarcus was only 14, but he was dedicated, perhaps just as much as I was at that age.

"You know who I saw there?" Trey asks.

"Who?"

"Salvatore Breeze."

I nearly spit out my food. "C'mon! What was he doing in town?"

"Said that his grandmother passed away. He was asking about you. Wanted to come see ya, but he's leaving tomorrow."

"Dang, it's been years since I saw that dude."

Salvatore Breeze had been one of my closest friends at the gym. He was a great sparring partner, and he always got the better of me in the ring. He was the one person I could never beat. He moved away a long time ago.

"He turned pro, you know – 2-0 with 2 knockouts."

"Maybe one day we'll meet in the ring," I say with a grin, looking at Trey.

"Man, you couldn't beat that dude for four years, what makes you think you can now?" Trey stands up, looks around the kitchen then stares over at me. "You sure you ok?" he asks again.

"Yeah."

He isn't buying it. I can't even taste the food anymore because I'm so used to eating the same things. He paces around the kitchen before walking out the back door onto the patio. I clean up real quick and follow him out. He's sitting on a table. The night is warm and the moon looks as big as the sun as it shines brightly in the night sky.

"You know, you're the last hope for that gym. You know that, right?"

I look up at the stars and smile thinking of Coach. The Star Boxing Gym. The smile is the first sincere one I've given in a long time when the subject of boxing is brought up. "There's always another star, Trey."

"No, not this time. You are it, man. You're the one that can bring this town new hope. Everyone is looking for you to be the next champ, to put boxing back on the map in this city and in Buffalo. Even the rich people think you can do it. You have a chance, Aiden, a chance to get out of this place. A chance to not be poor, to not have to worry about money for the rest of your life. It's not a dream anymore,

Aiden. It's real. I don't want to see you throw it all away."

"What am I supposed to do, Trey?" I say in frustration. "My back is on the ropes and the shots keep coming. Every time I try to get out, I get thrown right back on the ropes. I have no money, the gym is struggling to stay open, and every time I get the chance to get ahead, I just fall farther behind. The furnace went last week. I got another notice saying I owed taxes from three years ago that I have no idea how. I'm barely keeping up with the mortgage. I'm actually not keeping up with it. Life isn't about boxing, Trey. And if it is, then I am losing. Bad."

"That's what I mean, Aiden," he says, leaning forward on the table. "You're too damn good. You're better than Travis could have been. Better than we all could have been. And you're at a point in your career where your next fight can be your big break."

"You think I want to work 50 to 60 hours a week just to still be broke? I'm making minimum wage and it's the only job I can get. You think I want to train every single night after working all day, just so I can exhaust myself to the point that I can't even open my eyes? I wish I could train all day and be ready for these fights like I used to be. I just can't right now."

"What about Vanessa? Her dad? Don't you think he would help you?"

"No, I would never ask or accept anything from her. This isn't her problem, it's mine."

"Well, now you sound like Coach," Trey mocks. He's right. I do sound exactly like Coach. He has said the exact same thing to me before.

"Hi," a woman's voice says.

We both turn to see Vanessa standing there. I hope she didn't hear what we were saying. By the look on her face, I don't think she did.

"Oh, hi Trey," she adds, catching sight of him.

"What's up!" he says with a grin.

She smiles at both of us. "Am I interrupting guy talk?"

"No," I immediately respond. "We're coming in now."

"Actually, I'm taking off," Trey adds quickly.

"Ok, I'll be inside," she says, disappearing into the house.

Trey shakes my hand and gives me a half-hug.

"You know, when a great fighter gets their back against the ropes, they weather the storm. No matter how many shots are thrown their way, they stand their ground. And when the opportunity opens up to strike back, they seize it, and never let it go again."

He smiles and throws his fist in the air, nodding his head.

I'm not sure I'll ever get that opportunity. Right now, I felt like the fighter on the ropes, waiting for the Referee to come in and stop the fight. It's a funk I need to break out of as soon as possible.

Chapter Fifteen

I throw two body shots, both of which get blocked by Garcia. He throws a combination – two uppercuts followed by a hook that lands on my gloves. I throw a cross down the middle, landing cleanly on his chin. It hurts my hand but the sting fades away. My guard is up even though my back is against the ropes. Quickly, I clinch up and turn Garcia around, then push him away. The bell rings.

Heading to my corner, I wipe off the sweat that's falling from my head. Coach Kay sits me down and pours water all over my back. Trey walks up to the side of the ring and hands Coach the ends-swell to keep my face ok. My breathing is heavy.

"Aiden, listen to me, son. You are losing this fight. Do you understand? There are only two rounds left. I need you to win the last two rounds to have a chance to win this fight. Do you understand me, son?"

"Yeah," I mumble. My body hurts, my legs are almost gone, and I can't seem to get out of the way of Garcia's punches. I can see them coming but my body isn't reacting the way it usually does. I'm not in proper shape and it's showing. Coach is worried; I can see it in his eyes. I need to do something to win this fight, but I just don't have the energy. I'm losing? He's right. I have to be.

"I need four- to five-hit combinations. He doesn't move when you throw punches. He sits there with his hands up because you are only throwing one and two punches at him. If you make that four and five, you will connect with the last two, ok? C'mon, son, let's do this!"

I nod my head and the bell rings. Despite Coach's words the only thing I can bring my mind to embrace is that fact that I'm exhausted. Two more rounds I say to myself. I can do this. I can't believe the minute is over already.

As I take a deep breath, it feels as though someone is pressing their hands on my lungs. I walk to the middle of the ring. I do exactly as Coach says. The first three punches are blocked, but the second two get through. Coach is right. Garcia doesn't move his head or body. When I throw he just stands there with his hands up looking to block and counter. I back up and two seconds later I do it again. The same thing happens. I throw two body shots and land both of them. Everything is working but now I am tired and I can't keep throwing these combinations. I'm angry with myself. The power behind my punches has faded throughout the fight along with my speed. Garcia is taking my shots and still coming forward as though I can't hurt him.

The crowd is back and forth on their feet at the action packed fight taking place in front of them. They are loving the action. People cheer as we go back and forth. I find myself on the ropes again, going blow for blow with Garcia. His punches don't hurt as they land across my jaw. I duck a few punches to land some more body shots. Again, I push him out.

The fight gets back to the middle of the ring. I stick my jab out to keep him away. He tries to come forward but I move side to side, sticking out the jab. The fight slows down a little, allowing me to catch a little bit of wind. My legs are shot. I am fighting on pure will now. I cannot lose this fight.

He jumps forward, cutting me off from moving to his left, and he throws a hook to my body and comes back up, landing at the top of my head. I can't believe I'm allowing him to land this many punches on me. Again, he lands a jab-cross on my head, making it hurt even more than it already does.

Stepping back, he comes forward, throwing another combination, but I block it and step around him, tossing the jab out. The crowd is starting to boo as the fight slows down. This time I come forward again, throwing another five-punch combination. Four of the five punches land and he seems hesitant to come forward. I can't tell if I've hurt him. I throw a jab, followed by a cross down the middle that again lands on his chin. He comes back, immediately throwing a hook to my body, hook to my head, and cross down the middle, landing all three punches juggling my head. The bell rings. I can barely walk back to my corner, my legs hurt so bad. They feel like jello.

"Ok, ok, that's better. Deep breaths. He's hitting you too much."

I take a sip of water, trying to breathe, but I can't. I don't even know how I'm going to go another round. I feel like I'm about to throw up.

"You see that, those combinations work," Coach continues. "You got that round. I need you to do that again."

I nod my head but I know there is no way I can do it again, although I would never say that to Coach. He can probably see the look in my eyes, which is reflecting what I am thinking, defeat. I feel discouraged that I let this happen. I know I'm better than this guy. This fight shouldn't have taken this long. If I were in the shape I should have been, I would have knocked him out earlier. I can see the openings and when I throw punches they are landing, but I can't muster the endurance or strength to throw enough to hurt him. I've allowed him to land too many shots. I glance at Trey who gives me that look. 'Damn Mexican fighters have so much heart.' That's what Trey would say if Coach wouldn't kill him if he decided to speak. This guy just keeps coming.

"This is the last round," Coach says. "Give it all you got."

The bell rings and Garcia comes out wailing. He isn't playing around now; he's trying to knock me out. I fire back a flurry of punches. We are both landing some and the crowd is going nuts. There is no way I can continue fighting like this, but Garcia can. I back up finally, throwing my jab to keep him away. He keeps coming forward. I don't have time to rest. He is throwing punch after punch, trying to make this a slugfest. I block a few, and a few get through. I have nothing left to fire back. Instead, I just keep backing up, trying not to let myself get on the ropes.

It doesn't work for long. I find myself on the ropes again, taking shots from Garcia. He keeps putting the pressure on. Again, we fire an exchange of punches. He lands a few good shots that make my head dazed. I can't help but think that if he had any power behind these punches, he would have knocked me out by now. I'm trying to breathe and punch at the same time, but I'm getting hit with clean shots. I grab him long enough to catch myself from tumbling over, not because I'm hurt, but because my legs are gone.

The Referee separates us, and again Garcia is in my face, throwing punch after punch. I finally let my hands go and land a few good shots. As he presses forward, I continue to throw punches to fire back. The crowd is going crazy. I can't breathe, my legs are gone, but I just keep fighting. Heart, determination, will power, this is my biggest test for those three, because it's the only thing that's keeping me from falling over. Finally, after a few exchanges Garcia again backs me into the ropes, where he unloads a barrage of punches. I try to fight back but I can't keep up. I hold again.

As the Referee separates us, I stay off the ropes, throwing my jab to keep Garcia away. He's still coming forward but my jab is keeping his punches at bay. This three minute round feels like thirty minutes. Is it ever going to end? It will if I get knocked out. My jab is my savior. He can't seem to get to me. I wonder if his legs are tired. Trying to cut the ring off, he jumps quickly to the left and throws a cross straight down the middle, which lands on my nose. I step back and again he is in my face, leaning his sweaty body into mine and throwing combinations.

I decide to not back up and to just defend. I have no energy left to throw punches. The only thing I can do is defend, finish the round, and make sure I don't get hit with any more clean shots. Finally, the bell rings.

The crowd is cheering as Garcia raises his hands. I walk back to my corner, disappointed at my performance, to say the least. Coach grabs the wet towel and wipes me down.

"It's going to be close," he says, but I know his words are false. I've definitely lost. I can't even speak because I'm still trying to catch air. Each breath hurts my chest and the only thing I can think of is how happy I am that it's over.

"You got heart, bro, I'll give you that," Trey says as he leans against the rope.

"I had nothing left," I'm able to say.

"Shit, you didn't have anything left after round five and you still fought through it," Trey replies, smiling and rubbing my head.

"He was a tough fighter," Coach admits. "Don't be discouraged. You did good."

I don't believe him, but this isn't like other sports, where the coach rips the team after a losing game. In boxing, the criticism comes weeks later when training begins for the next fight. That's what Coach always did. Discouraging a fighter right after a fight can break him. Most trainers will never do it.

"Ladies and gentlemen, the judges' scorecards," the Referee announces. I can see everyone watching closely.

My heart begins to race, and Coach and I exchange worried glances as I walk over to the middle of the ring.

"All three judges score the bout the same, 76 to 74," the Referee continues. I lost, I lost, I lost. I know I lost. It's all that goes through my head. "For your winner, and still undefeated, Aiden Walker!"

I raise my hand as Coach Kay and Trey applaud. Some boos come from the crowd and I can see that Garcia is upset he lost. He didn't lose, however; I did. The judges had given me a gift. I may have been raising my hand, but not for one second did I believe I had done enough to win the fight, even though it had been close.

"Good fight," Garcia mumbles and quickly walks away. He knows he won too. For some reason the judges allowed me to win this fight. I have no idea why.

The locker room is quiet after the fight as though we lost. Coach walks around, gathering everything together so we can watch the rest of the fights. We have been given ringside seats.

I sit on the bench with my head down. I feel weak; I've never felt like this after a fight. Trey is singing to himself, trying to lighten the mood. We are sharing the room with other fighters and they all stop to congratulate me. I can't even say thank you with a straight face.

"That's ok," Coach Kay tells me. "We had a tough fight. You pulled it off. Now we just have to look forward to the next fight. We'll get you in better shape and maybe even a rematch."

"I could have knocked him out," I reply, shaking my head. "I should have knocked him out."

"You can't knock out everyone, son. Some fighters have granite chins. No matter how many times you hit them, they just keep coming forward. This was a good fight to test you."

Coach's confidence seems legit, but I'm not convinced.

"I lost Coach." I whisper.

"No, no you didn't. You won. It was close and you pulled it off at the end."

"No, I wasn't in shape," I say angrily. "I can't get in shape, working the way I am and trying to train. It's too much."

"Well, we will get you in shape," Coach replies. "We'll figure out a way around it."

I shake my head and begin to pace.

"This was my chance, Coach, my chance to impress the promoters. There are so many important people out there. I failed. They will never sign me now. The only chance I'm going to get is if they match me against their top guy. My purse will be low and I'll be on the opposite side of a bad decision." Deep down, I know that even with all of that against me, I would still take the fight and hope to knock out a top prospect. But it won't solve my problem of how to train properly.

"They saw you," Coach says. "That's all that matters. So, what, they can put us against their top guy? You can beat him. You know you can. I know you can."

"I can't beat anyone if I can't train!" I shout.

The locker room goes quiet. I take a deep breath. Trey is looking at me and so is Coach. I shake my head. Something has to be done. Work is killing me but if I don't work then I will be hungry and homeless. I'm not going to be that. No matter how much I love boxing. I'm not even sure I love it anymore. With work and boxing together, I have begun to hate both of them. The truth was, I just couldn't afford to fight right now. I must get rid of one, and right now it has to be this. "I'm done," I whisper.

"Wait, what? Done what?" Trey asks.

"I'm done boxing. I can't do this right now. I need a break."

"What kind of break?" Trey demands loudly.

"I don't know. I just need to focus on one thing right now."

"No, you can't be done!" Trey argues. He looks over at Coach, who remains silent. "Coach, say something. You can't let him quit." Coach resumes packing our supplies. "Coach?" Trey asks again.

"It's his decision, Trey," Coach says simply.

'Not even a little bit of fight from Coach?' I think to myself. It seems odd. Then I realize – Coach hasn't given up on me; he understands everything I've been going through. He has seen it in training camp and in my last few fights. Coach knows how hard it's been for me.

"You're not even going to try and stop him?" Trey demands angrily.

"Trey, please," I interrupt. "Nothing is going to change my mind. I can't fight another fight like this and I can't keep working for something that may never happen. Right now, I need to give up something – and it has to be boxing."

"I can't believe you two! I'm out of here, man!"

Trey runs from the room, leaving me and Coach alone. Coach finishes gathering our things. I'm still in my shorts and shoes. I'm upset with myself for making this decision, but right now there is no other way. Coach looks at me as he picks up the bag.

"You, um…you did a good job, son. And you're a hell of a boxer. But you're right. Without one hundred percent dedication, there's no way you can ever be as great as I believe you can be. I want your heart and your soul into it, every ounce of it. I don't know if anything will ever change that will allow you to box the way you want to, but the door is always open for you."

"Coach, I'm still going to be at the gym and give you money and stuff."

"No, no, I don't want your money," he says. "I'll be ok. I'm always ok. You take this time to find yourself. Find out who you want to be and what makes you happy. In the end, I just want you to be happy, Aiden, and if that's not in boxing, then that's ok with me."

I'm stunned by Coach's reaction. In that moment, for the first time since I was a boy, I realize what it is like to have a father figure in my life. Coach isn't just my boxing coach. He is much more.

Chapter Sixteen

It is easier to work at the factory without having to worry about boxing. What isn't easier is dealing with Vanessa. She is upset that I quit. I didn't tell her it's about money or being exhausted. She knows I'm not rich but she assumes I'm making enough to pay for everything I owe. I am even buying her things and taking her out to dinner, just to impress her. I can't afford to and each time it means not paying the electric bill or another debt.

"Tom and Wes are excited to see you," Vanessa says as we walk up to the club. We are going to Wes's birthday party at a place called The Vine.

"It's been about six months," I say. "Why'd they stop coming to the gym?"

"I don't know. Last time I talked to Tom was about two weeks ago when he invited us to come to the party. Before that, I hadn't seen him in months. He's been working for his dad a lot, I think."

That makes sense. Tom is probably making tons of money working for him. I wish I could go work for him. An office job would be less tiring on my body, and I would be able to train hard when I left. My factory job involves tons of lifting, which is making my body take a very cut form but exhausting me.

"How do you like the outfit?" she asks, checking out the black shirt and light blue jeans she had bought me for the party. Vanessa doesn't like my clothes; they aren't expensive enough. She will never say that, but I know that's why she buys me new clothes all the time. Every time we hang out with her friends, she politely asks me to wear something she gave me. I know why but I don't want to ruin it for her.

"They are nice. Very comfortable. I love the shirt. Thanks."

"Good, I'm glad you like them. You look really good. You better stay away from all the other girls in here." She laughs, nudging my arm.

"I mean, I can't make any promises, but I'll try my best." My mocking remark draws a harder nudge this time. She still makes me smile. Right now in my life she was the only thing that did.

"Hey!" I say, laughing. It's the first true laugh I've had in a long time. "How is this place?" The outside looks a little rundown like an old building that hadn't been used in years but the patio is crowded with people. It's not the usually downtown Buffalo scene, just some private bar off of one of the main streets. It may actually be a nightclub judging by the music and people dancing that I notice through the foggy windows.

"It's fun. Tom paid for the entire club to shut down so it's a private party."

Of course he did, I think to myself. Must be nice to have money to do whatever you want.

"I don't get why they waste money like that, just to party."

"Some people don't appreciate money the way they should," she replies, smiling. I love her beautiful smile. Even when I can't focus on anything and my thoughts are filled with anger, being around Vanessa makes me feel better.

Her friends, on the other hand, make me feel out of place. It's going to be a nightmare getting through this night dealing with her rich friends and all these people. We pass the bouncers and they both look at me awkwardly. I'm not sure if it's because they don't like me or because they recognize me. My professional record is no secret to the area.

There are people everywhere. There is a huge dance floor off towards the back and the bar circles around the entire downstairs. Above us is another floor that is just as packed. The club is very nice, looking as though it had just been remodeled. Vanessa sees a few of her friends and drags me over to say hello. She introduces me to the ones I don't know.

"Aiden, this is Jenna, Brooklyn, and Catherine. Girls, this is Aiden." They each smile and shake my hand. Catherine, for some reason, gives me a hug.

"We have heard so much about you," she says. "It's so nice to finally meet you. You're just as cute as you look in the paper."

Each of the girls is pretty and well dressed. I wouldn't expect someone of Vanessa's stature to hang around any other type of girl. They all seem to run in a clique of rich, good-looking people.

"Aiden!" Wes yells above the loud music. I smile as he runs through the girls to get to me.

"What's up, bro? Happy birthday," I say, shaking his hand.

"Chillin', man, thanks. Good to see you. C'mon, let's go do some shots!"

He grabs me and pulls me away from the girls. I look back at Vanessa, who is laughing. I can read her lips as she says "I'll see you in a little bit."

Within seconds, Vanessa is out of sight behind a huge crowd

of people. I'm not big on drinking but I figure I need to loosen up a little.

"Dude, I've been trying to get back into the gym. Been busy with work and all that. Congratulations on the fight. That's good shit. 14-0 now, right? I saw the newspaper kind of down you a bit. The dude that wrote the article is an asshole. Said he thought you lost."

I try to forget about it, but everyone I talk to brings it up. Jerry Shank is the editor who wrote the article. He said I looked "sloppy, outmatched, and exhausted." People come up to me all the time, telling me not to worry about it and that he is a jerk. They hadn't seen the fight, though. If they had, they would know he is right.

"Yeah, well, it was a close fight. Everyone has their own opinion."

Coach has drilled one thing into my head: Never admit to a loss. If the judges give me a fight and I know it's a bad decision, I should never admit to it. It will only cause craziness among the public. I shouldn't go around telling everyone I won though. I always take the safe response like 'It was a close fight' or 'He was tough' or 'The judges decide it not me.'

"Dude, you're the best fighter that we've had in this city in years," Wes continues. "Maybe more than that. Don't listen to what those clowns say. Two shots of tequila!"

As the bartender pours the shots, I look around for Vanessa. I don't see her anywhere. People are flooded on the bar making me uncomfortable as I keep getting bumped into or am always leaning up against someone.

"Make that three." Tom sneaks up behind me rubbing my shoulder, smiling. "What's up?" he says, smacking my hand.

"Nothing at all. How are you?"

"Good, good. Same old. Just working a lot. I'm trying to get back into the gym." He jokes around, throwing some punches at me. "I'm out of shape."

"Well, you don't look it," I say, feeling his arms. He's always been a big, solid guy. Tom lifted weights for years before coming to the gym to learn how to box.

"How's Coach Kay doing?" he asks.

"He's doing good. Still sounds like a drill sergeant when he trains everyone."

"That guy is going to die with that gym," Wes says. "I love him, though. Best man I know."

Wes hands us the shots. The scent of tequila makes me cringe a little.

"To Coach Kay," Wes announces, as we all raise the shots in

the air then drink them down. The taste is bitter. I shake my head, trying to get rid of the taste in my mouth. One thing is for sure, it definitely wakes me up.

"That ain't no joke," Tom says, doing the same thing as me.

"That's a man's drink!" Wes exclaims, slapping me on the back. "Rally them up again. Let's go."

My eyes widen. There's no way I can keep doing shots with these guys. I'm not going to back down, though. Some part of me feels I owe it to myself to have a fun night out. It isn't something I get to do often.

"Man, you guys are gonna kill me with these shots all night," I say.

"Oh, c'mon," Tom says, "even a dedicated fighter like yourself deserves to have a night out!"

"Round two," Wes says, handing us our shots. The pretty black haired bartender shoots me a smile. I try to ignore it. The second tequila doesn't go down any smoother than the first. The television above the bar is showing highlights of football games from earlier that day.

"The Bills aren't playing around this year," Tom says. "They're 7-1 now. I never thought they would be on top of the division after eight games."

"No one did," I say.

"The Jets are still going to beat them," Wes adds.

"Are you crazy?" Tom argues. "They are 5-3 and look like shit. Both their star wide outs are hurt. Johnson is playing awful at QB. They don't have a shot!"

"Put your money where your mouth is," Wes fires back. "500 says the Jets beat them next weekend."

"You're on!"

Five hundred dollars on a bet! I can't imagine wasting that amount of money on something so stupid. Do these guys have any idea what I could do with five hundred dollars? I need to get out of here.

"Well, guys, I'm going to go find Vanessa," I say. As I start to walk away, Tom grabs my arm.

"Hey, look," he says, pointing at the television. Dominick Cayman is on the screen. They are showing highlights of his fight. He scored a fifth-round KO over undefeated number-one contender, Viktor Santiago. Santiago was the only person in that weight class that posed a threat to Cayman and he had been annihilated.

"He's unbelievable," Wes says. "You think you can beat him?"

"Hell, yeah, he can," Tom interrupts. "This is Aiden 'White Boy' Walker. Ten more fights or so and you can take him on."

"I don't know," I say, looking up at the television. "I may never know."

"I heard he got paid $30 million for that fight," Wes chuckles. "One hour of boxing. That is insane. You have to get to that level, Aiden."

"I'd be happy making 100K in a fight," I admit. My response draws laughter from both of them.

"Aren't you that poor white trash boxer?"

Startled, I turn to see a man approaching. He's about 6-foot-1 and well built, with straight blonde hair and dark eyes that look like they mean business. He stumbles a little as he walks towards me. He's drunk.

"Johnny, wait…" Tom says to him, but the man pushes him aside.

"Get out of my way, Tom," he says, looking at me. "Yeah, that's you. I read about you in the paper. They said you are broke and poor. Little white trash man thinking that he's tough." He laughs. "What are you doing here? You don't belong in a place like this punk ass."

I don't move as he steps closer. He's drunk. I doubt that he's ever been in a fight before and if he has I doubt he knows what to do. He's coming forward at me straight, and his beer is being held in his right hand, which means there's a good chance he's right handed. That will be the first punch he throws. "Listen, I don't want any trouble," I say calmly. "I'm just here to have fun."

"Pfffft," he sputters drunkenly. He's much bigger than me, but nothing I can't handle. "Do you hear this kid? Big, bad boxer don't want no trouble."

I can see people's faces go from happy to concerned as they form a circle around us. Wes cuts in front of Johnny and pushes me back. "Just back off and go," he says in my ear. "This dude is going to fight you."

"Wes, what you doing, brother?" Johnny slurs. "Trying to protect him? Move out of the way and let me whoop this big bad boxer's ass."

"Johnny, chill, dude," Wes says. "This is my party and you're drunk. You need to get out of here."

Three of Johnny's buddies come behind him to back him up. Wes looks intimidated but stands his ground.

I smile at Wes and move him out of the way. "I got this," I tell him.

"No, Aiden, don't."

I walk over to Johnny and stand face to face with him. He hands his beer to the guy next to him. I smile again and watch as the grin disappears from his face.

"Johnny, stop it!" Vanessa appears out of nowhere and stands in between us.

"Oh, wow, she finally steps in to save her boyfriend," Johnny taunts. "You plan on keeping this clown around longer than you kept me?"

"You know this guy, Vanessa?" I ask her.

"Yes, he's my ex-boyfriend," she admits. "I'm so sorry. I didn't think it would be a problem."

"You knew he was going to be here?" I ask. I can't believe she would bring me to a party that her ex was going to be at, especially if he was some rowdy, drunk guy.

"I didn't think he was going to say anything, I swear."

"Don't you worry," Johnny chimes in. "You'll be out of here in no time. After I beat your ass, you can leave."

He tries to push his way through the people holding him back. I look at Vanessa angrily and push her aside as well.

"Aiden, don't!" she yells as I approach Johnny. I'm trying to stay calm but I'm having a very hard time holding back my emotions. The fact that I haven't fought in a month doesn't make it any easier. I actually have an itch to fight, whether it's inside or outside of the ring. The need to punch someone has been bothering me since my last fight. I want to knock him out.

Johnny's friends finally let him go and we stand face to face again. "That's good, poor boy," he says. "You can't take care of her the way I can."

"I tell you what I'm going to do," I say to him, taking a step back. "I am going to let you throw the first punch. And you better hope you hit me. And if you hit me, you better hope you knock me out. Otherwise, my face is going to be the last thing you see before you wake up on that floor."

Without hesitating, Johnny throws the sloppiest, wildest punch I have ever seen. From his right hand, as I suspected. I easily step out of the way. I throw an uppercut and land it on his chin. His eyes immediately roll back in his head and he falls to the ground, knocked out cold.

His boys run towards me and all hell breaks loose. The bouncers join in, too, and I'm left swinging for my life. Everyone is fighting; I'm hitting people I don't even know. I take a few shots myself from different directions and fall to the ground to protect myself. Punches are coming from all angles and I block them the best I can.

Finally, the bouncers grab me, pull me outside, and throw me onto the street. I'm bleeding from my head and I wipe my hand across it to make sure I don't have any deep cuts. I just appear to be brush burned.

My heart is beating so fast, I feel like it's going to burst out of my chest. My hands are shaking and so is my body. It's the first bar fight I've ever been in. I can't believe it happened. For some reason, it felt good to knock someone out again. Like something I had been waiting to do for a long time. My hand hurts, I hope it's not broke. I don't have health insurance. More bills.

I begin to walk, and just then Vanessa runs up behind me.

"Aiden, stop!" she demands. I keep walking. "Aiden, stop, please!" Finally, I stop and turn around to look at her. "Oh my God, you're hurt," she cries. She tries to get closer but I back away.

"I'm fine. Leave me alone." I turn back around and start to walk again.

"Aiden, stop, please. Just talk to me." She grabs my arm and turns me around.

"I don't want to talk, Vanessa. I want to go home."

"You can't walk home, Aiden. It'll take hours. Let me drive you."

I stare into her sorrowful eyes. "You set me up! You brought me here with your stupid friends and your ex-boyfriend, who was obviously going to start trouble as soon as he saw me!"

I've never yelled at Vanessa before. As much as I don't want to, I can't control my anger. Why would she bring me here? I know it was Wes's birthday but that Johnny dude was waiting for the first chance he had to see me. They should have known.

"I didn't think it would be a problem," she says. "We've been civil to each other since I started dating you. Please, just let me drive you home."

"He knew a lot about me, Vanessa."

"Only what he read in the papers."

"I don't belong here. I don't belong with your crowd."

"Aiden, what are you talking about? Yes, you do. I don't want anyone else or any of them. Please let me drive you home so we can talk about this." Her pleading isn't changing my angry mood.

"He was right, Vanessa," I say quietly.

"No, he wasn't, Aiden."

"YES HE WAS! I AM POOR!" I scream at her so loudly that she jumps. My anger subsides a little as I stare into her frightened eyes. For the first time since I was a boy, I feel like crying. "I'm poor. I'm broke. All of my bills are behind and I'm losing everything. I quit boxing 'cause I need to work more just to survive. I can't give you what you want, Vanessa. I can't buy you things, or take you out to nice dinners, or go to nice places with you. I have nothing to give you. And you deserve someone who can give you the life that you want and that your father has given you. I will never be that guy. Please, let me go."

"Aiden, I don't..." she begins.

"Stop, please," I tell her. "We may live in the same city, but we are from two totally different worlds. Your friends, your cars..." I pause, looking down. "...These clothes...none of this is who I am or who I will ever be. I just want to go home, and I want to walk."

I turn again and resume walking. This time, she doesn't follow. I've lost her, and perhaps it is a good thing I did. She lives in a world that I can't be a part of. I'm upset and I have a long walk to think about it. I've lost boxing and I've lost Vanessa – two of the things I care about the most.

I don't know what I'm doing or if any of this is a good idea. But I'm used to losing the things in my life that I love. I will get over this and bury it in the back of my mind, just like I do everything else.

That night, when I got home, I almost did it. I had thought about it before growing up but never had I been so close. Sitting on my bed I thought about my life. Everything in it had fallen apart. It was empty, it was broken. I lost everything. Boxing, Coach, Vanessa, a part of me. All of me. What was there left for me to do if not fight? Work a job that I hated just to pay bills that I hated even more. What was the point of life? Nothing. That was the answer. We live and we die. The lucky people get to live with wealth, love, and families. The people like me, well we get to live with nothing. We zombie our way through life, working long hours for terrible pay in the hopes that we will be better one day. That was not the way I was going to live my life. I would not be like the rest of this world slaved to work a full time job just to live a life that I hated being in.

I thought of Coach, he would miss me. Through all of the training and fights we had some good times. I thought of Trey. What would he do? My career was the only thing keeping that boy out of trouble. My guess would be that he would follow Sergio's path to hang with John. That was bad news. John visited me a few days back offering his help to make my money problems go away. Hell, I was a fool to turn him down. If I was going to go through with this, right now, then why not give a few runs with John a try. What could it hurt?

Swaying my thoughts back to my mission. I play with the gun sitting in my hand. I am trembling. My hands shake as though someone is waving them. Slowly, I move my finger to the trigger as I tremble the barrel and place it on my head. The shaking begins to immense as if I'm on a rollercoaster. I start to get dizzy, and all the thoughts of my life begin to fill my mind. My mother, my father, Coach, Trey, Vanessa, all of my fights replay in my head. There was no point to live in this life.

Just as I'm about to do it, or at least think I'm going to, the damn doorbell rings. I let out a huge scream as I throw the gun up against the wall in anger.

Running downstairs as fast I as I can I don't even look out to see who it is first as I open the door in haste. And to my greatest surprise, I look to see no one. Taking a few cautious steps outside onto the porch I look down the street to see some kids running from door to door, ringing the doorbells and running in laughter.

Chapter Seventeen

Three months later, everything is starting to look better. My bills are almost caught up. I can finally afford cable. Watching television isn't something I do a lot but it is good to keep up with the news.

Since I am putting in 70 hours a week at the factory without any distractions I can afford some of the nicer things in life. I grabbed a cheap iPhone off one of the dealers on the streets. My 40-inch flat screen television only cost me $50 from a crack addict that strolled by the house every so often. In no way do I support stealing, but this is the ghetto. People need to do certain things to get by. Passing up a $50 flat screen wasn't something I was going to do, regardless of my beliefs.

John came by the house a few more times after he heard I had quit boxing. His offer was the same one he gave every other poor ghetto kid in the hood: Work for him selling drugs and soon I'd be making so much money that boxing would be a thing of the past. As much as I wanted to listen to him, and as much as it took for me to gather the strength to say no, I couldn't bring myself to do it. A huge part of me regretted not going with him. He was rolling in expensive cars, living life as though he had no boundaries. It was hard seeing someone who didn't deserve to live that life, get to live it.

I am getting by, though. My new television and smart phone are helping me kill the little free time I have. I am addicted to educational shows. Animal shows always grab my attention too. There are a few reality shows that, no matter how hard I try, I cannot turn off. I'm addicted to Googling everything I can think of on my iPhone. My nights are often filled with looking things up on the Internet, watching the Learning Channel, and catching the late news. It's a boring life. Maybe even a sad one. But it was working.

As I stop to take a breath, I look out across the calm falls. Bright colors light up the water that passes over into the river making the night look amazing. Niagara Falls. The one place where my mind can be free. The one place I feel tranquil. Running is one thing I never stopped doing. Even though I'm not going to the gym anymore, nor am I training in any sort of boxing activity, I am always running. On average, I run a five-minute mile. Staying in great shape helps satisfy my itch to get back in the ring.

I notice someone in front of me looking at the water as well. The darkness has impaired my vision so I can't make out the person. I take a few steps in the person's direction and my heart skips a beat as I realize who is standing before me.

"Well, at least you're staying in good shape," Coach Kay says, grinning. I walk up to him cautiously, somehow afraid to get too close.

"Yes, well, I don't have time for anything else. Running only takes a half-hour of my time. On a good night I can do six miles."

"Six miles in a half hour? Looks to me like you're still in fighting shape."

"Just because I stopped boxing doesn't mean I stopped training," I reply, wiping the sweat off my face.

"Most people wouldn't be able to keep the commitment to it."

"Well, I'm not most people. What are you doing out here, anyways?" He hesitates. I know something is wrong. "Coach?"

"Sergio passed away today."

I feel my heart stop. "What? Oh my God!" I cry out in shock. Sergio? No way! "What happened?"

"Drive-by. So the cops say. He was involved with some bad people, Aiden. You know that. That's why he stopped coming to the gym."

I can hardly believe it. Coach doesn't seem upset, but he never does. My guess is he never even cried at his own mother's funeral. Sergio had been a good friend of mine for years. Me, Sergio, and Trey. That was the three everyone in the gym knew about. For the past couple years though our relationship had diminished. He spent his nights in the streets and I spent them in the gym.

"I just can't believe it?" I say quietly. "I don't even know what to say." I think about crying but not the slightest bit of emotions come to surface. I will miss him though. Regardless of the troubles he had in his life he was a good friend.

Sergio had had it coming, that's for sure. Just because I'm not chilling with John and the others doesn't mean I'm oblivious to what's been going on. The word on the street was that Sergio had been making enemies, fast. Chances are no one will ever find out who did it. The cops don't give a shit. A drug-dealing ghetto punk killed in a drive-by isn't even worth their paperwork. Who can blame them? They don't want to deal with all the crap, they don't want to even be there, and the ghetto doesn't want them there.

"Some of the guys said they see you running here every night," Coach says. "I figured since you don't come to the gym anymore, even for a visit, then I have to come see you."

His comment makes me feel bad. Even though I quit boxing,

I should still go hang out with Coach. He is, in fact, the only person alive that I can truly call family.

"I'm sorry." I know my apology isn't enough but at least he knows I care. Poor Sergio. I think of some of the times we had together. Some of the laughs. It's sad to think that I will never see him again. Almost surreal. "I've just been so busy with work. Last week I worked 7 a.m. to 7 p.m. for six days straight."

"I do not condemn the working man, son. Especially one that continues to send me money when I specifically told him not to."

His comment makes me uneasy. "The gym needs the money. Yes, I know, you don't care about living in the gym and losing everything you own. I get it. You probably like living in the gym. But I don't like the fact that you are still having a hard time keeping it open. I know it's not much but you've been cashing the checks so I know it's helping."

"I know that trying to get you to stop supporting the Star Boxing Gym is a losing battle, Aiden. You're about as stubborn with that as you are a fighter."

"I learned from the best." I smirk

We begin to walk down the path along around the falls as it gets farther away from us. One thing that never gets farther is the sound of the water crashing down. It's believed on a very quiet night the falls can be heard pouring over the edge of the cliff through the entire city.

Being with Coach brings me back to the times I did this with my father. I can see myself running as a boy and still hear him telling me not to get too close to the railing in the fear that I'll fall over. I miss being around Coach. Even though it's only been a few months since I was last at the gym, it feels like years ago. I grab my phone to check the time. Coach's eyes widen.

"Nice phone."

"You like it? Check this out." I start to open apps, showing him the cool things they can do. "This one is the news. I love to check the USA today and CNN apps. Yesterday, a father walked into his house and killed his entire family then sat on the couch, cooked dinner, and ate it. Police said he was in the house for five hours before he called the police and admitted to killing them. Crazy, isn't it?"

"It's a crazy world out there. That's why I stay away from TV, news, and all that nonsense. It poisons the mind."

"I mean, how could a father just come home one day and kill his entire family, with no motive, no reason? Just walk into his house and do that? Then sit there, like nothing happened? They are trying to say he's insane. That's an understatement. Two white guys killed a black guy last week claiming self-defense, yet the black guy had no weapon. You know what is going to happen to the white guys? Nothing! The media is backing them up, saying that they aren't going to convict the killers. How is that even possible? All these crazy stories, I could go on for hours. How could people do stuff like this?"

"Drugs, alcohol, depression – pick one. People are unhappy with their lives. They look to escape it by doing dumb things. Some people just go crazy and kill. Others cheat on their lovers, husbands, wives in the search for something better. Some drink a lot, do drugs…anything to make them feel more important than they really are."

"I just don't understand it," I say, looking at the water. "Most of these people in the news have money and families. Hell, I didn't grow up easy. My parents weren't there, I was poor, I didn't have anything. There were nights I didn't eat dinner because there was no food in the house. I had to go to school in the same clothes every single day for weeks and get made fun of by the other kids. My socks had holes in them, sometimes even my sneakers did. If anyone has a reason to kill themselves, do drugs, or kill other people, it's me." I had come close to taking my own life, but didn't. It was a dark experience that I will never forget.

"But you became obsessed with something else…boxing," Coach says. "You channeled your anger and hatred into that ring. That's how you were able to avoid all that. That's why you were so damn good. You had nothing to lose. No fear. No fear of getting hit, no fear of losing. Then, your obsession became making money, which is why you can go to that factory for 70 hours a week without even thinking twice about it."

"It's not about either one, Coach," I say softly. What was it? What drove me to live? I don't think it's a question that I could ever answer, nor anyone can for that matter.

He pauses for a long moment. "I saw your mother today."

His words shock me stopping me in my tracks. My mother – I haven't seen her in years. Stories have spread about her, very bad stories that I try to avoid for the most part. I can't believe he's bringing her up to me.

"Guess she hasn't died yet," I reply in an icy tone taking another view of the falls as we pass the second set of falls.

"No," he says. "No, she hasn't." He walks over to me, sharing my view of the falls. There's a long moment of silence. "She's an addict, son. It's a disease, a sickness that only love and caring can control."

"No," I argue, shaking my head and gritting my teeth. "It's a choice. She chooses to do drugs. She gave up on the people that tried to be by her side during the hardest time imaginable. She chose to leave. I had to sit at my grandmother's funeral alone. She didn't even have the decency to show up to her own mother's funeral!"

"This from a man who hasn't gone once to the grave of his own father," Coach states quietly.

His words stun me worse than any punch. I feel anger coming on, but not towards Coach. I want to be mad at him for calling me out. Who is he to judge anything I do? But he's right. I haven't gone to see my father's grave since the funeral. My hatred for him is beyond repair.

Coach is not making eye contact. Instead, he focuses on the water.

"He lied to me, Coach. And he never had the chance to make it up. One night I was lying in bed. I had school the next day so I had to get up early, but I couldn't sleep. He came in the room, asking me what I was doing up so late. I told him I couldn't sleep. So he sat down on the bed like he usually did, smiled, and said that he was going to be ok. Told me not to worry about him and he'll be home in eight months."

I take a deep breath before continuing. "I asked him how he could go fight a war that he didn't believe in. How could he go and kill people that did nothing to him? And he said that it was his duty. He had to protect the country."

The lake water shimmers as I stare at it. "He had to go into a country and fight a war that no one in this country believed in, not even him. And you know what happened? He didn't come back, Coach. He died. Later, I found out that he had volunteered to go. He didn't have to go. He wanted to. And I can't get that out of my head. He chose to leave. I hate him for it."

Pausing momentarily, I catch myself.

"My mother couldn't handle it. She tried everything. Took her one year to blow his life insurance and retirement money on drugs. Money that was supposed to take care of us. Then, she left. Told me I'd be staying with grandma for a while and that I'd be 'better off' with her. Never came back. She was right. With all the drugs and strange men that were coming in and out of her house, I couldn't handle it. I was close to being one of those kids on the news that killed their mother. I hated her. I still do."

As I finish, I realize this is the first time I have ever talked about it. Twenty-one years and I have never mentioned a word to anyone. I don't even know why I am saying anything now.

"He didn't abandon you, Aiden. The oath to serve your country is a powerful one that is not to be taken lightly."

"My father died serving a country that did not care for him. He was a number. One of two thousand lives lost for nothing. There was no honorary funeral. It wasn't on the news. He died for a country that didn't even know he existed. You know what I think? I think that if the country you live in wants to go to war with another country then its leader should be the first one on the battlefield. Then we will see how important the war really is."

Coach put his hand on my shoulder. His strong touch was comforting. "Spoken like a true warrior." He begins to walk away.

"I'll be back, Coach," I cry out to his back. "I want to be the champion of the world. Don't give up on me."

He stops, without looking back at me.

"Boxing is a sport like no other because it challenges the fighter in every way a man can be challenged. Training to be physically tough is easy. Training to be mentally tough…now that is where most fail. If you remember only one thing, remember this. The road to the championship isn't just based on winning the fight inside of the ring, but by winning it outside of it as well. When you understand that, you will understand what it means to be a champion."

Chapter Eighteen

I hear the timer as I rush into the kitchen to open the stove. Smoke comes out of the oven, filling up the kitchen. The smoke alarms start to go off. I had totally forgotten about the chicken. Waving the smoke away, I grab a mitt and pull it out as fast as I can. Burned. Damn! I place it on the stove and rush back into the living room.

I was so into the fight I hadn't even noticed the alarm going off. The PPV bout featuring Dominick Cayman is the best fight I've seen in a long time. It's the first time in years I have seen someone get close to beating him; it isn't close, however. Boxing is an odd sport that way. According to the judges, Joel Estrada won three rounds of the twelve-round fight. I had him winning five rounds. Estrada could have won eight rounds and he still would have lost the fight on the judge's scorecards. There was no way that promoter Grey Bones was going to allow Cayman to lose to someone like Estrada. Call it corruption, bad judging, or whatever. Cayman needed to be knocked out to lose a fight. Cayman, the poster boy of boxing, now holds a record of 48-0. No one in the boxing world is going to let him lose to a washed up ex-champion.

Estrada is upset. In the post interview he says he believes he did enough to win the fight. The crowd boos Cayman, as they usually do. I didn't believe Estrada won the fight, by any means, but he sure as hell made Cayman think twice about fighting him again. It's the first time in years Cayman has been pushed to the brink. His speed and power didn't affect the continuing pressure that Estrada imposed throughout the fight. I had noticed that Cayman was dazed by an overhand right in the eleventh round. The announcers hadn't mentioned it, though; they wouldn't say anything against Cayman unless he was clearly losing. They were on the payroll of HBO, who would disown anyone who threatened their million-dollar man.

Dominick is worth too much to boxing to allow him to lose. He is the star. Making $30 million a fight is worth a lot to a lot of people. At the top of the hierarchy is Grey Bones, the shadiest promoter in the industry. Overall income is over $100 million every time Cayman steps into the ring. People think that him winning is the key to him making all this money.

After the fight, Dominick gets on the microphone in his usual cocky fashion. He keeps saying he is the best, that the fight wasn't even close, and that no one will ever beat him. I can't stand to hear him speak. He is a great boxer and has earned his take; I have no problem with that. But this is a man I have followed his entire career. I saw his very first fight. I remember when he wasn't cocky, when he believed in morals and things that he wouldn't even speak of right now. Fame has changed him. The money has changed him. Those aren't things I envy in any man. He needs to be brought back to reality.

My doorbell rings. Who is coming to my house at midnight? I can't even remember the last time I had a visitor at all. I walk over to the door. I have no peephole so I try to look out the window, but the darkness shields my view. I see a person standing there. For a second I'm hesitant to open the door. It could be someone trying to rob me, although I have nothing to take. I will take my odds against one man any day. It's been a while since I hit someone so I feel sorry for the man if he's coming to my door looking for trouble.

The face I see in front of me when I open the door stuns me. It's the last person I would ever expect to see.

"Hello, Aiden," he says. I don't know what to say. He has a suit on and a backpack hanging from his hand.

"Uh...hello, Mr. Brass," I say. Vanessa's dad is at my door – all I can think is that something has happened to her. "Is everything ok?"

"Yes, yes, I'm sorry to startle you. Can I come in?"

"Sure." I'm sure he can hear the discomfort in my voice. "Do you want a drink or something?" I walk around the couch, grab the remote, and turn down the television. "Actually, I think I only have water."

"No, that's ok." He sniffs the air. "Have a cooking issue?" He smiles, looking towards the kitchen.

"Oh, yeah," I say, shaking my head. "I, um, was cooking some chicken and it stayed in the oven a little too long. I don't think I have a career in the kitchen."

"Well, at least you can cook," he says, laughing. "I wouldn't know the first thing to do in the kitchen."

He sits down in the chair and places the bag next to him.

"Trust me, I can't," I admit. "As you can see, it's not turning out well. Chicken is easy to cook, anyways. Rice, salad, that's about all I eat."

"You'll live to be a hundred if you keep eating like that." He takes a look at what's on television. I sit down on the couch across from him. He seems interested in the post conference of the fight. I forgot that he is a huge boxing fan. "He won again, huh?" he asks. "I had my wife order it and record it. Guess I just spoiled it for myself."

"Sorry, I can turn it off."

"No, that's ok, I didn't expect him to lose anyway."

"It was closer than his other fights, if that makes it any more interesting. He's beatable."

"Everyone is beatable. One way or another." He looks around. "This is a nice house."

No it's not, I think, not compared to your house. The living room in his mansion is bigger than my entire house and backyard.

"My grandmother left it for me," I say. "But I know you're not here to talk about my cooking and my house, Mr. Brass."

"You're right. I'm not."

"Is everything ok with Vanessa? Are you mad at me for what happened that night?"

I wasn't sure she had even told him. It was so long ago, why would he be here right now if that's what he was coming over for, and why at midnight?

"You mean for knocking out her egotistical, bone-headed ex-boyfriend? There is no one in the world that was happier to hear that than me." His grin makes me a bit more relaxed. "And Vanessa's fine. She's upset that you two aren't together anymore, but other than that she's ok. She did, however, bring up certain things to me, which is why I am here."

"What things?" I ask. Did I do something wrong? I knew I had treated her with the utmost respect. There is no way he's here because I did something to hurt her. He leans back in his chair.

"I looked into some things going on around here. Financial things. The gym doesn't seem to be doing well. In fact, I don't even know how it's still open. The IRS is ready to shut him down but somehow Coach Kay keeps them at bay."

I shake my head. Vanessa told him about the gym's problem.

"Obviously, you aren't surprised by any of this," he continues. "The deeper I started to dig, the more I realized the hardships going on with your Coach. Lost his house, his car, and everything he has. He's living at that gym. As soon as the IRS takes that building from him, he's going to be homeless."

"I send him money every month but it's not a lot and not enough," I explain. "It's all I can do. I'm not worried about Coach. He can live here. I asked him to live here but he likes living at the gym. I won't allow him to live on the streets, though, that's for sure. I'll drag him here by his feet if I have to."

Coach won't accept my offer to live here with me. There is an extra bedroom that is empty. I'm holding it for him because I know the day is going to come.

"Working 80 hours a week isn't a life for you, Aiden. Not for someone as talented as you are. Giving up the thing you love most in this world to work in a factory and give money to a gym that you don't even go to anymore…why would you do something like that?"

Oddly enough, no one has ever asked me that before. I look at the television for a moment.

"I don't know," I finally answer with a shrug. "Because if they stay open, one day I can go back. I am going back, actually."

"You are?" He smiles. I make my decision right there. The Cayman fight boils me. He can be beat. I can beat him. I just need the chance. I have to go back.

"Yes. No more messing around. It's time to get back in the ring."

I see Dominick's face on the TV and it reassures me that it's time to get back into the gym. I can beat this man. I know I can.

"Did you know when I was 18 years old I was a dishwasher in a restaurant?" he continues. I didn't know, nor would I have guessed. "I dropped out of school at 16 so I could work. I used to walk three miles to work every day just to earn minimum wage. Forty, fifty, sixty hours a week, it didn't matter. Do you know what I did with my checks when I got them?" He shakes his head. "I gave them to my parents because they needed the money to be able to afford to live. We were poor, so poor that if I wasn't working or had tried to move out on my own, they would have been living on the streets."

He now had my full attention.

"One day I was walking to the dumpster to drop off some garbage. A car pulls up. A nice one, you know. Lexus, brand new. You could see it shining as though it had just been driven off the lot of the dealership. I was smoking a cigarette. The man in the car rolled down the window and said 'A boy your age shouldn't be smoking.' I laughed at him. My response was bold: 'A man your age shouldn't have to drive a Lexus to make yourself feel like everyone else in the world actually cares about who you are.' I'll never forget the look on his face. He was shocked. What was more shocking was two days later my boss pulled me into his office and the man was sitting there with him. He was a devoted customer of the restaurant. I thought I was going to get fired. Instead, the man said he was going to double my pay and all I had to do was come work for him. So I did. Twenty years later, I bought his company."

"And here you are today."

"And here I am today." Mr. Brass smiles. "Later on in my life he would tell me that the reason he wanted me to work for him was not because of my honesty, or because he wanted to work me like a slave for making a rude remark to him. It was because at that moment in his life an 18–year-old boy had taken one look at him and known more about him than he did himself. And any boy who could do that, could one day be something brilliant. There isn't a day in my life that goes by that I wonder where I would be had I not run in to him that day. It was a moment in my life I never saw coming, but it changed it forever. You can say it was God, or fate, or simple coincidence. Who knows. What I do know is that my heart was good. I worked my ass off to help the people I loved and because of that something great happened to me."

I figured there must be a moral to his story. "That's an amazing story. So you think something good will happen to Coach Kay or me if we keep doing this?"

"I don't think, I know." He stands up and pulls a folder from his suit jacket, placing it on the table. "I stopped by the gym earlier and gave these papers to Coach Kay. These state that I am the new owner of the Star Boxing Gym. I paid all the back taxes and bought the building and placed Coach Kay in charge of everything that happens there."

My mouth drops open in shock. I don't know how to react. I take the papers and begin to look through them, stunned. There's nothing in them that I really understand, but it doesn't matter.

"I…wow."

"There's more." He sits back down and grabs the backpack. "If you are going to box again, I want you to come work for me."

I'm even more confused now. "I don't know," I say. "I need the factory money, and need to find a way to work in my hours at the gym again. Plus, I don't really know anything about business. I'm not even sure I know what you do."

"You won't be doing that. I'll pay you double what you make now and it's less than 80 hours a week."

My eyes widen. Now that sounded good!

"What do I have to do?" I ask.

He opens the backpack and slides it over to me. I look inside. At first, I don't understand.

"What you do best, Aiden – fight."

Inside the bag is a pair of brand new Grant boxing gloves, the most expensive kind there is. I pull them out, smiling. It feels good just to look at them. I've never had a brand new pair of gloves before. Digging more into the bag I see a new pair of boxing shoes, wraps, and all kinds of other gear in it.

"Every week you'll receive a check for double what you were making," he continues. "You can keep the money from your fights and help Coach Kay run the gym."

"I don't even know what to say, Mr. Brass." My hands are trembling. None of this feels real; it's like a dream come true. I have never felt this before: joy, happiness, true happiness.

"You don't have to say anything," he insists, standing up. "Help comes in all forms, Aiden. Sometimes you just need to get lucky."

"I'm going to pay you back. I swear I will. I'll give you back every dollar that you give us."

"You don't have to pay me back anything."

"Well, I may not have to, but I'm going to."

Mr. Brass laughs as he heads towards the door. "I think you should call my daughter. She would be happy to hear from you."

"You still want your daughter to date me after seeing my rundown house in the middle of the ghetto?" I ask. "She's better off with someone that can take care of her." Mr. Brass turns slightly more concerned as he gently sighs.

"Wealthy people may live a life where money isn't an issue. Their kids grow up thinking the same way. They don't know what it's like to have nothing; they don't know the sacrifices in life that most people have to make. Every time there's a problem, money bails them out. You gave up the thing you loved most in this world to work for survival. I would rather have my daughter end up with a man that knows how to survive than a man who only knows how to buy her things. Because when the day comes that the rich man loses everything, he will not know how to live. He will crumble."

"Thank you. You don't know how much this means to me. And I'm still going to pay you back."

I open the door for him. He looks back at the television.

"You can pay me back by letting me be in the corner the day you knock him out," he answers.

I turn to see a smiling Dominick Cayman in the post press conference. Tomorrow I will be going straight to the gym. It's time to be what I was born to be. Cayman better be ready, because I am coming for him.

Chapter Nineteen

I stand outside the gym with my bag over my shoulder, staring at the sign. This is it. I'm finally going to start my boxing career with no financial problems holding me back. I don't have to worry about anything but fighting. The break Mr. Brass has given me is more than I could have dreamed of. With a deep breath of relief, I walk up to the doors of the Star Boxing Gym.

I remember the night Coach Kay made me pull over to the side of the road on the way home from a fight. That's when he explained to me why he named the gym the Star Boxing Gym. I hadn't wanted to be the fighter whose star had become dark, never to be seen again. For the last few months, I had been that. Starting now, my star was ready to shine again.

To my surprise, when I open the door I hear music, but not the loud music we usually play in the gym to keep fighters motivated. I see a young, beautiful brownish colored girl singing inside the ring. Everyone is gathered around, watching her sing Whitney Houston's, 'I Wanna Dance with Somebody.' Her voice is absolutely amazing. People are dancing with her and sitting around the ring, clapping with the beat and cheering her on.

Coach Kay is sitting on a chair outside the ring, his face lit up with joy. I have no idea what is going on, but her performance is the most entertaining thing I have seen in a long time.

"I leave this place for a few months and look what happens," I say, sitting on the empty chair next to Coach. He looks over at me for a moment then turns his attention back towards the ring.

"She needed a place to practice," he says simply. "She's trying out for American Idol next month."

"Really? Well, that's good. What's her name?"

"Lakesha Banks."

"I don't know anything about singing but her voice is amazing. She's hot, too."

"Boys will be boys," Coach says, shaking his head.

"Well, she is. Good looks and amazing skill can take you far in this country."

"Did you learn that by watching television and playing on your phone?"

"No."

The performance ends and everyone applauds. Coach Kay stands up with a smile and begins to walk towards his office. I follow. His office is cleaner than usual. He sits down behind his desk and I pace, staring at the posters of all the great fighters of the past.

"I'm ready to come back," I announce.

He looks at me with determination in his eyes, leans back in his chair, and folds his hands.

"I've been running every day," I continue. "Shadowboxing, too. I need to build a little boxing stamina back as far as hitting the heavy bag and things, but it won't take long to be back to where I was."

"I'm not worried about that, Aiden."

"Ok, good. So get me a fight and let's get started."

Coach sighs at my words. He doesn't seem as excited as I am.

"Is something wrong?" I ask.

"I don't trust Mr. Henry Brass."

"Well, you should."

"Why should I? Do you know anything about him to make me think otherwise? Other than the fact that you dated his daughter."

"No," I admit.

"What's to stop him from waking up one day and looking at this place and shutting it down?"

"He won't do that. He loves boxing more than anything. There is nothing more he wants than to see this place succeed, to see me fighting in the championship fight against Dominick Cayman." I don't know what Coach is thinking but I don't like it.

"People of Mr. Brass's stature are only influenced by numbers. If he sees that this place is failing to, at the very least, pay for itself, he will shut it down."

Coach doesn't trust anyone. I know that. There will be no convincing him that Mr. Brass is a man he can trust. I'm not sure if he told Coach about the monthly allowance I am getting for fighting.

"Coach, it's all we got. If we can't put our trust in this man, then we'll lose everything. The IRS is on the verge of taking the building from us. Then you'll really be homeless and we will never be able to get the chance to fight for the championship. This is the only option that we have."

"I don't trust him," he says again. "We can find another way. He's still waiting on my signature."

"I'll buy the building back from him when we start making some serious money. You don't have to trust him. I am going to make it to the top of the boxing world. I swear I am. I'm going to be the champ. Just trust me."

He doesn't seem convinced as he gazes around the room. "Right before he died, Tracey Jury was going to leave me."

Coach's words shock me. I stop pacing, suddenly frozen in place.

"What?"

"Tracey was the most gifted fighter I had ever seen. I took him under my wing when he was five years old. He was dedicated, determined, and talented. There wasn't a day or minute that went by that he didn't think of boxing. Just like you. Our relationship wasn't the best, but it worked. Then one day he came to me and said he had received an offer from Bones Promotions. I was so happy. Finally, all the hard work had paid off. We would get our chance to rise to the top, just like we had always dreamed."

"What I didn't know was that his offer didn't include me. Bones Promotions wasn't going to allow him to train under me anymore. Part of the deal was that he had to move to Las Vegas and train under one of their trainers." Coach chuckled. "I wasn't even allowed to come if I wanted to. The money was too much for Tracey to turn down. I didn't blame him. Any man would be insane to turn that type of money down. I didn't want any money for what I had done for him, I just wanted to be next to him when he raised his hand as the champ of the world. I held no anger or hate towards him for it. But I was shocked. I didn't think it would be so easy for him to do."

"I'm sure it wasn't easy," I say.

"I would never find out. We got into a huge fight right before he was supposed to fly to Vegas. He walked right out that door. I thought that he would be able to come back to see me before he left, so that we could leave on good terms and all that. That night, he died." For a moment there was a silence. "The point is, Aiden, just because Mr. Brass is going to take care of us financially doesn't mean that there won't be other problems. The world of boxing is the shadiest, most corrupt, disloyal world a man can enter. Every second, someone is trying to take something from you, to better their profits or themselves. Promoters are constantly fighting with each other, judges are always ripping people off, and money and fame are the root of all the industry's flaws. The more successful you become, the more involved you are in all the b.s. that comes with it."

"This is why you didn't care when I quit, isn't it?" I ask. "It wasn't because you wanted me to make my own decision, but because you were scared of what would happen if I ever did make it to the top."

"Part of it was, yes. I know what these promoters can do to fighters. They will use you to make the most money out of you, until someone else comes along. Then they will take it all from you."

"I won't let them. And I will not leave you. Ever. I promise you that you will always be my coach, no matter what they say or do. I don't care what they try to do outside of that ring. Inside of it, there is only one goal – victory. They can do everything they can to try and sway things, but when the time comes to fight, there is only me and one other person in that ring. All I have to do is keep winning, and nothing can stop us."

"Very well, son," he nods, standing up from his chair.

"So you going to get me a fight soon?" I say, looking out his window into the boxing gym. I hear a folder slam onto his desk.

"Already done. Six weeks from today. All you have to do is sign."

I can't help but smile. The son of a bitch had everything planned already.

Chapter Twenty

My boxing career is back. I'm stronger than I have ever felt and I'm in the best shape of my life. My last four fights in as many months haven't gone past two rounds. Coach is worried that I'm not getting enough work. By ending fights with early knockouts, he isn't sure how I will react in fights that go eight to ten rounds. My record is now 18-0 with 16 knockouts. My last fight against Eddie Herrera was the fight before a televised HBO card. I don't know how Coach managed to get me on that. The impressive first-round knockout caught the attention of a few promoters, who are now offering me fights all across the country. Coach is carefully choosing my next fight from a list of great shows.

I finish hitting the bag, breathing heavily. My workout for the day is over. Trey tosses me a towel and I wipe off my face. Carefully, he begins to unlace my gloves. Mr. Brass has been good on his word. Every week I receive a check that is more than enough to pay my bills, save money, and have enough left over to enjoy some of the finer things in life, which I'm not used to.

"Let's go eat," I say to Trey.

"I'm one-hundred percent down for that," Wes agrees, walking over. Wes and Tom have both returned to the gym since my comeback. The local papers are rolling with interviews and articles about my recent fights. People in the city are beginning to recognize me everywhere I go, more so than before.

"What's your weight?" Trey asks. My weight. The one thing I hate about boxing. Lately though it hasn't been a problem.

"I'll check. It's been pretty consistent. I barely ever reach 170, even when I eat like a pig." My weight hasn't been an issue since my return. Since I fight at 168, I like to keep my weight around there. I always eat healthy and I'm burning enough calories to eat everything off the menu at any restaurant and still not gain a pound.

"You should think about dropping a weight class," Trey advises. "Imagine your power if you could make 160."

"I don't want to have to worry about dropping water weight before fights. Right now, I walk around at 175, even when I'm not training. I feel comfortable at this weight and not having to lose 10 pounds the day before a fight gives me the advantage."

A lot of fighters tried to suck weight before fights. They

would lose five to 10 pounds of water weight to fight a division below their actual weight, so they could fight guys that were smaller than them. Some even lost 15 the day before the weigh in. To me doing that sounds crazy. That can't be good for the body and I'm sure it doesn't help towards the end of a brutal twelve round battle. Being bigger than their opponent gives them an advantage making some fighters feel like the risk is worth it.

"You could move up. Dominick Cayman is at 175," Tom jokes.

Dominick isn't the champion in my weight class, but he is the champ of the world. He's the celebrity that everyone thinks of when boxing is brought up. "The face of boxing" is what the media call him. Champs were barely defined by belts anymore, not like the good old days of boxing. These days there were more belts than there were fighters. The object was to become the people's champ. They were the ones that paid to see a fight.

"If I get that chance to fight Cayman," I reply, "I'll move up." There was no question about it. Not only would the money set me for the rest of my life but beating him would mean I'm the new champ. The real champ.

"Where we going?" Trey asks.

"I don't know," I answer. I'm trying to take off my gloves and shoes but I'm so tired that I just need a minute to relax as I plop down on the hard bench.

"Don't even start this again," Wes adds. "Last time, it took us an hour just to figure out where to go."

"Well, that was 'cause your stupid ass kept saying no to every place we offered!" Tom cries, smacking him on the arm.

"You offered four different pizza places after I told you I didn't want pizza!" Wes says, pushing him.

"Guys, please, let's just pick a place and go. I'm starving." There is no way I'm going to sit here and listen to these two fight again.

"I say Chinese," Trey offers. "We haven't gone there in a while."

"No, I always get hungry an hour after I eat that crap," Wes chimes in.

"See, here we go again," Tom complains.

"What about filet mignon at the Mountain Steakhouse?" Wes asks. "Man it's been a few weeks since I've been there. I can already taste it in my mouth."

"A what?" I say. Wes and Tom turn to me, confused.

"A filet mignon. A steak. You've never had one before?"

Tom looks dumbfounded as I shake my head. "You can't be serious!"

"I've never even heard of it," Trey admits as we both laugh.

"Wow, this is blasphemy," Tom says, shaking his head throwing his hands up in the air.

"Us ghetto kids don't know about that. We just call a steak a steak. A fliet mi... mig...I can't even pronounce it," Trey says.

"This isn't just any steak," Tom says. "I can't even listen to this anymore. We are going. I'm paying. It's a little expensive." He looks at the way we are all dressed eyeing us up with a little disgust in his tone. "We are going to have to shower and change too." He smiles.

After a long car ride far away from home, we pull up to a restaurant on the lake that is the size of a mansion. A valet takes Tom's car and we walk up to the entrance. All of the workers are dressed in suits and ties, including the waitresses. Trey and I look around; we have never been to a restaurant this nice before. In fact, it feels like an entirely different world. What I do love about the place is the water that it resides in. The sight of the lake is amazing. Since the place seems to be somewhere in Buffalo, I can't tell which way the Falls lies.

"You guys are going to love this place," Wes says as the waitress takes us to our table. The tables are covered in brown cloth and the number of glasses and silverware is more than I have in my entire house. The waitress pulls out all of our chairs and opens up the menus for us to look at as we casually sit down. Wow.

"Your server will be over in a minute," she says. "Can I get you something to drink besides water?"

"Um, excuse me," Trey asks. I don't even have to look up from the menu to know the next thing that's going to come out of his mouth. "But there are two forks and two spoons here. You can have these back." He grabs them and puts them in the waitress's hand.

The waitress looks confused.

"No, Trey, they are both for you to use," Wes says, holding back a laugh while grabbing the silverware back.

"Why? I don't need two forks."

"One is for your salad and the other is for your meal," Wes explains.

"Well, why do I need to use a separate one for both?" Trey asks.

Tom chuckles as the hostess continues to look confused. "I'm sorry, you can go," he tells her. "He'll be fine." After she leaves he looks at Trey. "Have you ever been to a nice restaurant before?"

"The nicest restaurant I've been to is Applebee's," Trey says loudly, "and when you get to the front door, you need to dodge two crackheads before entering the place." His statement attracts the attention of a few tables around us. I can't help but laugh.

"You better get used to places like this, Aiden," Tom says. "When you start making millions of dollars, you'll always be eating here."

"Fifty dollars?!" Trey exclaims, looking at his menu.

"Will you be quiet?" I tell him. "You're being loud."

"You see this?" he whispers, leaning over to me. "This salad is $13. What kind of damn salad costs $13? A piece of damn lettuce. I can get a whole head for 1.99."

"I told you it was expensive," Tom says, laughing.

"Thirteen dollars for a damn salad and 50 for that filet mignon? That's not expensive, that's rape. I could eat McDonald's dollar menu for a month for that type of money."

"He's got a point," I agree. "I've never seen prices like this before."

"Guys, don't worry," Tom says. "Order whatever you want. I got it. And stop complaining about everything."

"Ok, but you damn white people are crazy."

After we all order, we sit around the table and talk about sports and other meaningless subjects. One subject gets brought up, though, that puts the attention on me. It's something that's been in the back of my mind for a long time.

"So, you still haven't talked to Vanessa since that night?" Wes asks.

Vanessa. I haven't even thought about what I will say to her the next time we see each other. If I did ever see her again. My iPhone has her number stored in it, but I can't bring myself to make the call. I've tried a few times. Sometimes I sat at home on the couch just looking at the number. Then I remember the last time we saw each other. The argument, the pain. I didn't belong in her world. It's ironic to think sitting here actually.

"No," I admit finally bring myself to answer the question after what seems like an eternity.

"Why not?" Tom asks.

"I don't know. I just need to stay focused, you know? The less distractions I have in my life, the more I can focus on boxing." That wasn't a total lie but it wasn't the main reason.

"Yeah, but she's not a bad distraction, bro," Tom insists. "Having someone else in your life with a positive outlook is a good thing."

"Then there's Mr. Brass," I continue. "I mean, if something

bad happened with us and he got mad at me, it could hurt the gym and my financial situation as well. I can't afford to ruin everything that I have going for me because of that." That's another extreme I try to add. Who am I trying to convince them or myself?

"Now you're thinking like a businessman," Wes laughs. "That's ok. She's been on a few dates lately, from what I hear. She'll be fine."

"What kind of dates? Serious ones?" My response is swift. Faster than any punch I have ever thrown.

My reaction draws grins from both Wes and Tom. I know what they are trying to do, and it's working. It's been over eight months. And while it hasn't seemed like a long time to me, I know that it's a long time not to talk to someone. I can't expect her to wait around for me to be ready.

"Oh, you know, regular dates," Wes says casually.

"If you miss her, and you love her, you should make the attempt," Tom advises. Love her? I didn't even know what the word meant. "Don't wake up one morning and realize that you lost the one person in the world that you want to be with."

"Um, excuse me." Our conversation is interrupted by a man in a suit standing above us. His fine, black hair perfectly complements his tanned, clean-shaven face. He's looking at Tom but sneaking over glances to me. He almost seems nervous.

"Mr. Pender," Tom says, standing up to shake his hand. "Sorry, I didn't recognize you."

"No, it's fine." He looks over at me. "You are Aiden Walker, right? The boxer?"

"Yeah," Tom answers. "Oh yeah, I'm sorry. Guys, this is Vincent Pender, one of my dad's work associates. This is Trey, Wes and, as you already know, Aiden Walker."

Tom's dad is a millionaire, so it is safe to say anyone associated with him is important as well. I stand up and formally shake his hand.

"My son is a huge fan," he tells me. "Do you think I could get a picture and an autograph?"

"Absolutely, sir," I answer.

"Thank you so much. He's going to be thrilled that I met you."

It's strange that a man of his stature is so excited to meet someone like me. The best part was, he was actually nervous to ask as if I was going to say no. I can see the other tables starting to point and look as they recognize who I am. After I take the picture and sign an autograph, a few more people come over. Mr. Pender even tells the waitress to pay our tab.

"Get used to it, Aiden," Tom whispers. "The bigger you get, the more this will happen."

The waitress brings our dinners and the commotion subsides.

"Excuse me, Miss," I hear Trey say. "I think this is wrong."

She looks at her pad. "You said filet mignon, right?" she confirms.

"Yeah, but where's the rest of it?"

His words make everyone at the table laugh and Wes nearly spits out his food. I can't help but smile.

Chapter Twenty-One

Sticking the jab as hard as I can, I step back so Kyle's counter cross will miss. As he comes forward, I take two more steps back. I throw a quick double jab at him. He blocks the first one but the second gets through and lands cleanly on his cheek. A counter cross comes flying at me, followed by a left hook to the body, which lands. Immediately, I counter with a cross and a counter left hook to his head, landing both punches against his hard skull. I step forward into his body with my guard up and throw two more body shots that land flush into his stomach, followed by a left hook to the head that he partially blocks.

Kyle backs up, trying not to engage on the inside anymore. I don't let him go far. I quickly get back in his face and throw a few more shots to his head. He throws back, staying on the inside with his head leaning against mine. A right uppercut straight down the middle lands on his hard chin, hurting my hand for a second. I follow that with two hooks to the head, which both land.

He tries to back up by throwing a jab, but his jab has gotten weaker over the last few rounds. The lazy jab is easy to throw over and I land a cross against the side of his head, followed by another hook to the head, which he blocks.

I throw two or three punches at a time and they feel amazing. I think Kyle is beginning to understand why people hate sparring me so much. As a professional fighter with not much experience, he's holding his own. I have landed some pretty clean, hard shots and they haven't hurt him as much as I thought they would.

Kyle comes forward again, throwing a jab and a wild cross, which I easily avoid. Instead of trying to counter him, I back up a few steps and allow him to bring the action to me. He comes forward, throwing a jab to the body, and I easily counter it with a cross. Catching him off balance, I jump forward, throwing a four-punch combination to the head. Every single punch lands and he staggers a bit, falling into the ropes.

The action-packed round ends as the bell rings. Kyle looks exhausted after six rounds of intense sparring. My breathing is normal. I feel as though I could go another six rounds if Coach asked me to.

"Nice work," Coach tells me. "That was intense. You need to go to the body more. You are starting to head hunt too much."

"I went to the body for nearly three rounds straight," I argue as he takes off my headgear.

"Then do it for six rounds," he insists.

"Body shots don't count when the judges are looking at who is winning the rounds," I tell him. "They want to see fighters get hit in the head."

"I understand that, but body shots weaken the opponent's movement and endurance. When a fighter isn't moving, he is easier to hit. With your speed and power, once the ability to move gets tough, they don't stand a chance. Start with the body and come back to the head. Three-to four-punch combinations, always."

He has been saying that since I was a boy. I usually don't listen, however, lately he's been right. Since the knockouts are coming so quickly, I haven't really wanted to attack the body of my opponents.

"Yes, Coach," I agree as my gloves come off.

"You look good, kid. The entire gym stopped working out just to watch. I even think I heard Kenyon Martin speak after that." Trey steps up to the side of the ring and hands me a bottle of water. I look over at Kenyon, who stares at me for a second before turning back to his bag. The man not only doesn't speak, he usually doesn't look at anyone, either.

"Speed is there, power looks good," Trey announces. "Your defense still sucks, but whatever."

I throw my water bottle at him hard and he catches it right before it lands across his face. He shoots a mean glare. "Thanks," I say, trying to dismiss his sarcastic remark. I feel amazing – the best I have in a long time. Putting in six to eight hours a day is helping. Coach is making sure I take days off here and there, since he believes it's very important to rest the muscles.

"Offensive fighters can seldom be taught defensive stances," Coach Kay says in response to Trey's statement. "You have great head movement, which is your defense, but when you get into these battles you forget to use it."

"I feel like it's easier to block with the gloves than to move my head. Moving my head too much throws me off and makes it harder to see the openings."

"Then you need to move your head when a fighter comes at you without thinking of countering. That's what sparring is for, to understand how to do new things. Learn how to be comfortable with moving away from the punches first. After that starts to feel natural, you can worry about countering off of it. Moving your head creates openings as well. We need to learn how to counter off of that to make you a better fighter. We'll get there. You're never going to do everything perfect."

"Well, I need to be damn close."

There's no way I am going to beat the top-level guys with the defense I have now. My speed and power will always be the tools that lead me to victory. However, to beat guys like Dominick Cayman, I have to learn to avoid being hit when it isn't necessary. Plus there is the issue of long-term health. I have never thought about it before Coach started nagging me about it. Taking too many shots to the brain isn't good. You don't want to be sick when you're sixty. Blah Blah Blah. He says it so much I just ignore it now.

"Good job, brother," Kyle says, walking over with his nose bleeding. I can't tell if his face is red from the heat in the gym or the punches I continuously landed on him. He's a red-haired Irishman with freckles. In my experience, the Irish are tough-ass fighters. Kyle affirmed that.

"Thanks, man," I respond. "You, too."

"I'll tell you what, I've been to a lot of gyms in this country and sparred some of the best fighters in the game. I have never seen your type of speed, power, and combinations rolled into one. You can go a long way, bro. Stay focused."

"Thanks, I really appreciate it."

Kyle is in town for a few days for his cousin's wedding. When he heard about the boxing gym, he came here wanting to spar. His record as a pro is 6-1. That one loss will haunt him his entire career unless he finds a way to get past it, which most fighters don't. When promoters search for opponents for their "stars," they often look at guys like Kyle. They give him a good payday to fight their top guy, but it's a sucker's bet because it's usually a fight he can't win. Once the losses start piling up against the top guys, he will become known as a "journeyman," a label in boxing that no top fighter wants to inherit.

Some journeymen are tough. Some find a way to beat the top guys by upsetting them. That usually means they get another good payday against a top fighter. It isn't a bad thing, but it's a road that usually ends before getting to a championship. Very rarely did a journeyman find his way to a title.

There's one thing I've noticed in the sport of boxing: It isn't really about winning a title anymore. These days, there are more belts than there are fighters. It has become more about winning big fights and gaining the interest of the public, which paves the way for the next one. And the pay isn't as bad for a journeyman, especially an exciting one. Plus, they always get those shots to become a champ.

Avoiding the journeyman route is my main goal. One loss could send me there, which is why I cannot lose. I will not lose. At the same time, the fights I am offered are not good ones. I keep beating guys who either don't have the experience that I have or lack the skills to be in the ring with me.

"What's wrong?" Coach asks, noticing my preoccupation.

"Nothing, just a little headache," I reassure him. "You know how it goes."

Getting hit in the head regularly can lead to headaches here and there. The headgear sometimes presses on the head too hard, which causes light bruising in certain places. Nothing serious.

"Trey, go get the Tylenol in the medicine drawer in my desk," Coach Kay demands.

"But I just got my gloves on," Trey argues, throwing his hands in the air. Coach Kay gives him a disgusted look.

"I got it," I say, putting my hand on Coach's shoulder to keep him from ripping Trey a new one.

Running into his office I look through a few drawers in his office but can't find the medicine. Moving aside some papers, I see the bottle at the bottom of a drawer. I grab it and glance quickly at Coach's desk. A paper with the heading "Bones Promotions" catches my eye. I look over the paper and my jaw nearly drops.

"I was actually hoping I'd get to tell you myself," Coach says, appearing in the doorway. "Don't get too excited. We're not taking it."

"Wait. What?" I ask. Is he crazy? Like hell we are not taking it. Coach always worried about something and I already knew what he was thinking. There was no way I was going to let him talk me out of this one.

"Tony Rocks is Grey Bones number-two guy. He's the guy they are bringing up to be the successor to Dominick Cayman. He may be young still, and not as experienced, but it's a dangerous fight."

"This contract offers us $25,000 and a main event on ESPN Friday Night Fights. There is no way we can turn this down."

I can't believe Coach doesn't want to take this fight. I know my anger is showing in my eyes.

"Did you not hear what I just said, Aiden?" he says. "He's Bones' number-two guy. Which means there is no way the judges are going to give you a decision, even if you win the fight."

"If I win it convincingly, they'll have to – it will be on national television."

"No, they won't. How many fights have we watched on

national television where the other guy got ripped off and we all knew it? They aren't going to overturn it or change it, either."

I understand his point, but there is no way we aren't taking this fight. It's a risk. I know it is. A huge one. But at this point, it's one I have to take. I've seen Tony "The Terror" Rocks fight before. I was on the undercard on one of his fights, my last fight before I quit. I know I could beat him!

"Then I have to knock him out," I insist.

"We aren't taking this fight, Aiden. It's too dangerous right now."

"Coach, we have to. I'm sick of fighting these meaningless fights. Beating him will put me on the map. Think of the people who will be watching! Everyone who's watching this kid and following his career will begin to look at me. This could be the big break we've been waiting for my entire career."

"And what if you lose? What if you get ripped off? You are not a national champion or an Olympic boxer, Aiden. We don't have a promoter backing us up. Nobody knows who you are. If you lose one fight, just one, there may be no coming back from it. The boxing world will bury you like you don't exist and we'll never be able to get the great fights we want."

"This is the great fight we want! Coach, I will not lose this fight. I promise you, I will knock him out."

Coach sighs as he looks over the contract. He knows I'm right.

"Coach, please," I continue. "Our entire lives we have been waiting for this opportunity and here it is sitting right on your desk. We have to take this fight. I can beat him I know I can. I'll die in that damn ring if I have to."

"That's what I'm afraid of, Aiden."

Coach just stands there, staring at the contract, which pushes my anxiety to the brink. "It's five weeks away," he says, still trying to change my mind.

"That's fine. I'd fight him this weekend if I had to." That was the truth. I'd fight him in twenty minutes if they asked.

There is no convincing me otherwise. This is the chance I have been waiting for, the chance Mr. Brass has given me, the chance Coach is waiting for as well. I am not going to mess this up.

"Very well, son, very well," Coach says reluctantly.

I smile as I walk out of the office. It suddenly hits me that Coach isn't worried about what will happen if I lose. He's worried about what will happen if I win.

Chapter Twenty-Two

I sit in the locker room, awaiting my entrance. Coach is just as nervous as I am, although he tries to make everyone believe he's calm by pacing around and finding things to do. He always tries to act so composed. But I know Coach better than he thinks. Better than he knows himself even. Those butterflies are stirring in his stomach just as much as they are mine.

I'm sweating after completing a 20-minute pad workout to warm up. My power feels amazing tonight. This is the most conditioned I've ever been for a fight. This is the most important fight of my career. I cannot lose. I will not lose. Losing doesn't even exist. Losing means everything is over. That's what I have to believe. Everything that I worked so hard for my entire life relies on this fight. Coach is right. I won't get the decision even if I do win the fight. Not in Tony "The Terror" Rocks hometown.

"This is almost as nerve-wrecking as the flight here," Trey says, sitting on the bench across from me. I want to smirk but my anger keeps it at bay. Smiling is weakness. Never show weakness before a fight. I think of my father and mother. They still give me my anger.

Trey is scared of flying. He kept asking the stewardess how long the flight was, if the plane was safe, and if she was sure the plane was checked thoroughly before we took off. He refused to look out the window until we landed. He annoyed the hell out of Coach the entire plane ride to New York so bad that Coach moved his seat to an empty one farther away from us.

It was amazing to see New York City from the air and even more so from the ground, as this was my first visit to one of the greatest cities in the world. The skyscrapers, the people, and the atmosphere were all so different. Everything was fast paced and there were people everywhere. Coach has been here plenty of times. He didn't seem amused by all the activity in the streets. He was more concerned with winning and getting out of there.

We wouldn't be leaving as soon as we expected though. The promoter allowed us an extra day to stay after the fight before flying us back home. He knew it was my first trip to the city and said that we should enjoy an extra day. It is unusual; most promoters want you to fly in, fight, and leave immediately afterwards. Apparently, Bones

Promotions allowed a few extra perks.

I haven't allowed the city to distract me from what I came here to do, though. I spent most of the day in the hotel room watching movies, playing on my phone, shadowboxing, and napping while waiting for the car to pick us up and bring us to the fight.

All of the attention is on Tony Rocks. ESPN did a special on him before the fight. I was ignored, for the most part. ESPN did a five-minute segment on me, but spent at least twenty minutes on Tony. He was the featured fighter that everyone was coming to see.

For me, it was my first interviews with some real boxing analysts. Guys that have studied boxing their entire careers and knew the sport better than I did. Not the fighting part, not the pain, not the suffering, but they knew the politics. They knew the fighters. They knew the game of boxing. The interviews put me on the defensive. I wasn't used to being asked about my career and the reason I started boxing. Most disturbing were the personal questions about my past. Fighters with good back stories are more intriguing to the public, so questions about my father dying in the military and my mother being a crack addict made up the bulk of the interviews. They ate it up.

"You guys are walking down in three minutes," the commissioner says, briefly sticking his head in the locker room. I stand up and start to shadowbox weighing my thoughts on how to beat this guy.

"Showtime, baby," I say to Trey. I try to smirk but my face won't draw the look.

"Water?" he asks. I nod and he pours some in my mouth. "He looked scared of you at the weigh-ins."

"Really? His mouth never stopped so I didn't realize."

Tony is a cocky fighter who's been running his mouth about how he is going to knock me out, embarrass me, and end my boxing career. At the weigh-ins, all he did was talk about how much of a mismatch the fight was. He reminded me of Dominick Cayman. It is no surprise they have the same promoter, and apparently are friends.

Tony isn't bigger than me, most fighters weren't. Working at the factory had developed muscles in my body that I didn't even know existed. He had the build of a boxer though. His firm jaw structure can obviously handle some punches. He's bald so at least I don't have to worry about sweaty hair rubbing all over me. His skin was pitch black too, not brown like Trey. He is an inch taller than I am, with a two-inch reach advantage. I will have to move my head a lot to get in on him because he'll be using his superior speed and height to keep me away from him. He is faster than me…much faster.

"I know Coach don't like it when I say this, but please knock his ass out," Trey whispers in my ear. Coach's disapproving grunt lets us know he overheard the remark.

"Look at me," Coach says walking over. He starts to put Vasoline on my face, which acts as a counter measure so punches slip off the face. I hate it because it makes my face feel greasy, but it is a legal measure of protection in boxing – not required, but recommended.

"Don't let all the cameras and people make you lose your focus, understand?" Coach continues. "This is the first big fight you've had. People will cheer when you land a good shot and when you get hit with one. You need to avoid getting caught up in that. Just because you land a good shot and they cheer doesn't mean you go after him recklessly. And if you get hit with one, don't recklessly go after him and try to get one back. You must stay focused."

"Yes, Coach." We've gone over this again and again. He's been here before, though, so he has good reason to keep drilling it into my head.

"Ok, you're up," the commissioner announces. My heart beats faster as we follow the commissioner out of the locker room. I can hear loud noises coming from the arena a short distance away. Bouncing up and down, I try to keep my legs fresh. The sound of rapper 50 Cent fills the room as I step into the arena. My refusal to pick my own entrance music leaves Trey with the decision, a duty he absolutely loves.

The lights and cameras are in my face and people boo when I enter the arena. The atmosphere, the crowd, the cameras – all of it seems surreal. Coach is right, this could be a huge distraction. People yell all sorts of things to me, mostly negative since I'm fighting in Rock's hometown. With Coach leading the way, I finally enter the ring.

The atmosphere is amazing. My heart is racing faster. For the first time in my life, I am fighting on national television. I jump up and down and shadowbox, waiting for my opponent to arrive.

Tony Rocks makes his way to the ring. All of the focus is on him, but I ignore his extravagant entrance. The only thing missing is fireworks as the music blasts and the lights dim to showcase their top fighter. I shadowbox in my corner with Coach and Trey, trying to keep loose, ignoring all the hype. I'm wearing black and gold, as I do every fight. They are my favorites and so far have been my lucky colors. Never in my life had I thought superstitions would affect me but lately certain things had come to light and maintaining the color of my attire had become an important superstition of mine.

The cameras are rolling. Out of the corner of my eye I see the announcers table. Legendary announcer Kelvin Reynolds is calling the fight. If I impress him, I will have accomplished part of my goal for the evening. He doesn't know much about me, other than the YouTube videos I had uploaded to the Internet that he most likely studied. From what I had heard earlier, he is impressed by my style even though he doesn't think I can win this fight.

After our official announcements to the crowd the Referee calls us to the center of the ring. I stare at the ground to avoid looking my opponent in the eyes as I always do telling myself the same thing before every fight. By doing so, I refused to acknowledge who he is; he is just another fighter that I need to beat. We listen to the Referee's instructions and touch gloves. I go back to my corner and await the bell to signal the start of the first round. My heart is pounding. I have to win.

"Composure," Coach says, standing on the outside of the ring. "He's fast and throws quick combinations. Your jab will neutralize the speed but you need to time it right because he's faster than you. Once you get his timing down, counter his punches. Go to the body! He can't fight on the inside so keep the fight tight. I know his reach is longer but it shouldn't be a factor with the way he fights."

Coach jumps down and I nod my head. The bell sounds.

Advancing to the center of the ring, I immediately throw a couple of jabs. With my first punch, all my distractions and nervousness fade away. The crowd ceases to exist as usual. It's time to get down to business.

Tony backs up and most of my jabs miss their mark. I walk him down again, throw two more jabs and land one. He continues to back up without throwing a punch, taunting me as he moves side to side. As I continue to back him up, he quickly counters with a cross-hook to my head. I block both and counter with two hooks to the body, landing both of them. He repeats his move and I follow with another two hooks to the body. Grunting, he seems frustrated already. My hard, firm jab keeps him backing up. Quickly, I add a cross to my jab and it gets through, landing down the center of his face and snapping his head back. The crowd sounds. I ignore it.

Tony finally decides to open up. He stands his ground and throws a four-punch combination. I block most of them, except the last one, which lands across my chin. I realize what little power his punches have. By focusing on speed he doesn't step into punches the way most fighters do, therefore his power is lacking. Even the ones that land on my gloves don't exert any impressive force. He tries another combination, but because of his lack of power, I throw two body shots in between his combo and come back with a hook to the head that lands flush on his chin. Tony stops moving around. His face is angry. He decides to sit in the middle of the ring and exchange now.

I step in with him and he doesn't back up. I throw two more body shots and come back to the head. He blocks the headshots and throws a five-punch combination to my head. A couple of them get through due to his extreme speed, which is truly amazing. I have never seen such a fast fighter. Half of his punches I don't even see coming; I just keep my hands up, hoping they don't get through. As I throw quick combinations with him, we are drawing the fan friendly fight that I always seem to get myself into.

One thing I notice is that he doesn't attack my body. I throw a cross-hook-cross combo to his head. All the punches land and he fires back immediately, landing a few punches on my chin.

The crowd is going crazy as we both stand in the middle, exchanging blows. My punches are landing clean on him. I can tell I'm getting the better of these exchanges. The round ends.

I return to my corner and sit down as Trey ices my back and Coach gives me water.

"Good job," Coach says, looking down at me. "He's frustrated. He's afraid of your jab, which is backing him up. Keep throwing it and tear them shots to the body. This is a 10-round fight, so if you keep landing body shots like you did last round, you're going to wear him down. Keep doing what you're doing."

"Don't expect him to stay on the inside this round," Coach continues. "He just found out he can't beat you there. He's going to start running around the ring again, so go after him. Time his jab and throw over it. Timing will beat his speed."

I nod as the second round starts.

Tony comes out better this round. He begins to throw his jab, which counters mine. His speed is better so I can't quite get to him the way I want. I continue to land body shots, though. His combinations to my head don't hurt but they are frustrating. The crowd cheers every time he throws one.

With his jab beating mine, I can't seem to box him in the center of the ring. He's dancing circles around me, keeping me away with the jab. Every single time I try to step in he throws a jab, cross straight at me and is gone before I can get off. My jab to his body lands every time though. So I continue to press the fight to his body. Then I realize that he tends to back straight up when I do it.

Rushing forward behind my jab, Tony backs into the ropes, where he stations himself. I don't know if he's just tired already or if he feels like being against the ropes gives him an advantage. If he thinks that, then he's wrong. I lean up against his body, throwing body shots and coming back to the head. I'm landing punches while he is trying to counter off the ropes with speed, but with his back on the ropes he can't go anywhere. I continue to throw body shots and come back to his head. He is throwing as well, landing almost all of his punches. His punches do have a certain sting to them. The crowd is going crazy as we stand there toe to toe and fight on the ropes. The bell rings.

"What are you doing?" Coach yells. "Move your head on the inside – don't just let him hit you! He's dropping his left after he throws the hook on the inside. Counter it with the overhand right. You might have to step back to get more power behind it, but you can hurt him with it. Let's go!"

The third and fourth rounds are the same. Rocks spends most of them trying to jab and stay away from me, but I'm applying pressure and making him fight on the inside and off the ropes. His energy seems to be fading. Most of the time he's leaning on the ropes; here and there he counters with speed combinations, but not enough to keep me away.

The crowd loves the action of the fight. At the end of each round they get to their feet and applaud.

After each round, Coach tells me to do what I'm doing, while at the same time yelling at me for not moving my head.

In the fifth round, Tony comes out a little stronger. I think his corner is telling him he's losing the fight. Coach keeps telling me I'm winning but it's hard to tell what the judges are thinking. Rocks doesn't want me to keep battering his body on the ropes so he takes the fight to the middle of the ring, using the speed behind his jab and combinations to keep me away. I try to get in on him and make it an inside fight, but he doesn't let me. He's running away from me, drawing boos from the crowd but definitely winning the round. I still feel good. My legs are strong, which adds to the power behind my punches.

At the end of the round I head back to my corner.

"Ok, he's scared of you now," Coach says. "He don't want this fight, you hear me? He's going to try and run. Cut the ring off on him to back him up into the corner again. Those body shots have worn him down, so keep throwing them. In a few rounds he's not going to be able to move like he is now and will be easier to trap."

The round begins. Tony's eyes no longer have the same confident, cocky look I saw at the weigh-ins. He seems worried. It's starting to set in that I am actually winning this fight. Tony throws a lazy jab and I counter with mine straight down the middle. He backs up and I jump forward, landing two hard body shots. He throws a jab-cross combo, which I block, and at the end of the cross I counter with my own cross and land right on his chin.

He backs up into the ropes and I unleash a barrage of punches to his body and then his head. He throws another four-punch combination, landing three of them across my face. My jaw hurts a little as a result, but the punches aren't powerful enough to keep me away. I continue to land punches to the body and keep leaning my body into his on the ropes cutting him off each time he tries to move around. He's not grabbing though, he's fighting back.

He pushes me away and throws a combination that lands two more punches. I back up to the middle of the ring and he comes at me.

Tony then makes the mistake of throwing a lazy cross. I back up and cock back an overhand right that lands square on his chin, sending him crashing down onto the canvas! I can't believe it! I just knocked him down! The crowd surprisingly erupts. I can't tell if it's a good eruption in my favor or one that says 'I can't believe our fighter just got dropped.'

As I run to the corner and await the count by the Referee I can tell by the way he lands that he isn't getting up. I jump up and down, cheering. The Referee waves his hands after counting to five; he also knows Tony isn't getting up. The fight is over – I have won!

Trey runs into the ring and Coach stands on the edge, casually clapping and smiling. The crowd is going crazy, cheering and applauding my victory. I can't believe it – I just knocked out one of the top prospects in the sport of boxing!

I hug Coach and Trey as we celebrate. Out of the corner of my eye, I notice the well-dressed Grey Bones staring at me oddly. This is the chance I have been waiting for. The country got to see me in an exciting fight. I'm not sure what will happen after this, but I do know one thing: I've gotten the attention of the boxing world.

Chapter Twenty-Three

The morning after the Rocks fight, I roll out of bed and shuffle to the bathroom. I gingerly touch the bruises that are now visible on my face. They don't look bad, but it's obvious I've been in a fight.

I'm still on a high. All night, people had congratulated me, telling me how much they wanted to see me fight again. I checked all the boxing websites and twitter feeds after the fight. Articles and tweets raved about how I had beaten one of the best up-and-coming boxers and how exciting I was to watch. The biggest thing was the shock it sent to the boxing industry. One tweet stuck with me: *Great fight. That Aiden Walker kid is someone to watch. Great speed, power, and explosive combinations. He can be the champion one day.*

I gained 2,000 new Twitter followers as well.

The announcer Kelvin Reynolds said he was surprised by the power and speed behind my punches. He was impressed by my skills and called me "someone to look out for in the future." After the fight he came up to me and congratulated me telling me that he was looking forward to watching me in the future. Reynolds was known as one of boxing's toughest critics, therefore, his review was not to be taken lightly. He could look at a fighter and quickly pinpoint his flaws. Mine, he said, was defense, yet he complimented my ability to take a punch and please the crowd.

I stroll around the room, bored and restless. The city of New York is spread out below my window. My ninth-floor room provides a stunning view of Times Square. Grey Bones sure knows how to take care of fighters. Trey and Coach had walked down the street to grab some coffee and donuts. I can't pinpoint what time I had heard them stumbling around the room, trying not to wake me up.

Sitting on the desk is a check in the amount of $25,000 made out to me. When I first got it, I couldn't pull my eyes away. I had never in my life seen a check for that much money. It seems unreal.

The question is what will I do with it? Mr. Brass is taking care of my finances. He is also taking care of the gym. I have to pay him back for everything he's done for me. I'll start a savings account for all the money I'm going to owe him. The rest of it I'll use to buy some new equipment for the gym.

Trey had suggested we spend some money in the city. It

wouldn't be a bad idea to buy some new clothes, including some for Coach Kay. He wore the same thing every day. Even now, he was wearing a Star Boxing shirt, with black pants to match.

I could get Coach an apartment. Even though he earns fifteen percent of my money, I could give him more to get him out of the gym. Then I really take a thought at it. Yea right. He's going to fight with me about giving him the fifteen percent as it is. There's no way he's going to take more.

I guess at the moment I don't need to worry about any of it. Although I want to enjoy the victory, more than that I want to get back to what I do best – fighting. Tomorrow I want to be back in the gym, training for my next fight.

A loud knock on the door startles me out of my thoughts. Unless I have a serious lapse of the sense of time it can't be Coach and Trey. Looking through the peephole, I see a boyish hotel worker.

"Mr. Walker?" he says when I open the door.

"Yes."

"Grey Bones would like to meet with you. He's down in the lobby. Would you like me to take you to him?"

"Uh...sure." I'm immediately nervous. Grabbing my key, I follow the young man.

Maybe Grey is pissed that I knocked out one of his top fighters. Tony Rocks was supposed to be the next big thing in boxing. It isn't often someone comes along and knocks out this level of fighter. In fact, I had heard Grey Bones was mad at his matchmaker for putting Tony in with a fighter they didn't know much about. There is no rematch clause in the contract, so I don't think he wanted me for that. I clearly dominated the fight, anyway, so a rematch would not be in anyone's best interest. Maybe he wanted to sign me?

As we approach the lobby I see Bones in the lounge area with his laptop open in front of him. Several security guards hover nearby. He smiles when he sees me and stands up. He's about three inches taller than me and well built. He has long arms. As a fighter, I notice these things about people. Long arms, build, and height. That's how I size everyone up.

"Aiden," Bones says as he shakes my hand. "Congratulations on your impressive victory. I'm sorry I didn't get the chance to say it earlier. I was a little preoccupied after the fight last night."

I can't tell if his face is actually deceitful or if it's because I've heard so many shady things about him. For one thing, I find it odd that Bones would pay someone $25,000 for his services and then show so little interest in him afterwards.

"Thank you, Mr. Bones, I appreciate it."

"Do you want something to drink? Water, coffee, pop?"

"No, thank you." I politely reject hesitant to engage.

"Beer?" he persists.

"It's a little early to be drinking," I answer with a smile.

"Not for some people," he chuckles, looking towards the bar. "Please, sit."

I take a seat in the chair across from him.

"Exciting night!" he continues. "I haven't seen the crowd that pumped up in a long time. How are those bruises?"

"They're ok. They only hurt a little."

"That's usually how it works. Where's Joe Kay?"

"He went to get coffee and food. We're walking around the city later so he needed some energy."

"New York City is an amazing place. There's so much to do. You got paid a good amount last night, too, so take some of that money and explore the city. It's much different than where you come from." He takes a sip of his coffee.

"It's like a whole new world here. Everywhere you turn, something is going on, so many people and businesses. I mean, you see it on TV and stuff, but until you actually come here you don't realize what it's really like." He's actually not a bad guy to talk to. Bones's tone makes him easy to warm up too. I'm surprised by it.

"I was much like you – a small-city boy cut off from a vast world I didn't even know existed. Now these cities are my life. Every week I'm in a different town or city. I wouldn't have it any other way. It's truly amazing how the world works." He takes another sip of his coffee. "Now, the reason why I asked you to come down here. Your performance last night was impressive. You beat one of my top guys like he was an amateur. A performance like that cannot go overlooked."

"I was just doing what I do best. I love to fight."

"Yes, but you're different, Aiden. You're exciting, energetic, and very talented. Most important of all, and forgive my phrasing of this, but you are white. 'White boy' is what they call you right?" He laughs. "Fitting name."

"What does that have to do with anything?" I immediately think of my name 'White-Boy'. The interviews touched on it every time I did one. How did that name come to be? I usually laughed when I told them.

"It has everything to do with everything, Aiden. You're a very good-looking white boy. Hence you're professional name. Now don't get that twisted, I don't go the other way, if you know what I mean." He takes another sip of coffee. I notice his black hair is peppered with grey. "Anyways, right now boxing is a sport that minorities control. The fans, the fighters, trainers – they are all black or Hispanic. They run this sport in every aspect. White people in America have lost interest in boxing. They have turned to MMA. You, however, could bring them back. You could be the next Juan Riviera, except you'll actually make it."

"Juan Riviera was Mexican," I point out. Riviera had been one of boxing's most elite fighters. Everyone loved him. He had been on the receiving end of a brutal knockout as soon as he became a superstar. One fight and it was all over. He retired at the age of 26 and became a huge promoter in the industry.

"Yes, but his fan base was white," Bones argues. "And the girls loved him, just like they will you. My point here, Aiden, is that you are very marketable. Not just your style of fighting, but your attitude and your character. Last night, I had hundreds of people asking me about you, 'When is Aiden Walker going to fight next?' Models and ring girls were asking me if you were single. The marketing potential you have is limitless. You can be the next big thing in boxing. You can bring back people who have lost interest in the sport. Countries in Europe have elevated boxing to the number two sport in the world, behind soccer. If we can add the interest of white Americans to that of the minorities, you can't even dream of how big this could get. Even bigger than Dominick Cayman."

Is he serious? I can't believe he's saying all this to me after knocking out just one guy. Maybe he's lying. But what does he have to gain by lying?

"Thanks, I suppose," I reply. He looks me dead in my eyes without the slightest twitch.

"Which is why I want to sign you." The words shock me.

I can't believe it – Grey Bones wants to sign me as one of his fighters! I'm frozen; I don't know what to say or think. My entire life I have been working towards winning the one fight that would make a big promoter notice me. Now it has happened. And Grey Bones isn't just any promoter. He is, arguably, the best in the industry.

"Now I think I need a drink," I say after a long moment of silence.

Bones chuckles. "So is that a yes?"

"Yes, of course it means yes." My reaction is immediate but I realize something. I think back to what Coach said about Tracey Jury.

"I mean…I want to, yes. There are a lot of details to go over, though, aren't there?"

"Absolutely. I understand you can't say yes right away. The main things are simple: two years, at least five fights. I can guarantee you'll make at least $1 million for all of those fights. And if everything goes well, there will be a fight against Dominick Cayman that will guarantee you at least five million. Oh, and a $300,000 bonus just for signing with Bones Promotions."

My heart is racing faster than it did before the fight. Is this really happening – $300,000 just to sign the papers? I can pay Mr. Brass back and buy the gym. I can buy Coach a new house; hell, I could buy a new house. Coach and I can go back to normal. I've dreamed about this moment my entire life.

"What about training? I don't want to leave my town and I don't want any other trainer but Coach Kay."

My request dampens his excitement. He leans back in his chair.

"To start, that would be fine," he begins. "However, as we get you going, we will feel better having you train in Las Vegas under our preferred trainers. Coach Kay can come if he wants. We'll set both of you up nicely." And now the famous Bones catch. I didn't think he was a bad guy but he's comfortable with what he knows.

"But would Coach Kay be my head trainer?"

"Aiden, I don't think you quite understand the opportunity I am giving you. Some things need to be sacrificed in order to get better. If you want to beat Dominick Cayman, we need to teach you different things, like defense. Fighters need to experience new trainers in order to learn different things. This is how they get better. It's what turns them from a good fighter into a great fighter. I'm not sure Coach Kay can teach you those things."

This is what has worried me from the minute I heard Grey Bones wanted to speak with me.

"I can't leave the man that has trained me my entire life. He isn't just a trainer to me. He's much more than that."

"This isn't the first time I've heard that, Aiden. I understand the connection a fighter has with his trainer, which is why I don't want him totally out of the picture. Obviously a man like me, who has signed dozens of fighters, has to go through this a lot. You will see that replacing him as head trainer will work to your benefit. He can still be around, just like I said. Your best chance of making it to Dominick Cayman and beating him is by trusting me to do what I do best."

Bones has given me a dream offer, but with a consequence I'm not willing to accept. That isn't the only thing that bothers me.

"That is, even if you let me beat Dominick Cayman," I say. He raises an eyebrow, pretending to pay no mind.

"I'm afraid I don't understand what you mean." He shyly

replies.

"I know I was down on the judges' scorecards four rounds to one before I knocked out Tony, even though I had clearly won every round except maybe the second. Kelvin Reynolds had me up four rounds to one and so did the press row scoring."

"The judges' scorecards have nothing to do with me," he replies, his anger beginning to show. "After the offer I've given you, you're gonna sit there and call me corrupt to my face? Who are you to judge me? You're a pity fighter that was lucky to get the shot you did."

"I know this business, Mr. Bones. More importantly, I know how you run things." I stand up, looking around at his security. "I'm sorry, but I must deny your offer. You have a nice day." I can't believe I just did that! 300,000 thousand dollars turned down. I basically took the money and threw it right back in his face. Maybe I should go back? It was just a misunderstanding. I really didn't mean to call him corrupt. Maybe I could say I'm sorry and work it out. Coach would still be in my corner, he promised. No. It didn't feel right. It needs to feel right and that didn't. Holy shit! I'm such an idiot.

I walk towards the elevator. This isn't the way I want it to end, but there is no way I am going to leave Coach. I won't be like Tracey.

Chapter Twenty-Four

"So let me get this straight," Trey says scratching his head as he paces around Coach's office like a child ready to explode. "Not only did you turn down a $300,000 signing bonus, guaranteed $1 million over the next two years, and a chance to fight Dominick Cayman for $5 million, but you told the most powerful man in boxing that he is corrupt and fixes fights right to his face." Trey's words almost make me laugh despite the seriousness of the situation. He turns around to look at Coach. "And you always call me the stupid one."

"Trey," Coach smirks, "Get out of here."

"I'm just sayin'," Trey mutters as he walks out of Coach's office, "Could've got me one of them BMWs or a Lexus. Could have been rolling like Wes and Tom. Damn."

"So how bad is it?" I ask as Coach shuts the office door and shakes his head.

Coach looks over the papers on his desk. "Doesn't look good. Not too many people can call Grey Bones corrupt to his face and survive much longer in the boxing world."

"I didn't call him corrupt. I just implied that he was the reason why I was behind on the cards against Tony. It's not like I was lying." Technically, I hadn't, but I should have known I would eat those words. There are things that you just don't say to people, and that was one of them. I was an idiot!

"Yeah, well, we're back to a bunch of small, local fights that probably won't be for another month or two at best. I emailed and faxed a few promoters that were interested in bigger fights but nothing has come back. I'll bet every dollar I have that Grey Bones has blacklisted you."

They aren't the words I want to hear.

"All that hard work for nothing," I say, pacing around the office. "I'll never get a big fight again."

I slam my hand against the wall. Boxing politics is something I have always hated. Now that I'm part of it, I hate it even more.

"It's not for nothing," Coach says. "You beat Tony Rocks on ESPN. Thousands of people around the nation watched it. Something good will come out of it. We just have to give it time."

"So what now?" I ask in frustration. "We just sit around for the next couple months and wait to get lucky?"

Coach has always had a fight lined up. Before this, we had at least five other fights we could have taken. Now, no one wants me except some guy with a 10-15 record and I have to wait two months to even get that.

"Yes," Coach replies calmly.

"Well, I can't sit here and wait. I just beat a top prospect! I don't want to go back to fighting on these shows that no one knows about, for no money, and against somebody that is just using boxing as a secondary income and doesn't even train properly for it."

"I know you're upset, Aiden, but we can build your record up a little more. You have to trust that another big fight will come along. Not everyone likes Grey Bones. In fact, most people don't like him. We can try to reach out to some other promoters and see what they say. There's no way you can be blacklisted for long after your performance against Rocks."

As frustrated as I am, I have to believe in Coach. Maybe I could use a little break after five fights in six months. Most fighters didn't get the opportunity to fight that much.

"You know what bothers me the most, Coach?" I continue, shaking my head and sitting down in the chair across from him. "If Bones had given me that offer before Mr. Brass came along, I would have taken it. I would have left this place for Vegas in a heartbeat and left you here with the hope that one day you would forgive me. That's how broke I was. I would have done anything for money."

"And if you had, son, I would have understood."

His words make me pause. "So, wait, you would have been ok with me signing with Grey Bones?"

"No, I said I would have understood. Just because you understand someone's actions doesn't mean you agree with them. If you were broke, struggling to pay bills and keep a house, and that offer had been given, no sane man would have turned it down. I would have been happy for you, regardless of what I think of Bones Promotions."

"Why, though? I don't think being broke is an excuse to make bad decisions."

"No, son, it's not. But it's necessary sometimes, to better yourself. Making a bad decision doesn't make you a bad person. Sometimes it makes you a better person." Coach stands up. "Don't get me wrong, though. I'm glad you told Grey Bones that he's a corrupt promoter. There is nothing more I want in life than to see you go into that ring and knock out Dominick Cayman...to hold that belt above your head and say 'We did it.' Luckily, Mr. Brass prevented you from making the bad decision."

Again, his words surprise me. "I thought you didn't trust him."

"I don't," Coach answers without hesitation. "For now, though, his good deed prevented you from having to do something you didn't need to do. The decision he made to help us can change the rest of your life, Aiden, for better or worse. Such is the flow of life. I believe in my heart that you will be the one to knock out Dominick Cayman."

"Thanks, Coach."

"And thank you, Aiden, for thinking of me first. I would have never thought you'd become so loyal to me. I truly thank you for that." His shocking words hold. Did he just give me a sincere compliment? Did he just actually thank me for something? Coach must be losing his mind.

"I just don't trust anyone else to be a pain in my ass and yell at me to train the way you do, that's all." My sarcastic remark brings a smile to Coach's face. "So now what?" I ask.

"You relax. Keep training, but don't overdo it. We'll see what happens in the next couple weeks. Meet a girl, go out to dinner, spend some of that hard-earned money you just got. Boxing isn't the only thing in life, son."

"Coming from a man that lives in a boxing gym?" How can he tell me it isn't the only thing in life? He once said that you must live, eat, and sleep boxing. It must be your life. I remember those words. I'll never forget them. Coach Kay's life is boxing. He goes to church and trains fighters. That's it.

"I like living here," he protests. "I got a room, a kitchen, and a television upstairs now, thanks to Mr. Brass. This is my home."

"You really like living upstairs from this smelly place?" I joke. "I don't know. Oh, and I want to donate $2,000 to the Boys and Girls Club over on Frankly St." One of the kids at the gym had said that they were looking for money to sponsor their basketball program. It totally slipped my mind.

"Maybe we shouldn't go donating money yet. You're not making millions of dollars."

"If there's one thing I am going to do with my money, it's help other people. Whether I make twenty thousand or twenty million. Just help me do it."

He shakes his head with a determined look. I can tell he's not mad – maybe just a little protective of blowing money like that so fast.

"Fine, one thousand," I relent. "That's enough for now."

"Ok, ok, one thousand to the Boys and Girls Club," Coach

agrees. He's been helping me handle my finances. He was way more experienced with handling it than I was.

"Um, Aiden?"

The voice startles me and I turn to see Julius Grimm walk in. He's an amateur boxer who lives up the street. His rugged face and tiny body do not reflect his amazing skills as a boxer. Nothing about his clothes was extraordinary. Lately I've been helping Coach hold pads for fighters, and sparring with the amateurs. It was a great feeling to train fighters. Grimm was one of the guys that I was training.

"Someone is here to see you," he continues.

"Can you tell him to wait a minute?"

It's probably another reporter. They've been coming to the gym all week and asking for interviews. I know I have to get used to it, but they often come at the worst times.

"Yeah, but it's a her."

"Her?"

"Yeah, says her name is Vanessa."

Coach smirks then pretends to bury himself in some papers on his desk. I look out the window and see Vanessa standing next to the boxing ring, looking through the glass directly at me. Trey is in the ring, pointing to me and then to her, and laughing.

"I, um, I'll be right there," I tell Julius.

As I leave the office, I see her looking at me with a smile on her face. Her long, blonde hair is beautiful and her green eyes sparkle. It's been so long since I've seen her, I actually forgot how gorgeous she is. I suddenly realize how stupid I've been to let her go for so long. My heart races a little as though it's the first time I have ever met her.

The last time I saw her, I'd ended it with her. I was broke and believed she deserved better. I'm still broke, compared to the amount of money she is used to, but I feel different now. It's not the money, though, that makes me think I might be able to make this relationship work. It's my confidence in myself as a person that's stronger.

"Hi," she says softly, casually.

"Hi," I answer, in awe that she's standing in front of me.

"I saw your fight on ESPN. My, uh, dad had a big party. There was no way I could miss it. Congratulations, by the way."

"Thanks. Actually, I haven't had a chance to talk to your dad since then. Did he like it?" Mr. Brass had called me the night of the fight. I tried calling him back and I left a message, but he never responded.

"Are you kidding me?" she laughs. "The entire night he was

telling all his friends that you were the next big superstar in boxing. He was betting on how long it would take you to knock the other guy out. He was like a little kid again."

I laugh, too. It's hard to imagine someone of his stature being so excited to watch me fight.

"You guys look so cute together when you're laughing," Trey's voice rings out loudly as he walks to the corner of the ring. Even though he is in the middle of a sparring session, he still finds time in between rounds to make comments.

"I'm sorry, do you want to go outside?" I ask Vanessa.

"Yes," she laughs. As we turn to walk outside, I look at Trey and mouth the words "You're dead" so he clearly understands me.

When we reach the outside I realize that night has set in. The moon is shining brightly and stars are filling the sky. The air is a bit cooler as fall is approaching.

"You look beautiful," I murmur.

"Thank you," she says not being able to hold a smile. "You always were full of pleasant things to say Aiden."

"Not the last time I saw you," I admit. "I said some things I probably shouldn't have."

"That's ok. I understand what you were going through. I didn't realize at the time. I should have paid more attention. Perhaps I should be the one apologizing."

Her amazing smile gets to me every time I look at her. I can't believe I've been able to stay away from her for so long. Now that she is here, I'm getting all the feelings back that I used to have for her.

"You told your dad, didn't you?" I ask.

"It took me a while. First, I had to tell him that we broke up, which took about a month. Then when he asked why, I told him the reason." She laughs. "He was actually thrilled that you knocked out my ex-boyfriend. He hated him more than anything. Once I told him about your financial troubles, I could see the look in his eyes that meant business."

"Well, I should thank you then. What he did – what you did – has changed my life. More than you will ever know. And I promise to pay him back every dollar he gives me."

"I'm sure you will, but he won't accept it."

"Well, he's not going to have a choice. I'll sit outside your house with a check until he takes it."

She stops walking.

"Aiden, he didn't do it because he expects you to be a star that will one day pay him back. He did what he did because he saw what I saw in you: compassion and determination. He did it because he believes in who you are, not just your ability to box. You think about helping others before yourself. I never wanted money from you, Aiden. I just wanted your love. That was enough for me. You were the first boyfriend I ever had that made me feel as though nothing in the world could hurt me. And if it tried, you would be there to protect me. You were the first person that put me first, above everything else. Even though I knew boxing was your life, I felt that I was first."

"But I couldn't provide anything for you."

"You just had to provide yourself. If you had understood that, you wouldn't have run off the way you did."

"Why did you stay away for so long then," I ask, "and why come back now?"

She begins to walk again.

"After that day I was so upset. I was most upset that I didn't know what to do to make you happy. I asked my friend to help me find out some stuff about you. You were so secretive about your past and your parents. Then I caught up on some past articles. Once I found out about your mother and father, I didn't even know what to think. I knew that there was nothing I could say or do that would ever make you happy because I knew nothing about the pain that you were going through. I figured it would be best just to stay away."

"I'm glad you're here now," I admit. Looking back at the gym, I see Coach Kay beginning to close things up for the night. "I was actually just finishing up. Do you think that I could interest you in dinner?" She stops to turn around, grilling me directly in the eyes.

"Oh, I don't know. Are you sure you're here to stay this time?"

"Of course. And to prove the truth in my words, we can go to any restaurant you want. Even that Mountain Steakhouse place."

"You've been to the Mountain Steakhouse?" She shockingly inquires.

I already know what she is thinking. It's a romantic place and she probably isn't going to believe the next words that come out of my mouth.

"Yes, but not with a girl – I haven't been on a date since I was with you. With Wes, Tom, and Trey. Don't even ask how it went." I laugh. "Besides, you're the only one going on dates with people, or so I hear."

"Checking up on me, are you?" She nudges my arm. "Well, for your information, none of them got a second date, or even a kiss."

"Oh yeah, why is that?"

"I don't know. Maybe my heart was somewhere else the entire time."

It is a good feeling to have her back in my life. I hope she stays. It's like Coach said, boxing isn't the only thing in life. If I need to learn to balance it with other things, Vanessa is a good place to start.

Chapter Twenty-Five

Weeks pass without a single phone call for a meaningful fight. We decide to pass on two offers against opponents that have no business being in the ring with me. One had a record of 24-13, and the other a guy that was 13-20. The money was horrible and it wasn't worth the training to take those fights.

I am what the boxing world calls "on ice." So instead, I try to turn my focus on my social life, and put boxing in the back. I work out but not hard. Often I just go to the gym to help Coach with the other fighters, and teach the upcoming boxers everything I know.

The gym is fun. We laugh, joke, and train hard. I always mess with the little kids coming in. They all love me and try to be like me. I spar the amateur boxers trying to teach them everything I know. Parents of the children that come to the gym love me, and apparently word has gotten out that I'm this amazing person outside of the ring. The gym is starting to get packed with all sorts of people every day. Just being around all the people is awesome.

Everything is going well with Vanessa. We are hanging out a lot, going out to a lot of dinners. I am managing to keep my weight down even though every night is spent eating out somewhere, whether it's with Vanessa or the boys. I'm thinking of moving up to 175. My upper body is very ripped and I'm not sure how long I can fight at 168 anymore. What I don't manage to keep is my money. I am blowing through it faster now than I ever did before. I try to pay for everything with Vanessa, because that is what I was taught. I guess I still respect what my father tried to teach me. He never allowed my mother to pay for anything.

She is getting used to the publicity that is the result of my fights, especially the last one. No matter where we go, someone wants an autograph or a picture. I can't go out to a peaceful dinner without at least five people coming up to me. Everywhere, people look at me strangely. I think some aren't sure if it is truly me so they stare until I am out of sight. It's an odd feeling to be so popular.

"No, you have to tie the bow this way," Vanessa explains. I'm sitting on the floor of her room, which is about the size of half of my house. When we first approached the house, I couldn't even take in the entire thing, it's so enormous. There are tennis courts in the backyard and a pool so big that sharks could swim comfortably in it.

Every room in the house is an amazing sight. The kitchen is huge, about five times the size of mine. It is hard to believe people actually live like this.

"I have no idea how to do this," I admit.

"Look. Loop it over, tie it, and then loop it again. It's simple."

"It's not simple. It's hard." Frustrated, I toss the rope over. Vanessa laughs as she grabs it and puts it back in my hand. "Can we try this again? Watch, I'll show you one more time."

"Why can't you just tie all the baskets and I'll stuff them with all this crap?" I ask. For the past hour, we've been putting together these auction baskets for a benefit her father is throwing. There are over 50 baskets that still need to be done.

"Because you don't do that good, either," she answers with a grin.

"Great, so I'm completely useless." My self-pity doesn't move her. She grabs the rope and makes me tie the basket guiding my hands gently through the process.

"See, it looks perfect," she says. It's the first one out of 25 that I've done right.

"What's this for, anyways?" I ask. There is a lot of cool stuff in these baskets, some of which I want to keep for myself. One has $1,000 worth of jewelry. Others have a $500 gift card to Target, $1,000 in auto repairs, an all-expense paid trip to Mexico. I've been to a few benefits with Coach, but never anything like this. With my sudden popularity in the area I've been getting asked to go to a lot of these things.

"One of my dad's old friends has a son who's very ill. They can't afford his medical bills because he lost his insurance after losing his job last year. My dad's been trying to help him, but it's tough, ya know?"

"Yeah, I know." I didn't need Vanessa to tell me what it felt like to be broke. "How sick is he?"

"I don't know exactly what the term is. He was diagnosed a few years ago. He only has a certain amount of time to live, and that time is running out. That's why his father lost his job. He wanted to spend time with his son before he died."

"So, wait, this boy is going to die no matter what we do and how much you raise?"

"Unfortunately, yes."

"That's awful."

"I know. He's put himself into so much debt that even after he loses his son, he will have a million other things to worry about. I feel so bad for him. My dad is going to pay off the rest of his bills after the benefit money is applied, but he hasn't told him yet."

Mr. Brass doesn't mess around, I think to myself; he just gives his money away. I know Coach doesn't trust him, but from what I've seen of the man, he is very caring and helpful. He told me the story of how broke he'd been when he was my age, and how lucky he was to meet his eventual boss. Maybe he felt he could give that luck to other people.

"Well, I want to donate money and a basket," I decide. "At least $1,000."

Vanessa looks at me and smiles.

"Aiden," I suddenly hear Mr. Brass say, sternly. His is standing in the door staring. I wonder how long he's been there?

"Yes, sir," I reply, looking up.

"For the hundredth time, please don't call me 'sir'," he complains.

"Sorry, Mr. Brass."

"Actually, you can call me Hank. I'm tired of hearing Mr. Brass and I'm tired of hearing sir. Just Hank will be fine."

"Can I call you Harry?" I joke.

"Absolutely not," he fires back. "Anyways, I need to talk to you for a second. Vanessa can come, too."

He walks out of the room and we exchange curious glances.

Following Vanessa into his grand office, I can't help but look around in astonishment. The office is amazing. The marble floor alone is probably worth more than the entire boxing gym. Windows the size of church doors reveal a stunning view over the hills, where the buildings of downtown Buffalo can be seen in the distance. Giant shelves holding enough books for a lifetime of reading line the walls. His desk is messy with stacks of papers, just like Coach's. Pictures of his wife and kids line one side of the desk. That is something Coach doesn't have, not one picture of anything. For Coach's birthday I had been planning to get a photo of him and I to put on his desk.

Mr. Brass sits down and we sit across from him.

"What's up?" I ask.

"I talked to Coach Kay a few days ago," he replies.

"Oh, so you heard?"

"Heard what?" Vanessa cuts in.

"Yes, I heard," he continues, looking through some papers.

"What is going on?" she persists. I haven't told Vanessa anything about what is going on in my boxing career.

"Aiden has been blacklisted," Hank tells her.

"What does that mean?" she says, staring at me.

I smile and look over at her father.

"It means Aiden called the biggest promoter in boxing corrupt right to his face, and now he can't get a good fight," Mr. Brass explains, grinning.

"I didn't call him corrupt." It's useless. No matter how hard I try I can never explain myself.

"Well, that's neither here nor there," Hank says. "Anyways, I've been working my ass off for the last couple days on this and I think I got something."

His words get my attention. The fact that he is so obsessed worries me, but if he's found a way to get me off this blacklist I want to hear about it.

He hands me a poster. "That's just a sample of what it could look like."

I look the poster up and down in disbelief. "You have got to be kidding me!"

Vanessa grabs the poster from me.

"That's about as real as it's going to get," he says. "If we can't get you a big fight, we'll bring a big fight to you. This is something I have dreamed about for years."

"Is that Banks Arena, where the hockey team plays?" Vanessa asks, looking at the background of the poster.

"Yes, the Arena fits 30,000 people," her father replies, "and we are going to hold a fight there."

I can't believe it. The idea is brilliant.

"Do you really think we can sell it out?" I ask.

"Aiden, there are over one million people within a hundred-mile radius of here. Not to mention Canada where boxing has become huge. They have been waiting for a champion boxer to come out of this area. You honestly have no idea how popular you have become around here. If the hockey team and football team can do it, I can. I could sell 50,000 seats if I had the room. Just leave it to me."

"Who's the other guy on the poster?" Vanessa asks.

The fighter's twirled mustache is as big as the words on the poster. His skin is pale and the look in his dark eyes is resolute. The strength he exhibits in the ring is exemplified in his tough face.

"Kenny Harbinger," I say. "Which brings me to my next point, Hank – there is no way he is going to agree to it."

"Who is he?" Vanessa asks.

"Five years ago, he was the champion of the world," I explain. "He's a great fighter. Very talented. But he lost to Dominick Cayman and since then he hasn't been the same. He's well past his prime but still very dangerous. A fight against him would grab the attention of a lot of people around the country, even if it wasn't on national television. The thing is, I can't see him agreeing to come to my hometown for the amount of money we will be able to afford to give him."

I remember watching Harbinger fight when I was younger. I like him. His attitude is very professional. I just don't see him taking a fight like this.

"He's desperate," Hank says. "He's fighting for money now – but no one is offering him fights. His last three fights have been overseas because no one here wants to watch him. People still follow him." 500,000 followers on Twitter I think. Yes, I'm obsessed with social media. I could probably give a list of every popular boxer and how many followers each one had. Hank pauses and looks at me before continuing. "He's already agreed to the fight; he's been guaranteed $100,000. If we sell this thing out, which I am one hundred percent positive we will, you will walk away with the same amount."

I exchange looks with Vanessa. With money like that, who needs a promoter?

"I don't even know what to say," I tell Mr. Brass.

I'm in shock. My next fight is against a man I've not only respected my entire life, but who I look up to. Although he's not the fighter he used to be, Kenny will come to fight. He won't be boring, by any means. I'm confident he will stand in the middle of the ring and go toe to toe with me for 10 straight rounds.

For this fight, I have to be completely focused and in better shape than I have ever been before.

"Who's promoting it?" I ask.

"You let me worry about all that stuff," he replies. "You just worry about the fight. Remember, Harbinger has never been knocked out before. If you can manage to do that, even Grey Bones won't be able to keep you away from bigger fights."

I like the sound of that.

Chapter Twenty-Six

"You're joking, right?"

The morning sun is making its way through the cloudless sky as I hold back a big yawn. Being extra tired this morning has a lot to do with Trey coming over last night and staying up with me, watching fights. We were trying to break down Kenny Harbinger's style.

"Not even a little," Coach responds. The sound of the river running behind me is soothing and would give me comfort if I were here to visit. Following the trail all the way down takes you to the bottom of the world-famous Niagara Falls. The gorge is what the locals call it. It's oddly my first time down here, though I feel like I may have heard about it. A path of trees, rocks, and natures finest things that lead the river all the way to one of the greatest wonders of the world. The gorge is one of the greatest things about Niagara Falls. It is just as dangerous too. There are no railings that prevent one from getting too close to the fast paced river, which estimates its speed at nearly 40mph. Perhaps higher. People have died, mostly because of carelessness.

"How many stairs is it again?" I ask, stalling. For me, though, the gorge will be my own personal hell.

"399."

"They're not even real stairs." The path leading down into the gorge consists of manmade stairs about three-feet wide. Most of them are broken in half from years of cold winters. Staring towards the top it feels like miles away to get back up there.

"I don't care what they are," Coach persists. "Your job is to run up…and to run down. Three times to start. Kenny Harbinger is going to be a brick wall in there. You will have no breaks, no time to regain yourself. There will be not time to box him. He will walk you down and fight you every minute of every round. Endurance will be how you win this fight, not skill."

His stern words scare me. I try to ignore my fear.

"How did you even find a place like this?" I ask, beginning to stretch.

"My parents took me down here when I was child. As I grew older, it became a fun place to drink and smoke pot with friends. People used to throw parties down here."

"Smoke pot? You? C'mon!" Not one ounce of me can picture

Coach smoking pot. He is so serious, so stern, so in control. I wasn't even sure he ever drank.

"What, you think I didn't know how to have fun when I was your age? Back in my day, I could have out-drank your boys Tom and Wes."

"Coach, you flip out when you see a cigarette bud on the ground outside the gym. Now you're telling me you used to smoke weed and drink. Forgive me if I'm caught by surprise."

When Coach sees a cigarette outside the gym, he picks it up and goes up to every single person in the gym, smells them, and asks if it is theirs. Once he finds out who the person is, if it's a young kid, there is serious hell to pay. Even the adults are not let off.

"Just because I did it doesn't make it right and doesn't give anyone the right to go do it themselves," he explains. "I have to set a better example than what I used to be. Therefore, I must be against everything I used to do to make the kids that come to the gym better. They must strive to be better than other people out there. It's harder for them because many of them come from bad situations. That is what I teach. Discipline. You think I don't know that 80 percent of the kids in the gym are smoking pot and drinking every night? That they are out selling drugs? I know that. I tell them it's wrong and that I'm against it. As long as they know that, there is a chance they can stop."

I continue to stretch, dreading the task that is in front of me. I can run 10 miles a day, but running stairs for 10 minutes is something I hate. I have a feeling these particular stairs are going to give me serious trouble. Three times? Has he gone mad?

Collecting my thoughts, I realize that he is right. Kenny Harbinger is not coming to play around. He's coming for war. So am I.

"You know, this is the first time I've heard you talk about your parents," I say quietly.

In all the years I've known him, he's never mentioned his family. Never said anything about his past. He is a mystery to me when it comes to that. I can name his favorite foods, colors; I can tell you the first thing he does when he wakes up in the morning and how he will react to most situations. But I can't tell you the name of his parents, or how he became a boxing trainer. I can't tell you anything about who he actually is.

"Is that something that interests you?" he asks.

"Yes. I mean, you always say a man's parents determine his outcome, don't you? That's what you said about me. So I would assume your parents are a big part of the reason you are the way you are today. I would like to know more about them."

"I guess you have a point there," he admits. "Get started. When you come back, I'll tell you what you want to know."

"Sounds good to me."

It doesn't take more than 50 stairs for my legs to start burning. My iPod plays Lil Wayne, which motivates me to keep going. Rap music usually does. I try to think of other things to distract me from the burning sensation in my legs. I've learned that taking your mind off of situations helps you forget about them. Right now, I need to forget how much my legs hurt. Coach is going to make me run these stairs every day, so I'd better get used to it. In the last weeks of training camp, he is going to make me do this at the end of the day, not the beginning. And I'll be doing it six times, not three.

I run up and down the first time. Coach stands at the bottom, timing me. Once my foot touches the bottom stair, I pause breathing as though my heart is about to explode. I can't believe how tired I am. It's only been one time.

"Don't rest! Let's go! Let's go! Let's go!" His shouting motivates me to press on, even though I feel like I'm going to pass out.

This time, I try to focus on the wildlife. It's very peaceful down here. I can see myself getting used to running these stairs every day, despite my legs feeling like they are going to collapse and my heart giving me the sensation that it may stop. I might throw up. A few older people walking down the stairs glance at me strangely. I am covered in sweat. They must think I'm crazy. I am.

The scenery is amazing. Trees tower over me and a small creak of water flows from the top of the gorge to the bottom. It's comforting in a way. More so than the falls itself.

I finally complete the run and bend over, trying to catch my breath as I hit the bottom of the stairs for the third and final time. I feel like throwing up but I try my best to hold it in. Coach stops the timer.

"Not bad for the first time. By the end of training camp, I want this time cut down by two minutes. We'll be doing it at least six times."

I am too tired to argue. I can barely catch my breath; I remain hunched over.

"Stand up," Coach orders. "Put your hands above your head, high."

I do so, and after a few minutes I can finally speak.

"I thought I was in shape. I've never felt this way before."

"You are in shape, son. But this is what we need to do to get the extra punch out of you."

"I'll do it every day in training camp from now on," I say, glancing up the stairs. "My goal is to conquer these damn things."

I need to be able to run these stairs without feeling the way I am right now. Coach is right: Kenny Harbinger is not going to back down and I haven't gone 10 rounds yet. Chances are, Harbinger is going to take me to the end.

"Let's walk the path, shall we?" Coach suggests. "You can let your lungs breathe a little."

I follow him, looking over at the river water, which seems to be moving 100 miles an hour. I've heard stories of people falling in, only to be found miles down the river. I turn my attention back to Coach. There are paths that lead down to the water. People can be seen with fishing poles sitting on the edge of the rocks. Fishing? It seemed so tranquil. I wonder if I should give it a try. Who would teach me though? None of my friends seem like the fishing type.

"So, about your parents..." Coach waits a few seconds before responding. He looks around cautiously, as if someone is watching us.

"My father was a boxer. Buddy Kay. He wasn't a great boxer. He was a journeyman, so to speak. He trained me my entire amateur career. Our relationship was perfect. My mother supported everything we did. Every win was like a holiday at home, filled with excitement and joy. The losses were met with strong advice and determination to keep pushing. They both supported me the best way parents could."

He pauses for a moment. "Then came the day I wanted to go pro. We did everything we were supposed to. But when I went to get my license, I was denied. The doctor had found something wrong with my brain. Not enough to require any sort of medication or treatment, but enough to say that I would never be able to take shots to my head again. If I tried to go pro, I could end up dying; I would end up dying. So he wouldn't approve my physical. We tried some other doctors, to no avail. I was done." Damn, that was sad. Coach didn't even get a chance to try a professional career.

Coach looks out over the river. "My father, man, was he disappointed. I always felt like that day changed our relationship. It was like without boxing we had nothing to talk about, nothing to do together. I tried everything to save our relationship. He wasn't interested."

He pauses. "I was ashamed of myself for something I had no control of. I felt like he was disappointed in me. I moved out and began to train people while working in the automobile industry. I didn't see much of my parents after I began my new life; just holidays, a few weekends here and there. Then one day I received the call. My dad had died. He was 67 years old. My mother died a year later, at 67 as well."

I listen intently, feeling my body slowly returning to normal as we walk.

"At the time my father died, I hadn't seen him in five years. After my boxing career had ended, I couldn't face him the way I wanted to. So I stayed away. It was the biggest mistake of my life. When I got the call that he had passed, it was a Sunday night. I was sitting on the couch watching old fights and football, like I did every Sunday. That's what he and I used to do. I couldn't help but think that I could have been at the house watching it with him all those Sundays, and that by sitting there alone in my house, I had given up thousands of quality hours I could have spent with him. I didn't want to make the same mistake with my mother, so I went to see her every single day I could, until the day she died."

Coach pauses. "And there's my story. I always felt that me and my father should have experienced different things in life than just boxing, but I never gave us the chance."

I took a seat on a fallen tree limb. "Was becoming a professional boxer his dream, or yours?"

"Don't sit," Coach advises sternly, and I immediately stand up. "I'm not exactly sure anymore. He pushed me into the sport when I was younger and I just did it, without ever thinking if it was something I wanted to do. I remember the feeling I had when I was told I couldn't fight anymore. Part of me was relieved; it was as if I didn't want to do it anymore. My biggest disappointment was about how upset I knew he was. Sure I wanted to be a fighter. It was all I knew. But was it what I wanted. I don't know."

Coach takes a deep breath as we approach the car. "It doesn't matter now. I love what I do and I'm thankful he pushed me into this sport. I can't imagine doing anything else in life."

"Well, if you ever want to do something other than boxing together, just ask," I say. "A vacation, basketball game, bingo, strip club...whatever you want."

His laugh seems to echo through the entire gorge.

"How about 10 rounds of pads, a five-mile run, and some bag work?"

He smiles as he says it, but I'm not amused. I'm exhausted, but I know I have to keep pushing.

"That's not exactly what I had in mind," I say.

Chapter Twenty-Seven

"Posters are all over every city from here to Rochester," Trey says. I continue as I hold pads for one of the kids in the gym. Oscar Grenado is his name. A young Puerto Rican kid from down the street where I live. He's not bad for only a few months of being at the gym. "There isn't anyone within a 100-mile radius that isn't going to hear about this fight. Coach says 10,000 tickets are already sold and it hasn't even been two weeks."

"You need to step into the cross a little more, and keep the left hand up higher when you do or I'm going to hit you in the head." I say to Oscar as he nods. He does exactly as I say, and his right hand is actually pretty hard for a fifteen year old. Trey circles us in the ring as I work with the young kid who is surprisingly as tall as I am.

"Fifteen," I say, between the kid's punches addressing Trey. "Fifteen thousand."

Trey's eyes widen. I can't believe it myself. It's only been one month since promotion of the fight started. Everyone in Buffalo and the surrounding towns is talking about the fight. It's in every newspaper and on every radio station. The media are following my training. Reporters are in and out of the gym every day.

"We have interviews lined up, too," Trey says. "Mr. Brass has a list of days, times, and places where we need to be. We should really think about buying a car."

"Why do you always say 'we'?" Wes screams, walking over to the edge of the ring.

"What you mean, 'Why do I always say we'?" Trey yells. "Because it is 'we'. Aiden isn't going anywhere without me!" He smacks me on the back before exiting the ring. I laugh.

"Why do you always have to mess with him?" I ask. "Jab, Cross, Hook." I yell at Oscar. Wes chuckles.

"Because it's funny. He's funny. Where did you find him, anyways?"

"Here. He was the first person that I ever sparred."

"Really? Wow, that's crazy. And you're a seasoned professional boxer set to become the champ and he's...well, he's him."

"I'll tell you what, he could have been something. That boy was talented, that's for sure."

I remember when I first sparred him. He was so much faster than me, so much more experienced.

"What happened?" Wes asks.

"It's a tough sport. Dedication is the key to everything. He wasn't dedicated. Plus, he was always getting in trouble. He'd come here for a few months then disappear for a year, come back, fight a couple times, and disappear again. The day I went pro, he decided to stick around. Hasn't left the gym since." Maybe I saved Trey's life. I don't know where he would be without me. I don't know where I would be without him. He was my best friend.

I try to maintain my focus while participating in the conversation. Coach hates it when we talk to each other while we're working out. Holding pads for kids was helping me with my ability to see punches coming at me, and it was a part of my training. Also, I loved to do it. But Coach would be pissed if he saw us talking even as I did this drill. If he had seen this, he would be yelling at both of us.

"But he don't fight anymore," Wes says. "I only see him sparring."

"No, I just think he likes being here. It keeps him out of trouble. He's been the best friend a man could ask for. Even if he is going to mooch off of me for the rest of his life."

"I heard that!" Trey shouts. I hadn't even seen him come back. We all laugh as the bell rings to end the round. "Here," he says, handing me a glass of cold water. I give the kid the water.

"Thanks. Good job Oscar. Go practice that on the bags."

"All right, my dad bought tickets for him and the entire company," Tom says as he walks over. Me and Trey exit the ring as I put on my gloves to do some bag work. He's dressed much differently than I'm used to seeing him. His fine tailored suit is out of place at the gym. He is working hard at selling tickets. "I can't wait to see this fight," he continues. "This is going to be awesome."

"Man, you ain't allowed to wear suits in this place," Trey says to him. "Who you think you are, Donald Trump?"

Tom ignores him. "You nervous to be fighting in your hometown?" he asks me.

"I don't know. I haven't really thought about it. I've just been trying to focus on the fight."

"You haven't thought about it?" Trey says in disbelief. "This is a hometown fight! Everyone is going to be there. All your friends, family." He hesitates for a second. "Well, you don't really have that many friends." He raises an eyebrow. "I guess you don't really have any family, either."

"Thanks," I respond, sarcastically, but Trey is right. My only

162

friends are at the gym and they see me fight every day. I have no family, although I consider them my family. I'm going to be fighting in front of a bunch of strangers, as usual.

"Trey, you really need to learn to think before you speak," Wes says, shaking his head.

"That's all beside the point," Tom interrupts. "Trey is right. This is the hometown fight. Everyone is going to be supporting you, watching you. You are going to come out of that locker room and 30,000 people are going to be rooting for you. It's a little different than your other fights."

"If I hear one more word come out of any of your mouths, I'm sending you on a 10-mile run with Aiden," Coach barks, approaching us unexpectedly. "Then you can talk about all the things you want to talk about. Let my boy train!"

Everyone mutters apologies as they quickly scatter. Coach sighs. "Those boys will be the death of me one day. I wish they were all like Kenyon – speechless."

The bell rings to start the round and I begin to hit the bag as Coach watches. He gets behind it, holding it so it doesn't move away from my punches.

"Everything looks good so far," he says. "Kenny is having weight issues. They might have to do it at 172. I told them it may cost them but it shouldn't be a problem. Weight isn't an issue for us, so I'm not worried."

"Don't take anything from his purse," I answer. "If he wants it at 172, that's fine. I want to move up to 175 after this fight, anyway."

If a fighter can't make the weight agreed upon in the fight contract, there is a clause stating they could lose some of their purse money. I know Kenny is struggling to make ends meet as it is, so I'm not going to take anything away from him. I know what it feels like to struggle.

"You having trouble making weight?" Coach asks.

"No, I just want to move up." I lie. I was having some weight issues. The muscle that I had built was giving me issues. But that wasn't the reason I wanted to move up. "That's where Dominick is. If I'm going to get a shot against him, I need to get used to that weight."

Fighting Dominick is my ultimate goal. I need to be comfortable at a weight that's close to getting me a shot at him.

"Well, moving up would give you a speed advantage over most people in that weight class," Coach agrees. "Also, you hit hard enough to fight at 175. Hell you hit hard enough to fight at heavyweight. So if that's what you want to do, then we can do it. I might actually like you better at that weight."

Coach has mentioned this to me before. He is concerned about it at the same time, though.

"How much am I guaranteed for this fight, anyways?" I ask. All the excitement about fighting at home against Kenny Harbinger has distracted me; I hadn't even asked how much I would be making for the fight. Mr. Brass told me if we sell out, I will make $100,000, which is amazing. Apparently, with the proceeds from the tickets, food, drinks, and everything that would be sold that night, they are expecting to bring in over one million dollars.

"Fifty thousand, guaranteed," Coach answers. "More than the ESPN fight."

"If I had known that, I would have done this a long time ago," I say, hitting the bags harder.

"This isn't something that happens every day, Aiden. You are lucky to grow up in an area that has missed the sport of boxing; perhaps even luckier that this area craves sports. You've built a good record, fought on ESPN, and the public sees you as a good man that they want to support. Everything needed to fall into place for something like this to happen – and it did. Plus, there isn't anything else going on around here. The football team sucks every year and the hockey team is only good once in a while."

"That's a good thing, I guess," I admit.

I turn to look at Coach and immediately stop hitting the bag as I notice a woman standing at the gym entrance. Coach looks over, too. The woman has long, black hair and brown eyes, and she's very attractive despite her ragged clothing. She is slowly looking around. Her eyes eventually meet mine and I stare at her in disbelief.

"Aiden!" she cries, bringing her hands to her mouth.

Coach puts his hand on my shoulder. I know he must be as stunned as I am. I'm frozen for a moment as though I am looking upon a ghost. I try to make a move, any move, however I can't. The look on my face must be priceless. It's definitely a look that no one has ever seen before.

"Mom?" I say quietly. I can't even remember the last time I saw her. I must have been about nine years old. "What are you doing here?"

"I saw the posters," she explains. "Everyone is talking about it. I just…I had to see for myself. I couldn't believe it – my boy, a boxer."

"I'm not your boy," I say angrily, taking off my gloves and throwing them to the ground. I'm trying to control my emotions but I'm not sure how long I can stay calm. Everyone in the gym is pretending to work out, but I can tell their focus is really on me. I walk over to her quickly.

"I deserve that," she says. "I'm not here to apologize for what I have done or to ask forgiveness."

Not here to apologize? My rage flares and I can't stop it. This woman is not my mother; she is a fraud.

"You damn well should apologize and you should ask for my forgiveness!" I yell as I stop a few feet away from her. "So, what, you see my face on a poster and suddenly you decide to come say hello? What, do you need money or something? Is that it? That's the only time you ever wanted to talk to anyone in your life, anyways."

My shouting has gotten the attention of the entire gym.

"I've been clean for six months now, Aiden," she says, her eyes tearing up.

I feel no remorse, only anger. Her mere presence fills me with anger and hostility.

"Six months, huh? What about the other 15 years? You abandoned me! You left me to live with a poor old lady who had nothing. You took all the money we had and spent it on drugs. It was your choice to abandon your family. Don't walk in here with six months' clean and expect me to be happy for you."

"I don't expect you to forgive me," she replies, choking up. "I don't. I know what I did was wrong. You have no idea what I've been through."

"You? What you have been through?" My entire body is shaking with rage. I can't even believe what she's saying. I actually laugh out loud. "Let me tell you what I've been through, Mom. I grew up poor. The only time I ever ate a good, wholesome meal was when I stole it. At school, when teachers told the kids to have their parents come to their games or to help them with homework, I couldn't because my father was dead and my mom was a crack addict."

I know I'm screaming but I can't stop myself. "I couldn't even buy a new pair of sneakers so I wore the same ones for years until the holes in the bottom of them gave me blisters. All the kids in school made fun of me. I couldn't join any sports because no one was there to teach me how to play. When all the kids were going to the mall and buying clothes, I was sitting at home, knowing I would be wearing the same shirt to school for the next three days."

I see the tears streaming down her face, but I feel no pity for her. "Don't tell me about going through things. You made the choice to do drugs. I didn't choose to grow up the way I did."

The gym is silent. I look around, finally being able to calm down as everyone stares upon us. "Walk out that door and don't ever step foot in here again."

Biting her bottom lip, tears falling from her eyes, she nods her head, turns around, and walks out.

Coach Kay stands silent as he watches my mom leave.

I don't even look at him.

Chapter Twenty-Eight

I sit down in the new locker room that Mr. Brass had built in the gym and place a towel on my head. The sauna has relaxed me. With everything going on, I haven't paid attention to all the improvements Mr. Brass is making. The gym now has showers, a sauna, and women's and men's locker rooms. In eight months, he has turned this place into a fine gym. New people are signing up constantly. Some of them want to fight; others are just trying to get a good workout. Parents are bringing their kids in to help them train for school sports. The gym's new vibe feels good.

Mr. Brass also ordered treadmills, weight machines, and other workout equipment that is supposed to arrive within the next month. Surprisingly, Coach supports all of this. His demeanor has changed over the last year, that's for sure. Before, if someone had tried to put a treadmill in the gym, Coach Kay would have kicked them out and left the treadmill outside on the street for any random person to take. Lately, though, he seems to welcome the changes.

Fight week is here. In four days, I will step foot in the ring to face my biggest challenge to date, in front of my home crowd. Everyone in the city is talking about it. My number of Facebook friends has jumped from 400 to 2,000 in the past two months. My Twitter feed is gaining new followers every single day. Social networking is a huge vehicle for me to promote the fight. The support I'm getting is unbelievable.

Tom, Wes, and Vanessa have helped promote it in ways I never would have thought of. We've sold 22,000 tickets. Mr. Brass is still predicting a sellout.

I'm closing the gym tonight but right now I can't move from this bench. Everyone is gone. I am exhausted. I trained a little longer than usual to work on my endurance. I am going to need it for this fight.

Coach is meeting with Mr. Brass to go over some final details before the fight. They have become close over the past few months. I'm starting to believe Coach actually likes him. He'll never admit it, though, stubborn old man that he is.

I am ready for this fight. I know I am. I've run those damn stairs every single day for the last two months. My legs feel like I could run across the country without stopping. My wind will hold out as well. I'm not the underdog for this fight like I was for my last.

Kenny Harbinger's skills have deteriorated over the years. He isn't as fast or as strong as he used to be. However, Kenny will come to fight. From the time the bell sounds until the time it ends the round, he will be in my face, throwing punches. I'll have to outbox him, outfight him, and have enough endurance to do it for 10 straight rounds. If I can't go punch for punch with Kenny without getting tired, I will lose this fight. Also, Coach is worried about my habit of getting into brawls. Even though the fans love the way I fight, it's dangerous.

We have watched tapes of Kenny's last few fights. His technique seems pretty standard. He comes forward, throws a lot of punches, and tries to outlast his opponent. His jab has slowed, his feet don't move a lot, and his defense is probably worse than mine. It will be easy to land the jab. Even Grey Bones had admitted I have one of the best jabs and left hooks he has ever seen, even better than Dominick Cayman's.

I stand up in the darkened locker room and stretch my arms. I haven't been sleeping well. My mother's sudden appearance a few weeks back continues to trouble me and interrupt my sleep with crazy dreams. Dreams of us being together as a family when I was little. Memories. I still can't believe she had the nerve to come back into my life after all these years. After everything she did to me as a child. And before the biggest fight of my career. My anger erupts every time I think of her. I wish my grandmother was still alive. She was the only person in the world who understood everything I had gone through as a child. I never blamed Grandma for us being poor; she had to make do with what we had. My mother took my father's military pension after his death and blew it on drugs. She was the reason we had been broke – she was the reason for all of it. That's why I hate her. I punch my fist against the locker and slam the door shut.

For some reason, I look to my right. I'm startled to see Kenyon Martin sitting on the bench.

"Sorry, I thought everyone left," I mumble. Kenyon, who is known to stay late, must have slipped by me when I was closing up. Since the man never speaks, it's not hard for him to go unnoticed, despite his enormous size.

"You are angry," Kenyon says.

"Yes, I'm…" Suddenly I stop looking at him oddly. I can't believe it! It's the first time I've ever heard his voice! His accent is very pronounced and his voice is even stronger than Coaches. I would guess he is from somewhere in Africa. In 15 years, no one in this gym has ever heard him speak. No one is going to believe this.

"You speak?"

"You are angry with your parents?" he asks, looking up at me.

"And apparently you know what goes on in the gym," I say shaking my head.

"Just because I do not speak, does not mean I do not listen."

I pause, deciding whether I should continue.

"Yes, I am angry," I finally say. "My father died fighting a war for this country, a war he did not believe in nor did he have to participate in. My mother took his money and spent it on drugs, leaving me to grow up with nothing. Now, over 15 years later, she decides to show up on my doorstep and claim that she is clean. And expect me to open my arms with joy. Yes, I am angry. I am very angry."

I have no idea why I just laid out my feelings to a stranger. Then again, Kenyon isn't a complete stranger. I remember seeing him through the window when I first discovered the boxing gym. Besides, since he doesn't speak, there is no one he is he going to tell.

"Sit, please," he replies. "I want to tell you a story."

I hesitate. His accent is very strong, but I can understand every word he is saying.

"Please," he repeats, motioning for me to sit across from him. "I will tell you of the last day I saw my parents."

He now has my full attention. I sit down on the bench.

"When I was five years old, I was living in a village called Haiku in Uganda," he begins. "My parents were loving parents. They raised me to have a strong back for whatever problems would come our way. Uganda was a terrible country, plagued by wars and murder. Our village was a small one in the middle of the forest. We kept it small, because if the revolutionaries found us, terrible things would happen to our people."

I stare at him, still not believing I am actually listening to him speak.

"One night, my father ran into the tent. I woke up in fear. People were screaming and yelling. I could hear gunshots. I knew that the revolutionaries had found us. As fast as we could, we gathered our things and began our escape. But it was too late. The soldiers captured us and brought us to the center of the village."

A scene enters my mind as I listen.

"It was customary for them to kidnap the children, turn them into murderous soldiers, and make them fight in the army. The parents would either be killed or turned into slaves. The man leading this particular group of soldiers was a hateful, evil person. They called him Massa. That day, he decided to kill all of the parents in our

169

village in front of their children as punishment for hiding. He matched up each family, pulled the kids aside, and shot the parents one at a time. I can still hear the cries of my friends as the soldiers went down the row, murdering in cold blood."

"I don't know what it was, but when they got to me, the leader made the soldier stop. For a second, just one second, I was joyed. I thought he would spare the lives of my parents. Massa looked me in the eye. I don't know what it was he saw in them that day – defiance, hatred, or maybe nothing. Maybe he was just proving a point. He took the gun from the soldier, gave it to me, looked over at my mother and father, and said to me, 'I want you to do it. And if you do not, they will suffer a fate far worse than death'."

Kenyon pauses for a moment. I haven't taken my eyes off of him. In fact, I feel his pain as though it is my own.

"I looked into the eyes of my parents," he continues, "as they waited for me to kill them. My mom, she was crying. Not because she was afraid to die, but because she was afraid of what I would become. My dad did something that I will never forget. He smiled and nodded. I could not understand it back then. I was angry with him for it. But years later, I understood. He smiled because he knew I would never become what they wanted me to. Years later, I escaped and came here."

I keep my gaze on him. "I am so sorry," I say. I have watched documentaries about what goes on in Africa. But never had it felt so real as hearing it from someone who lived through it.

"Do not be," he says. "I am not. I tell you this story because you should understand that your father fought so that this country would never be like the country I grew up in. The people in this country do not understand what the rest of the world is like, because they themselves never have to live it. Your father chose to protect this land and he should be honored for it, especially by his son."

Suddenly, I understand. I feel so selfish. What right did I have to be mad at my father for all these years?

"You know, you should speak more often," I joke.

For the first time since I've met him, Kenyon smiles.

"Often, a man of few words, has more to say, than a man of many," he says.

I think of my father. He is right. Damn it, he is right.

Chapter Twenty-Nine

"Will you come somewhere with me, Coach?" I ask, taking off my boxing shoes and tossing them in my bag. I wipe the sweat from my face with a towel. My body feels the best it ever has. I'm ready for this fight.

"Yeah, sure. It's about time I get to ride in that new car of yours."

I look over at Kenyon Martin, who is just finishing up hitting the bags. It is because of him that I am doing this. For some reason, I can't do it alone. Not entirely. I want Coach with me.

I used part of my advance from the upcoming fight to buy the Nissan Maxima. Mr. Brass had been right – 27,000 tickets have been sold, almost a complete sell out. In addition, sponsors had dished out tons of money so their company names will be mentioned or posted somewhere in the arena. I know Kenny Harbinger and I are getting paid a lot for this fight, but I can't even imagine how much Mr. Brass is going to end up making. I still don't know how he managed to get a promoters license, or even if he did. He may have been working with someone that already had one. I wasn't paying much attention to the details.

I love my new car. It's the first time in my life I've been able to purchase something so expensive on my own. Walking into a dealership and laying down half of the balance in cash had been one of the best feelings in the world.

I can still remember the days when I couldn't walk into a local grocery store and buy the things I wanted. That feeling will never leave me. Because of it, I will always donate money to the poor. I even spend some weekends volunteering down at the church, helping to feed the homeless. They like me down there. I sign autographs and serve them food while enjoying laughs with the other aids and people.

No matter where my life takes me from here, I will never forget where I came from.

"Ready?" Coach asks as he watches Kenyon grab his things and walk out the door.

"Yeah." I put on my sneakers, grab my bag, and we head out.

"Those are nifty," Coach says, smiling and looking down at my feet.

"I just got them."

"I'm not used to seeing you with new things. New car, new sneakers, new gloves, new clothes, I feel like I'm looking at an entirely new person."

"Well, you're not. I'm the same person I always was. If you would accept anything I bought you and would wear anything other than the same old black pants and gym shirts that you wear every day you could have some new things, too."

"I told you, I don't need stuff like that. I'm perfectly fine the way I am." Coach is still living at the gym and says there is no way he's going to move. He's been offered places, houses, apartments. The money that is coming into the gym from new memberships is more than enough to get him out of there. Still, he refuses to leave. Stubborn as usual.

"Yeah, yeah. I don't even want to argue about it anymore."

We get into my car and I see Coach stare at the CD player and iPod hook up. He looks into the backseat. The black leather seats are very comfortable. He opens the sunroof above his head playing with it back and forth like a little kid discovering his first toy. The grin on his face in unforgettable.

"Impressive."

"Thank you."

"Has Trey asked if he can drive it yet?"

"Only a hundred times."

"We need to talk about the media," Coach says as we take off.

"What about them?"

"Well, you need to know what to say and what not to say. The media can be your best friend or your biggest nightmare. It's kind of like having a girlfriend. When you answer questions the way you are supposed to, everything is good. When you start to say things that could cause a bit of drama or trouble, they will exaggerate them to the point where what you said was entirely different from what you intended."

I smile at his explanation. Vanessa does that a lot.

"So I talk but I don't put myself in a situation where I might get myself in trouble," I say.

"Yes, although boxing is a little different because you can talk smack about your opponent. It's actually more compelling to the public if you do."

"But I don't want to do that."

"I'm not telling you that you have to, I'm just saying that it's more acceptable than it is in other sports. Take Dominick Cayman, for example. Much of his success is because of his attitude in front of the cameras. People want to hate him or love him. You don't have to be like him, but you have to be likeable. Those good looks of yours alone aren't going to help you."

"So just be myself."

"Yes. And don't say anything that will get you into trouble."

"Can you give me an example of something that would get me into trouble?"

He looks out the window for a second, thinking.

"No, I can't," he answers. "The media can take any little thing you say and turn it against you. Just be yourself. This fight is different because it's in your hometown and the local media are the only ones watching you. But as you get into bigger fights, you will find out what I mean."

After a silent ride afterwards, we pull up to our destination and Coach's face turns grim as he looks over at me. I know he's confused. I am, too. Part of me wants to turn back. But I can't. Kenyon was right.

I drive slowly through the tall gates and follow the curves of the narrow roads. Even after all these years, I remember where it is. It's like some part of my brain has stored it there for this particular moment. I park the car and we get out and slowly walk across the grass. The air is warm and the sun is going down. This isn't a place most people would like to be when it's dark.

Coach doesn't say a word. I know he knows where we are going.

Finally, we reach the tombstone that says 'Barry Walker 1968–1997'. We stand in silence for a while.

"This is the first time I've been here since the funeral," I say quietly, staring down at the grave. Coach doesn't say anything. "I don't know why I stayed away so long. I was so angry with him. And now, I don't know why I was. I shouldn't have been. I was wrong."

"Anger has a way of making us do things we shouldn't, say things we shouldn't," Coach responds. "It clouds our perception of what is going on. It is necessary sometimes, however."

Coach comes to stand at my side and we both stare at the grave.

"I miss him, Coach. So much. I was never mad at him because of how he died, or what he died for. I was mad at him because he left me. I just didn't know how else to channel the fact that I missed him more than anything in the world. After it happened, every single day when I woke up I would walk over to his bedroom, thinking he would still be there, that maybe it was all a dream."

Standing there, I can almost feel my father's presence. I hope

173

it isn't just my imagination.

"Aiden, if your father was here today, he would be proud of the man you have become," Coach says. "I can guarantee that, son." He puts his hand on my shoulder. "And your mother is proud of the man you have become, too."

"Don't," I say, shrugging his hand away. "My father didn't choose his fate, but she did."

"And now she has come back, clean, and wants to be a part of your life."

"Well, she can't be. She doesn't deserve to be."

While I know my anger toward my father was my fault, my anger toward her is hers. Even Kenyon's story did not sway me to forgive her. I'm not ready. I don't know if I ever will be.

"I'm going to head over to the car," Coach says. "You come when you're ready." He pauses before leaving. "Aiden, don't let hate for your mother leave you standing here years from now, regretting the same thing you are now."

"If you take away my hatred for her, too, what will I have left to fight with?"

Coach has always said that my anger over my past has made me a fighter. Now I feel like he is trying to take that away from me. The darkness my parents left me in, the hatred that boiled deep inside me every day and every night, has made me the fighter I am. Every single time I step into that ring I want to kill.

"All fighters have anger towards something, Aiden. Most people start boxing because of hate, and most people will never make it to the pros. You don't want to be most people." I can hear his voice fading as he approaches the car. "Anger made you a good fighter. Love will make you a great one. A great man is only a bad man that has overcome his darkness." Coach disappears with those words. Could I be the fighter that I am without my anger? Every single time I step into that ring I change. I want to kill. I want to destroy the man standing across from me.

Looking up at the sky, I wonder again if my father is watching me. What would he say if he was standing before me? I think he would be mad at me for the way I reacted towards my mother at the gym. He would be angrier about that than he would about me being mad at him. He'd be smiling. He was always good at that.

If there is one thing I will never doubt, it was his love for us. I couldn't remember a day that he didn't come home with a smile on his face or when he didn't kiss my mother goodbye or hello.

"Now, Aiden, don't give your mother a hard time, ok?" he

would say. "I know it's hard to obey rules and do work you don't want to, but those are two things you will have to do your entire life, whether your mother makes you or not."

Those words have stuck with me. Man, I had hated homework. I had hated all the rules and all the chores she made me do. Now, I hated myself for hating those things. I would have given anything in the world to grow up having to follow her rules and to do my father's chores.

I know what I need to do.

"I, um, I don't know if you can hear me," I begin. "I'm not sure if you even know I'm here. But I just wanted to say that I'm sorry. I'm sorry for staying away all these years. I was angry, and now I'm not."

I pause, hanging my head. "I miss you. I know if you were here, you would be at the gym every single day, watching me. You'd probably get there before me and leave after me. I'm sure of it. I know it wasn't a long time, but I couldn't have asked for a better man to be my father. "

I lean my head back and close my eyes.

"Watch over me. Protect me. Give me the strength to overcome the obstacles in my life. Be there for me, as you always were."

When I open my eyes and turn my attention back to the grave, I suddenly notice something I hadn't before. Coach must have seen it, too. I shake my head. Damn Coach, always one step ahead of me. On my father's gravestone is a quote: *A great man is only a bad man that has overcome his darkness.*

Chapter Thirty

Nothing outside of the ring diverts my attention. Not even 30,000 screaming fans chanting "White Boy". When the bell signals the end of the round, I'm relieved. I take a deep breath, trying to regain my wind, but when I reach my corner and sit down, I'm still breathing heavily. My arms feel like they've gained 100 pounds each. My legs are exhausted. I try to gain composure but I am exhausted. I've been rocked a few times in this fight. I still feel like I don't entirely know what's going on at times from the punches that dazed me earlier. It's hard to tell if the fans noticed.

I would like nothing more than for the fight to end right now. I glance over at Vanessa and her dad, who are cheering as loudly as they can. Coach comes up on the ring with Trey, who rubs my neck with ice to cool me off. I look into the eyes of Coach for a brief moment and I know he can see exactly what I'm thinking.

"Three more rounds," Coach tells me calmly, squirting water from the bottle into my mouth. It's so refreshing that I could beg for more. "How do you feel?"

"I'm tired," I admit quietly so that no one can see or hear what I say. "It's like fighting against a brick wall that keeps coming forward."

"You're winning the fight by a lot," he says. "I don't think he's won one round. Stop fighting him on the inside so much. Box more. Stick the jab to him and stay on the outside. Every fight doesn't need to be exciting and end in a knockout."

His words are reassuring. The reason I'm keeping the fight on the inside, though, is because I'm too tired to back up and move around. Countless hours of watching tape and training could not have prepared me for what is happening in the ring. Yes, I am winning – but I feel like I'm losing. Kenny Harbinger's jaw is made of steel. I can feel it with each time I punch him. His body is rock solid even years after his prime. His punches don't have much behind them, thank God for that.

"I can't believe I'm this tired."

"Listen to me, no matter how hard you train, you will get tired. You are in shape. You just need to fight through it and get another wind. Stick the jab and move. Outbox him. He's coming straight forward, with no head movement. He is very easy to hit with

176

the jab. You just have to throw it and stop brawling him."

Taking another deep breath, I stand up and the bell rings.

I stick the jab and back up, allowing Kenny to chase me down. The light glinting off his rough beard and pale skin plays tricks on me at times. He comes straight forward, just like Coach said he would. I throw a jab-cross-hook combination really fast and back up. All three punches land without him attempting a counter. I can feel the strength in my punches still. I can't believe this guy is still standing. Any other person in the world would have been knocked out rounds ago. I do it again, except I add a cross at the end. Again, all the punches land without him being able to counter me yet he still comes forward as though he cannot even feel them.

If there is one thing I remember about Kenny, it's that he never gets tired. He has been in my face all night. The fight has drawn excitement from the crowd as most of it we have been exchanging punches. I could have fought him in an eight-by-eight ring for the last seven rounds. Even though I am clearly winning the fight, and I have gotten the better of him on all of the exchanges, he has not backed down. My punches don't seem to phase him, no matter how fast I throw them or how much power I put behind them. The man doesn't appear to be human; he is like a robot with no emotion or sense of pain. I keep throwing punches, and he keeps coming forward.

His punches don't hurt me anymore. I've been able to sit on the inside for most of the fight and bang with him other than a few times he rocked me. I felt really good, until the fifth round. That was about the time I started to lose my composure. My wind was giving way on me. It was becoming harder to breathe and my legs were heavier every time I tried to move away. The problem had continued into the sixth and seventh rounds. The crowd hadn't seemed to notice; with every punch thrown and landed, they cheered. However, I was having a hard time keeping pace with him. I was fighting on pure instinct.

This round, I feel different. I'm able to keep him at a distance while throwing the jab. At times, I jump in with a combination and back out. He is unable to keep up with me and I can't believe the beating he is taking. I figure at the end of this round, his corner might stop the fight. He hasn't landed a single punch this round. I'm getting refreshed just like Coach said I would. Breathing is starting to feel a bit normal, and my legs are getting the bounce back into them. Now I'm ready to go.

Suddenly, I hear the bell. I'm surprised the round is already over.

"See!" Coach says, meeting me at the corner. "You can box

177

when you want to. There's no reason to take all that damn punishment working inside all the time. Two more rounds. Still tired?"

"Hell, yeah," I say, half joking. "But I feel better than I did the last two rounds."

"Good, this is what we needed. You never fought 10 rounds before. This is what it feels like. We are in round nine. Two more rounds. Don't get careless, ok? One punch can change an entire fight. Keep boxing and backing up. There's no reason to get caught in any more exchanges. He looks tired."

The next round begins. I take a couple big breaths of air and continue my jabbing. Kenny comes at me with a little more determination this time, throwing punches as I jab and stay away. My speed is too much for him. He can't seem to get anything going, yet he continues to back me up and walk me down. I think about trying to back him up but I know he won't. He'll just stand there and trade punches with me until I have to take a step back. He's been doing it the entire fight.

Staying away from his barrage of punches, I back up, throwing combinations to keep him away. I land a left hook across the top of his head. He staggers a bit before coming forward. I can see in his eyes that he is a little dazed. For the first time since the beginning of the fight, I can hear the crowd. They are going ballistic. I glance into his eyes briefly. I think he's hurt!

Instead of backing up, I stand and throw two hooks to the body. Kenny throws a cross to my head, which I block. I counter with a cross-hook-cross combo. All three punches land and he staggers more, backing up for the first time in the fight. He's definitely hurt! I rush after him, throwing punch after punch as hard and fast as I can. He doesn't counter with anything; he just falls into the ropes with his hands up. Finally, an uppercut-hook combo sends him crashing to the canvas. I can't believe it! I knocked down Kenny Harbinger! A man that has never seen the canvas before!

The eruption from the crowd can no doubt be heard throughout all of downtown Buffalo. Kenny stands up before the Referee finishes his 10-count. I have to knock him out! Even though he isn't as good as he used to be, knocking Kenny out will send a strong message to the boxing world.

Rushing after him, I throw a barrage of punches again. Suddenly, I feel a powerful punch land on my chin, sending me back a few steps. My head is aching and my vision blurs. Damn, he caught me. The sound through the crowd is negative as they can see I've been stunned. Two more punches land on my face as I back up, trying to avoid Kenny's assault. He has hurt me. My legs stumble and I lay against the ropes. Kenny comes after me and I throw a left hook, landing it on his chin. He staggers back. We are both hurt. People are screaming. I feel myself getting back to normal as the blurry image of Kenny becomes clear. He throws two body shots, and lands a hook across my skull that I partially block. I'm dazed. I immediately counter with an uppercut that lands right on his chin. Again, he staggers.

He's really hurt now as he actually takes a few steps back. The punch has helped me regain my composure.

I rush after him again, continuing my assault. Coach is going to kill me for going after him like this after being hurt the way I was. Kenny stands there and our bodies lean into each other. He's still staggering a bit. Laying my head into his, I throw two body shots and come back with a cross-hook to the head. For the second time, Kenny goes down as the crowd erupts in cheers! He rolls over and tries to get back up. Instead, he reels into the corner and falls again. This time, the Referee won't allow him to get back up.

The Referee runs over to Kenny and waves his hands to call the fight. The fight is over! Beating Kenny would have been big news in the boxing world – knocking him out is going to be huge!

Everyone is cheering. "White Boy" "White Boy" "White Boy". Coach jumps up onto the side of the ring, calm and smiling after a victory, as usual. Trey, Mr. Brass, and Vanessa all enter the ring, screaming with happiness.

After hugging everyone in my corner, I head over to Kenny Harbinger's corner to pay my respects. His coach, a young, rough-looking black guy, smiles and pats me on the head.

"Great fight, kid," he says.

"Thanks. You, too. He's one hell of a fighter." I walk over to Kenny and give him a hug. "Thank you for giving me the opportunity," I say to him.

"I've fought a lot of guys, but none of them stayed on the inside with me the way you did tonight," he says. "For the first time in my career, I was beaten at my own game. Stay focused. You're going to be a champ one day, kid."

Once, he was one of my favorite boxers, a man I have looked up to since I was a kid. For him to say something like that to me, well it hits a different spot in my soul.

"Thank you, I will, I promise," I say, then return to my corner.

Vanessa comes up and gives me a kiss. "Ew, you're all sweaty," she says with a laugh.

The cameras are in my face and the local news stations want interviews. I am going to be here a while. Then I notice that no one in the crowd has left; they are all staying and cheering for me, chanting the name that had been given to me by the gym years ago. I raise my hands to the crowd and look up to the sky. The feeling is astounding.

Chapter Thirty-One

Coach's text message on my phone makes me grin.

"What's so funny?" Vanessa asks. I look down at the field where her little brother's football game is being played. He's excited; he keeps pointing over at me. The Harbinger fight made me an instant celebrity in Western New York. People constantly ask for autographs and take pictures with their phones. It's not just four or five people coming up to me at a restaurant anymore; dozens of people now come up to me everywhere I go.

Strangers come up and congratulate me on the fight. Local papers run my picture, speculating about what is going to happen next. Who should I fight? Should I fight at the Arena again? Since the football stadium holds double the amount of people, should it be held there? What I will do next is the question on everyone's minds.

The spark hasn't just peeked around here. All around the nation people heard of Harbinger's knockout loss. And while many thought that he was just too old to be boxing, it was my name that was still mentioned as the person that beat him. The national media was taking a light interest as of right now.

The local media however, was treating me like I was some sort of God. When we arrived to watch her brother play, I thought I was in Hollywood, being attacked by fans wanting autographs.

"Coach tells me to take a week off. Not even two days later, he says I need to be at the gym in two hours." I shake my head and put my phone back in my pocket.

"Maybe he misses you," she says, grinning.

"After two days?"

"Yes! I miss you after two hours."

She grabs my hand. It's nice being able to see her more often, although despite my week off I have been very busy. There were over a dozen benefits I had promised to attend. The Mayor had asked me to be present at the Italian Festival that they have every year in the city. Both cities actually. I had to make an appearance in Buffalo as well. There is a five-mile run for cancer I am supposed to lead. Never in my life had I been this busy with activities.

I had had radio and television interviews to do back to back to back. One thing that troubled me was the questions the radio hosts and other interviewers asked. They loved to bring up my childhood –

my father dying for his country, my mother falling victim to drugs. When I told them I grew up poor, eating only rice and chicken, they brought up the subject over and over. I remained composed during the interviews, but it bothered me to talk about it so much.

Both Coach and Mr. Brass had explained that my past would be the focal point of the interviews. It was a story that would sell, that people wanted to believe in. The media loved the fact that I grew up with nothing, that I had to quit boxing at one point in order to focus on work. The story about my father dying on the battlefield had caught their attention. Some of them even wanted to bring my mother in for an interview, but that's where I drew the line.

"Coach doesn't miss anyone," I assure Vanessa. He is emotionless when it comes to things like that. Nothing will ever break through the hard exterior he wears so well.

"Aiden, you're like the son he never had. I'm sure he misses you. But you're definitely right, he would never call you to the gym just because he wanted to see you. Maybe you have another fight offer. And does this mean dinner is off?"

Damn, I totally forgot I promised to have dinner with her and her family.

"Well, dinner's at 5, right? I think I can be there in time. Coach wants me to meet him at 4. It's actually weird that he wants me to meet him on a Sunday, now that I think about it. I should be able to make dinner, though."

Her phone vibrates. She looks at the text, then at me.

"Actually, dinner has been moved back an hour," she says. "My dad just texted me. He says he has a meeting with Coach Kay at 4."

We exchange glances. Something is up. My anxiety kicks in after hearing that, and I suddenly don't want to wait until 4 to find out what is going on.

I can call Coach and ask him, but I doubt he will pick up. Even if he does, he will just tell me to come to the gym and won't say anything until I arrive.

"Looks like I'll be making dinner after all," I smile trying to refocus my thoughts. What the hell is going on?

The crowd in the stands starts to cheer and we look onto the field to see her brother running with the ball. He carries it into the end zone and we all start yelling. His teammates go crazy.

"He's fast!" I yell in Vanessa's ear, above the cheering of the crowd.

"Yesterday he told me he wants to be a professional athlete, just like you," she says.

He wants to be like me? Never in a million years would I have expected a kid to say that – at least someone who isn't from the Star Boxing Gym, anyway. The kids there always say they want to grow up to be like me. It's only because I'm an undefeated professional boxer. Having a kid playing football saying the same thing was odd. I knew he liked me from all the times I had visited the house over the past few months. We always played games together. He smoked me in football on the Xbox.

But to grow up and want to be like me?

After the game ends, we go down to the field to congratulate the team on their victory. The team asks me to take a picture with them. I hear one of the parents call me a "genuine man with a good heart."

I say goodbye to Vanessa and drive to the gym. I can't wait any longer to find out what is going on. Mr. Brass and Coach don't meet face to face unless it's something big, especially on a Sunday.

I had gone to church that morning. I thought Coach would be there, but he wasn't. That was odd, too. It was the first time I'd gone since he took me there over two years ago. For some reason, I had felt I needed to go. But I had felt odd and out of place. I didn't know any of the prayers or when to sit, stand, or kneel. Luckily, the lady next to me had helped me out.

After mass was over, I stayed there alone, asking God to forgive me for all the ways I had neglected him. I prayed for Him to always watch over me and the people I love. I prayed for Coach the most. For the first time, since the day he found me snooping around the gym, I can see that he is finally happy. We have money, a successful boxing career, and others wanting to take up boxing. The gym is filled with kids, girls, older women, and young fighters. It is making money on its own, now that Mr. Brass revamped it. Coach still lives upstairs, though. Oddly enough, it is his home. He loved his life now.

I feel I have to thank God somehow. All my years of boycotting church have only clouded my mind more than it already is. I need to believe there is a higher power watching me. I have begun to read the Bible and understand life in a way I never did before. It is my belief that my duty in this world is not only to reach my personal goals, but to help others reach theirs as well. I had been down on my luck, and someone had come along and helped me. I need to do the same.

I made a promise to God that I will donate 25 percent of my earnings to people in need. Whether it's paying a dying kid's medical bills, supporting a charity, or doing something nice for someone I love, I will do it. Hell, I could buy nice things for strangers, too. I need to do something with my earnings to help people, the way Mr. Brass had helped me.

Pulling up to the gym, I notice a few more cars there than I'm used to seeing on a Sunday afternoon, since the gym isn't usually open. I see Mr. Brass' white Mercedes parked next to an unknown black Cadillac Escalade.

I walk into the gym. I thought nothing could surprise me anymore, but when I look into the face of the well-known man standing next to Coach and Mr. Brass, I'm in shock. They all look over at me and smile as I approach.

The man is flanked by two massive bodyguards.

"Aiden," Coach says.

"I can't believe it," I reply, in awe.

The man puts his hand out. "Well, I guess you know who I am," he says, chuckling.

"Yeah, I mean, yes. It's such an honor to meet you, Mr. Riviera."

Juan Riviera was once boxing's most elite fighter, and had become one of the sport's top promoters. His good-looking features don't seem any different than when I saw him years before on television. He is my height, with thick black hair and brown eyes.

"The pleasure is mine, Aiden."

"What are you doing here?" I ask, looking over at Coach and Mr. Brass, who is holding a folder.

"Mr. Riviera is offering you a contract," Mr. Brass says, shaking the folder.

"In all my years of boxing, I have never seen a fighter sell 30,000 tickets without a well-known promoter backing him, even in his hometown," Riviera explains. "What you did was not only remarkable, it was nearly impossible. Word spread that Kenny Harbinger had been knocked out on an untelevised card. I had my men do some research. I was coming home from a fight I held in New York City and I had to come see for myself what all the fuss was about."

Juan Riviera wants to sign me! I try to hold in my excitement. I have been here before and it didn't turn out the way I wanted it to. Juan Riviera was Grey Bones' biggest competition in the promoting business.

"I truly appreciate the offer, Mr. Riviera."

"Please, call me Juan," he insists.

Pausing, I try to think about what I'm going to say.

"I just…there are some things I need to make sure of first," I begin.

"I know about the offer Grey Bones made you," Riviera says glancing over to Coach with a smirk. "I know you denied it. To be honest with you, it wasn't the smartest thing to do." He looks at me closely. "But I understand why you did it. Do you know what the biggest mistake of my career was?"

I shake my head.

Juan looks at Coach. "It was getting rid of my trainer after coming close to losing my first championship fight. I blamed him for everything, and it wasn't his fault. After that, my pride wouldn't let me go back, but every day I wished I could. I would never ask you to leave your trainer."

"So I can stay here and train?" I ask, just to make sure.

"Yes, I will send sparring partners here for training camps," he confirms. "If you ask me, Grey Bones was a fool to let you go. We've studied your tapes, your attitude, your surprisingly good looks for a white fighter. Aiden you are exactly what boxing needs right now. You have everything it takes to not only be a public icon in the sport, but to beat Dominick Cayman."

Coach seems confident. He has probably already read the contract from beginning to end.

"How long before I can get Cayman?" I ask.

"Six fights, maximum," Juan answers quickly, almost too quickly, "provided you win against whoever we put in front of you. Dominick doesn't have many opponents left. I need to get you on HBO for a few fights so people can get to know you. Then you can headline your own HBO card. If all goes according to plan, you'll have Dominick in two years. He's still young and he's not fighting a lot. I don't see him losing at all, either. He'll still be there."

Two years is a long time. This is boxing, however. I have to earn my shot with Cayman. That doesn't mean becoming the number one contender, either. It means I need the public to demand it. Only then will he fight me.

"I've looked over the contact with Coach," Mr. Brass says. "Everything is in order. You'll get a $1 million signing bonus. Plus..."

"Wait...excuse me?" I ask, nearly gasping for air as I stare at Juan. "Did you just say $1 million signing bonus?"

Coach says nothing, but a smile tugs at his mouth. Mr. Brass just looks at me. I can't believe what I'm hearing. Is Riviera serious?

"Can I talk to you alone for a second, Aiden?" Juan asks.

I glance at Coach and nod. Riviera motions me to follow him.

"What are you thinking?" he asks as we start to walk around

the gym.

"I…I don't know. I can't believe this is happening."

"Do you know what I did when Gavin Hunter offered me my first contract?" he says with a laugh. "I threw up."

"Really!" I say, laughing, too.

"Yes, really! I didn't think it was real. I couldn't believe it. He did it, though, because he believed in me. And I believe in you. I know you can beat Dominick. It's my job to get you there – and it's your job to win the fights. One million dollars will be nothing if you can beat him. You're already a star here. I can make you a star across the country, even the world. I'm willing to spend $1 million on you to take that chance. I have financial advisors at my beck and call if you want advice on how you should invest it. My fighters don't worry about money; they worry about training and winning. That's all I want from you."

"You know, when Grey Bones offered me that contract, I don't think he truly believed I could beat Dominick," I say. "Standing here now, I believe that you know I can. As long as Coach and Mr. Brass agree, I'll sign the contract this week."

"That's exactly what I wanted to hear. I don't say this a lot, Aiden, but you have the biggest potential for becoming a superstar of any fighter in the sport today. It's the reason I came here myself." He pauses and stares into my eyes. "Let's get that dream fight with Dominick Cayman and show him who the new champ of the world is going to be."

I've always looked up to Juan as a boxer and a promoter. I never thought he would take an interest in someone like me. I have to take this opportunity. This is the dream we've always wanted, and it has finally come true. He and I walk back to the group and Juan says his goodbyes, explaining that he needs to catch his flight.

"I look forward to hearing from you," he tells me before he leaves.

The three of us watch him walk out the door then turn to each other.

"Well?" I ask.

"I don't see anything wrong with it," Mr. Brass says. "The signing bonus alone is enough to start a new life, God forbid something happens and you can't box anymore. It's what you've always wanted, Aiden." Mr. Brass was right. This type of money changes my life forever. With or without boxing. I fought so hard to achieve this, and finally I have gotten it. I can't even explain the joy that I am feeling. This is all surreal to me.

"Two years," is all Coach says.

"It's a long time," I agree.

Chapter Thirty-Two

Glancing down the street, I run across quickly while gazing up at the skyscraper that towers before me. The sun reflecting off the glass is scorching on this beautiful clear day. It was a good idea to wear my sleeveless Everlast T-shirt and shorts; it was a horrible idea to wear black. Downtown Buffalo is crazy this morning.

Everlast is sending me free items every week. So are Title, Ringside, and every other boxing gear company in the country. As long as I wear their brand during my fights or training, they say, they will keep on doing so. I have enough clothes in my closet to go through an entire year without having to wear the same thing when it comes to boxing gear. All for free too. Finally I received a contract where I could pay for all this stuff and these guys send me free things. It's so weird.

I walk through the enormous doors of the building and notice the sky-high ceilings, beautiful tiled floor, and amazing waterfall from the second floor of the building into the main lobby. I head to the reception desk.

People gaze at me a little longer than normal. I can't tell if it's because they know who I am or because they're dressed in suits and dresses and I'm wearing workout clothes.

"I'm looking for Henry Brass," I say to the receptionist. She's very attractive, with expensive glasses and a nicely fitted green dress, but she snarls at me without even making eye contact.

"Do you have an appointment?" she demands.

"No, I don't. Can you just tell him…"

"If you don't have an appointment then you can't see him," she interrupts.

"Trust me, he will want to see me if you just tell him that…"

"Why do you think he would want to see you? Especially coming in off the street, looking the way you do. He's a very busy man. We aren't giving away donations at this time for any sort of business or charity so you can please leave or I can have you escorted out of here."

I smile to hide my anger. "Listen, lady…" I begin, a bit more firmly.

"Aiden?"

I turn around to face the voice behind me. I look at the well-dressed, clean-shaven man. Vincent Pender. I have no idea how I remember the name. My first time at the Mountain Steakhouse with the boys he had asked for my autograph. It seemed so long ago.

"Mr. Pender, nice to see you again," I say, shaking his hand.

"Here to see Henry?" he asks.

"Yes, but this lady won't let me up without an appointment. I tried calling him but he hasn't answered since this morning and he doesn't know I'm coming."

Mr. Pender walks over to the receptionist. "Do you like your job, Miss Halls?" he asks.

"Yes," she answers, nervously.

"Then I highly suggest you let this young man in to see Mr. Brass. If he finds out that Aiden Walker was here and you did not let him up, you'll be looking for a new one."

Fear covers her face as she looks over at me. I can't help but smirk.

"I'll have someone take him up," she says.

"Thank you," I say. "Oh, and thank you, Mr. Pender."

"No problem. I saw you on HBO a few weeks ago. What a knockout. Keep it up, kid." He smiles as he walks away.

"Thanks."

I can't believe it's already been a little over a year since I signed with Juan Riviera. He has given me everything he promised and more. All three of my fights have been on HBO – and all ended in stunning knockouts. I am 23-0 with 21 KOs. The boxing world knows who I am. My Facebook page has blown up, I have over 35,000 followers on Twitter, and we are getting offers from all over the world.

Most important, my fans love me. I follow their tweets every day asking when my next fight is, how my training is going, and other questions I can't even begin to know how to answer. I try my best to keep in touch with them. They support me and I need to let them know I care.

Coach hates social media. He hates the media, in general. Although he isn't opposed to open workouts, he isn't a big fan of them, either. He allows the media to do their segments but quickly closes the doors when they're done. There is no way he is going to allow all the hype to distract me from my training. I admit, without him it would be hard to stay focused. Everyone wants to divert me from my training for one reason or another. Coach makes it known there is no skipping, even for a charity event. When it comes to training, I have to stay focused.

Training is different now. Because I only fight three times a year, I'm able to take more time off. We have official training camps that run six to eight weeks before fights. When I don't have a fight scheduled, I don't need to train as hard. I still work out every day, whether I am in camp or not, but when I'm not in camp it isn't as big of a deal. I can run a few miles a day, hit the bags for an hour, and enjoy my life. I'm the happiest I've been in a long time.

Stepping out of the elevator, a man escorts me into Mr. Brass's office. He is on the phone, staring out the window. Turning around, he sees me standing in the door. He puts his finger up and then quickly finishes his conversation. His office at his house is nicer than this one, but this one is still amazing. He has a stunning view of downtown Buffalo and the water that surrounds it. Again, I notice the library of books that outline his office. When does he have time to read all of them?

"Aiden, what a pleasant surprise. Please, sit down."

"How are you doing?" I say, taking a seat across from his enormous desk. His office is bigger than my entire house. I don't know why I haven't moved. With the $1 million signing bonus, and the $200,000 per fight that Juan is paying me, I don't need to live there anymore. I could pay cash for a nice house in a good neighborhood. But home is home for me. I'm having a hard time thinking about leaving it.

"Good, good. Work, as usual. What brings you here? I know you said you needed to talk this morning but I didn't think it was important enough for you to drive into the city."

I smile. He stopped giving me money after I received Riviera's signing bonus, but he still owns the gym. I pull the check out of my pocket and hand it to him.

"This is all the money you gave me with interest, up until the day I signed with Juan Riviera. The rest of it is to buy the gym from you. I looked up how much it's worth, and if I'm off a few numbers I'll pay whatever I have to."

I'm not sure why it has taken me this long to give him the money. I could have paid him the day Juan gave me the bonus. I guess I had been so busy training for fights and doing other things, it had slipped my mind.

He looks at me and shakes his head.

"I told you before, I don't want you to pay me back, Aiden. I just want to be in your corner when you knock out Dominick Cayman."

"And you still can be. But I have the money to pay you back and I want to. There is no way I could ever keep the money you gave me. I wouldn't be able to live with myself."

"Well, I can't take back money that I already gave you."

"You can sell me the gym. Just take the entire check as a payoff."

"This is three times what the gym is worth. I'll let you buy the gym from me, but not for this amount." He tries to hand me back the check.

"I'm not taking it," I say, grinning. "If you don't want to take it, then donate it to something. Trey will take it."

"Oh yeah, and what would I call that?" he asks with a laugh.

"Special needs for the mentally challenged?"

My joke makes him laugh harder. I stand up and he shakes his head.

"Fine, I'll take the money back and get the paperwork in order for you to buy the gym. This is obviously an argument I will not win."

"Well, I'm not very good at losing."

"No, I guess you're not."

"Except to Vanessa, for some reason."

He smiles. "Well, son, you'll learn that's a battle no man can win." He laughs again then suddenly turns serious. "Aiden, I have a question to ask you. But I don't want you to get angry, not until I know what is going on."

What is he talking about? Is it something with Vanessa? I suddenly feel nervous.

"Last week, I went over all the papers for the gym for the last five years. I calculated the money that you gave Coach Kay, plus all his income, the house that he lost, everything. It doesn't add up."

"What do you mean?"

He pauses. "It means he wasn't paying bills with all that money. He wasn't paying any bills with any of the money, even the extra money you were giving him. None of that money got applied to any of the bills to keep the gym open."

"I don't understand. How did he keep it open for so long?" I can't believe I'm hearing this. Mr. Brass has to be making a mistake.

"He was making minimum payments. He would get behind, make a deal with the bank or the IRS, and pay small stuff – enough to keep it but not enough to get caught up. Don't get me wrong, eventually even with the money you were giving him, he would have lost it, but he would have managed to stay open and actually be comfortable for a lot longer than he was. I tried calling him to have him come down here, but when I mentioned what we needed to talk about, he hurried me off the phone and hasn't answered since. I mean, it's not a big deal now but…"

"If he wasn't paying any bills then where was the money going?" I ask.

"Exactly."

"I'll find out."

"No, I don't want you to start anything. I just wanted to know for banking reasons. If you're buying it back then it doesn't matter to me."

"Mr. Brass, he's the closest thing to family that I have. I can talk to him about anything. I'll ask him what is going on and will have an answer for you."

I'm not sure if I'm angry or disappointed or confused. I don't know what to think.

"You don't have to tell me anything, Aiden. The gym is yours again. If it's something that bothers you then you can take it up with him. But the gym's yours again."

I try to smile, but it's fake. What had Coach done with all the money I'd been giving him? As a matter of fact, what is he doing with it now? He is still living upstairs at the gym, still hasn't bought a car, and still has nothing to show for it. Do I approach him about it or ignore it?

Something isn't right, and I need to find out what it is.

Chapter Thirty-Three

I jump out of the brand new Infiniti and glance over at Wes with a smile on my face. The black interior smells fresh and the dove-grey exterior glimmers in the sun. Trey is smiling, too. Wes and Tom exchange glances. Coach isn't happy to be dragged outside the gym on this warm day.

"Why do you guys look like you're up to something?" Wes asks, raising an eyebrow.

"I'm not up to anything," Trey says.

"New car," Coach nods. "Very nice."

"It's not mine," I say, dangling the keys.

"Well, whose is it?" Coach asks, looking at each of us.

I walk up to him and hand him the keys. "It's yours."

Coach looks stunned. He looks at me, then looks at the car, then looks at me again. It's the first time I have ever seen him confused.

"Mine?"

"Yes, Coach, it's yours. Happy Birthday!" He must have thought I'd forgotten. Coach tries to hide his birthday from everyone at the gym but there is no way he's getting away with hiding it this year. Certainly not after the great year we've had.

Everyone wishes Coach a happy birthday. He stands in silence. Trey goes up and gives him a hug, but Coach is too shocked to hug back.

"How old are you now?" Wes asks.

"Sixty-two," he answers, his voice barely above a whisper. "Mine?" He says again. I actually think he's in shock.

"Grey Infiniti, black interior, moon roof, tape player and CD player, satellite radio, everything you said you wanted," I say, patting him on the back.

"I can't accept this, Aiden." He puts the keys back in my hand and walks toward the gym. "Take it back."

We all stand without moving. Wes and Tom don't know how to react. Trey walks over to me and stares at the car.

"I'll take it," he jokes.

I punch him in the arm then head into the gym and into Coach's office. He is standing at the window, staring into nothing since all that's behind the gym is garbage, broken down houses, and trees. Carefully, I shut the door behind me.

"What's wrong, Coach?" I ask. "I know you're afraid of getting old and all, but that's no reason to turn down an expensive, very thoughtful, and very expensive gift."

"I'm not afraid of getting old," he says, turning around. His face is sad. "You should spend your money on something better than me."

"I've been spending money on you since the day I was able to make money, Coach, even when I was broke. Now that I have the money to buy you something nice, you throw it back in my face." I sigh and walk over to the window. "Not to mention, I know you didn't use the money I gave you all these years to pay the gym's bills."

He has no reaction. He just stands there, looking out the window.

"Mr. Brass told me," I continue. "Said that none of the numbers add up. When he asked you about it, you blew him off." Again, I pause, but he still doesn't respond.

"I don't care, Coach. I don't care about the money. I just want to know where it went. I want to know why you haven't bought one damn thing with the money you've earned for training me. Why do you still live here? You have enough money to pay for that Infiniti and a brand new house, in cash."

When Coach still doesn't respond, I sigh and head towards the door. I don't know why he's not telling me what happened. But if he doesn't want to talk, there is no way I can force him.

As I reach the door, he finally speaks. "There was a point in your life where you didn't have a dollar. And I told you that money isn't everything, that no matter how much you have, it will never be enough. And that happiness comes from a place far greater than your bank account."

"I understand, I really do," I reply. "But we have money and the ability to buy nice things now. I want to use that opportunity, Coach. And you should, too. I wasn't happy when I was broke. I am now. I don't know if it's the money, or Vanessa, or because I'm doing something I love to do. But I'm happy, Coach, and you should be, too."

"I'm glad it makes you happy, Aiden. No man on this earth is happier for you, son. I'm just in a different place than you, that's all."

"What kind of place is that? One that doesn't allow you to enjoy nice things, a nice home, maybe even a girlfriend? C'mon, Coach, I see the way some of the ladies around here act towards you. You just shove them away like they are nothing. You once told me there is a life outside of boxing, and you made me live it. But it's not my life that this sport has taken over, it's yours."

Boxing is all Coach knows. I want him to see the world and enjoy his life, the way I am. Maybe it's his father. Maybe that story he told me down in the gorge has gotten a hold of him. Does he think that without boxing our relationship is nothing to him?

"It's not that simple, son."

"Then explain it to me!" I shout in frustration. I'm not going to allow him to get out of it this time. "Why can't you have a life outside of boxing?"

"It's none of your business!" he yells back.

"Yes, it is! It is my business! We've been together for over ten years!"

"You think because you sit there with your nice car, all that money, and your exciting life that you know everything now?! That you can just walk into this office and change the way I have been living my life for the past 25 years because you've changed the way you live yours?! I don't want to change my life, Aiden. I'm happy the way it is."

"You are not happy!" I argue back. "What happened to the money I've been giving you? What are you not telling me? What is the matter with you?!"

"I'm sick, Aiden!" he shouts. His face softens as he looks into my eyes. "There, does that make you happy. I'm sick! That's what I did with all that money from before. I was paying all my hospital bills." Suddenly there is a calmness over the room. A sense of nothingness as if something has driven the anger right out of the gym.

My anger ceases immediately. Sick?

"Sick, what do you mean sick?" I ask. I think of it. I remember the doctor at the church that wanted to talk to him in private so many years ago. The way he has acted the last few years. Allowing Mr. Brass to come to the gym and make all these changes. "Coach, what are you not telling me?"

"I mean sick, Aiden. I've been sick for 10 years."

"Well, you got health insurance now, right? So you can pay for the medications and get better with what's going on. It's been easier this last year, hasn't it? We don't have anything to worry about now Coach. We can take care of it."

"No, Aiden, it hasn't. It won't get better. Because money can't buy my illness away." He walks over and puts his hand on my shoulder.

"You're scaring me. It's ok though right?" I say trying to assure myself. His eyes give way as he doesn't move his hand. "We are gonna be good right Coach?" I can feel my words tremble as my mind think's the absolute worst.

"I'm dying, son."

My heart sinks to the floor as I stare into the sorrowful eyes of Coach Kay. My legs nearly give out on me. It's the words I thought he would say but didn't want to hear. There was no way. Not my Coach. This can't be happening.

"Coach...that can't be," I argue, on the verge of tears. "You said you've been like this for ten years. I mean, you can go on another ten years right?"

"Perhaps, but it's catching up to me, and fast." He says quietly. "The meds are helping, but my time is running out. The doctor said I have a few years left, if I'm lucky. I'm saving my extra money to donate to the gym for when my time has passed. That's why I don't want to move into a house; that's why I don't want a new car. I just want to live my life the way I've been living it. I'm happy this way."

I can't believe it. All this time, all these years, he's been sick – and he never said a word.

"How long have you known?" I can barely speak but with every ounce of energy that I have I refuse to allow the tears that are begging to come out show. I was going to have to live life without Coach? It didn't even make sense. I had never even thought about it.

"I was diagnosed 10 years ago. I can remember the day as though it were yesterday. I went to the gym after I found out. Opened it up, just like any other day. I was sitting there, holding pads for one of my fighters, and I looked out the window and saw a little boy standing there, looking through."

My eyes widen. There was no way!

"I thought it was a ghost at first," he continues, "or that God was watching me. But that boy kept coming back to that window. Every single day. Then one day I walked out and met the boy, and he changed my life forever. What you have become wasn't by some chance son, you were destined to be champion. I believe fate brought us together and I believe we have some good years left. I believe that you will be the one to beat Dominick Caymen." He walks back around his desk and shoots out a casual smile. "Don't let this change anything we've been doing. I'm still going to work your ass like no other. This old man still has a lot of fight in him."

"Coach, you can't die, you're my Coach." I shake my head. His playful words will draw no happiness from me. "I won't let you."

"Everyone dies, son."

"But not so soon."

"Aiden, listen to me. I'm not dead yet, you hear me? I don't want you to worry about me, you understand? We will continue business as usual. You will train hard. Do not bring it up. Don't mention it. I don't want you to feel sorry for me. I just want to live as normal as possible, without sympathy from everyone around me. Do you understand?"

"Yes, Coach." My reluctance is shown.

"I know this isn't easy. God, I know it's not. I've lived my life the way I always dreamed of, Aiden. Every kid that comes in that door brings me excitement. I love to train, I love to coach. That's what I love to do. No amount of money, or fame, or anything can take that away from me. Every day that I spend in this gym is a day fulfilled. I go to sleep every single night with a smile on my face. And taking you to where we got you in your career makes me the happiest man alive. I could die tomorrow and I'll die a happy man, title or no title. Do not focus on the few years left in my life, but the many left in yours."

"I'm going to win the title with you right by my side, that I promise you," I say. I need Juan to get me that fight, and I need it right now.

"I would like that." He smiles. "That is the only gift I want from you."

I nod my head, trying to hold back my tears. "I don't care what you say, Coach, you're taking the damn car." I try to smile but I can't.

He chuckles. "Ok, I'll take the car. Now go enjoy the next week off. We have to start camp on Monday." Suddenly I'm stunned as my mood changes back to boxing.

"Camp? I don't have a fight scheduled."

He walks over to his desk, grabs a paper, and hands it to me. "Yes, you do. I took the liberty of accepting the fight without asking you. I didn't think you would refuse it."

I look over the paper. "Ricardo Barrios!" I exclaim.

"Number one contender, HBO main event, undefeated. Juan called me. You beat Barrios, and Dominick Cayman could be next."

My excitement is clouded by what I now know about Coach. I have to be as normal as I can, but how? How can I look a man in the eyes, knowing he is dying, and act like everything is ok? I could wake up any day and get a phone call saying he is gone.

I can't let Coach down. We are too close to Cayman. Barrios is going to be a huge fight for me. I have to win this fight then Dominick will be next. He has to be.

Chapter Thirty-Four

Emotions are running high at the gym. Everyone is excited about my recent victory over Ricardo Barrios. Nobody will say it but I know everyone is thinking it: Is the next offer from Juan going to be a fight with Dominick Cayman?

I hadn't knocked out Barrios like I'd hoped. My 12-round, unanimous decision victory was a tough, hard-won battle that has the boxing world talking. Once again, I managed to get myself into a thrilling slugfest, which grabbed the attention of more boxing fans in the country. They are calling for me to fight Dominick.

Juan told me there are two types of fans. The first are the hardcore boxing fans. They watch the sport with a close eye and know a lot of the good fighters coming up. I had built up this type of fan base by winning tough, exciting fights that enticed people to want to see me in action. My fights on HBO had made these fans love me. These fans will watch me fight whoever, and pay for it.

The other type are what he calls the "fair weather boxing fans." They know who Dominick Cayman and the other Pay-Per-View stars are, but that's about it. This type wouldn't know who I was if I walked up to them in a grocery store and offered my autograph. These are the fans I needed to earn to be a Pay-Per-View star.

My hardcore fans are calling on Dominick to fight me, although that doesn't mean he will. There's a good chance Cayman doesn't even know how who I am. It's up to his promoter, Grey Bones, to make the fight happen – and I don't exactly have the best relationship with him.

An advantage I have is that people not only believe I should fight Cayman, they believe I can beat him. He is running out of opponents, meaning I have a better chance of getting the fight than other contenders in the division. He is also arrogant. If he knows people think I can beat him, he might sign the fight. He doesn't want doubt in anyone's mind that he is the best light heavyweight in the world.

Twitter and Facebook have exploded with fans. I'm over 100k followers on Twitter. I've been doing interviews with all of the top reporters of boxing from all over the nation. Radio shows, and even some television shows. Juan has been doing an amazing job at getting my name out there. He says it's my good looks and great personality that the people love. Also my action packed style of boxing helps. He believes we are ready to take that next step and that the pressure is on Cayman to take interest in the fight.

Coach seems to be doing well. He's acting the same as always. The excitement from the last fight had made me temporarily forget what he is going through. However, no matter how hard I try, no matter how much I distract myself with other thoughts, no matter how many interviews I do or how busy I try to make myself, it is always in the back of my mind.

"I'm not sure I like it," I say, snapping out of my daze and looking around the empty room. The ceiling is high, making the tiled floor look distant. Just as I'm about to walk out to the patio to check out the in-ground pool again, I hear my phone ringing.

"Of course," the agent murmurs, shaking his head and looking at the pocket where my phone is. I don't really like him. His flashy suit reflects his arrogant personality. Vanessa gives me a dirty look as I grab my phone. Instead of answering it or even looking to see who it is, I silence it and put it back in my pocket.

"I'm just saying. How much is it again?" I ask.

"Can we have a moment?" Vanessa asks the agent. He grabs his things and walks into the other room. She smiles and turns to me. "Ok, talk to me. What's wrong?"

"I just don't like it," I say, looking around. "The ceiling's too high, the kitchen is too far away from the family room, the bedrooms are all upstairs, and I'm not sure how I feel about that. Do I even need an upstairs?"

She grabs my arm. "Aiden, we've looked at over a dozen houses. Each one has something you don't like. I don't believe that every single house has this crazy thing wrong with it that makes you not want to buy it. What's wrong?"

"I just don't want to be so far away from Coach," I finally admit.

She doesn't know about his situation – no one does. We are keeping it a secret. But the house was at least a thirty minute drive from the gym. All of the houses we've looked at are far away from the gym. They are in nice neighborhoods that I'm not used too. I'm not even sure I'm comfortable living in a house with no crack head sitting on the porch when I get back. Weird.

"You're the one that wanted to go look at houses," she says. "If this were for both of us, I would have driven myself mad already."

"Maybe I'm just not ready to move yet."

"Which is understandable, but you can't live there forever.

The neighborhood is falling apart. With the amount of money you have saved up, you can pay for any one of these houses we are looking at, in cash. The gym is only 30 minutes away. I mean, the cost for gas is not exactly going to break your bank account." Her joke does draw a smile. Vanessa. I cherish her.

"I'm just not ready to move yet. I'm sorry."

I leave the house and walk to my new Jaguar. Cars are the only purchase I've made lately. This one cost me $65,000; I absolutely love it. I felt guilty buying it. The salesman was pushing me worse than any drug dealer I had ever known. The money could have went to a charity, or the boys basketball club. Or someone that needed it. I traded in the Maxima for it. It's not like I had five cars just sitting in my driveway. I tried to justify that buying a nice car was something I deserved for my hard work. Was I just fooling myself?

Vanessa walks out with the agent and gets in the car. I'm sure she's pretty mad, but I know I'm not ready to move. I know the agent is mad but I don't give a shit about him. Coach needs me. Of course, he would have my head on a silver platter if he knew I am basing my decision on him.

"Are you mad?" I ask as I start the car and pull out into the street.

"No, I'm not mad. I know how hard it must be to leave. But you need to realize that you can't live there forever." She grabs my hand. "I know that's where you grew up, Aiden, but you need to get out. Coach and Trey need to get out, too. Coach wants to live at the boxing gym not because of you, but because that's what he wants to do. Trey, well, you know Trey. He will probably end up living with you." He sure would. Right on the couch too. He probably wouldn't even take his own bedroom.

She falls silent and I start thinking about Coach's sickness. I've tried to find out everything I can about it online. I've met with doctors, done research, even found other people with the same illness. Nothing has made me feel better. It's like watching a timer count down and the only thing I can do is wait for it to hit zero. Not being able to help him is the worst feeling in the world. No amount of money will fix this. I once thought money was everything. Those days seem distant. I was wrong. Life was everything. I think back of the time I almost took my own life. I was a fool.

The ride back to the city is quiet. My phone rings again and I answer it. It's Trey.

"You need to get to the gym – now!" he yells and hangs up.

My hands start to shake. I drop my phone on the floor and start to feel nauseous.

"We have to go to the gym! Trey just said I need to get there, now."

I pick up speed. My instinct tells me something has happened to Coach. My heart is beating faster than it does before a fight.

"What's wrong, Aiden? Relax," Vanessa says. "You're going too fast."

"I have to get there. What if something happened?!"

I'm going double the speed limit but I'm not worried about getting pulled over. Every cop in the city knows who I am. They would never give me a ticket. Weaving in and out of streets my heart is racing. No. Not yet. We are so close to Cayman. This can't be happening right now.

"What could possibly have happened?" she asks.

"I don't know. Trey just sounded like something was wrong."

"Aiden, you're going to get us into an accident. You need to slow down!"

She's right. Luckily, we're almost there.

I don't see any cops or ambulances as I pull up to the gym, but that doesn't mean everything is ok. I run into the gym, not knowing if I've left the car running. Vanessa follows.

I see Coach in his office – he's fine. My heartbeat finally slows. After all I did to get here, nothing appears to be wrong.

Trey walks over to me, smiling.

"What the hell is wrong with you?!" I shout at him.

"What?" he asks, looking at Vanessa. They both look confused.

"You made it seem like something was wrong," I explain, beginning to calm down.

"No I didn't, I just said to get here as quick as you can. Coach has something for you."

"Well, you should have told me on the phone that's what it was," I say angrily.

I walk into Coach's office. He's on the phone.

"Ok, I'll talk to him," he says and hangs up. Thank God he's all right.

"You look like you just saw a ghost," he jokes.

"I just...I thought something was wrong," I reply, knowing I still sound jittery. I really thought his time had come. Trey had seemed so worried, and I'd been far away from the gym. There is no way I'm going to buy a new house. I can't go through that again.

"Trey gave you the old 'Get here now' and hung up, huh? And you thought something had happened to me." He leans forward on his desk, looking over some papers.

201

"I was worried, that's all. It's different now. He can't do that."

"I told you to stop worrying about it. I'm fine, ok? I went to the doctor last week and he said everything looks good. So you have nothing to worry about for at least a few more years, got it?" He looks over at me. "Got it?" he demands.

"Yeah, but maybe next time I should go with you." Coach rolls his eyes. "You know, to the doctor. I'm just saying, I might have a few questions."

He continues looking through the papers.

"Well, we got the next fight," he says, ignoring my comment. "It's a little lower than Juan wanted, and he still wants to try and negotiate your cut for the fight, but he wanted me to run it by you first. You'll get some of the PPV revenue, which should increase the…"

"Tell me you're going to say what I think you're going to say!" I say excitedly, walking around the desk.

"Are you going to let me finish?" he smirks.

"Coach, don't mess with me right now. You're messing with my emotions and you know how much I don't like it."

"I just want you to make a rational decision, that's all."

"Coach, I don't care if the fight is for free, please tell me that's the contract to fight Dominick Cayman."

"We could fight one or two more times. You've only been 12 rounds once and only have 24 fights. He's got twice as many fights and way more experience."

"I don't care. If that's the contract to fight Dominick Cayman then that's what I want. It's what I've always wanted. And you are seriously messing with me right now." I'm so excited I can feel my nerves tingling throughout my entire body. "So…is that the contract to fight Dominick Cayman?"

"Yes," he answers finally, handing it to me.

"Yes!" I yell, grabbing it and engulfing him in a hug. I jump up and down. "We did it!"

Trey and Vanessa walk into the room and I notice Mr. Brass has arrived, too.

"Now you know why I did that," Trey says, folding his arms and shaking his head. He's mad at me but he'll get over it.

"I'm sorry," I laugh, waving the contract around.

"Is that what I think it is?" Mr. Brass asks with a grin. Coach must have called him to come down.

"Sure is," I answer. "In four months, I'll be stepping into the ring against Dominick Cayman!"

Everyone in the room screams in excitement. This is it – the fight I've always wanted. I don't care how much I'm getting or how much I could get; I just want to fight this man. Now is my chance to show the world I am the best fighter in the sport.

Chapter Thirty-Five

The countrywide tour to promote my fight with Dominick Cayman took me to New York City, Las Vegas, Los Angeles, and San Francisco. It was my first time in three of the four cities. There were even talks of heading to Europe for a few weeks, but that idea had been thrown out at Dominick's request. He doesn't believe there is any interest in the fight over there, at least enough to send us. One thing I've learned over the last few weeks is that Dominick is in control of a lot of what happens.

The tour was exciting. Traveling from city to city to promote the fight was exhausting, especially in a five day period, but it was all worth it. I signed autographs, met tons of people, and got to travel the country. It's surreal to me how much national attention the fight is getting and how the fans came out to all of our conferences. They asked simple questions at the conferences. How was I going to beat Dominick? Did I think I could beat him? Has he ever faced a power puncher like me before? It was all about my style, and then a few questions about my personal life but nothing about bringing up the past. I'm not used to any of it. Dominick, on the other hand, knows how to act in front of the cameras. He knows how to answer all the questions and do it with star power written all over his face. He absolutely loves it. They were really promoting the fact that we were both undefeated, and that I was a young contender. Undefeated bouts tend to draw more attention in the boxing world.

Coach didn't like it. He didn't like any of it. He's focused on getting ready for the fight. He spent most nights in the hotel room watching all the videos of Cayman he could get his hands on. Lucky for us every single one of his fights could be found on YouTube. A few times I stayed up with him, hoping to notice some new vulnerabilities in Cayman's boxing style, but nothing stood out. I have to apply pressure and outpunch him. His speed and power are excellent. His combinations are super-fast. His defense has some exposures, though, which can only be brought to light by applying pressure. He tends to keep his head up while he's on the ropes. I may have my shot there. I just had to put him there. It's the only way I stand a chance against him.

When I finally met Cayman in person, he wasn't what I expected. He is toned, but he's not bigger or taller than me. My upper body is a bit bigger than him as it is with all my opponents. Most people say I don't have the build of a boxer because I have a big upper body. But I think it's just deceiving to the normal eye because when I stand toe to toe with most of my opponents I don't look that much bigger than them, especially now at the light heavyweight division. We stand pretty even when we face the cameras. He shows me genuine respect. It isn't until the cameras come that he starts acting like his usual arrogant self. Coach tells me to ignore his intimidation and the way he talks crap in my face when we stare each other down. I heed Coach's advice and just smile when Dominick talks about how I'm a nobody, how I'm not at his level, how I should be grateful to even step into the ring with him.

Grey Bones is respectful of me as well, talking me up to all the interviewers. This is their way of selling the fight. They need to prove to the public that I'm a worthy opponent. The media seems to have taken in all of the hype as well. Some people are giving me a chance to win this fight. Nobody sells a fight better than Dominick, that's for sure. He loves being in front of the cameras and talking about how great he is. He loves claiming to be the best in the sport, how he cleared out two weight classes.

Nothing he says is untrue. I truly believe he is the best boxer in the sport. But when the night comes when he and I face off in the ring, I have to be better.

HBO is running a show called "Behind The Corner" that captures the final weeks of our training camp. The show runs interviews, shows me training, and exposes my life behind the scenes. The cameras are placed in the gym and follow me around at home during certain times of each day. I don't find it to be a distraction. In a strange way I actually like it. I hear the ratings for the show are the highest ever with me on it. Coach Kay hated it. He didn't like anything that interrupted training. In order to get the fight, however, we had to do the show. It is good publicity for me so I wasn't entirely against it. Plus, if it was in the contract then I was going to do it, no matter what. Like I told everyone, I would fight this man for free, if necessary. I meant that, 100 percent.

It's three weeks into training camp and my body feels like it's been run over by a semi-truck, twice. Coach isn't holding anything back this time. I'm running the stairs at the gorge five times up and five times down. After that, I'm running five miles on the road. Everything is intensified. Hitting the bags has jumped from one hour a day to two. Sit-ups, push-ups, medicine ball drills, running cones – everything has been doubled. At the end of each day, I feel as though I could sleep for weeks.

We thought about moving training camp to Las Vegas or Los Angeles. That is what most fighters do. Juan had advised it actually. There was more of a boxing culture in those areas of the country. I denied the offer. Coach's sickness was one reason. He didn't need to be travelling like that. Juan could bring the sparring partners here. I would even help pay for them, even though he would never let me. The other reason was that I wanted to get Buffalo and Niagara Falls on the map with this Behind The Corner show. It was a perfect way to show off the city and show where I came from. With little opposition Juan was ok with it.

Juan has so many people flying into the city, I can't even remember half of their names. He got me a conditioning coach, who is monitoring everything I eat. I have a cut man, an assistant trainer, and Juan himself is flying in and out, watching my camp. Three days into training camp, I noticed he had seemed less high-strung after witnessing the way I trained. In fact, I heard him say he felt I might have been over doing it. Coach advised him that this is the way we always trained and were doing a little more to prepare for a fight of this magnitude.

Sparring starts next week. Juan is flying in a few fighters who have a style similar to Dominick. None of them fight exactly as he does, but they should help me with the speed problem I'm facing. He will be the fastest fighter that I have ever faced. I had heard they are excited to spar me. For some reason, I underestimate my popularity among boxers around the country. I don't realize young fighters coming up are looking up to me.

"Time!" Coach yells. I stop punishing the bag in front of me and take a deep breath. "We are done for today."

Tonight's the night. I look at the clock. It's seven p.m.

"I'll be back at 1 a.m. for another training session," I say, as Trey takes off my gloves.

"You serious?" Trey says. "Damn, man. I got a hot date tonight, too."

"You don't have to come Trey," I mutter.

"Phew, thank God," Trey says. He looks over at Coach, who gives him a brutal look. "I'll be here," he sadly adds.

"No, it's really ok, Coach. Just me and you will be fine."

Coach has no problem getting up and training me. He doesn't care what time of night it is. He would just claim he wasn't sleeping anyways.

"Ok, then," Coach says. "The fight is five weeks away. I've been studying Dominick's style. He doesn't like his back being on the ropes. His hands are high when he is allowing for clean body shots.

We have to put him there and bang with him."

"Body shots don't win rounds in the judges' eyes," I argue, as Trey finally gets both of my gloves off. I wipe my head with a towel.

"No, but they will drain his energy."

"I have yet to see him drained in a fight." I argue again.

"That's because no one goes to his body. He's not hard to back up against the ropes because he doesn't like to be pressured. He goes straight back and then tries to quickly move to the right or the left. And when you get him on the ropes, you can throw combinations to the body and then to the head. The judges will like that and the crowd will go crazy, even if you're not landing good shots. His defense is his speed. We need to take that away. Body shots will drain his energy for later in the fight."

"So just attack his body, even if we lose a few rounds because of it?" I question.

"Yes. His entire game is speed and footwork. We take that away by draining his energy. You need to be able to walk through his combinations and punches with head movement."

"Well, your defense sucks so you can leave the head movement part out," Trey jokes, inspiring a spiteful look from Coach.

"It's getting a lot better!" I say, shooting Trey a dirty look.

"It is. I'll give you that." He smiles and rubs my head.

"Get out of here," I joke, pushing him away.

I look over at Coach, who grins. "That's the first smile I've seen all training camp," I tell him.

"Don't get used to it," Coach smirks before his serious, hard-driven face returns.

"So, body shots," I state. "What about when we are in the center of the ring? What if I can't push him to the ropes as easily as we think? I'm not sure I'll be able to time his punches because he's so damn fast."

"I haven't figured that part out yet. Some of this stuff we're going to have to see when we're in the fight, and adjust as the rounds go. That's what great fighters do. The main part is to keep the fight on the inside, which you are good at. And while I hate the way that idiot friend of yours says it, he's right: Your ability to take punches and keep pushing forward gives you an advantage here."

"So you're saying my defense sucks, too," I mock.

"No, I'm saying you like to take unnecessary punches to get where you want to be. The difference is, I think you are as fast as Dominick. We just have to see if it's true. Speed can be deceiving sometimes. Just because you don't throw your jab and cross fast at a distance, like he does, doesn't mean you are slower. If you can get the fight on the inside, you will be faster. And Dominick likes to get in on the inside sometimes, even though he's not very good at it. The crowd loves his fights because he bangs on the inside too. But you are better than him at that. You have to draw him into your fight, which is on the inside. And get him away from fighting his fight which is staying on the outside."

I nod my approval. "I'll watch some more tapes with you later," I say, picking up my things. "Maybe we can look at some of the rounds he's lost in previous fights and see what they did to make him lose the round. Right now, I need to be somewhere. Then I'm going to rest before coming in later."

"Hot date with Vanessa?" Trey asks.

I shake my head. "Not exactly."

Once I get home, I jump in the shower and get ready. Then I start the long, nerve-wracking drive that starts my thoughts swirling. My only hope is that the information I received is correct. I'd hate to be this nervous, only to arrive and find out no one is there. I shuffle through radio stations to find a song that calms my nerves. Before I realize it, I'm at the church.

Stepping out of the car, I look at the huge building.

"Give me the strength to deal with this," I pray as I head into the church. As soon as I step inside, I see that my source is correct. She is sitting in the front pew, alone.

For a second, I feel like turning around. Am I ready for this? And so close to my fight? Should I be messing with my mind right now? No. This is something that needs to be done, before the fight. I needed to get rid of this pain. Or at least start too.

The church is empty except for the sound of classical music playing over the speakers. The sound is soothing and helps build my courage to go through with this.

Slowly, I walk towards the front, gathering my thoughts. I can see her holding a rosary as she looks ahead. I make myself known by trying to be loud as I walk up to the front of the church. Then she turns to look at me, her face resembling mine.

"Aiden," my mother says haltingly, standing up. I can tell she is shocked to see me, but not as shocked as I am to actually be here.

"I...I thought I would never see you again, at least in person, anyways," she continues. "Your picture is everywhere so it would be impossible not to see you."

For a moment I stand without moving. I'm still not sure I want to press forward. She has stopped, too, and stares at me. She can see the hesitation in my eyes.

"What are you doing here?" she asks quietly.

I take a deep breath and begin. "I know that I didn't handle our first meeting well. I apologize for acting the way I did at the gym. I was just caught off guard."

"I completely understand. It's my fault. I should have called or gave you a notice or something. I should have known that you would be angry."

Her apology seems sincere. She sits back down and stares up at the altar. I feel like all the statues of Jesus, Mary, and even God himself are up there staring down at us. Why am I here? I hated this woman.

"Please, sit," she offers.

I look down the aisle and take a few steps into the pew, keeping a good distance between us. I'm not ready to get too close yet.

"I just want to know why," I continue, delving straight into what I need to know. There is no reason for small talk. "Why did you leave me to live with Grandma? Why did you do the things you did?"

My anger starts to rise but I try and keep a cool head.

"I was lost," she says. "I was hurt. Confused. I didn't know how to raise you. When your father died, I felt so helpless. So alone. And you were so angry at him, I didn't know how to make you happy. Then I got involved with the wrong people. My life changed forever. I tried to be the woman he would have expected me to be, but I just couldn't do it. I failed him. I failed you. And I live with that regret every day of my life. Not a morning starts nor does a day finish that I don't think about you."

She pauses. "The people I was hanging with – drug dealers, crack addicts – they loved boxing. When they mentioned a local fighter that was beginning to make waves in the boxing world, I noticed they said his name was Aiden. When I found out it was you, I nearly had a heart attack. I spent the entire night sitting up in my bed, thinking about my life. That night I left that wretched neighborhood, and I never looked back. I went to rehab with the help of some friends in the church, got healthy, got a job working at a clothing store, and now I'm here."

"A clothing store?" I ask.

"Yes. It's not the greatest pay but it pays the bills, most of them anyway. The church gives me food and stuff when I can't afford it."

She smiles, looking up at the altar.

"If you need money, then I'll give it to you," I say quietly. I don't know why I offered it to her. She deserved to be poor, to be hungry. But, she was my mother. And for some reason I felt that my father was smiling at us right now. He would be happy to see this.

"No, no," she replies. "Absolutely not. I built this house and now I will sleep in it. I don't want your money, Aiden. The only thing I want is you back in my life."

"I don't know if I'm ready for that," I admit. "This is a small step to a very large set of stairs."

"I understand and I'll wait my entire life for you to be ready. I don't care. I messed up. I know I did. I can't even imagine the pain and suffering you had to endure growing up. Hell, you've taken up a career where your sole purpose in life is to beat someone to a pulp! That alone makes me realize how hard it was."

I stand up and look at the familiar statue of Jesus. The blood trickling down his face from the pain and suffering he had to withstand makes me feel a little vulnerable. No one had it worse than him. Could I forgive this woman? That was the main question. The question that had haunted me since she stepped back into my life. Perhaps, I could.

"You know, there were times in my life that I hated everything, everyone," I say. "Even Coach. There was a time that I thought about killing myself because I had given up. In my memory, buried somewhere in all the darkness that clouded my thoughts, I could remember when Dad was alive. When the three of us would go to the park, play games, and do fun things. Those memories never left me. I held onto them during my hardest times. Maybe it was because I felt that one day I could be reunited with you, that maybe one day I would have my own family to love and that I would be able to redeem myself by raising them well."

I look her straight in the eyes. "My hatred for you, and my hatred for him, stemmed from my even stronger love for both of you." I pause for a second. "I may never forget the painful life I lived, getting to be the man that I am today, but I forgive you for it, because without it I wouldn't be who I am today."

"You have become a great man. Just like your father was. He would be so proud of you." Tears begin to fill her eyes as she looks up at me. I reach into my pocket and take out an envelope. She looks at me awkwardly. "Aiden," she says, "I don't want your money."

"It's not money," I assure her. "Well, not really."

"What is it then?" she asks. I hand it to her.

"The second step," I say, finally smiling. She opens it and her mouth drops open. "I want you at the fight," I continue. "There are two plane tickets, a hotel room, and spending money for you and whoever you want to bring. I can't promise I'll see you a lot, but I feel it's right that you be there."

She rushes over to me and gives me a hug. I wasn't ready for it but in a way it soothes me. All of the memories of hugging her when I was a child run through my mind. I haven't hugged her since I was a little boy.

"Of course I'll be there!" she cries letting go.

I nod my head as she stares at the tickets in disbelief. "Good. Well, I have to get going now."

"Ok. I'll, um, see you at the fight, I guess," she says, smiling.

"Ok," I say. I start to head toward the entrance then I stop and turn back to her. "What do you think Dad would say about this fight if he were here?"

I know the answer. I'm just wondering if she will. When we played games, he always said the same thing.

She looks up at the ceiling as if talking to him then at me, shaking her head and chuckling.

"That's simple," she says. "What he always said…'Go get 'em, champ'."

Chapter Thirty-Six

I sit at the edge of the ring and wait for Coach to come down. Usually, he would have already been up waiting for me. The fact that it's 2:00 in the morning never stopped him before. I feel bad that he gets up to train with me. With him being sick, I don't like waking him up when he sleeps. There is no telling him that, though. The man would slap me upside the head if I dared to think about not waking him up during one of my early morning sessions.

The last couple weeks have been intense. The national reporters like to get interviews in between camp too which has become a bit of a distraction because we have to plan our training around them sometimes. This training camp is by far the best I have ever taken part in though. It's only 10 days until the biggest fight of my life. Over and over again, I fill my mind with tapes of Cayman's last couple of fights. I try and play out how I want the fight to go, the things I will do to counter what he does. It feels like my first fight all over again. But no matter how many tapes I watch of this man, there is no way to know how to attack him until he's standing before me in the center of that ring.

My usually carefree mood has changed in the last few days. That's how everyone knows fight day is getting close. I'm edgy and snap very easily over the littlest things. Vanessa hates being around me for training camp. For the most part she stays away, limiting her visits to twice a week, mostly on the weekends. I understand why fighters move away from their homes for training camp. My angry mood makes even my closest friends not want to be around me. Everyone knows not to mess with me this close to the fight.

The distractions in the gym have been even greater, as of late. The camera crews for HBO's "Behind the Corner" have been documenting my every move. We have to stop training, sometimes right in the middle of a session, because they want me to explain to the viewers what I am doing and how it helps me prepare for the fight. They've been involved in a few of my late-night sessions as well. The story of my life growing up, how I slept in the gym for a year, and my parents has exploded on national television. Coach hates the fact that they are here and he even got in a few fights with some of the producers. He feels the distraction is making me lose valuable training time. I know the real reason he's mad is that he doesn't like all the publicity on him. He also doesn't want anyone to find out about his illness. If the media gets a hold of that, they will expose the story to the public. Sadly, my stock in the industry would probably skyrocket if they did find out. Sad stories make great marketing strategies to the public.

According to Juan, the first episode of the show raked in nearly double the amount of viewers than ever before. Even Dominick is impressed. Juan told me it's because of me. Dominick hasn't faced an undefeated fighter in about two years, mainly because he's beaten everyone at least once already. Juan also says that the amount of people contacting him about me is more than he could have imagined. Women are noticing me – women who are not even boxing fans – and they absolutely love me. They love my story, my face, and my poise in front of the cameras. *Sports Illustrated* told Juan that if I win this fight they will feature me on the cover. He said that would only be the beginning. Juan had said that I could be the future of boxing when we first met. He was not lying. Even with a loss to Dominick, Juan believed that I could still be a PPV star. I did not intend to lose though.

"Everything alright?"

Coach's voice startles me. "Yeah, why?" I ask.

"You are usually shadowboxing or jumping rope." He's right. I never wait for him to get up. I'm usually working out right now waiting for him.

"I just got distracted in my thoughts, that's all," I admit. I don't get up as he approaches me. I don't know if my body is just tired or if I'm procrastinating.

"Maybe we should take it easy tonight," he advises as he leans up against the ring next to me. "You've been working hard. One night off may be good for you."

"We can take it easy in 11 days," I insist, finally jumping off the ring. My body doesn't hurt like it used to. Juan's men have been setting up ice baths, electric shock messaging, and other things that are helping my body get through training.

"Rumor has it Dominick is a little worried about this fight," Coach says, grinning. "And I think he damn well should be."

"That's not what I heard. The first episode of 'Behind The Corner' aired last week and apparently he was his same cocky self. In fact, he's more confident about this fight than he ever has been." Trey had told me everything that happened on the show.

"You didn't watch it?" he asks in surprise. "You watch that show before every big fight. Now that you're on it for the very first time, you decide not to watch it?"

"No, I'll watch it after," I confess as I begin to shadowbox. "I don't need to mess with my head more."

"You shouldn't believe everything you see on television," Coach says. "He's acting more confident because he's more intimidated. People talk, especially the guys you've been sparring. Sparring partners get around. They see the things in training camps and they go tell people and before you know it everyone is hearing about it. Your sparring partners, in particular, used to spar Dominick, too. They are going around telling people that they think Dominick is in trouble. Obviously, that gets back to his camp, which worries them. The power behind your punches scares him."

"The public doesn't seem to think so," I argue. "I'm a 5-1 underdog. The boxing experts are saying I only have a puncher's chance."

"No, you have a fighter's chance son." He smiles. "A puncher's chance means that your only chance is to knock him out in one punch. A fighter's chance means you're going to fight him for 12 rounds straight. That's what you are going to do."

"Well, you're right. He should be worried. Like I told the cameras, I'm going after him for 12 rounds straight. From the time the opening bell rings to the time it stops, I will be in his face. He's never faced a fighter like that before." My confidence for this fight is at an all-time high. I know I can beat this man. I believe I know how to do it. No, it won't be easy. Fighting never is.

"Those wretched cameras," Coach says. "I can't wait until they're out of my gym."

"You know, they are not that bad," I argue. "It hasn't messed with my training like you think it has."

"I know, because you're disciplined. And unlike me, that face of yours was made for the cameras." He smiles.

"You know, after this fight, regardless of the outcome, we are all going on vacation. I've been looking at some spots you know. Australia, Hawaii, Mexico. They all look amazing." We needed a vacation. A very long one.

"Well that would be nice for you but count me out." His immediate denial is expected.

"It wouldn't hurt to get you out of here for a few days Coach."

"I belong here Aiden. No vacations. This is what I love. Besides, someone has to keep those degenerate friends of yours in line. If I left this gym for two minutes, God only knows what they would do to it." He stops, looking around. "Speaking of Trey, shouldn't he be here right now?"

"Yeah, he's not coming. Another hot date. Apparently, he's using my celebrity status to get girls interested in him."

"With your money, too. Friends like that are hard to come by." He shakes his head, making me laugh out loud.

"I know everyone thinks he's a mooch. Actually, I know he's a mooch. But he's my best friend. He's been there for me through it all, just like you have. You both became my family when they were lost to me. I'm willing to do whatever he wants, and in all honesty, he doesn't ask for much. He still refuses to leave his mom's house. God bless that woman for dealing with him every day. I'm sure his reason for staying home is so he doesn't have to cook and clean his own house." I can't imagine having to live with Trey my entire life. Although he's my best friend, he's very eccentric at times, which makes me want to strangle him. "Now that I think about it, his mom is very pretty – and single, too," I add.

Coach turns his dark eyes on me. He's not impressed. "Don't even," he says, shaking his finger.

"What?" I ask, laughing as I jump back onto the edge of the ring and sit down to face him. "I'm just saying, Coach. You could adopt him."

"Oh, I could," he grins. I laugh hysterically. "It wouldn't be fair to involve a woman in my life. Not to me and surely not to her."

His comment changes my mood. I look down to the ground, saddened. "Have you heard anything else?" I mumble.

"Nothing that matters." His short response lets me know he is lying. The doctor could tell him he is dying tomorrow and Coach still wouldn't tell me. I have to win this fight for him. "I told you before not to worry. We have the biggest fight of our lives coming up." He grabs the gloves and comes over to start wrapping me up. I can't help but look at his face. When that day comes, the day that he passes away on me, I will feel a pain I've never felt before, greater than any punch, any knockout, any sort of training that I put myself through. The bond I share with him is not just as a Coach, but as a father figure as well. I never had the chance to say goodbye to my father.

"It's really here, isn't it, Coach?" I ask as he wraps my hands.

"You're not getting the butterflies on me now, are you?" he mocks as he carefully wraps through each finger.

"I always have the butterflies." My nerves don't leave my stomach before a fight, not until I'm in that ring, fighting for my life.

"Ah, yes." He finishes one hand and starts the other. "Well, if you weren't nervous about stepping into the ring with Dominick Cayman, then I would be worried."

"Thank you, Coach," I say.

215

"For what?" he asks, glancing at me.

"For everything – for believing in me, for giving me the chance to show my skills to the world. And for bringing me to this fight."

"You brought yourself to the fight. I only guided you there. But you're welcome," he says. Giving a glance into my eyes, he gives way a little. "You know, I don't care what happens in this fight. Win, lose, get knocked out, or knock him out, it don't matter, son. You'll always be the champ in my book." He smiles, letting a little emotion show through this usually stern face.

"Promise me something, Coach," I say. "When it does happen, when you feel that it's coming, give me a chance to say goodbye."

"Aiden…"

"No, you don't have the right to argue with me about this. Not this time. Just make this promise to me."

I'm holding back tears. I know that death cannot be stopped. I know that Coach has no control over the day or time his illness will finally get the best of him. But he is a man of determination. Somehow, some way, I know that by making this promise he will hang on until I have the chance to say goodbye to him.

"Ok, son," Coach says. "Ok."

Chapter Thirty-Seven

In all my years of fighting, I have never experienced the intensity of the prefight like I have in the last few days. As I sit in the locker room, the lights seem to sparkle differently while I pace back and forth, awaiting my grand entrance into the arena. I know I don't look nervous; I look prepared, determined. However, I am almost shaking. Watching the television, I can see the cameras finding their way to the celebrities in the crowd. Celebrities I watch in movies and on television are sitting at ringside. I can't believe they're here, about to watch me fight. It doesn't seem like any of this can be happening.

My white and gold trunks have my name stitched across them. It's the name my father carried: Walker. My shoes are stylish, matching the color of my trunks. It only took a few days to break them in the way I wanted. I'm wearing white Reyes gloves with matching gold lettering.

In every fight leading up to this one, I had worn black and gold. That changed today. To me, black represents darkness and sorrow, which is everything I was growing up, everything I used to be. That color needed to be put to rest, along with my past. That's why I chose white for this particular fight. It reflects power and goodness, and symbolizes that I've overcome my darkness and turned it into something extraordinary. Coach says I look like a prince with my robe coat, which matches the rest of my boxing attire. On the back of my coat in gold lettering is a very fitting phrase: "In God We Trust." It's ironic; no one had hated God and money as much as I once had. People try to keep them separate, but it's impossible. The saying incorporated into our money defines this world. God and money are what we live for, and what we die for.

Yesterday, I had tipped the scales in front of millions of viewers on ESPN, weighing in at 174. Dominick had come in at 175 on the dot like he usually does. He will likely weigh about 185 when he steps into the ring, from what I'm told. I will probably be around 177. His weight advantage hadn't been obvious when we stood face to face after the dramatic step on the scale. He had been running his mouth, as usual. I hadn't held back this time. Our heated exchange nearly turned into a fight.

Las Vegas is the boxing capital of the world. While we had discussed fighting in the huge football stadium in Los Angeles, it is no surprise that the fight landed at the MGM in Las Vegas. This is my first trip to Sin City for a fight. The city's reputation can't capture how miraculous it truly is. They say that the weekend of a big fight is one of the best times to be in Vegas. My picture is everywhere in the city, alongside Dominick's. People come up to me everywhere I go, asking for pictures, autographs, interviews, whatever they can get from me. Juan had to hire bodyguards to keep them away, although I try to sign everything I can.

Juan had been right about one thing: The amount of women interested in this fight had nearly doubled, according to the stats. He had always said that my looks and personality would result in a whole new fan base for the sport of boxing. So far, he has been correct. This fight is projected to sell more PPV buys than any of Dominick's other fights. Juan thinks it's because of me; boxing experts believe it's my undefeated record and my 22 knockouts in only 24 fights. These stats make the public think Dominick is in trouble, even though most boxing analysts have picked me to lose the fight. They feel I'm not fast enough to keep up with his speed and that my defense leaves me vulnerable.

A boxing expert came up to me when I first arrived at the MGM earlier in the week – ESPN's own Kelvin Reynolds. He saw me on ESPN back when I upset Tony Rocks. He told me he is predicting that I'll beat Dominick. Dominick, according to him, hasn't recently been in a true test of will and determination that requires him to dig deep in order to win a fight. I am going to be that test, and it's a test Reynolds doesn't think the champ will pass. Later on in the week, he went on ESPN to make his prediction, saying the exact same thing he told me. The prediction caused a stir in the boxing world. All over Twitter, people were retweeting his pick, inspiring debates that will last until we step into the ring.

"Vanessa says 'good luck'," Trey says, walking over to me. She had come into the locker room earlier, wishing me luck. I don't know if she's trying to reassure herself or me. Nerves have gotten the best of her. My safety is her main concern; no matter what happens, she doesn't want me to get hurt. I'm lucky to have a girl like her. Emotions, for me, are very hard to express. She knows how I feel about her, though. I'm happy she's in my life. Trey jokes about her being on national television. The cameras always find the fighters' significant other. She will no doubt wear a look of nervousness if they do. She'll probably be too scared to even cheer.

I have kept a promise to another man. Mr. Brass stands by Coach as they discuss some pre-fight issues. Coach is probably suggesting how he can help out when they are in the corner. He came into my life unexpectedly and offered me the opportunity to showcase my skills to the world. Most young boxers don't get the chance to meet a man like Mr. Brass, to help them the way he has helped me. I can never thank him enough for what he's done. I may have gotten this far without his help, but I will never know.

"Commissioner just walked in," Wes tells me as he and Tom enter the locker room. "You're up in five minutes. Right after the national anthem."

"This is it, kid," Tom says. "Time to show the world who the real champ is!"

I made sure my two good friends who have been with me for years weren't left out. While they couldn't stay in the corner with me, they had ringside seats right behind me. They are also going to be part of my entourage as I enter the arena.

Coach looks over at me and I nod. We hear the national anthem begin.

"Everyone come over here," Coach announces. My cut man, a rugged, well-built man named Hector Guiro, is new to the group. Although he's only been in my training camp a few weeks, he has said numerous times that we make him feel at home. He and my conditioning coach, William Nest, loved our training camp. William is a good-looking man with a flair for style. He's 45 years old but takes care of himself in the manner of a 30-year old. They both join our little circle around Coach.

"Listen up, this is the fight we have all been waiting for," Coach begins, "the championship fight against the world's best pound-for-pound boxer. No matter what happens tonight, I want you all to know that I appreciate what each and every one of you has brought to the table. This fight tonight is not just about winning a title; it's about fighting as hard as you can to get where you want to be in life. It's about believing in yourself and the people around you. It's about striving to accomplish your goals, no matter what obstacles you may face on your way there. No one believed we would be here tonight. No one believes we will walk out of that ring victorious. Let's prove them all wrong."

"Hell, yeah!" Wes yells. Everyone stares at him. "Sorry."

"You guys go out there," Coach says to the group. They leave the locker room and head toward the arena entrance.

I take a couple deep breaths; Coach gives me a sip of water. I'm warmed up and sweating. I jump up and down to make sure my legs are under me. I feel great. Training camp was tough, but my body feels amazing. The cameras show me in the locker room during the national anthem.

"Stick that jab in there hard and fast in the first couple rounds," Coach tells me. "He's not going to expect you to come out and box. He'll be confused. A good jab neutralizes speed. While he is faster, he has never seen a jab as good as yours. Stick it to the body and to the head. Then I want the cross thrown off of it, into the body as well. If you see that your jab is backing him up into the ropes, step to the right and cut the ring off. Keep him on the ropes and attack the body and go back to his head. I want every punch to be body first."

"Yes, sir," I say, taking another sip of water.

"Don't let the crowd get you excited. Pace yourself. I know you can throw a lot of punches, but don't overdo it too early. Save the assault for later in the fight when the body punches have taken their toll on his movement."

We have discussed this game plan at least 10 times in the last two days. Coach always feels the need to repeat himself, mainly because when I get in the ring I don't listen. He doesn't like that.

I hear the national anthem come to an end. The crowd is out of control, cheering and screaming. This is it. The commissioner walks in and signals that it's time for us to enter the arena. I take a deep breath, glancing at Coach. He nods to the commissioner, then says a last few words.

"You got this," he reassures me, putting his hand firmly on my shoulder. "Let's go show the world who the real champ is."

The nerves in my body start to take over and my heart races like it's my first fight all over again. This is what I've trained for, I keep telling myself. Through all the pain, all the suffering, through every obstacle placed in front me that I overcame, I am finally about to walk down the aisle to fight the fight I have dreamed about since I was 13. The images of me growing up through my life to get hear play in my head, from the time I entered the ring for the first time as an amateur up until now.

The cameras are waiting for us as Coach and I exit the locker room. The music playing is from the movie *Gladiator*. It's a mellow tune that actually gives me goose bumps. I glance over at Trey. He knows exactly what I'm thinking, and he smiles. No rap?

"I thought that maybe it needed a change up." He smiles.

I can hear the noise of the crowd getting louder as I approach the entrance. Despite being the underdog, I'm still the crowd favorite. I'm not sure if it's because people actually like me or because they hate Dominick so much.

As I finally enter the arena, new music kicks in. I smile on the inside, although I remain serious on the outside. It's the theme from the movie *Mortal Kombat*. When the crowd hears the music, they go nuts. The music pumps me up. My entourage leads the way. I can barely collect my thoughts over all the screaming and cameras in my face. Millions of people are watching my entrance. It's hard to believe.

People are shouting at me.

"You are going to lose!"

"Knock his ass out!"

"You're going to get knocked out!"

"You are going to be the new champ!"

I try to ignore them. I need to focus only on the fight. Coach is right; I've never been in this type of environment before. Being on the undercard of a HBO PPV isn't nearly as intense as this; the main event against the world's top fighter is as big as it gets. I'm beginning to feel the stage fright Coach was talking about.

After what seems like miles, I get to the ring. I run up the stairs. Before entering the ring, I walk along the outside of the ropes. Turning towards the crowd, I smile, make the sign of the cross as I look towards the sky and ask my father to protect me, and then enter the ring. The crowd cheers even louder. As odd as it sounds, I am finally in my place of peace: the ring. Circling around to keep my legs warm, I await the entrance of Cayman. There are so many people in the ring I can barely move from my corner. I try to ignore all the celebrities that are watching me get ready. This is by far the most intimidating crowd I've ever been in front of.

"Ignore them," Coach tells me, giving me a sip of water. "Don't worry, son. Once the fight starts, everything in your mind will cease to exist except Dominick."

I nod as I bounce on my legs a bit. Coach is right. When the fight starts, none of these people will matter – not the pre-fight interviewers, the announcers, the boxing experts, or the crowd.

Dominick's music starts as he makes his grand entrance to the arena. I don't recognize the rap song he comes out to. People are booing and cheering at the same time. To Cayman, this is all normal. He smiles as he walks down the aisle, greeting the fans as though he's making his way down the red carpet. In fact, as he jokes with people before entering the ring, he looks like he doesn't have a nervous bone in his body. I try to make eye contact with him as he enters the opposite end of the ring, but he ignores me. To him, I'm just another opponent he is going to walk all over. My job is to change his opinion.

I am announced first: 24-0 with 22 KO's. Even though I don't have any belts, the announcer gives me a thrilling introduction that keeps the crowd on their feet, applauding.

I take off my coat, go to my corner, and kneel down. "God, give me the strength to overcome my enemy," I pray, "to endure pain and suffering, and protect the health of not just me, but my foe as well. Amen."

Next up is Dominick. After announcing all of his belts and the fact that he is, pound for pound, the world's top-ranked fighter, his 48-0 record with 32 KOs is stated. He has twice as many fights as me and more knockouts than I do fights.

"Ok, remember, stick the jab, go to his body," Coach says in my ear so he can be heard above the screaming crowd. "Get his timing down on that speed of his."

I can tell Coach is just as nervous as I am. Trey, Wes, and Tom all wish me luck, giving me a quick hug and tapping my gloves.

Finally, the ring is clear. The Referee calls me. I take one last look at Coach, as if I'm never going to see him again.

"Go get our title, son," he says.

I enter the center of the ring. Dominick comes over to meet me and the Referee explains the rules to us, just as he did in the dressing room.

Cayman and I are face to face; not even an inch separates us. There is no fear in his eyes, just confidence – confidence that I need to break. I need to hurt this man in a way he has never been hurt before. I want to knock him out. I want to kill him. Even though I have made peace with my past, there is anger burning inside of me. It's what keeps me motivated. All the money and all the love that has been given to me is not enough to completely overcome my years of pain and anguish. Years of being alone and broke had built up my hatred of this world. It was that pain that I held onto because it allowed me to keep fighting. When I stepped into the ring, all of that pain resurfaced, and my only objective is to destroy the man that is trying to destroy me.

I walk back to my corner, awaiting the bell. Seconds later it sounds, and the fight begins.

Chapter Thirty-Eight

I come out sticking the jab, just as Coach advised. Surprisingly, the first jab I throw to Cayman's head lands square on his hard chin. He eats the punch with a smile. The crowd goes nuts. For the most part, I have blocked out everything to focus on Dominick. However, to say the cheering of the crowd doesn't affect me would be a lie. After the second punch lands the crowd erupts again, making me want to go after him. This is what Coach was talking about; I can't allow the crowd to dictate what I do.

My jab is working well. He throws a very fast jab-cross combo down the middle, which lands on my face. While his punches sting, they are not overloaded with power. He does it again. I move my head away from the cross this time, allowing only his jab to land. I go to throw a counter cross, but he is already gone so my punch wildly misses. His speed is amazing! I barely see him throw his jab; by the time I do, it has already landed and another punch is coming. When I try to counter, he's gone.

Stepping towards him, I throw a jab to his head that lands and then come back with two body shots that both land cleanly. Again, the crowd goes nuts. As Cayman throws a three-punch combo to my head, every punch lands cleanly. However, I come back with two hard body shots. I jab again, throwing it as fast and hard as I can. Both of them land, pushing him to the back of the ropes. I immediately lean my body into his and throw two hard body shots, then come back with a hook, which lands on the top of his head. Dominick stays with his back on the ropes and throws an uppercut, which I block, and he follows with a hook-cross combo that partially lands. Again I lay into him, throwing two vicious body shots, then I come back to his head with a cross-hook combo that grazes off his gloves.

The action of the fight has the crowd on their feet, screaming! Dominick is not backing down as he tries to trade blows on the inside with me. While he lands a few clean punches, my body shots, followed by my combos to the head, are giving him hell. The bell sounds, ending the first round. The crowd remains on their feet.

"That's what I'm talking about!" Coach yells as he, Trey, and Mr. Brass clean me up. Even though Cayman has landed a lot of punches, they don't hurt. Despite his speed, his defense isn't that

223

good. I find it easy to land punches on him when I lay him on the ropes.

"You see that?" Coach continues. "Jab, jab, jab. When you have him backed on the ropes, lay into his body. He will not be able to last 12 rounds like this! Don't let him keep the fight in the middle of the ring. His speed is too fast. If you allow him to box you, he is going to dance circles around you. I think you won that round. Let's go!"

The announcers are surprised at the first round. I can hear them when I'm in the corner since they're right next to me. All three of them think I won the first round, which is shocking. It's a good start.

As the bell for the second round rings my confidence has built. I begin to stick my jab into Dominick's body, even moving my head a little to avoid some of his counter punches. My hands are held high as usual which is catching a lot of his jabs. He's not going to win rounds by just throwing ones and two's against me. That was part of our plan, to make him attack. We dance a little in the center of the ring as he uses his superior speed to keep me away from him. I continue to have success with my jab as he backs away every time I throw it.

When I see that I have him close to the ropes, I jump at him, throwing two body shots and coming back to his head. Dominick doesn't back down as he stands there and throws an uppercut that lands flush on my chin, hurting my jaw a bit. I throw two more body shots and a hook to the head that lands on his skull. The crowd is erupting as we go toe to toe on the inside with no one backing down. I land a cross, hook combo on his head as he counters with a uppercut, hook that both land. Again I throw two body shots, and come back to the head with two more as he continues to fire back. Defense has ceased to exist as we just fire away. The noise from the crowd cannot be ignored as the bell sounds.

"Good, good!" Coach yells as I take a seat on the stool. Trey ices my back as Coach takes the endswell to my eyes. The sensation of both is soothing. I can't believe that Dominick is exchanging on the inside with me and I'm surprised at his ability to take my punches. "He's fighting your fight. That's good. Keep using the jab to push him back. When he is close to the ropes, step to the side you see him going towards to cut the ring off and put him on the ropes and bang that body! You've won these first two rounds. Let's go!"

Round three begins and I do exactly as Coach says. By now the crowd is astounded and I can hear the announcers at ringside saying that these are the most exciting first two rounds that Dominick has ever been in. I hear them say that they also have me up two rounds to zero.

Instead of backing up when I jab Dominick shocks me by stepping to the side and throwing a cross right down the middle the lands flush on my jaw. The punch staggers me a bit as the crowd explodes. It hurts, but I'm not dazed. He thinks I'm hurt as he rushes forward to try to finish me off. I stand on the inside, throwing two body shots as hard as I can as he counters with a cross, hook combo where only the cross lands. We stand in the middle of the ring, not backing down as we both throw combinations. This time it's easier to block some of his shots, and he does the same by moving his head making me miss a lot. The action however seems to have enticed the crowd once again.

As I see an opening in his defense I land a hard cross on the side of his head that makes him step back. The crowd erupts as I rush after him, throwing a left hook to the body then coming back to the head with another left hook. He blocks the one to the head and fires back with his own lead cross that I catch on my gloves. I can't tell if he's hurt but I pressure him anyways, leaning my shoulder into his to keep him on the ropes, and continue my barrage of body shots. Our sweat is starting to get mixed up as I feel the sweat coming off his body seep in with mine. He's having success landing the uppercut on the inside as once again he hits me with it. I immediately counter with a right uppercut, and the round ends drawing a standing ovation from the people.

"Just keep doing what you're doing," Coach says as I stumble into my corner at the end of round three. He's calmed down a little since the first round. I have, too. My nerves have vanished. I don't feel any pain in my face, despite being hit a lot. "Listen, he's not going to let you keep him on those ropes anymore. You need to push through him. Keep the jab going. Eventually he's going to start boxing and keep this fight away from the ropes. He knows he can't beat you on the inside now."

Round four begins, and Coach's words couldn't be more true. Instead of backing straight up when I jab, Dominick begins to move left to right, tagging me with punches as I try to get to him. He's not letting me anywhere near him. I keep my gloves up, trying to push him back with the jab, but he refuses to get into a brawl with me. His speed is overwhelming when I try to engage in the middle of the ring. There is no way I can let him get away with beating me up for an entire round without being able to land anything back. I continue to jab, landing a few, but I'm not able to follow up with much. I get a few body shots in, but his movement is troubling. I am taking a lot of shots, and even though none of them are landing cleanly, it doesn't look favorable in the judges' eyes.

The fans aren't as intrigued this round but Dominick is dominating it. I can't even get close enough to get a second punch off. My jab ceases as I just try to rush him a few times but that doesn't work either. The bell rings through my thoughts.

"Do not stop jabbing!" Coach exclaims. "I told you he would be hard to get too when he started boxing. Jab, jab jab! That's how you neutralize his speed." He pulls me close to whisper. "Body, body body. I don't want you to throw anything to the head unless it's wide open. We need to wear him down even if we lose a few rounds on the scorecards." His words surprise me. Lose rounds on purpose?

As we enter the fifth round, I listen to Coach sticking my jab to his body and sometimes following with the cross. I can hear the announcers say that Dominick is going to start pulling away as he boxes more each round. I can't let that happen. Jabbing and going to the body is not winning me the rounds.

He continues using his superior speed combinations to land punches and keep me away from him. There is no way I am going to get him to fight me on the inside as he did the first three rounds. I've stopped jabbing and going to the body as the round wears on. For now I've become somewhat of a punching bag for him. His punches don't hurt, and I'm catching a lot of them with my gloves, but I can't get any of my own punches off. The judges are not going to favor me at all if I can't throw punches.

"I can't get to him," I tell Coach at the end of the round as Trey puts the stool out for me to sit on.

"You need to cut the ring off with the jab!" Coach demands, pouring water down my trunks and all over my body. "Why aren't you listening to me?"

"I'm trying," I respond.

"He's not throwing any body punches, Aiden. When he throws the combination to your head, you need to dip and lay into his body. Don't worry about coming back to the head for now, because he'll be gone when you try. Keep backing him up with the jab. We have to wear him down." I nod but I don't think Coach is convinced. "Do you trust me son?" He asks looking me dead in the eyes.

"Of course I do."

"Then listen to what I say." The bell rings.

I nod as we enter the sixth round. I do exactly as Coach says, drilling into his body as he uses his masterful speed to hit my head. Good thing Coach believes in my ability to take his punches. I jab hard and the jab is still landing as well as it was in the first round. I just can't do anything afterwards.

For most of the round, Dominick doesn't get close to the ropes; he continues to throw two- to three-punch combos and backs up. It isn't until about 20 seconds are left in the round that I throw a lead left hook over his cross, which lands flush on his chin. Surprisingly, Dominick's legs dance a little then he stumbles backwards. I've heard the crowd go wild before, but now it sounds like a volcanic explosion! I realize he's hurt!

Every person in the place jumps up, screaming at the top of their lungs. I hurt him! Immediately, I rush over, throwing a barrage of punches with no sort of plan behind them. The only idea is to knock him out now that I have my chance! He fires back, then grabs me to hold on, then fires back. I land two body shots and another left hook that makes him grab me. He's strong when he holds me, strong enough so that I can't get my arms out to throw a punch. When we get close, I can see it in his eyes that he's dazed! I just can't get the punches off to finish him. Suddenly, I see blood. Taking a step back I look to his eye to see that it is bleeding. I need to finish him right now! Then, a horrible thing happens, as I hear the sound of the bell ring, the round ends. Damn it!

"Listen to me – do not get careless, understand?" Coach yells before I even get the chance to sit down. "He's hurt, Aiden, but he's the champ. He knows how to weather this storm and he is smart. Don't punch yourself out. Do not stop jabbing and do not stop going to the body, do you understand?"

I nod, my excitement fading. I had the chance to knock him out, but I missed it. I take some deep breaths. I feel great and my legs are strong. My endurance is still good. Coach's advice is in accord with the announcers calling the fight. I hear them say that Dominick has never had someone with a firm, strong jab push him back the way he has been pushed back in this fight. They also say that the number of body shots landed on him is the most in any of his past fights, and it's only the sixth round. They are fascinated at the way this fight as played out, and I even hear one of them say that Dominick may be in trouble as the fight wears on. Their confidence in me has grown. I am halfway through the fight, and it might be even. I have the chance to beat him. I have to beat him!

Chapter Thirty-Nine

The faded image of my father is gone. I've taken away my eyes from my mother. Coach's words finally ring through my head. I have to win these last two rounds to win the fight. Yes, the journey to get here has been tough. The story of my life is a story that only I could explain. I had been through it all, and finally had overcome all the demons that haunted me since I was a boy. It wasn't over though. Not yet.

The signal for the start of the eleventh round rings through the crowd. The last four rounds have been exciting to say the least, and if anyone could say that they know who decisively won them, then they would be lying. As we enter the center of the ring, once again I look into Cayman's eyes, and for the first time in his professional career I see desperation in them.

Everyone has taken their seat for the time being, but that will likely change as soon as Dominick and I start exchanging punches once again. I advance cautiously, throwing my jab hard but not coming forward, as I have been. I am using the jab to keep him from being able to land a combination while we stand in the middle of the ring. I'd be lying if I said I'm not tired and that his punches have had no effect on me throughout the fight. My legs, however, seem to have gained a boost of energy. Immediately, I press the fight forward again.

Dominick isn't moving side to side anymore. The body shots seem to have worked, according to plan. I step in behind the jab and follow with a cross and hook. All three punches land without him countering. Instead of him dancing around like his usually self, he backs up into the ropes, where I unleash a barrage of body and head punches. The crowd erupts again, as they usually do when I have him on the ropes. Dominick fires back, landing a cross on my chin that may have shattered a bone. It's the hardest punch he has landed on me and I feel it, but I do not move. Instead, I land two more body shots and throw an uppercut to his head, which he blocks. He counters with an uppercut that lands flush on my chin, making me take a step back.

The crowd is going crazy. I am not hurt but I can feel the pain of his punches in my face. Two more rounds. I have to win them! As he comes forward, he gets sloppy, throwing wild hooks that are landing on my gloves. He thinks I am more hurt than I actually am, and he tries to get the Referee to stop the fight. I immediately counter him with a hook-cross-hook combo that lands across his head. Cayman backs up, surprised at my attack. I don't allow him any leeway as I push him back into the ropes and land a hook to his head. He manages to block my follow-up cross then counters with one of his own, which lands on the top of my gloves.

This level of excitement has been going on for the last four rounds. I have no idea if the judges are giving me these rounds or not. They've all been really close; the entire fight has been close. My face is bruised, as is his. Dominick's corner has done a great job closing up the cut over his eye but I continue to try and land every punch right on it. Blood is seeping through, getting all over both of us, but it's not enough to stop the fight. The crowd once again is on their feet.

It's been a long, exhausting round; Dominick begins to hold a little bit. The referee breaks us up a few times. He's still lying with his back on the ropes. The man is as tired as I am. If this round ends, he will have time to rest; I need the rest, too.

When the referee signals us to engage again, I rush after him. He throws the jab to keep me away but it's lazy. Loading up on an overhand right, I land my fist fiercely across his chin. His legs falter and the crowd explodes louder than it has all night, with everyone in the arena on their feet. The bell rings. Shit! Every time I hurt him I don't have the time to finish him.

"Leave the stool!" Coach shouts at Trey as I come to the corner. Coach looks at me resolutely, not even blinking as he speaks. Leave the stool? Coach doesn't want me to sit. It might actually be a good thing. "Listen to me, son. He is hurt! Do you understand me? He is hurt! I need you to go after him right now. Do not let him finish this round, do you understand me?" I nod my head as Coach pours water over me. "Everything in your life has led you to this moment, right here. Every moment, every memory, every ounce of hate and love in your soul. This is the moment of greatness that you have always waited for. Right now, you need to dig deeper than you ever have before. I don't care if you're tired, I don't care if you can't feel your legs. This man is hurt! You have broken him. Do not stop throwing punches until his face is on that canvas, do you understand me?! The next three minutes of your life will define you as a champion."

He pauses as the referee takes the center of the ring. "Go get him, champ," he adds. His words shock me. My father? That's what he used to always say. I feel like he has spoken to me through Coach. I know that it's time to give it everything I got and more.

Three minutes left. I have to go after him. The bell rings to start the final round. No one is sitting down. Dominick comes out throwing hard. His corner must have told him he needs to win this round. I dip my head away from his barrage and land a hook to the body. He steps back.

Again, I come forward behind the jab. He tries to move to his right but I land a left hook that makes him go straight back. He tosses out the jab and I throw over it again with my right hand, landing on his head. He's on the ropes now, covering up. I heave two heavy body shots. Instead of countering, he stands there, lying on the ropes. I throw two more and come back to the head, landing a left hook and an overhand right across his face.

Suddenly, he counters with a barrage of punches that land on my gloves. One of them gets through, crashing into my chin, but I don't feel the power. His speed is gone, his power is gone, and his legs cannot move. I land a cross to the body and follow with an uppercut to his head that lands flush on his chin. His head dangles.

Dominick keeps throwing punches off the ropes as we once again exchange in an explosive barrage of punches. Neither of us are backing down. His punches daze me but I keep fighting. I'm not even sure I am seeing just one person in front of me anymore. Suddenly, as I land a cross across the side of his face I notice his eyes give way. He's really hurt! Stepping back, I throw a left hook as hard as my exhausted body will allow. I can feel the bones in his chin slam against my knuckles. His eyes roll and he falls to the ground. The roar of the crowd may blow the roof off the arena.

"Dominick Cayman is down! Dominick Cayman is down!" I can hear the announcers yelling. "Cayman is down! Unbelievable!"

The fans watching on television must be going crazy as well. I run over to the corner, waiting for him to get up. I'm too tired to be excited. I keep my composure as I wait. He's struggling to rise to his feet as he finally beats the 10-count. I can tell by looking in his eyes that he is hurt. His spirit to keep fighting has made him rise to his feet, but he's out of it.

When the Referee signals us to fight again, I run over to him, pushing him into the ropes and laying into him, punch after punch after punch. He tries to fight back and he lands a few shots on me, but the drive in my soul keeps pushing me forward. I will not allow him to back me up. I land another hook to the head and he's out on his feet. As the Referee runs over, I follow with a cross across his chin, which sends him to the ground again.

The referee begins the count as Dominick struggles to make it to his feet. Six, seven. The seconds seem forever, but it doesn't look like Dominick is going to make it. Finally, the referee counts to ten, and Cayman tries to stand but falls back into the ropes. The referee waves his hands! Cayman can't continue! It's over! I won!

Everyone in the arena is screaming! The announcers are going crazy! I run into the middle of ring, shouting with joy! Trey, Coach, Tom, Wes, and Mr. Brass run into the ring, jumping up and down.

I fall to my knees and place my head on the canvas as tears begin to fill my eyes. I DID IT! Everyone jumps on me, yelling and screaming the exact same thing that I am thinking. Even Coach is jumping up and down. I did it! Everything that I have dreamed about growing up, everything that I have worked so hard for my entire life. I beat Dominick Cayman! It doesn't even feel real. With everyone on top of me I can barely move but I don't care. I'm so exhausted I just want to fall asleep in this spot right in the middle of the ring. The place is in an uproar.

When they finally get off of me, I stand up and hear the crowd chanting my name: "Walker! Walker! Walker!"

"Hell, yeah!" Trey yells, hugging me along with Tom and Wes. My smile doesn't leave my face.

Dominick walks over to me and embraces me. "Good fight, champ," he says, grabbing my glove and raising my hand to the crowd. "You're one hell of a fighter."

"Thank you, champ," I reply. "Thank you for giving me the opportunity to fight you." He nods his head and disappears behind all the people in the ring.

"Yes, baby!" Vanessa yells running over. I had lost her in all the excitement. I give her a hug and kiss. "I still don't like you getting beat up like this," she says, laughing, putting her hands on the bruises covering my face.

"Well, you better get used to it," I say as Mr. Brass walks over. He hugs me as well.

"I knew you could do it kid," he whispers in my ear. Everyone in the ring is coming up to me congratulating me. I'm not even sure who half these people are but I thank them and go with it.

"Thank you," I reply to Mr. Brass looking over some of the people congratulating me. "Thank you for everything. I don't know if I would have ever made it here without your help."

"Yes, you would have," he says, nodding.

Juan comes over and puts his hand on my shoulder. "Congratulations, champ," he tells me, poised as always. "I always knew that it was going to be you."

"Thanks!" I respond giving him a half hug.

I look for Coach and realize that he's standing in the corner, smiling as he watches everyone congratulate me. He seems to be taken in awe at everything around me. I'm not even sure he ever left the corner now that I think about it. He's looking around with the biggest smile on his face that I have ever seen. I meet his eyes then walk over and give him the biggest hug I can manage. "We did it, Coach," I whisper to him.

"Yes, we did, son." He's holding me tighter than he ever has before. "Yes, we did."

Chapter Forty

The fight has changed my life. I'm getting interview offers for every television show, radio station, and magazine across the country. Mr. Brass is trying to handle all my affairs but he's getting overwhelmed. When Oprah called him to arrange for me to appear on her show, he was so excited that he accidently hung up on her. I laughed when I heard the story. I'm going to have to hire a manager.

The picture of me winning the title from Dominick spread across every paper and magazine in the country, and even in other parts of the world. Everyone wants to hear my story. Not only are they calling me the future superstar of boxing, the fight has been deemed the Fight of the Year by much of the media. Some are calling for a rematch but I hear that Dominick is on the verge of retiring. His career is complete. Mine is just beginning.

Juan is getting calls from all over the world asking when my next fight will be. Promoters are offering up their top guys for me to battle. There are a few on the list that have piqued our interest. Juan claims that from here on out, all my fights will be PPV main events and my average draw will be $20 to $30 million per fight. I can hardly believe it. Money like that was just a dream growing up. It's a dream right now. Never had I thought that boxing would bring me that type of money. Yes, I wanted to fight Dominick, and I wanted to beat him. I had achieved that dream. Truth be told, I never actually thought of life after that dream was accomplished.

What will I do with all that money? I don't even know what to do with the $7 million I made in the Cayman fight. I'm going to have to hire an accountant and someone else to tell me what to do with it all. I hear all the time of people making bad investments. Trey has already offered me six different business ideas that he plans on starting. I'm lucky to have friends like Tom and Mr. Brass that know business ethics. I'm sure that I'll be ok. My focus needed to be on boxing, and right now, that focus was shattered.

It's been two months since the fight. I've been around the country doing interviews, appearing on television shows, and spreading my face and story across the country. I've appeared on the cover of at least five magazines, and my followers on social networks have reached hundreds of thousands. I was on top of the world, but at this moment, it felt nothing like it.

I stare at the ground, speechless. The shiny tile floor, which looks as though it's just been polished, shows my reflection. Vanessa holds my hand, trying to comfort me. Trey sits across from me, next to Mr. Brass; both of their faces are stricken with a tender sadness. Tom and Wes just look around trying to keep their focus.

There are hundreds of reporters outside trying to get in but the police are blocking their way. Rumors are circulating on Twitter and Facebook, but no one really knows what's going on.

"Aiden," the doctor says as he approaches me.

I stand up. "How is he?" I ask.

"Not good," he responds. "He's awake and talking, but it won't be for long." The doctor looks around at all of us, then back at me. "He only wants to see you right now, Aiden."

The doctor walks up to the nurse's station and drops a folder on the counter. I follow him. "Doctor, you have to tell me what's going on," I demand. I had met Dr. Brudge the first time I attended church with Coach. He and Coach are good friends and I can see that he's holding back tears. Even that day, so long ago, both of them knew what was going on. I remember the private meeting they had.

"I'm sorry, Aiden. He's lucky to have lasted as long as he has. He's waiting for you. You should go say goodbye."

My heart sinks to the floor and I feel my knees almost give way. This is it – the moment I've been dreading since I found out. He had waited until the fight was over, until we had brought home the championship. That was the time table that I was given. Doctor said that he should have passed over six months ago.

For a minute, I stand in a daze, thinking of all the good times Coach and I had together. In fact, every memory of my life revolves around Coach. From the time he took me into the Star Boxing gym until I beat Dominick, I saw the man almost every day. We ate together, trained together, and even when I was sleeping at the gym after my grandmother had died he would sleep on that little cushioned chair in his office making sure that I was ok. Now it's all going to end. I'm no longer going to go to the gym and see Coach waiting for me to get ready. He isn't going to be there, training kids all day long.

I try and regain my composure as I walk slowly to Coach's room. It almost feels like I'm walking toward my own death. It's more nerve wrecking than walking down the aisle to a fight. Everything is grim, and as people pass me by and look at me, I feel like they know as well. That they can see the pain in my eyes.

I open the door and see Coach lying in bed. He looks comfortable. The windows are shaded not letting any of the outside light in. I can't take seeing him like this; he was always so strong. I walk over to the bed and sit down in the chair next to it.

"What are you doing here, son?" Coach says angrily shuffling around. "I told the doctor not to let anyone in until I'm gone."

"Well, it looks like he listens to you about as good as I do," I answer. Coach struggles to shift himself in bed so I help adjust his body and pillow. I have never seen him so weak. I can't bring myself to remove my eyes from his.

"Foolish man," Coach mumbles. "I pay him thousands of dollars over all these damn years and he still can't listen to my requests." He coughs a little.

I hope the pain he's feeling right now isn't as powerful as what I'm experiencing. How am I going to do this? Every moment I spend in this room brings a misery so deep I can't grasp it. I'm helpless. There's nothing I can do to help the man I love more than anything in the world.

"The doctor said you'll be out of here in a few days," I tell him. "You just need to rest. We can start training for the next fight in no time. We can get some burgers and fries, eat like pigs for a few days before I have to worry about making weight again. I was thinking of getting you a house, too. Can't be staying at that gym anymore, Coach." I choke on the lies as they come out of my mouth.

Coach relaxes a bit and looks at me with a smile. "A house? Been a long time since I stayed in a house. What kind of house are you going to buy me?"

"Whatever kind you want. Maybe a mansion on the water, with a little white picket fence and a dog." We both smile even as I feel the tears coming to my eyes. "Don't matter to me."

"One on the water, on the lake, actually. That would be nice…" His voice trails off and he looks out the window.

I grab his arm as we embrace a moment of silence.

"You take care of that gym, ok?" he says, still staring at the outside world. "Take care of Trey, too. Don't you be letting him do what he wants, you hear? You tell him if he acts up in that gym, I'm coming down to smack the back of his head."

"Yes, sir." I can't hold back my tears as I let out a laugh; they fall from my eyes and trail down my cheeks.

"Vanessa, too," Coach continues. "She's a good girl. Don't you go breaking her heart, you hear me? And her dad's a good man. You tell Henry I said thank you for everything he did for us."

Even on his deathbed, Coach is still barking out orders. He wouldn't have it any other way.

Finally, he takes his gaze from the window and looks directly in my eyes. I smile through my tears. "We did it, Coach," I sputter.

"Just like we always said we would."

"We sure did, champ," he agrees, grabbing my hand and squeezing it hard.

"I can't do this without you, Coach. I can't fight without you by my side." I bury my head in the covers as tears pour from my eyes. He can't leave me. How am I going to fight again?

"Look at me, Aiden," Coach demands. I refuse to lift my head. "Look at me," he says again. Slowly, I raise my swollen eyes. "Yes, you can," he continues. "You're a fighter, Aiden, that's what you do. You fight. You fought your way through your father's death. Fought your way through those streets. Fought your way into that ring. Everything that has ever stood in your way in life you fought through, and were victorious. Don't you stop boxing because of this, you hear me? I mean it. Your entire life you have been a fighter. You were born to fight, son. You will fight your way through this, too."

His strong words only bring more tears. "I don't want to fight without you by my side, Coach. I can't. Who's going to yell at me when I'm messing with the new kids? Who's going to push me when I feel like I can't fight anymore? Who am I going to argue with when I disagree with the game plan?"

I shake my head, looking away from his familiar brown eyes. "I'm sorry, Coach, I really am. Because the one thing I never told you after all these years was how much I cherish you. How much I can't imagine living my life without you pushing me through it. I know life goes on, but I don't want it to, Coach. I don't want it to go on without you."

"I will always be by your side, Aiden. I never got the chance to say this, but thank you. Thank you for everything you did for me. Thank you for allowing me to live the life I always dreamed of. Thank you for taking care of the gym. And thank you for being the son that I always wanted. I've lived a good life. A damn good life. And I accept this."

He squeezes my hand tighter and I look at him through the tears pouring down my face. He starts to cry, too.

"I love you, Coach."

"I love you, too, son."

I embrace Coach, not wanting to ever let go. After a minute, I reluctantly release my hold on him and wipe my face with his blanket.

"Now go," he tells me. "I don't want you sitting around here, watching this old man fade away."

"No, not this time," I argue. "You will not be alone through this. I'm not leaving this room until you do."

He grabs my arm, looks into my eyes, and nods his head.

"None of us are." The voice of Mr. Brass startles me as I turn to see them all standing at the door. They all walk into the room and Coach looks towards all of us.

"Ok, son," he says. "Ok."

Three hours later, Coach passed. It was the hardest thing in my life that I ever had to go through. Thousands of people came to the wake and funeral. An unending line of people waited for blocks at the funeral home and church to pay their respects to Coach.

There is a steady flow of gifts and condolences. I'm running out of space to put everything. People sent punching bags, treadmills; one man even sent an entire boxing ring. The amount of love and support I've received from the community and the boxing world is overwhelming. Letters from all over the country fill my house. I had no idea how I was going to read them all.

"This had your name on it." Mr. Brass says as he walks up from behind. We are both staring at the fresh grave that Coach has gone in.

"What is it?" I strangely ask grabbing the rectangular wrapped object from him.

"Not sure." He admits. It reads:

To Aiden
From Coach

I unwrap the brown covering slowly as me and Mr. Brass exchange awkward glances. As the paper falls to the ground I look upon a hand drawn picture looked to have been drawn by a pencil. It's a picture of me sitting on a bucket in the corner of the gym, that actually sort of looks like the corner of a boxing ring. My gloves are lying on the ground, and my wraps are starting to come off.

"Who knew, Coach was an artist." Mr. Brass pats me on the back as he walks away. Coach was always full of surprises. In the picture, I look determined, but broken. It was an image of affliction. Of the hardships that I had experienced. It was perfect. When had he drawn it? God only knows. For it reminded me of my life, and what I have had to overcome to get where I was, and what I was still overcoming with each passing day.

Life was not to be taken for granted. That was by far the biggest lesson I had learned, and I had not learned it truly until recently.

As I stand among the close friends who have accompanied

me on this journey, I think about whether I should retire. I don't know if I can ever fight again. In my heart, though, I know that if I make that decision Coach will come back from the dead and yell at me. For all I know, he's up in heaven right now, cursing me for even thinking about it. He was right, though – I have a lot of fight left in me.

Staring across at my mother, I can't help but smile. I'm no longer the angry boy I was. I learned that being angry all the time didn't enhance my ability to fight. In fact, it hindered my performance in the ring. My entire life has changed. I'm happy. I'm not alone in the world. The support of my fans, my loved ones, and my Coach have made me the fighter that I am. And despite all the pain and suffering I went through growing up, I now know I can always depend on my cherished ones – especially the one man in my life who always believed in me – to be there for me and protect me.

Once everyone has gone, I stand alone, looking down on the grave of a man who changed many lives. On his tombstone are the words I will never forget, the motto we live by in the boxing gym: "When life throws you a punch, throw two back."

THE END

Special Thanks

Without a great team a lot of this would be difficult to accomplish. So I'd like to thank a certain group of people for their hard work in helping to make all of this happen. Cindy Mantai for editing and proofreading. Paul Clifton for drawing the cover.   Mike Del Zappo for modeling for the cover. Derrick Chamberlain for the graphic design. Also to Don Tanguay and Eva Berney for their support. To No Frills Buffalo for allowing this novel to happen. And to my parents who always have been great supporters of everything I do in life.

About the Author

Gabriel Gonzalez was born in Niagara Falls, NY on September 21st 1982. He likes to make it known that he was born on the same day as famous writer Stephen King, often stating that great minds were born on the same birthday. He graduated from Niagara Catholic high school in the year 2000, and then went on to attend Buffalo State College until 2005 where he graduated with a Bachelor's Degree in Sociology and a Minor in Religious Studies.

When Gabriel was fifteen years old he and his friend were paid to clean out the upstairs of an abandoned building. The reason for this was because a boxing gym was going to rent it out. Now he was no tough guy, in fact, he didn't like fighting at all. Yet, his interest could not be swayed. When the gym moved in he signed up to see how he would like it, and never looked back. He loved it. Boxing taught him how to be self-confident, disciplined, and patient. These characteristics didn't just bind themselves within the ropes. They translated into his life as well. The sport changed his life.

Fifteen years later he still goes three days a week and now helps train fighters alongside his Coach. He has seen many kids walk in and out of that gym with so many different stories. While the novel is fictional, it sums up what all young fighters go through trying to make it in one of the world's most brutal and dangerous sports. What he has seen over the years in the sport of boxing, and the dreams that he has seen both shattered and accomplished, has inspired him to write this story.

www.ingramcontent.com/pod-product-compliance
Lightning Source LLC
Chambersburg PA
CBHW072226170626
46813CB00003B/1113